# The MX Book
of
# New Sherlock Holmes Stories

Part XVII:
Whatever Remains . . .
Must Be the Truth
(1891-1898)

# THE MX BOOK OF NEW SHERLOCK HOLMES STORIES

### STORIES

## PART XVII
## WHATEVER REMAINS . . .
## MUST BE THE TRUTH
## (1891-1898)

SOUTHAMPTON STREET

359

EDITED
By
David
Marcum

OFFICES

TRADITIONAL HOLMES
ADVENTURES
COMPILED FOR THE
BENEFIT OF THE
RESTORATION OF
UNDERSHAW

ISBN Hardback 978-1-78705-506-3
ISBN Paperback 978-1-78705-507-0
AUK ePub ISBN 978-1-78705-508-7
AUK PDF ISBN 978-1-78705-509-4

Published in the UK by
**MX Publishing**
335 Princess Park Manor, Royal Drive,
London, N11 3GX
www.mxpublishing.co.uk

David Marcum can be reached at:
*thepapersofsherlockholmes@gmail.com*

Cover design by Brian Belanger
*www.belangerbooks.com* and *www.redbubble.com/people/zhahadun*

# CONTENTS

## Forewords

## Adventures

*(Continued on the next page . . . .)*

The following can be found in the companion volumes
# The MX Book of New Sherlock Holmes Stories
# Whatever Remains . . . Must Be the Truth

## Part XVI – (1881-1890)

*and*

## Part XVIII – (1899-1925)

*(Continued on the next page . . . .)*

The Murderous Mercedes – Harry DeMaio
The Solitary Violinist – Tom Turley
The Cunning Man – Kelvin I. Jones
The Adventure of Khamaat's Curse – Tracy J. Revels
The Adventure of the Weeping Mary – Matthew White
The Unnerved Estate Agent – David Marcum
Death in The House of the Black Madonna – Nick Cardillo
The Case of the Ivy-Covered Tomb – S.F. Bennett

*(Continued on the next page . . . .)*

*(Continued on the next page . . . .)*

## PART V – Christmas Adventures

*(Continued on the next page . . . .)*

## PART VI – 2017 Annual

*(Continued on the next page . . . .)*

## PART VII – Eliminate the Impossible: 1880-1891

## PART VIII – Eliminate the Impossible: 1892-1905

*(Continued on the next page . . . .)*

## Part IX – 2018 Annual (1879-1895)

*(Continued on the next page . . . .)*

## Part X – 2018 Annual (1896-1916)

## Part XI: Some Untold Cases (1880-1891)

*(Continued on the next page . . . .)*

## Part XII: Some Untold Cases (1894-1902)

## PART XIII: 2019 Annual (1881-1890)

*(Continued on the next page . . . .)*

## PART XIV: 2019 Annual (1891 -1897)

*(Continued on the next page . . . .)*

*The following contributions appear in the companion volumes:*
**The MX Book of New Sherlock Holmes Stories**
**Whatever Remains . . . Must Be the Truth**
**Part XVI – (1881-1890)**
**Part XVIII – (1899-1925)**

# Editor's Introduction:
## *"Whatever Remains . . . ."*
### by David Marcum

People like mysteries. We read books about them. We watch films and television shows about them. We look for them in real life. The daily unfolding of the news – *What's the real story? What is the truth behind these events that I'm following? What will happen next? What will tomorrow bring?* – is just another form of mystery.

Some people claim that they don't like mystery stories, instead preferring other genres. But consider for instance how often a mystery figures in a science-fiction story. I've been a *Star Trek* fan since I was two or three years old in the late 1960's and saw an Original Series episode on television, and I can say for sure that many – if not most – *Star Trek* television episodes or films have strong elements of mystery somewhere within the story, and in most cases the characters serve as detectives, leading us from the unknown puzzle at the beginning of the story to the solution at the end, working step-by-step and clue-by-clue to find out what happened, or to identify a hidden villain. *Is that harmless old actor really Kodos the Executioner? How exactly does Edith Keeler die? Why does God need a starship?*

To extend the Sci-Fi theme a bit: I don't like *Star Wars*, although I guess that one way or another I've seen just about all of it, so I'm certainly aware of the mysterious elements throughout the story. *What did the hints imply about Luke's father, before the answer was provided? What exactly was the emperor up to before all was revealed? Who are Rey's parents?* It's all a mystery, cloaked in space battles and pseudo-religion Force-chatter and light-sabre fights. In *Dune*, which I do like, mysteries abound as the story unfolds, with questions that must be answered, followed by more questions. These stories may not be a typical "mystery story" – a murder or a jewel theft, with a ratiocinating detective or a lonely private eye making his way down the mean streets, but they are mysteries none-the-less.

Look at other genres: Romance books and films? Who is the tall dark stranger, and how can his background be discovered by the heroine, layer-by-layer, using detective-like methods? The Dirk Pitt books by Clive Cussler, along with books about Pitt's associates "co-authored" by others, are most definitely mysteries, although clothed in incredible world-shaking plots. (I've lost track of the Sherlockian references that

1

continually pop up in the adventures of Pitt and his friends.) The original James Bond books, before Bond became so currently complicated and far from his origins, were each labelled as *A James Bond Mystery*. Stephen King, known for his supernaturally-tinged masterpieces, writes stories that are full of mysteries, and sometimes with actual detectives, showing just how much influence that the early mystery writers like John D. MacDonald had on him. Television shows like *Lost* or *Dallas* or *How I Met Your Mother* respectively asked questions like *What is the Island?* or *Who shot J.R?* or *Who is the mother?* None of these were specifically mysteries, and they are draped in all sorts of other trappings – time-shifting castaways, oil-baron shenanigans, or a typical sit-com group's antics – but the plot points that drive the shows are no different than what would be found in a mystery story. It's the same for stories that are nominally for kids like *Gravity Falls* or *A Series of Unfortunate Events* ask *What's Grunkle Stan's story?* and *What's up with that ankle tattoo and the VFD?*

And liking mysteries is just a step away from pondering greater unknowns. It's a human trait, as shown in cultures around the world. No matter what place, and no matter what era, we find stories of ghosts, and monsters, and questions raised about the nature of death, and whether there is more going on all around us than can ever perceived. It was that way thousands of years ago, when mankind squatted in caves around fires, waiting for the dangerous night outside to pass, and it's that way right now, as we hide in our fragile constructs of civilization and wires and thin walls and fool ourselves into believing that we've pushed back the night. (Look around. We haven't. The night is here.)

The Victorian Era, with its rapid strides in scientific knowledge, brought science crashing up against superstition and religion and spiritualism. Scientists had been gaining an understanding of the workings of the universe, and our little speck of it, for decades – chemistry, physics, astronomy, and so on – but the means for spreading that knowledge and educating the ignorant was very limited. Many people still lived much as their ancestors had a hundred years before, or longer, close to the land and nature, and uninterested in explanations about weather patterns or how atoms and molecules interacted. It was much easier to rely on superstitious explanations for natural phenomena, in the same way that the ancient Greeks and Romans had created their gods to explain the sun and moon and lightning. In daylight, all might be rational and modern, but when the sun went down, it was much easier to believe that *there was something out there* . . . .

The Victorians were gradually becoming educated, but the skin of knowledge was still thin, which allowed such things as the fascination with death and the spiritualism crazes of the late 1800's to take such a strong

2

hold, even luring in those who wouldn't be thought to be so gullible – Dr. Watson's *first* Literary Agent, Sir Arthur Conan Doyle, for example. It's common knowledge how he ruined his reputation during his later years by going over so whole-heartedly to the spiritualists. Additionally, he was shamed for his avid and naïve support of the Cottingley Fairies hoax. It can be taken as a fact that Mr. Sherlock Holmes, indirectly associated with Sir Arthur by way of Dr. John H. Watson's writings, was not happy that his reputation might be linked to such foolishness. Fortunately, there is ample evidence that Holmes forsook neither his beliefs nor his dignity.

Many people brought cases to Holmes throughout his career that seemed to have hints of the supernatural or the impossible about them. A few of these were published by way of the Literary Agent: "The Creeping Man" begins with the story of a girl's father who is seemingly changing into some sort of beast. "The Sussex Vampire" finds a woman accused of sucking the blood from her own baby. "The Adventure of Wisteria Lodge" has voodoo intruding into the supposedly modern English countryside. And of course there is *The Hound of the Baskervilles*, in which a curse from centuries past seems to have reawakened, killing a respected Dartmoor resident and threatening to destroy his heir as well.

These tales are part of the pitifully few sixty adventures that make up the The Canon. It contains references to many other "Untold Cases", some of which have seemingly impossible aspects – a giant rat and a remarkable worm and a ship that vanishes into the mist. We can be sure that Holmes handled each of these with his customary excellence, and that any sort of supernatural explanation that might have been encountered along the way was debunked. For Holmes, the world was big enough, and there was no need for him to serve as a substitute Van Helsing.

Holmes's stated his rule, with minor variations, for getting to the bottom of seemingly impossible situations several times within The Canon:

- "How often have I said to you that when you have eliminated the impossible whatever remains, however improbable, must be the truth." (*The Sign of the Four*)
- "It is an old maxim of mine that when you have excluded the impossible, whatever remains, however improbable, must be the truth." ("The Beryl Coronet")
- "We must fall back upon the old axiom that when all other contingencies fail, whatever remains, however improbable, must be the truth. ("The Bruce-Partington Plans")

- "That process . . . starts upon the supposition that when you have eliminated all which is impossible, then whatever remains, however improbable, must be the truth." ("The Blanched Soldier")
- "That is the case as it appears to the police, and improbable as it is, all other explanations are more improbable still." ("Silver Blaze")

Thus, the first part of the process is actually *eliminating the impossible*. And to a man with a scientific and logical mind such as Sherlock Holmes, this means that the baseline is established that "*No ghosts need apply*." So Holmes explains to Watson at the beginning of "The Sussex Vampire", asking, ". . . *are we to give serious attention to such things? This agency stands flat-footed upon the ground, and there it must remain. The world is big enough for us*."

If Holmes were to start every investigation with all possibilities as available options, including those beyond our human understanding, he would be finished before he even started. Imagine Holmes saying, "*This man may have been murdered – or he may have been possessed by a demon, overwhelming the limits of his body and simply causing him to expire. I'll sent you my bill*." Think of the time wasted if Holmes were an occult detective, with nothing considered impossible, all possibilities on the table, and virtually nothing that could be eliminated in order to establish whatever truth remains. The Literary Agent, Sir Arthur Conan Doyle, was willing to accept ridiculous claims about spiritualism and fairies and all sorts of nonsense. Not so for Sherlock Holmes – and thank goodness.

That's not to say that Holmes was closed-minded. There were many intelligent men in the Victorian and Edwardian eras who mistakenly believed that all that *could* be discovered *had* been discovered – but Holmes wasn't one of them. There is an apocryphal tale where Charles H. Duell, the Commissioner of U.S. patent office in 1899, stated that "*everything that can be invented has been invented*." In *A Study in Scarlet*, while discussing crime, Holmes himself paraphrased *Ecclesiastes* 1:9 when he told Watson, "*There is nothing new under the sun. It has all been done before*." And yet, with a curious scientific mind and an exceptional intelligence, Holmes would have certainly realized that there *was* more to be discovered, and that things are always going on around us that are beyond what we can necessarily perceive or understand – invisible forces and patterns of interaction on a grand scale beyond our comprehension. In relation to his own work, Holmes explained:

4

*". . . life is infinitely stranger than anything which the mind of man could invent. We would not dare to conceive the things which are really mere commonplaces of existence. If we could fly out of that window hand in hand, hover over this great city, gently remove the roofs, and peep in at the queer things which are going on, the strange coincidences, the plannings, the cross-purposes, the wonderful chains of events, working through generations, and leading to the most* outrè *results, it would make all fiction with its conventionalities and foreseen conclusions most stale and unprofitable."*

Thus, in spite of his statements that *"[t]here is nothing new under the sun"* or *"the world is big enough"*, Sherlock Holmes would have been open-minded enough to realize that – with our limited perspectives – the impossible isn't always easily eliminated when identifying the truthful improbable.

Sometime in late 2016, when these MX anthologies were showing signs of continued and increasing success, it was time to determine what the theme would be for the Fall 2017 collection. When I had the idea for a new Holmes anthology in early 2015, it was originally planned to be a single book of a dozen or so new Holmes adventures, probably published as a paperback. By the fall of that year, it had grown to three massive simultaneous hardcovers with sixty-three new adventures, the largest collection of its kind ever – until we surpassed that in the spring of 2019 with sixty-six stories, and a total of nearly four-hundred.

Initially, in 2015, I thought that it would be a one-time event. But then people wanted to know when the *next* book would appear, and authors – both those in the original collection and others who hadn't been – wanted to contribute more stories. So of course the original plan was amended, and it became an ongoing series.

It was announced that a fourth volume would be published in the Spring of 2016, *Part IV: 2016 Annual* – with the word *"Annual"* confidently assuming that it would be a yearly event. But there was such great interest by participating authors that I realized a Fall collection in that same year was necessary, beginning a pattern of two collections per year that has continued to the present – an *"Annual"* in the spring and a themed set in the autumn. And so I announced and began to receive stories for *Part V: Christmas Adventures*, published later in 2016.

These types of books have to be planned with plenty of advance notice for authors to actually write the stories. So halfway through 2016, the book for the following Spring, *Part XVI: 2017 Annual*, was announced, and very soon it was necessary to figure out what the Fall 2017 collection's theme would be.

That came to me while I was mowing my yard, where I do some of my best thinking. We have 2/3's of an acre, and I still have a push-mower, so that's good for a couple of hours of intense perspiration and pondering. And on that day, I had only been mowing for five or ten minutes when the idea of *Eliminate the Impossible* popped into my mind.

That title, *Eliminate the Impossible*, had been used before by Alistair Duncan for an MX book in 2010, something of a catch-all examination of Holmes in both page and screen. (In fact, this was the first Sherlockian title published by MX, and look what that led to!) This new anthology, however, would feature stories wherein Holmes's cases initially seemed to have supernatural or impossible aspects, but would absolutely have to have rational explanations – *"No ghosts need apply."* And yet, after the rational solution was explained and the case resolved, it would be acceptable if there was perhaps a hint that something more was going on beyond Our Heroes' understanding. I explained by paraphrasing Hamlet when soliciting stories from the various authors: *"There are more things in heaven and earth, [Watson], Than are dreamt of in your philosophy."* For instance, after the culprit is revealed, and Holmes and Watson could be departing, the investigation complete. Watson might look back and see . . . *something impossible.*

> *"Holmes,"* (he might say.) *"Do you see it?"*
> *"It is nothing, Watson,"* (would be Holmes's reply.)
> *"Mist. A mere trick of the light."*
> *"But still . . . ."*

And so the rational ending would be preserved, but the idea that there are more things in heaven and earth would be possible as well.

When I had the idea for the theme of the first MX collection of this sort, 2017's *Eliminate the Impossible*, I wasn't sure how it would go. I received a bit of sarcastic push-back from one person who referred to this as a "Scooby Doo book". I was disappointed at his reaction, and I'm glad to report that the success of both simultaneous volumes of *Eliminate the Impossible* proved that his assessment was incorrect.

Still, a few people were surprised that I would encourage a book of this sort. They shouldn't have been. I make it very clear that I'm a strict Holmesian traditionalist. I want to read more and more Canonical-type stories about Holmes and Watson – and nothing whatsoever never ever in any form about *"Sherlock and John"*! – with no parodies or anachronisms or non-heroic behaviours. That's what I collect, read, chronologicize, write, and edit, and also what encourage in others as well. There have been many times when I've started reading a new Holmes story, only to realize that, no matter how authentic the first part is, the end has veered off into one-hundred-percent no-coming-back supernatural territory – Holmes is battling a real monster, or facing a full-fledged vampire or wolfman, or perhaps a brain-eating fungus from another planet. There is a misguided belief that, just because someone wishes it to be so, Holmes can be plugged in anywhere like Doctor Who, or that he's is interchangeable with Abraham Van Helsing – and he most definitely is not.

As someone who has collected, read, and chronologicized literally thousands of Canonical Holmes adventures for almost forty-five years – and that certainly passed quickly! – I'm dismayed when this happens. As I make notes for each story to be listed in the massive overall Canon and Pastiche chronology that I've constructed over the last quarter-century, I generally indicate when a story has included "incorrect" statements or segments, and I include notes identifying those parts that were really and truly written by Watson, as compared with paragraphs or pages or chapters that were clearly composed and added by some later editor who has taken Watson's notes and either changed parts, or stuck in completely fictional middles and endings to fulfil his or her own agenda. Sometimes the story goes so far off into the weeds that even pulled-out pieces of it can't be judged as authentically Watsonian, and the whole thing is lost.

But the stories of *Eliminate the Impossible* – and now this collection as well – are fully traditional in the best Canonical way.

The idea of a story where Holmes and Watson were presented with circumstances that initially seemed supernatural but ended up having a rational solution was not new, and I can claim no originality for thinking of it. Before those volumes in the ongoing MX series appeared in late 2017 – *Eliminate the Impossible Part VII (1880-1891)* and *Part VIII (1892-1905)* – there were many other tales of that type. In my foreword to *Eliminate the Impossible,* I listed a number of them, and since then there have been more. As I explained then, there are far too many stories of that type to catalogue in this essay . . . but here are some of them for friends of Mr. Holmes to locate.

First, I have to recommend the stories in *Eliminate the Impossible,* Parts VII and VIII of this ongoing anthology series. They are some of the finest Sherlockian adventures to be found, and *Publishers Weekly* wrote of the two volumes: "*Sherlockians eager for faithful-to-the-canon plots and characters will be delighted*" and "*The imagination of the contributors in coming up with variations on the volume's theme is matched by their ingenious resolutions.*" Other MX anthologies in this series also have stories along these lines, although they are mixed in with more general Canonical adventures, in the way that "The Sussex Vampire" and "The Creeping Man" were included with Holmes's other non-*outrè* investigations.

While assembling the three-volume set that immediately preceded this current collection, the *Spring 2019 Annual*, containing general Canonical tales in *Part XIII: (1881-1890)*, *Part XIV (1891-1897)*, and *Part XV (1898-1917)*, I received a number of stories that could have just as easily fit into this current collection. I considered whether I should contact the contributors and see if they wished to hold those stories for publication in this Fall 2019 collection, *Whatever Remains . . . Must Be the Truth* (Parts XVI, XVII, and XVIII), but in the end decided to go ahead and use them in Parts XIII, XIV, and XV instead. And I'm glad that I did, because the inclusion of those narratives in the Spring 2019 books made for a really excellent set of adventures.

Among the many other places that one can find Holmes stories – some full-on supernatural and some that fit my own requirements – are *The Irregular Casebook of Sherlock Holmes* by Ron Weighell (2000), *Ghosts in Baker Street* (2006), the Lovecraftian-themed *Shadows Over Baker Street* (2003), and the ongoing *Gaslight* series edited by Charles Prepolec and J.R. Campbell. These titles include, *Gaslight Grimoire* (2008), *Gaslight Grotesque* (2009), *Gaslight Arcanum* (2011), and most recently *Gaslight Gothic* (2018). John Linwood Grant is editing a forthcoming book in which Holmes will team with noted occult detectives, such as Thomas Carnacki, or tangentially with Alton Peake, an occult investigator of my own invention who has appeared in some of my Holmes narratives, although always off-screen.

Holmes battled the supposedly supernatural in countless old radio shows, including "The Limping Ghost" (September 1945), "The Stuttering Ghost" (October 1946), "The Bleeding Chandelier" (June 1948), "The Haunting of Sherlock Holmes" (May 1946), and "The Uddington Witch" (October 1948). An especially good radio episode with supernatural overtones was "The Haunted Bagpipes" by Edith Meiser, (February 1947), later presented in comic form as illustrated by Frank Giacoia, and then again adapted for print by Carla Coupe in *Sherlock Holmes Mystery Magazine* (Vol. 2, No. 1, 2011)

And of course, one mustn't forget the six truly amazing radio episodes of John Taylor's *The Uncovered Casebook of Sherlock Holmes* (1993), and then published soon after as a very fine companion book. Then there's George Mann's audio drama "The Reification of Hans Gerber"

(2011), later novelized as part of *Sherlock Holmes: The Will of the Dead* (2013).

In addition to numerous radio broadcasts, there were similar "impossible" films with Holmes facing something with other-worldly overtones, including *The Scarlet Claw* (1944) and *Sherlock Holmes* (2009). Television episodes have tackled this type of story. The old 1950's television show *Sherlock Holmes* with Ronald Howard had "The Belligerent Ghost", "The Haunted Gainsborough", and "The Laughing Mummy". The show was rebooted in 1980 with Geoffrey Whitehead as Holmes, and had an episode called "The Other Ghost".

In 2002, Matt Frewer starred as Holmes in the supernatural-feeling *The Case of the Whitechapel Vampire*. Nearly a decade earlier, Jeremy Brett performed in a pastiche that was loosely tied to "The Sussex Vampire" entitled *The Last Vampyre* (1993). The supernatural elements were greatly played up in that film, although it had a rational ending. Brett's performance was extremely painful to watch, as at that point he had foisted his own personal illnesses – both mental and physical – so heavily onto his portrayal of Holmes and there was really nothing of Holmes left, but other aspects of the film were tolerable, if one looks past the acting and accepts that this was a separate story entirely from "The Sussex Vampire".

Brett's tenure as Holmes limped to an end the following year, and since that time, except for a few stand-alone films – three more Matt Frewer adaptations, a curiously odd and unpleasant version of *The Hound of the Baskervilles* (2002) starring Richard Roxburgh, a mild effort starring Jonathan Pryce called *Sherlock Holmes and the Baker Street Irregulars* (2007), and Rupert Everett's emotionless Holmes in *The Case of the Silk Stocking* (2007) – there have been no other versions of Sherlock Holmes on television whatsoever. (It's hoped that Holmes will return to television sooner rather than later, since it's been a very long time since 1994, when the last Holmes series was on television – not counting a few Russian efforts – and it's sure that when he does, a few seemingly supernatural stories will certainly be included as part of the line-up.)

In print, there are many other examples of this type of story. From the massive list of similarly themed fan-fictions, one might choose "The Mottled Eyes", "The Case of the Vengeful Ghost", "The Japanese Ghost", "The Adventure of the Grasping Ghost", "Sherlock Holmes and the Seven Ghosts", "The Adventure of the Haunting Bride", "The Problem of the Phantom Prowler", *That Whiter Host*, or "The Vampire's Kiss". There are countless novels, such as the six short works by Kel Richards, or Val Andrews' *The Longacre Vampire*, or *Draco, Draconis* by Spencer Brett and David Dorian. One shouldn't ignore the narratives brought to us by

9

Sam Siciliano, narrated by Holmes's annoying cousin Dr. Henry Vernier, all featuring supposedly supernatural encounters. Check out Bonnie MacBird's second Holmes adventure, *Unquiet Spirits*, and David Wilson's *Sherlock Holmes and the Case of the Edinburgh Haunting*. Then there are several by David Stuart Davies, including *The Devil's Promise*, *The Shadow of the Rat*, and *The Scroll of the Dead*. One can read Carol Buggé's *The Haunting of Torre Abbey* and Randall Collins' *The Case of the Philosopher's Ring*, and the different sequels to *The Hound*, including Rick Boyer's most amazing *The Giant Rat of Sumatra*, Teresa Collard's *The Baskerville Inheritance*, and Kelvin Jones' *The Baskerville Papers*.

Holmes has battled Count Dracula in too many encounters to list, but in almost every one of them, he finds himself ridiculously facing a real undead Transylvanian vampire who can change into a bat. Often, Holmes is simply inserted into the Van Helsing role within the plot of the original *Dracula* story. Although I own each of these, I've always ignored them, as the *real* historical Holmes would never encounter an *imaginary* creature such as this. The one exception so far that I've enjoyed and been able to finish has been Mark Latham's remarkable *A Betrayal in Blood*– finally, a Holmes-Dracula encounter that I can highly recommend.

A list of this sort is really too long to compile, and this shouldn't be taken as anywhere close to the last word. There are numerous supposedly impossible circumstances or supernatural encounters of one sort or another contained in many Holmes collections, tucked in with the more "normal" cases, and these are but a few of them:

- "The Deptford Horror", *The Exploits of Sherlock Holmes* – Adrian Conan Doyle and John Dickson Carr
- "The Shadows on the Lawn", *The New Adventures of Sherlock Holmes* – Barry Jones
- "The Adventure of the Talking Ghost", *Alias Simon Hawkes* – Philip J. Carraher
- "Lord Garnett's Skulls", *The MX Book of New Sherlock Holmes Stories – Part II: 1890-1895* – J.R. Campbell
- "The Bramley Court Devil", *The Adventures of the Second Mrs. Watson* – Michael Mallory
- "The Ghost of Gordon Square", *The Chemical Adventures of Sherlock Holmes* – Thomas G. Waddell and Thomas R. Rybolt
- "The Ghost of Christmas Past", *The Strand Magazine* No. 23 – David Stuart Davies

- "The Mystery at Kerritt's Rood" *Sherlock Holmes: Tangled Skeins* – David Marcum
- "The Devil of the Deverills", *Sherlock Holmes: Before Baker Street* – S.F. Bennett
- "The Case of the Devil's Voice", *The Curious Adventures of Sherlock Holmes in Japan* – Dale Furutani
- "The Adventure of the Haunted Hotel", *The Untold Adventures of Sherlock Holmes* – Luke Benjamen Kuhns
- "The Death Fetch", *The Game is Afoot* – Darrell Schweitzer
- "The Yellow Star of Cairo", *The MX Book of New Sherlock Holmes Stories – Part XIII: 2019 Annual (1881-1890)* – Tim Gambrell
- "The Adventure of the Devil's Father", *The Great Detective: His Further Adventures* – Morris Hershman
- "The Horned God", *The MX Book of New Sherlock Holmes Stories – Part X: 2018 Annual (1896-1916)* – Kelvin Jones
- "The Dowser's Discovery", *The Strand Magazine* No. 58 – David Marcum
- "The Phantom Gunhorse", *Sherlock Holmes: The Soldier's Daughter* – Malcolm Knott
- "The Adventure of the Winterhall Monster", *The MX Book of New Sherlock Holmes Stories – Part XIII: 2019 Annual (1881-1890)* – Tracy Revels
- "The Case of Hodgson's Ghost", *The Oriental Casebook of Sherlock Holmes* – Ted Riccardi
- "The Case of the Haunted Chateau", *The MX Book of New Sherlock Holmes Stories – Part XV: 2019 Annual (1898-1917)* – Leslie Charteris and Denis Green
- "A Ballad of the White Plague", *The Confidential Casebook of Sherlock Holmes* – P.C. Hodgel
- "The Adventure of the Dark Tower", *The MX Book of New Sherlock Holmes Stories – Part III: 1896-1929* – Peter K. Andersson
- "The Adventure of the Field Theorems", *Sherlock Holmes In Orbit* – Vonda N. McIntyre
- "The Adventure of Urquhart Manse", *The MX Book of New Sherlock Holmes Stories – Part I: 1881-1889* – Will Thomas
- "The Haunting of Sutton House", *The Papers of Sherlock Holmes Vol. I* – David Marcum

12

In the spring of 2018, it was time once again to start planning for the 2019 MX anthologies, and again while I was mowing – in pretty much the same spot, so there must be something buried there that radiates some kind of beneficial mind-influencing waves – I had the idea for these current books. If *Eliminate the Impossible* had been so successful, why not do it again? And what else could it be called but a variation from the same Holmesian maxim?

The three companion volumes that make up *Whatever Remains . . . Must Be the Truth*, like those in *Eliminate the Impossible*, contain stories where Holmes faces ghosts and mythological creatures, impossible circumstances and curses, possessions and prophecies, Some begin with the impossible element defined from the beginning, while others progress for quite a while as "normal" cases before the twist is revealed. Some are overt encounters with supposed monsters or phantoms, while others are more subtle, pondering the nature of existence and the vast patterns around us that we cannot perceive. As with all Holmes adventures, this collection represents one of the great enjoyments of reading about The Great Detective – the reader never knows where each tale will lead. And while each of the adventures in these volumes is categorized by Holmes *eliminating* the impossible to obtain, however improbable, the truth, the various impossibilities contained within these covers are presented in an incredibly varied and exciting manner. I'm certain that you will enjoy all of them.

As always, I want to thank with all my heart my patient and wonderful wife of thirty-one years (as of this writing,) Rebecca, and our amazing son and my friend, Dan. I love you both, and you are everything to me!

Also, I can't ever express enough gratitude for all of the contributors who have donated their time and royalties to this ongoing project. I'm constantly amazed at the incredible stories that you send, and I'm so glad to have gotten to know all of you through this process. It's an undeniable fact that Sherlock Holmes authors are the *best* people!

The contributors of these stories have donated their royalties for this project to support the Stepping Stones School for special needs children, located at Undershaw, one of Sir Arthur Conan Doyle's former homes. As of this writing, these MX anthologies have raised over $50,000 for the school, and of even more importance, they have helped raise awareness about the school all over the world. These books are making a real difference to the school, and the participation of both contributors and purchasers is most appreciated.

Next is that group that exchanges emails with me when we have the time – and time is a valuable commodity these days! I don't get to write as often as I'd like, but I really enjoy catching up when we get the chance: Derrick Belanger, Bob Byrne, Mark Mower, Denis Smith, Tom Turley, Dan Victor, and Marcia Wilson.

A special shout-out to Tracy Revels, Arthur Hall, and Kelvin Jones, who joined me in writing multiple stories for these volumes. When the submission deadline was fast approaching, I wrote to Tracy, who had written one story at that time for this set, and asked if she'd be interested in writing others to appear in the companion volumes. She took it as a challenge and wrote two more amazing tales in just a week or so. Arthur consistently pulls great tales from The Tin Dispatch Box, and I'm glad that they end up here. And I was a fan of Kelvin's work back in the 1980's, so I'm very happy that he's a part of these books.

There is a group of special people who have stepped up and supported this and a number of other projects over and over again with a lot of contributions. They are the best and I can't express how valued they are: Larry Albert, Hugh Ashton, Derrick Belanger, Deanna Baran, S.F. Bennett, Nick Cardillo, Jayantika Ganguly, Paul Gilbert, Dick Gillman, Arthur Hall, Stephen Herczeg, Mike Hogan, Craig Janacek, Will Murray, Tracy Revels, Roger Riccard, Geri Schear, Robert Stapleton, Subbu Subramanian, Tim Symonds, Kevin Thornton, and Marcy Wilson.

I also want to thank the people who wrote forewords to the books:

- Kareem Abdul-Jabbar – Along with your fame as a sportsman, you are a necessary, noted, and effective voice for improving society. And on top of that, you're a Sherlockian too! Thank you for helping to round out our understanding of Mycroft Holmes, and for participating in these books as well!
- Roger Johnson – It seems like a lifetime ago when I sent a copy of my first book to Roger, because it really mattered to me that he review it. He had never heard of me, but he was most gracious, and we began to email one another. I've been incredibly fortunate to have since met him and his wonderful wife, Jean Upton, several times in person during my three Holmes Pilgrimages to England. Roger always takes time to answer my questions and to

14

participate in and promote various projects, and he and Jean were very gracious to host me for several days during part of my second Holmes Pilgrimage to England in 2015. In so many ways, Roger, I can't thank you enough, and I can't imagine these books without you.

- Steve Emecz is always positive, and he is always supportive of every idea that I pitch. It's been my great good fortune to cross your path – it changed my life, and let me play in this Sherlockian Sandbox in a way that would have never happened otherwise. Thank you for every opportunity!

- Brian Belanger – Just a few days before I wrote this, I received a series of new cover designs from Brian for a forthcoming three-volume set that I edited, *The Further Adventures of Sherlock Holmes – The Complete Jim French Imagination Theatre Scripts*. What Brian sent was typical – excellent, brilliant, and with a great understanding of what needed to be conveyed. He's very talented, and very willing to work to get it right, instead of simply knocking something out or insisting that it be *his* vision. I'm very glad that he's the cover designer for these and other projects that we assembled together.

And last but certainly *not* least, **Sir Arthur Conan Doyle**: Author, doctor, adventurer, and the Founder of the Sherlockian Feast. Present in spirit, and honored by all of us here.

As always, this collection has been a labor of love by both the participants and myself. As I've explained before, once again everyone did their sincerest best to produce an anthology that truly represents why Holmes and Watson have been so popular for so long. These are just more tiny threads woven into the ongoing Great Holmes Tapestry, continuing to grow and grow, for there can *never* be enough stories about the man whom Watson described as *"the best and wisest . . . whom I have ever known."*

David Marcum
*August 7th, 2019*
*The 167th Birthday of Dr. John H. Watson*

*Questions, comments, or story submissions*
*may be addressed to David Marcum at*
*thepapersofsherlockholmes@gmail.com*

# Sherlock, Mycroft, and Me
## by Kareem Abdul-Jabbar

If you're reading this, there's nothing new that I can tell you about being passionate about Sherlock Holmes. You wouldn't have bought this book unless you shared that passion. It is a robust passion shared by hundreds of millions of fans around the world. There are over two-hundred-and-fifty international societies dedicated to the Holmes legacy. It is a testament to fans' loyalty that they persist in gobbling up new Holmes stories by literary interlopers such as myself, despite Sir Conan Doyle's own dismissive attitude toward Holmes, even to the point of killing him off in "The Final Problem". Explained Doyle: "*I have had such an overdose of him that I feel towards him as I do towards* paté de foie gras*, of which I once ate too much, so that the name of it gives me a sickly feeling to this day.*"

Fortunately, we don't share that feeling.

For eight years, Doyle fought against public outrage at Holmes' "death" and intense pressure to produce another story. And ever since he brought Holmes back, the character has become immortal. I am delighted to be one of the many authors who have contributed to his immortality through my three novels and graphic novel featuring Mycroft Holmes, Sherlock's smarter brother.

My love of the genre was inspired by watching Basil Rathbone and Nigel Bruce playing Holmes and Watson in the movies when I was a child. Later, when I was traveling so much as a professional basketball player, I read all the Holmes stories on the long plane flights. This in turn led me reading other mystery writers, which I continue to do today.

Why then did I choose to write about Mycroft rather than Sherlock? Part of the reason is that the stories barely mention Mycroft, except to say that he was smarter and less disciplined than Sherlock. This gave me leeway to create from practically nothing the character I wanted to write about. One of the things I like about mysteries is that they are, at their core, morality tales in which characters must grapple with choices of right and wrong. The best mystery writers offer layered detectives who struggle and who try to restore justice and order to the chaos created by murder. For me, that chaos was symbolic of the endemic injustice in society, so I wanted a detective who was willing to face those injustices head-on with courage and intelligence.

Sherlock is a bit of an anomaly in that he uses his remarkable abilities to quench his own intellectual thirst. If someone else benefits, that's just a

16

happy byproduct. Mycroft, on the other hand, uses his abilities to further justice and to benefit society. Sherlock is more like the amoral Sam Spade in Hammett's *The Maltese Falcon*, whose motivation for solving the case is that it would be "bad for business" not to. Mycroft is more like Marlowe in Raymond Chandler's novels or Ross Macdonald's Lew Archer. They also doggedly pursue the truth, but they do so out of a commitment to justice. Although I am entertained by brilliant loners like Holmes and Spade, I admire characters like Mycroft and Marlowe who want to better their communities.

In both my novels and graphic novel, I write about the young Mycroft. Basically, it's a superhero origin story about how he came to hone his skills and why he chose to use them to make the world a better place for everyone. Maybe it's my own origin story: Honing my basketball skills and using my fame as a platform to better society. And when the basketball days were done, honing my writing skills to tell stories about a young genius who time and time again faces moral crossroads – and each time chooses the right path.

It's not just that he chooses the right path, but that he uses rational thinking to do so. We are in an Age of De-enlightenment, when politicians openly lie because they know their followers don't care about the truth. We have smart phones, the most powerful educational tool in the history of the human race, and we use it send photos of our food rather than fact-check our leaders who control our economic and social futures. The Holmes brothers represent logic, rational thinking, keen observation – all the tools people need to seize control of their lives and improve their communities and country. They represent us at our intellectual best and present a benchmark that we should all strive toward.

More important, they're entertaining and exciting.

We all have our personal reasons for loving the stories of Sherlock Holmes. Whatever yours are, Dear Reader, you need only to turn the page with giddy anticipation because on the other side, the game will be afoot.

Kareem Abdul-Jabbar
*June 2019*

17

# All Supernatural or Preternatural Agencies are Ruled Out As a Matter of Course
## by Roger Johnson

In his preface to the 1928 anthology *Best Detective Stories of the Year* (London: Faber & Faber), Mgr. Ronald A. Knox wrote:

> *I laid down long ago certain main rules, which I reproduce here with a certain amount of commentary; not all critics will be agreed as to their universality or as to their general importance, but I think most detective "fans" will recognize that these principles, or something like them, are necessary to the full enjoyment of a detective story. I say "the full enjoyment"; we cannot expect complete conformity from all writers, and indeed some of the stories selected in this very volume transgress the rules noticeably. Let them stand for what they are worth.*

The second rule – "All supernatural or preternatural agencies are ruled out as a matter of course" – seems obvious, though it had already been successfully broken by William Hope Hodgson in his tales of *Carnacki the Ghost-Finder*, who applies proper detective methods to determine whether a supposed haunting is genuine or not. [1] The rule would be broken again, of course, most notably, perhaps, by John Dickson Carr in some excellent short stories and an outstanding novel, *The Burning Court*.

Knox's commentary on this particular rule reads in full:

> *All supernatural or praeternatural agencies are ruled out as a matter of course. To solve a detective problem by such means would be like winning a race on the river by the use of a concealed motor-engine. And here I venture to think there is a limitation about Mr. Chesterton's Father Brown stories. He nearly always tries to put us off the scent by suggesting that the crime must have been done by magic; and we know that he is too good a sportsman to fall back upon such a solution. Consequently, although we seldom guess the answer*

18

*to his riddles, we usually miss the thrill of having suspected the wrong person."*

That dig at G.K. Chesterton's most famous contribution to the genre is rather curious. It suggests that the identification of the culprit is the only point of a detective story. Mgr. Knox may have believed it, [2] and the term "whodunnit" unfortunately perpetuates that blinkered idea, but it ignores character, atmosphere and two of the essential puzzles posed by Chesterton and solved by Father Brown. To the question of "*Who?*" we should add "*Why?*" and – most important in this context, though dismissed by Knox as mere riddles to be guessed – "*How?*"

Like Sherlock Holmes in at least three indisputable Canonical exploits, the little priest is faced with situations that appear to be impossible and therefore the work of unearthly powers. But he knows, and we know, that magic has no place here: A human, or at least a natural, agency is at work. Despite Knox's censure, we are not deprived of "*the thrill of having suspected the wrong person*", *and* we have the additional excitement of trying to work out how the apparently impossible was achieved.

We know too that Sherlock Holmes was there before Father Brown. The tradition established by Arthur Conan Doyle in *The Hound of the Baskervilles*, "The Devil's Foot", and "The Sussex Vampire" lives and flourishes, as this collection proves!

Roger Johnson, BSI, ASH
Editor: *The Sherlock Holmes Journal*
*August 2019*

## NOTES

1 – One of Carnacki's investigations, a very neat little detective story called "The Find", doesn't even hint at the supernatural.

2 – His own mystery novels are rarely read these days, unlike the Father Brown stories.

# Stories, Stepping Stones,
# and the Conan Doyle Legacy
## by Steve Emecz

Undershaw
*Circa 1900*

The MX Book of New Sherlock Holmes Stories has now raised over $50,000 for Stepping Stones School for children with learning disabilities and is by far the largest Sherlock Holmes collection in the world - by several measures, stories, authors, pages and positive reviews from the critics. *Publishers Weekly* has been reviewing since Volume VI and we have had a record ten straight great reviews. Here are some of their best comments:

> *"This is more catnip for fans of stories faithful to Conan Doyle's originals"* (Part XIII)

> *"This is an essential volume for Sherlock Holmes fans"* (Part XI)

*"The imagination of the contributors in coming up with variations on the volume's theme is matched by their ingenious resolutions"* (Part VIII)

MX Publishing is a social enterprise – all the staff, including me, are volunteers with day jobs. The collection would not be possible without the creator and editor, David Marcum, who is rightly cited multiple times by *Publishers Weekly* and others as probably the most accomplished Sherlockian editor ever.

In addition to Stepping Stones School, our main program that we support is the Happy Life Children's Home in Kenya. My wife Sharon and I are on our way in December for our seventh Christmas in a row at Happy Life. It's a wonderful project that has saved the lives of over 600 babies. You can read all about the project in the second edition of the book *The Happy Life Story*.

Our support of both of these projects is possible through the publishing of Sherlock Holmes books, which we have now been doing for a decade. You can find out more information about the Stepping Stones School at:

You can find out more information
about the Stepping Stones School at:

*www.steppingstones.org.uk*

and Happy Life at:

*www.happylifechildrenshomes.com*

You can find out more about MX Publishing
and reach out to us through our website at:

*www.mxpublishing.com*

Steve Emecz
*August 2019*
Twitter: *@steveemecz*
LinkedIn: *https://www.linkedin.com/in/emecz/*

Undershaw
*September 9, 2016*
*Grand Opening of the Stepping Stones School*
*(Photograph courtesy of Roger Johnson)*

The Doyle Room at Stepping Stones, Undershaw
*Partially funded through royalties from*
The MX Book of New Sherlock Holmes Stories

**Sherlock Holmes** (1854-1957) was born in Yorkshire, England, on 6 January, 1854. In the mid-1870's, he moved to 24 Montague Street, London, where he established himself as the world's first Consulting Detective. After meeting Dr. John H. Watson in early 1881, he and Watson moved to rooms at 221b Baker Street, where his reputation as the world's greatest detective grew for several decades. He was presumed to have died battling noted criminal Professor James Moriarty on 4 May, 1891, but he returned to London on 5 April, 1894, resuming his consulting practice in Baker Street. Retiring to the Sussex coast near Beachy Head in October 1903, he continued to be associated in various private and government investigations while giving the impression of being a reclusive apiarist. He was very involved in the events encompassing World War I, and to a lesser degree those of World War II. He passed away peacefully upon the cliffs above his Sussex home on his 103rd birthday, 6 January, 1957.

**Dr. John Hamish Watson** (1852-1929) was born in Stranraer, Scotland on 7 August, 1852. In 1878, he took his Doctor of Medicine Degree from the University of London, and later joined the army as a surgeon. Wounded at the Battle of Maiwand in Afghanistan (27 July, 1880), he returned to London late that same year. On New Year's Day, 1881, he was introduced to Sherlock Holmes in the chemical laboratory at Barts. Agreeing to share rooms with Holmes in Baker Street, Watson became invaluable to Holmes's consulting detective practice. Watson was married and widowed three times, and from the late 1880's onward, in addition to his participation in Holmes's investigations and his medical practice, he chronicled Holmes's adventures, with the assistance of his literary agent, Sir Arthur Conan Doyle, in a series of popular narratives, most of which were first published in *The Strand* magazine. Watson's later years were spent preparing a vast number of his notes of Holmes's cases for future publication. Following a final important investigation with Holmes, Watson contracted pneumonia and passed away on 24 July, 1929.

*Photos of Sherlock Holmes and Dr. John H. Watson courtesy of Roger Johnson*

# The MX Book
## of
## New Sherlock Holmes Stories
## Part XVII:
## Whatever Remains . . .
## Must Be the Truth
## (1891-1898)

# The Violin Thief
## by Christopher James

The
thief
who
stole,
one
winter
night,
Holmes's
prized
Stradivarius,
holds it in his hands
like a sparrow's coffin;
feels its small weight,
its girlish waist; thinks
how its shape
reminds him
of a nibbled almond,
or a cello miniaturised
by an old, bored magician.
He waits for his payment
plucking the four strings
while someone hums
The Devil's Trill
Sonata
in
the
next room.

# The Spectre of
# Scarborough Castle
## by Charles Veley and Anna Elliott

### Chapter I

My story begins February 13th, 1891, the morning before St. Valentine's Day. I was barely awake at my home in Paddington when I received a telephoned request from Mrs. Hudson.

"He's just had a telegram and asked for you, Doctor," that good lady said. "If you might look in on him?"

Despite the bitterly cold weather I took a cab to Baker Street. Prior to seeing Holmes, however, I stopped in at Otto's, the Baker Street stationer's shop where I normally acquire my pens, papers, and notebooks, to purchase a Valentine's card for Mary, my dear wife. The aisles were crowded with male shoppers on missions similar to mine. Making my way among them, I selected a card with a strong red coloring and fewer lacy frills than most of the other offerings.

As I glanced over the cards and read their sentimental messages, I could not help but think of Holmes and his resolute detachment when it came to matters of the heart. It occurred to me that Holmes would likely never receive a Valentine's Day card, although there were countless individuals who were most grateful to him for the help he had provided over the years. It seemed to me a sad thing that Holmes would go through his life without the romantic affection that, for me, at least, made life most deeply worthwhile.

Putting such fruitless musings aside, I completed my purchase and walked the short distance to 221b Baker Street, where I let myself in using my own key. I mounted the seventeen steps to the rooms I had once shared with Holmes and opened the door to the sitting room.

A suitcase partially blocked my path. I saw Holmes seated calmly on his usual chair beside the fireplace. The golden glow from the burning coals lit up his aquiline features, accentuating the lines of his sharp profile.

He looked surprisingly fresh.

"Ah, Watson!" he said. "Do come in and warm yourself. I perceive you have been at Otto's to purchase a card for Mary. The stationer's emblem on the thin paper wrapper proclaims it."

"And you, my dear fellow," I replied, not to be outdone. "I perceive you are on your way to Paris. Your suitcase here and the stamp on the baggage label make their own proclamations."

33

"Indeed?" He gave me one of his small smiles. "Do you perceive more?"

Encouraged, I entered the room and continued, "Yes, I do, Holmes. Your freshly shaven appearance and alert demeanor indicate that you are engaged on a case of some sort. An important one, I would further conjecture, since you would not make a Continental journey merely for your own amusement."

Holmes nodded. "Brilliant, my dear fellow. You have observed well."

"Thank you."

"But regrettably, what you have described is not accurate."

*I might have known*, I thought.

I said, "Please enlighten me."

Holmes reached for his pipe and tobacco. "The suitcase at the door is not my suitcase," he said, "and it is not on its way to France. It has been sent to me, at my request. However, its contents should prove helpful to me when I do travel to Paris, possibly even today, on a very important matter for a very highly-placed individual. In truth, had it not been for a request regarding another case, I would have been on the Dover train by now. So you should take some consolation in knowing that you are partially correct in deducing that I was on my way to Paris, and that I am occupied with at least one case."

"Mrs. Hudson said you had received a telegram this morning?"

"Indeed. I am expecting a visit from a police commissioner, from a humble Yorkshire town called Scarborough. It is along the coast."

"I know of it," I said. "A spa there advertises spring waters with purportedly curative powers. All quackery, of course. But why should a Yorkshire police commissioner delay your important journey to Paris?"

At that moment our outside bell rang.

"That will be the commissioner," Holmes said. "I do hope you will remain. I believe that you may be of some assistance."

We heard a heavy tread on the stairs, and in a few moments the door was opened by a stocky, ruddy-faced man dressed in a thick gray tweed overcoat and suit, hatless, red-haired, and wearing elegant but somewhat scuffed calfskin boots.

He glanced momentarily around the room before his gaze settled on me. He gave me a broad grin. "I just saw you in the stationer's," he said. He held up a thin paper bag, identical to mine. "And judging from your wedding ring, I reckon we were on the same errand." He added, "For different ladies, of course."

His manner was so friendly and outgoing that I took an instant liking to the fellow. "Valentine's Day," I replied.

"And a good woman is hard to find." He held out a hand. "I'm George Marcus, Commissioner of Police in Scarborough."

His grip was firm. "I am John Watson. This is Mr. Sherlock Holmes."

Holmes remained in his chair, but he gave a cordial nod to the commissioner. "Your powers of observation are evident," he said. Our visitor removed his overcoat and settled into the chair opposite Holmes, who went on, "Your telegram mentioned that the matter was a sensitive one. What brings you to consult me?"

"We had best begin with this, Mr. Holmes." He took from his pocket a folded-up newspaper and passed it across to Holmes. "A story in the Scarborough *Gazette.*"

The commissioner continued as Holmes examined the newspaper. "That edition of *The Gazette* was printed a month ago. Wintertime is the slow season for our town, and for most other towns along the seacoast. We have our fishing, and our spa, but we do not really come alive until the weather is warm enough for visitors to visit our beaches and hotels. In truth, we rely on the income from summer visitors, made possible by the railway. Since the direct connection with York was put in, our town has grown dramatically in size."

"That is fortunate," I said, watching Holmes out of the corner of my eye.

"Yes, but the whims of a fickle public can be a two-edged sword, Dr. Watson. If the summer visitors no longer favor us with their custom, we would lose all we have gained. Thousands of our townspeople would be out of work and their families would be destitute. My own circumstances would be forever altered as well. It would be a great shame for both my wife and me if we had to leave, for the town is indeed a beautiful spot, even in the winter. The Grand Hotel, for example, overlooks the ocean, and I have planned a wonderful Valentine's Day supper there with my wife. The cold, of course, will not be a factor tomorrow night since we shall be indoors, overlooking the beach through the large glass patio, which is quite comfortably heated – "

"Mr. Commissioner," Holmes said. "Are you attempting to persuade me to come to Scarborough to enjoy the views of the ocean at night in February?"

The commissioner looked embarrassed. "Certainly not, Mr. Holmes. It is just that – well, I must admit it–I am trying to induce you to see the town as more than just a town. As something valuable that should be preserved. A town with a history, a jewel for all England – oh, what is the use? I cannot make you feel what I feel. My own love for the town is so bound up with my own happiness with my wife."

He turned to me. "Dr. Watson, you perhaps can understand. But Mr. Holmes, I fear I have got off on the wrong foot with you. I do have a problem that I believe will challenge your intellect. And I know that an intellectual challenge is what generally moves you to take action. I just wanted you to know what a great deal of good you will be doing if you take the case."

Holmes had finished with the paper by this time, and he passed it across to me. "I take it the article written by this Patrick Shinford is what you wished me to consider," he said.

"Indeed. Perhaps it would be well if Dr. Watson also had a look."

I ran my gaze over the headline:

*Spectre in Scarborough Castle*
*Terrifies Local Woman*
*by Patrick Shinford*

I skimmed the details of the account, which clearly had been written to emphasize the atmosphere and emotion of the incident. Setting those colorfully descriptive details aside, I noted the facts. A town resident had been walking her dog before bedtime in the vicinity of the ruins of the old seacoast castle, parts of which had recently been excavated. The moon was full. The dog seemed distressed, though there was no one else in sight. Then the woman thought she saw a ghostly figure bearing down on her. She and the dog ran home.

"Perhaps the dog was reacting to the moon," I observed.

"Perhaps," the commissioner replied. "We examined the area for footprints, naturally, but there had been rain by the time we were made aware of the incident. We found nothing."

"Do you have a file on the case?" asked Holmes.

"I do. However, I haven't brought it with me. The story is merely background for the matter I have come to discuss. In itself, as it is written, the story is harmless. Indeed, this sort of thing is good for business."

Holmes nodded. "People will visit locations of infamy hoping to see a ghost, or to indulge their fears of the supernatural. I know that Scarborough Castle has attracted a number of legends of troubled spirits, having suffered many horrors over many centuries of conflict."

"Quite right, Mr. Holmes. The paper relies on advertising from local merchants and hotels, you see, and so wants stories that help bring in more visitors. We are all in this together, one might say."

"But if increased business was the intent of the story," I asked, "why would the paper publish at the slowest time of the year? Why not wait until later, when visitors are more likely to be making their holiday travel plans?"

"My apologies, Doctor. I should have told you about the Bass Brewery excursion. The company provides an annual summer holiday for eight-thousand employees and their wives, and their children. They travel to only one destination each summer. Last year they hired fourteen trains, each with fourteen railway carriages. Each worker had his day's wages paid in advance plus up to a guinea in pocket money. As you may expect, that business can do a town like ours a power of good. We were victorious in the competition last year, and this year we need to win again."

"When will the Bass company select the winner?" Holmes asked.

"Two of their representatives are scheduled to visit Scarborough tomorrow, prior to making their recommendation to the full committee."

"You cannot believe this report of an imaginary spectre would harm your chances."

"No, Mr. Holmes. But an actual, physical attack would be most damaging. People expect safety on holiday. If the threat of an actual attacker were to be noted by the Bass committee – well, it is quite certain that they would look to other towns. Unless, of course, they knew that the attacker had been caught, or were reassured in some other manner as to the efficacy of our safety measures."

"I take it that a physical attack of some kind has recently occurred," Holmes said.

Commissioner Marcus hung his head for a moment. "Yesterday."

"Which prompted your telegram and your visit," said Holmes. "I do wish you had begun our interview with that fact, and not by attempting to sway my emotions."

"You are quite right, Mr. Holmes. And I shall beat around the bush no further."

The commissioner took a deep breath. "Yesterday evening, the *Gazette* reporter Patrick Shinford was found dead at the base of the wall of Scarborough Castle. His skull had been crushed."

Holmes sat silent for a long moment, his fingertips steepled, apparently lost in thought. Then his gaze cleared.

"How were you notified?"

"At my home. By telephone."

"When was this?"

"Around eight o'clock last night."

"Who called you?"

"Chalmers, the editor of *The Gazette*. He called me to report Mr. Shinford was missing. He was expecting Shinford at *The Gazette* offices.

Shinford had promised to deliver a story by seven, so as to be in time for the next morning's edition."

"What did you do?"

"I went straight to the castle. Took two constables with me. That is where we found the body."

"Why look for Shinford at the castle?"

"Shinford had gone there, according to Chalmers. To confirm something about the ghost."

"Did you examine the body?"

"I did not. It was dark and the weather was bad. Not much could be seen. My men have cordoned off the area, however, and I shall have the written report from the medical examiner today. When I return to Scarborough, of course. It is a four-hour journey from Kings Cross Station."

"I am aware of that," Holmes said. "I assume you wish me to travel with you."

"I should be most grateful – "

"But I should like to know why you thought to bring me into the case. You have competent people, no doubt, and you strike me as a competent investigator."

The commissioner leaned forward, spreading his arms and turning up his palms. "Your reputation, sir, is my reason for requesting your assistance. My position in the town is not all-powerful, and with the stakes so high, of such great importance to the Scarborough's future – "

"The Bass excursion people?" Holmes interrupted.

"Yes, exactly. They will require reassurance that active measures are being taken to eliminate the risk of another attack. I need not only to *do* all that I can, but to *appear* to do all that I can. You understand the distinction. Bringing in a man of your stature for this case will reassure the townspeople, and the newspapers – there is also an evening paper, *The Clarion* – will react accordingly. Perhaps they will even print something favourable. Or perhaps they may aid us in the investigation, by printing what we wish our quarry to read."

"You do not think the reporter died from an accidental fall."

"I do not."

"Your reason?"

"At dawn this morning, just before I sent you my telegram, I received a telephone call from our medical examiner. The examiner noted two fractures of Shinford's skull. One was at the front, where one would expect after a fall, and which was consistent with the fractures of the bones of Shinford's hands and arms. The second fracture, however, was at the base of the skull."

38

"Suggestive," Holmes said. "Not conclusive, since there could have been an impact with the ridge of the castle before the long drop to the ground. However, an intentional blow is a more likely explanation. Now, what can you tell me about Mr. Shinford? Who might wish to harm him?"

"There would be an extensive list of enemies," said the commissioner. "He was a notorious busybody. No one really liked him. He had a bad leg, some accident at birth, they say, and I expect he was pretty well roughed up about it when he was a boy. Once he'd grown, he still had to walk with a cane. Developed a pretty big chip on his shoulder, if you take my meaning. A nasty way about him."

"Then it seems we have a number of suspects from which to choose," Holmes said.

The commissioner's eyes widened in hope. "So you'll come back with me?"

Holmes shook his head. "Regrettably, as Dr. Watson knows, I am committed to another matter requiring me to sail at once to the Continent," Holmes said. He indicated the suitcase at our doorway with a brief gesture.

The commissioner's shoulders slumped in disappointment.

"However," Holmes continued, "Dr. Watson might assist you."

My surprise must have been evident, for Holmes deliberately looked away from me as he continued. "His medical expertise will be valuable in determining whether Mr. Shinford died solely as a result of a fall, or whether he was injured before a fall, or whether he was simply attacked at the base of the castle. Besides, Dr. Watson has experience in matters that appear to be supernatural. A few years ago, he was of invaluable assistance, in the county of Devon, in apprehending a murderer who, although diabolically evil, was unquestionably mortal. And the name of Dr. Watson is as recognized by the public as my own. He would be a perfect ally for your investigation. He might also send me reports, and I could reply with recommendations."

He paused and looked at me. "That is, if Dr. Watson is amenable."

Something in his glance, and his reference to our Devon adventure, gave me the impression that he wished to employ the same method he had used for that case.

At that time, he had pretended to be in London, while actually he had been nearby, investigating *incognito*, on the moors and in the small village near to the estate of Sir Henry Baskerville, our client, so as not to arouse suspicion and to keep the murderer off his guard.

I was inclined to accept.

But my thoughts turned to Mary. I had made a Valentine's Day dinner reservation for us tomorrow at The Criterion. Inadvertently, I looked down at the thin brown paper bag, which I still held in my hand.

"Will your wife be disappointed?" the commissioner asked.

## Chapter II

I took a hansom cab to my home in Paddington, intending to deliver my Valentine's card to Mary and then pack for the trip to Scarborough.

Regrettably, Mary was out shopping. I scrawled a hasty note and left it on our dining room table along with the card. It required only a few minutes for me to prepare my suitcase and make arrangements for Anstruther to attend to my patients for the next week. I then waited in my vestibule, glancing at my watch, hoping Mary would return and enable me to deliver my explanation and farewell in person. But she did not, and my watch showed that I would have to catch a cab and make haste to King's Cross Station if I weren't to miss the noon train. She would understand, I thought. My absence wouldn't be long, and she had always insisted that I help with any matters on which Holmes needed my aid.

The commissioner had booked seats for the two of us in a first-class carriage. As we rode, he told me some of the history of the castle, including the legends that had grown up around a number of traitors who had been beheaded there.

"Ah, yes," I said. "Holmes mentioned legends and horrors."

A shadow passed over the commissioner's face. "I grew up in Scarborough. My father was a constable in the Scarborough police force, and I began at the same rank, twenty years ago. One sees a lot over the years that one would like to forget, if you take my meaning."

He took out his pipe and a tobacco pouch, and for a moment I was under the impression that a further explanation would be forthcoming. But instead he said, "Now, let me tell you about the castle as it operates today, and about the schedule I propose we follow upon our arrival. I should like both of us first to go directly to the area where the body of the reporter was found. It will be approaching sundown by then, but we will still have an hour's daylight in which to examine the ground and the steps along the castle walls above."

So it was that at just a few minutes before five o'clock the commissioner and I found ourselves upon the precipice of the ruined Scarborough Castle tower, a stark barren shell of a structure, with no roof or interior floors, and with only three bare stone walls left standing. We had climbed what seemed like hundreds of stone steps that hugged the interior of those walls. I was unsteadily straddling one of the tower battlements, looking eastward towards the shining gray waves of the sea.

Behind us the setting sun was nearly at the horizon. In the fading golden light, the tall tower cast a long, jagged shadow.

Not far away to the south was the only active building in the area, the South Steel Battery, where, I had been told, ammunition and other military supplies were stored against the unlikely event of an invasion from the sea. Nearly one-hundred feet below us, white canvas tarps had been spread to cover the ground in order to preserve whatever impression remained from the impact where the reporter's body had fallen.

A short distance beyond, the ground dropped precipitously away. The seashore below, I thought, must be three-hundred feet below the base of the castle, and thus four-hundred feet below where I was now being buffeted by the wind. My cold wet hands slipped on the lichen-slick rocks. I dug my knees into the edge of the stone wall to steady my frame and prevent me from toppling over the edge to my certain death.

I was examining the area as closely as the waning sunlight and my precarious position would allow. Using Holmes's methods, I wanted to reconstruct how the *Gazette* reporter had come to fall – or whether he had been pushed. If the latter, had he and a companion climbed the long, narrow stone stairway, as the commissioner and I had done to reach this height? I had already examined the steps themselves for footprints, but so many visitors had trod those stones for so many years that the surface had worn smooth. It was impossible for me to determine whether the *Gazette* reporter had climbed alone to meet someone, or whether he had walked up with a companion.

"Anything?" the commissioner asked, his eyes downcast. He was leaning back against the wall, bracing himself against the wind, clinging to the slippery rock formation.

"I am looking for fabric," I said. "Where the reporter's coat or trousers might have scraped as his body went over."

"He was wearing a green wool overcoat," the commissioner said. "Hard to distinguish in this light, on these moss-covered rocks."

I wished that Holmes, with his keen observational powers, was with us. But he was not. It was up to me.

I said, "I see nothing here to indicate anyone fell from this place."

"Yet it is directly above where the body was found."

"Shinford would have been a very reckless fellow to climb over the top at this location."

"Or terrified by a ghost. Or something pretending to be one," the commissioner said. "But we had now best make our way down the steps, while there is still light to examine where the body fell."

41

We reached the grassy surface at the foot of the tower after about five minutes' careful descent. There, in the shadows, two uniformed constables pulled back the canvas tarp to reveal the surface of the yellow-green, sandy turf. The newly-visible area had sunk as though compressed by a great and forceful impact. The depression vaguely resembled the shape of a man.

I got down on my knees, as I was certain that Holmes would have done, and examined the concave area in the turf. When I had completed my inspection, the constables and the commissioner looked at me as if for guidance.

"The outlines are distinct," I said. "Here the hands and elbows struck. Between them, the head. Behind them there, the knees and the feet."

I stood and surveyed the perimeter. My eyes stung from the sharp chill of the sea wind. However, owing to the shadows caused by the low angle of the setting sun behind us, more slight indentations in the turf were visible near where the body had fallen. "I can see dim impressions of footmarks," I said, "but those are likely those of the persons who discovered the body, and the others who removed it from the scene."

"Your conclusion?" asked the commissioner.

"The body fell here and lay still. It was not dragged here and staged to appear to have fallen. At least that will be my interim conclusion. I may change it later, when I have examined the body."

In the police coach, the commissioner went over our upcoming schedule. "We have an hour at the mortuary," he said, "then another at the rooming house where the reporter was staying. Then, at eight o'clock, my wife has arranged a light supper event at our home where you can speak with several individuals who knew the deceased. I might add that they also have a keen interest in the economic prosperity of the town, and the successful visit of the representatives of the Bass Company tomorrow."

"They will want me to say that the reporter's death is an accident," I said.

"Indeed. That would be the path of least resistance. Yet if it is not the path of truth, we cannot follow it."

I was gratified to hear those words from the commissioner, though I didn't say so, since I knew that he expected me to take his professional integrity as a given, which of course I was inclined to do. I did feel somewhat uneasy at the way he was controlling our schedule, however. I doubted that Holmes would have submitted to such detailed direction.

I reminded myself that the commissioner was simply taking command of the situation, as his position required. And it was certainly improbable that he wished to conceal anything, since he was putting so much effort into the investigation. His late-night visit to the scene, his dawn railway journey to London and return, our late afternoon inspection, where we had both been knocked about by the chill February wind – these all evidenced his desire to find the truth.

The coach stopped. The wind lashed at us both as I opened the door. Waiting for us outside the mortuary entrance was a uniformed constable. He saluted the commissioner and handed over a yellow envelope which I could see contained a telegraph message.

"It is for you," said the commissioner.

Opening the message, I read these words.

*Telephone Mary at once. S.H.*

I showed the message to the commissioner and asked, "Is there a telephone connection to London?

"We have a telephone here at the mortuary," the commissioner said. "And we now can put calls through to London, via the new trunk line to Birmingham. Just installed last year – makes us more competitive with Brighton."

"Most convenient."

"I take it Mary is your wife?"

"Indeed."

"Doubtless she will want to know where she can reach you if needed. You will be staying at my home, if that meets with your approval. At least for this first evening. Our spare bedroom is quite comfortable, and my wife has already aired out the room and had the linens changed. Tomorrow you are perfectly free to change to one of the town's commercial establishments if you like. You will meet the managers of both the major hotels at our little supper tonight, and I expect they will vie for your custom."

"I shall attempt to be diplomatic," I said.

"Well, let us get inside and you can make your call," the commissioner said.

It took nearly five minutes for the operators to make the connection, but finally I heard Mary's voice.

To my surprise, she answered with, "Mr. Holmes said you would be calling."

"He telephoned?"

"No, he came here to Paddington. He said he was on his way to the Dover train. He wanted to apologize for taking you away from me on the eve of Valentine's Day. Isn't that extraordinary?"

"Indeed, it is – "

"I had already read your note and your card, of course, but I wasn't expecting *him*!"

"I wonder why he came," I said.

"I asked him that, of course. And he told me. He wanted you to send your reports to Mycroft, by telegraph if possible. Mycroft will be aware of his whereabouts, since it is a diplomatic mission that is taking him to France. He also said you were to be cautious, and to pay particular attention to the condition of the top side of the body. Whatever that means."

"I understand," I said.

"He also said this case would not be like Dartmoor, but that he would be with you in spirit."

I understood. After letting Mary know where I would be staying and wishing her good night, I rang off. I felt grateful she had omitted to ask me what Holmes meant by his reference to Dartmoor, for I did not want her to worry about me.

But now I knew. Holmes would not be nearby, hidden somewhere in the background, watching and ready to come to my aid. I really was on my own.

## Chapter III

The body of Patrick Shinford lay on the mortuary slab, face up, covered only with a sheet. The face was distorted and discolored beyond recognition, and stained a greenish-brown by the impact with the grassy turf below the castle tower. The room was cold. The commissioner and I were alone for a moment, but then Barrett, the medical examiner, stepped in. Small, balding, with a dark brown toothbrush-style mustache, he was carrying a brown pasteboard folder.

"My report," he said, after introductions had been made. "I thought you might wish to examine my findings as well as the body, Dr. Watson. I have inventoried the contents of the thoracic cavity in the usual manner before closing up. The skull cavity remains empty and unsutured in case you wish to examine the damage from the inside. The man's garments and the personal possessions recovered from the scene are in that box on the table."

I stepped forward and bent down to observe, first, the ruined forehead, nose, and cheekbones, and then the shaved crown of the head, which had been opened by the examiner's saw and scalpel. At the base of the skull the hair above the neck was matted and caked with blood.

"I believe you mentioned a fracture at the back of the head," I said to the commissioner.

Dr. Barrett spoke up immediately. "All the details on that are contained in my report. The damage in the lambdoidal area is severe."

"The connection to the spinal cord – ?"

" – was nearly severed. A powerful blow. Sufficient to crush that area of the skull."

"Not merely a fracture?"

"Probably done with a heavy object – a rock perhaps."

"An abundance of those in the area," the commissioner remarked.

"I cannot be certain, however, that the blow to the back of the skull was the only cause of death," said Barrett. "The bruising at the back is barely more pronounced than the bruising at the front. You will note here – " he pointed to the center of the sternum " – a round indentation and discoloration. That bruise is the only one with a distinctive pattern, indicating that it had enough time to develop before the circulation ceased. You will also note the legs – one being shorter than the other and with weaker musculature. But the bones of both legs were broken by the impact of his fall. The force required to do that indicates that the elevation from which he fell was considerable."

"Might we turn the body?" I asked.

We did so. Mindful of Holmes's instructions, I paid particular attention to the back, which would have been the top side when the body had been discovered. I saw nothing unusual. But at the base of the thighs, just behind both knees, there was a marked bruising, about an inch wide, the skin abraded but not quite split open. The marks were the same on both legs.

"A staff, or a long rod," I said.

The commissioner nodded. "He was taken from behind. Possibly while distracted by some supposedly supernatural phenomenon."

"Probably the attacker was hidden on one of the staircases," I said, "or possibly he dropped down on some pretext – tying a shoelace or the like – to pick up the weapon. Then he swung hard, bringing Mr. Shinford to his knees."

"Then the attacker swung again," said the commissioner, "also from behind, crushing the base of the skull. He then hauled the body to the edge of the parapet and tumbled it over."

"So, not an accidental fall," said Barrett.

"Though the attacker likely hoped to make it appear to be so," the commissioner said. "In fact, had the body landed on its back, the impact might have obscured these initial wounds."

"It would take a strong arm to wield a staff with such force," I said. "That may narrow our list of suspects." Then I recalled something. "I believe you said Mr. Shinford walked with a cane."

"Yes, he did."

"Was the cane found at the scene?"

"It was not," said the commissioner.

"Otherwise it would have been brought here with his clothing and other possessions," said Barrett.

"Did you notice anything about those?" asked the commissioner.

"Only that his right shoe had been specially built up to compensate for the shortness of his right leg. Nothing else. His garments are torn and stained from the fall."

We spent a few more minutes examining the clothing and personal belongings of the deceased, which included a cheap pocket watch, miraculously unbroken and still ticking, a wallet containing two of Shinford's business cards from *The Gazette*, and a latchkey, presumably from his place of residence. We found nothing inconsistent with the theory of the attacker wielding a staff or heavy pipe, although we added to these weapons the possibility of Shinford's cane having been used against him.

"By the way," said the commissioner as we were leaving the mortuary, "there is one other event on our schedule. If you approve, of course, and provided that you have the stamina after such a busy long day. I have arranged for the police coach to pick us up at my home at ten o'clock tonight, and to drive us back to the castle. It would be well, I feel, for you to see the scene of the incident after dark, as it was at the time the body was discovered. But now, let us see what we can learn from Shinford's rooms."

Shinford's former residence proved to be a large comfortable lodging house only two blocks from the beach. The landlady was a hard-bitten long-faced woman with unsmiling eyes. She showed us in and asked, "When will you have his things cleared out?"

"That will be up to you and the next of kin, if there is such a person," the commissioner said.

"How long had Mr. Shinford been your tenant?" I asked.

"Four years, now."

"A good tenant?"

"He didn't make disturbances, or annoy the others," she said. "Can't ask for more than that in a renter. Except he had fallen behind in his payments the past two months. A death in the family, he said. Needed to provide emergency funds. He promised he would have the money this week. Seemed very confident about it – not the usual kind of whining or wheedling, if you know what I mean. But that's no good to me now."

"Do you know where his relatives live?"

"London, I think. Probably *The Gazette* knows. I had a reference from a London landlord, but I haven't got it any more. I looked, of course, but as I said, it's been four years."

"We shall let you know what we find," the commissioner said.

"Well, I hope you'll be quick about it. I need to start showing the rooms right away."

With that she left us.

We set to work examining the two rooms and their contents, I in the sitting room and the commissioner in the bedroom. I tried to imagine how Holmes would proceed if he were with us.

Recalling other cases that we had shared, I pictured him in my mind. He would be down on the floor. Looking under the rug. Examining floorboards.

I got down on my hands and knees. I found nothing. I examined the baseboards. I found nothing.

Then I noticed a variation in the dust pattern around the circular base of a tall, empty, wooden umbrella and coat-rack stand. On one side of the marble-topped base, there was no gap between the dust on the marble surface and the wooden floor beneath it. But a crescent of cleaner floor showed on the other side. This indicated to me that the stand had recently been moved.

Grasping the wooden pole and gently lowering the stand to the floor, I examined the bottom of the heavy base. I found a metal plate, attached to the wooden frame by two screws. Each of the screws was cleaner than the metal plate to which they were attached. I used my folding pocket knife to loosen the screws and remove the plate.

A small notebook had been stuffed into a cavity within the base of the coat-rack stand. I picked up the notebook and stood to examine it, calling for the commissioner to join me.

There were perhaps thirty pages in the notebook, the first twenty-five of which bore notations, all in blue ink. The remaining pages were blank. At the top of each page that had been written in were initials, and below the initials, in neat columns, were a series of dates and numbers. The pages further in had fewer entries, and those contained more recent dates.

"What do you make of this?" I asked the commissioner.

He ran his finger over the initials at the top of several of the pages. "On this one we begin with *G.M., 1.03.87, 10.2*, followed by a check mark. Below that entry are similar numbers in each column, each followed by a check mark, except for the entry at the bottom, which does not have a check mark. On the next page, we have *R.B. 2.15.87, 15.0*, and a check mark. And below, the same arrangement of numbers, with the last lacking a check mark."

He paused and returned the notebook. "I believe these initials at the top of each page represent persons, and the numbers below represent dates and payments. The check mark indicates the payment has been made. The dates without check marks, you will note, all begin with 02 and end with 91, indicating they were due or are due one day this month."

"Could Mr. Shinford have been a money lender?"

The commissioner shook his head. "If so, there should be more columns, indicating the initial principal Mr. Shinford had advanced the borrower, and the balance remaining after each payment."

His expression became grim. "No, I believe that Mr. Shinford advanced no sums of money. He merely took money from those unfortunate persons whose names will correspond with the initials at the top of each page."

"He was a blackmailer."

"Indeed. Getting what he could, on a regular or irregular basis – you will see how the dates are not all at regular intervals – and never letting his victims get free of him."

"As a reporter, he would be able to investigate many activities in the town without arousing suspicion. You had said he was something of a busybody."

The commissioner nodded. "You realize, of course, that this notebook likely contains the initials of the principal suspects as to Mr. Shinford's murder."

"Each blackmail victim would have a strong motive."

"But the initials may be coded." He pointed to the last entry, which bore only a single "*E*" at the top of the page, and only a single date and number: *02-09-91, 10.0.* There was no check mark.

"His latest victim, it would appear. Only four days ago."

"Yes. But the initial could be anyone. My wife, for example, is named Elsie and you will meet her shortly. She is hardly likely to be a blackmail victim." He paused for a moment, then went on, "Though I do not see a reason to conceal the names, since the notebook was clearly meant to be seen only by Mr. Shinford."

"Evidently we have much to learn," I said.

"I concur. Our next task is to find where Shinford kept his evidence, and also where he kept his ill-gotten gains. The sums indicated on these pages add up to quite a substantial amount – far more than is indicated by the modest clothing and furnishings here in his rooms."

"Yet he was behind in his rent."

"Probably planning to do a runner, cheating his landlady, taking his money with him. Perhaps something may have given him cause." The commissioner looked thoughtful for a moment. "I shall inquire at the banks in town. Also, I shall see as to whether he traveled regularly to another town, where he might have opened another account. Or taken out a safe-deposit box."

He looked at me, "I don't suppose you noticed anything unusual about that built-up shoe of his, did you? Good place to conceal a deposit-box key."

"I didn't notice."

"Well, we can always go back. See if we can pry something out. Or find something sewn into his coat lining. Now we know there's money to be found and possibly a lock to wherever he stored it, we can be alert for a key. If we're fortunate, we will be able to recover the funds and return them to the parties involved."

He tapped the book with his forefinger. "Except for the murderer. No restoration of funds for him. Assuming that all our other suppositions prove correct and that the death was not accidental."

He glanced at his watch. "It is very nearly eight o'clock. I shall leave a constable here to secure the rooms. We can take the police coach to my home and the little gathering my wife has arranged. There, it will be quite natural to ask people what they knew of Mr. Shinford."

"We will say nothing of our discovery here, of course," I said.

He nodded. "Yet when you are introduced to our guests and learn their names, I am sure you will take particular note of their initials."

The inspector's home was only a short ride away, just across from a park. A modest, two-story structure, its brightly-lit windows cast a welcoming glow as we walked across the wide boulevard. Inside I was surprised to find the atmosphere warm and festive. In the parlor, a punch bowl had been set up, and perhaps a dozen guests were milling about, cups in their hands, chatting animatedly.

"I'll put your suitcase in your room upstairs," the commissioner said. "But first, here's Elsie, my wife. She can introduce you around, and I'll join you in a moment."

The commissioner's wife sparkled in a cream-coloured gown and white tiara, crowning an impressive arrangement of lustrous brown hair piled high in the latest fashion. Her dark eyes flashed as she greeted me.

"So delightful to meet you, Doctor!" she said. "You lead a most adventurous life!"

"Only on occasion," I said modestly.

"And your wife allows you to travel, even with Valentine's Day upon us!"

49

"She has always been most understanding." I smiled. "You, I know, will be getting a Valentine's card tomorrow. Your husband and I shop at the same London stationer's."

"I have already received all the gift I could wish for," she said. "I don't know where to direct my thanks, but I will be forever grateful to the person who removed that dreadful man Shinford from our world."

At my surprised look, she continued, "He was attempting to blackmail me, you know. He learned of a small indiscretion that would have harmed my reputation. But that is of no concern to me now. You may think it callous, or you may be shocked by my candor. Yet I know I can trust you, Dr. Watson. I feel relief, and my gratitude is genuine." She paused. "And I am sure you will help my husband find whoever is responsible. Now come, let me introduce you to the others in our party. I think you will find them equally grateful."

I smiled politely as she led me to a middle-aged couple who were sipping punch and chatting comfortably with a third man. My thoughts were somewhat jumbled, for I had expected a game of cat-and-mouse, attempting to interview people and recall their names, and then later match them with the initials in the book we had found in Mr. Shinford's rooms. But here was Elsie, whom the commissioner himself had casually suggested might be "*E*", the latest entry in the list of victims. And she had just volunteered that yes indeed, she had been.

I felt that if I had the notebook with me and read out the initials to the group, going page by page, there would be ready responses from the parties involved. *Oh yes, that's me! Let's have some more punch!*

This I supposed would have been an understandable private response from any of Shinford's former victims, whose burdens had now been lifted. But public celebration? I supposed it indicated that these people were all close friends who trusted one another.

But how ought I to proceed? What would Holmes do now?

Those were the questions at the back of my mind as Elsie introduced me to the couple and their companion.

"This is Dr. Watson, Mr. Sherlock Holmes's associate. Dear George brought him here to investigate – "

"What we're all toasting to?"

At this, the crowd clustered around me. The remarks came thick and fast, and I had no way of attributing them, since I didn't know their names. Yet, hoping to learn something from unguarded speech, I was reluctant to slow down the flow of conversation.

"You're hunting the man who's earned our undying gratitude?"

"If it's a man."

"You mean a woman?"

"I wouldn't ignore the possibility of divine intervention."

"The castle spectre, you mean. That's my idea of divine intervention."

"Old headless what's-his-name? Or the traitor to King Charles?"

"No supernatural forces are needed, if you ask me. The wretch could have just slipped and fallen."

"Unsteady on his pins, we all knew that."

"I think that was the root of his evil personality. Crippled from birth, he blamed the world."

"Yes. Wanted his revenge somehow. Get a bit of his own back."

"Got it back from us."

"Instead of earning an honest living."

"Who knew there could so much fun in speaking ill of the dead?"

"You hated him."

"Who wouldn't hate a man like that? Weaselly little sneak."

There was a momentary lull as the commissioner joined us.

"Ah, George," said one of the guests. "Our generous and honoured host. Here, have some of your own punch. Just been refilled for the third time."

The commissioner looked quite serious. "Thank you, one and all. But we are investigating the possibility that the death was not accidental. Dr. Watson here may have some questions for you. Your truthfulness will be essential, and most appreciated."

A hush fell over the group, but only for a moment. Then Elsie said, "He was a rotter and whoever killed him did the world some good."

"Hear, hear," said a tall aristocratic man. He turned to address me. "Dr. Watson, I am Ellis Chalmers, editor and publisher of *The Gazette*."

"We should drink to you, Chalmers," said another man. "You're the one sent that little snake to his death at the castle, weren't you?"

"Yes, but my motives weren't to benefit you lot," replied Chalmers. "I merely wanted another ghost story. Shinford hadn't given us anything since last month, and with the Bass people coming tomorrow, I thought it as well to give them something exotic. Something worth an overnight stay, rather than just the day train trip to and from the beach."

"Why did you assign Mr. Shinford to write about the castle ghost?" I asked.

"I didn't," he replied. "One day he came in with a tale of a woman walking her dog. That's what started it. There were ghost stories before, of course, but only legends. No reports from living citizens. At least not while I've been with *The Gazette*."

"Did Shinford witness that first incident – the woman with her dog?"

51

"No idea. For all I know, he found her in one of the pubs. Or made up the tale himself."

"Did he object to returning to the castle?"

"He didn't."

"No fears of the headless ghost?"

"He laughed at that sort of thing. He did complain about the grounds, though. The rocks and the slippery steps. Hard to navigate with that bad leg of his."

"When did you last see him?"

"It was around five o'clock, at the office. He was about to leave when I reminded him he had promised me another ghost story today, and that I'd want his copy on my desk by seven that night. He said he'd have it. Then he surprised me, rather."

"Why?"

"I expected he would just go to his desk and bang out something with a new cast of characters. Frightened young honeymoon couple, terrified mother and toddler, something like that. I never thought he would go to the castle again at that hour. But he said he already had something prepared and just wanted to check on a detail, after dark."

"What would he see after dark that he wouldn't have already seen?"

The commissioner spoke up. "Perhaps Dr. Watson and I will find that out within a few minutes," he said. "We plan a visit there to round out our day's investigation."

"I shouldn't disregard the ghost theory, Dr. Watson," said Chalmers. "In the fog, in the wind, in the weather – the mind plays tricks."

"But the weather on the first night was clear, at least according to the first article in *The Gazette*," I said. "The moonlight was specifically mentioned."

"The mist, though. Comes in on the sea wind. In the moonlight, a swirl of white mist – that could look like a spirit, couldn't it?"

"Come now, don't frighten the doctor."

"He's immune. Man of science."

"But what of Shinford's ghost? Anyone here afraid of the wrath of Shinford's ghost?"

"Of course not. None of us could have killed him," said Elsie.

"Why?" I asked.

"Because that night we were all here for The Browning Society meeting." Elsie said. "Except for Mr. Chalmers, and he was at *The Gazette* waiting for Mr. Shinford to deliver his story."

"I called the commissioner from our office," said Chalmers. "You can check on that with the telephone operator, of course."

52

The commissioner nodded. To me he said, "I left when I got the call. The meeting was winding up anyway. But as far as I'm aware, until that call, none of us left the room."

"Assuming we're all telling the truth," Elsie said brightly. She gave her husband a gay smile. "An assumption that has to include you too, dear, doesn't it, since you were here with all of us as well that night?"

"Another good reason to bring in an outside expert such as Dr. Watson," the commissioner said.

"Well, hurry back, both of you," Elsie said. "We'll stay and drink a final toast, to the end of Mr. Shinford. In the next world, may his soul receive the justice it deserves."

## Chapter IV

The police carriage was nowhere to be seen when we stepped into the cold air outside the commissioner's home. "Constables must have been called away on something more urgent," the commissioner said. Then he shrugged. "Maybe it's for the best. Just as quick for us to take my personal carriage, and we'll be home all the sooner."

I helped him hitch up his horse and sat beside him as he drove.

"Your wife told me Shinford had approached her," I said.

"So she really would have been '*E*', the final entry in his book."

"As to the others, we might check off the initials that correspond to those people we have just seen, since each of them provides the other with an alibi."

"That should narrow the field," he said. "We can do that in the morning. I know all their names."

"What are we looking for tonight?"

"We are recreating the scene, so to speak. Something may become apparent."

He said no more, and we drove the short distance to the seacoast park in silence.

In the darkness, Scarborough Castle looked even more foreboding than it had appeared at sunset. The jagged towering ruin rose up grim and black from the surrounding low walls and grassy clearing, silhouetted against the moonlight like a shadowy predator from an old legend. Out beyond the rocky walls, the darkened sea waves shimmered and writhed. Closer in, they dashed themselves into foam, booming and hissing.

"We can see, at least," I said.

"A cold light for a cold evening," the commissioner said.

We stepped down from the carriage and the commissioner tied the horse. I saw no mist and no spectre.

"No one else about," he said. "Hard to hear anyone, with the wind and the waves."

Something about his tone – cold, objective, but with a circumspect lilt, I thought – put me on edge. He was behind me. I was looking at the base of the castle ruin.

I saw movement. A shadow of something. A cloud passing the moon? Or was it my imagination?

I wished that I had brought my Webley revolver. I felt the reassuring heft of my pocket knife in my trousers pocket.

Then in my mind something clicked into place. I turned to face the commissioner.

"When Shinford died," I said, "You were here."

"I thought you might reach that conclusion," he said, very calmly and deliberately, and without a trace of fear or hostility. It was as if we were everyday colleagues discussing a historical case from long ago. "But why?" he continued. "You heard my friends. We were all together. They all saw me when the call came in."

"They were occupied with their poetry meeting. You could easily have gone out and then returned before Chalmers called."

"Why would I do that?"

"Elsie," I said. "Her initial was the last entry in Swinford's book. When we first found the book, you pretended it was an absurd idea to think that she was '*E*'. When I mentioned a few minutes ago that Shinford had approached her, you spoke of her being '*E*' as if you'd just considered it. But when she and I spoke, she was completely casual about what she called her 'indiscretion'. No guilty smile, no request that I keep the information from you. So she must already have told you of Shinford's blackmail attempt."

"What if she had?"

"You cared too deeply for her to let that pass. You went to Shinford directly."

"I did. Yesterday afternoon."

"What happened?"

"I was waiting for Shinford when he left *The Gazette*. He didn't recognize me, because I was muffled up and driving the carriage, something I rarely do. He thought I was a cabman until I showed him my pistol and arrested him for the attempted blackmail of my wife. Then he tried to bargain. He didn't mention that notebook, but he said there was a safety deposit box and that he kept the key hidden here at the castle. Said he could make me rich. So I drove him here. I told him that when I had the key and the name of the bank I'd let him make a run for it. Purely a figure of speech, of course."

54

"He was amenable?"

"When I showed him this pistol, he was."

There was a pistol in the commissioner's hand.

"So Shinford's key is here?"

"Beneath a loose rock in the stairs, he said, just at the top next to one of the upper walls – a perfect hiding place. No one looks at a slimy old rock when they're climbing."

"And he showed you where?"

"Oh, he tried to. He started up the steps, and reached the top, with great difficulty, me behind him all the way. I held his cane, so he couldn't use at against me."

"After you'd hit him with it, behind the knees."

"I admit I was furious with him for approaching Elsie. Still makes my blood boil, when I think of him trying to take advantage of her. Thank the good Lord she came to me first and didn't let her fears for her secret eat into her soul."

He gestured toward the peak of the castle ruin. "In any event, Shinford and I were up there last night. He was hobbling along the ridge towards the south end of the tower. Said his hiding place was just ahead. Then he stumbled and fell. Went over the edge at that crenellation there. All in an instant." He snapped his fingers. "Gone."

"Like that," I said.

"A pity," he continued. "Not for Shinford, of course. He deserved to die. But a pity he didn't reach the hiding place and give me the key. Maybe the climb had tired him out. I made my way back down the steps to where he had fallen. He was face down and not moving or breathing. But I still had his cane and gave him a good whack on the back of his head, just to be certain."

"What did you do with the cane?"

He gestured vaguely towards the sea. "When I'd pitched it away, I realized I couldn't prove I hadn't killed Shinford in a fit of rage and hurled him off the wall. It was only my word against anyone's accusation. So I couldn't let it be known I was here when he died. I drove straight home and joined the poetry club meeting. Didn't tell anyone where I'd been – not even Elsie."

"Didn't they notice your arrival?"

"It was just after six-thirty. The meeting was just beginning. And the call from *The Gazette* came nearly two hours later. When I'd finished talking with Chalmers, I hung up the receiver and told the group that Shinford had gone missing, last seen intending to do a story about the haunted castle ruins. The mention of his name caused quite a stir. Elsie said I'd better get over to the castle to investigate right away."

"Why not just send one of your men?"

"Elsie was afraid Shinford might have some letters with him that would expose her. She wanted me to hide them if I found him first."

"You didn't want to tell her he was already dead."

"Of course not. Later, when I came back and told her the body had been found, she was overjoyed. Called up all the people from her poetry club to give them the good news. But the mayor and the hotel manager were worried about what the Bass excursion people would say about a death at one of the town's biggest tourist attractions, especially when the victim had been writing about it."

"So you had to launch a vigorous investigation."

"But I had to control the investigation, in order to keep any blackmail materials against Elsie or my friends from coming to light. I couldn't do that with one of my own detectives on the case asking his own questions. That's when I realized I needed to bring in someone from the outside."

"Someone famous."

"Who could argue with my choice to bring in Sherlock Holmes? And you, of course, are the next best thing."

"You flatter me."

"Now, we've just one more task ahead of us here tonight. As I said, we need to find Shinford's key."

"Why tonight?"

"Someone else might find it. I can't go up there by myself. I – well, I'm afraid of heights. I come over faint."

I remembered. "You kept your eyes downcast when we climbed the tower this afternoon. You were clinging to the rock wall."

"And I'm nearsighted to boot," the commissioner said. "Come, now, I will show you the general area up on the top. We'll find the key, and return in triumph. You'll get a good night's sleep. Then I'll put you on the train tomorrow. When I find Shinford's safe-deposit box, everyone will get their money back – their fair share anyway. Thanks to you, we have Shinford's book to help us make those calculations."

He stepped back and gestured toward the castle. "Probably best if you lead the way."

"I think not," I said.

"Why not?" A half smile and a look of puzzlement was on his face.

"Not until you tell me the whole truth."

"But I did tell you – "

"No, you did not. Shinford did not die in the way that you described."

"How can you say that? You weren't here. I was."

"You never climbed the tower with Shinford. He would never have chosen such a difficult place to hide his key. A cripple, requiring himself to limp to the top of the castle every time he needed his key, making a dangerous climb on a regular basis in all kinds of weather? No, that is impossible. And when one has eliminated the impossible, what remains, however improbable, must be the solution."

"Poppycock."

"You were here on the ground when you hit Shinford with the cane. He fell to his knees. He pleaded for his life. He probably offered to split his money with you. Probably even gave you the key. Probably handed it over, when you were standing face-to-face and you were pointing your gun at him. But then you used the gun to knock him down again – that made the bruise I saw on his sternum – and rolled him over to grind his face into the dirt, so forcefully that you made his face nearly unrecognizable. Then you kicked him in the back of his head. And that was your undoing."

"Rubbish."

"I know what I saw on the mortuary table. The blow shattering the lambdoidal area came from beneath the base of the skull, not from above. That detail should be in the medical examiner's report, or if not, then Dr. Barrett can re-examine the body and confirm the direction of the impact. He might even match the contour of the fracture with the toe-cap of your shoe."

"That will never happen," the commissioner said.

"You waited a few moments after you had kicked Shinford, catching your breath, no doubt, while he lay motionless, face down. It gave you time to think. You wanted his death to look like an accident, so that the police wouldn't have to investigate Shinford's past. To make it look as though he had fallen from the tower, you jumped on his torso with both feet. Again and again. And then on his arms and legs. He was already dead from your kick to the skull, so more definite bruises did not develop on the body, protected as he was by his thick overcoat."

"You have no proof of any of this wild ranting."

"But I do. Along with the evidence from the mortuary, there is also Shinford's notebook. With Elsie's initial. It can be placed into evidence if needed. Unless you cooperate."

"The book is on my dresser at home. Elsie's indiscretion will never be made public."

"Also, I expect you still have the key Shinford gave you. Unless you dropped it?"

Involuntarily, the commissioner's free hand went to his waistcoat pocket.

He gave a momentary grimace as he realized how his own movement had betrayed him. But the pistol in his other hand remained steady.

"Too bad you won't live to make your case to the court." He drew back the hammer of his revolver. It made an ominous click.

"Surely you are not so foolish as to shoot me with your own police revolver."

"You're right about that too, Doctor. I took this gun from a dead thug twelve years ago. Thought it might come in useful. Well, now it has."

"But why bring me to the castle?"

"Because, Dr. Watson, one way or another, I need you to die here."

My heart pounded in my chest. Finally, I understood. "You need to take police attention away from the death of Shinford."

He gave a smile of acknowledgement. "I had hoped to report that you made the climb and then fell, like Shinford, apparently frightened by something. That account would also have strengthened the legend of the spectre."

"Good for business."

"But if you refuse to cooperate?"

"I do."

"Then I have another alternative that will suit. After tonight, the Scarborough police will be looking for a crazed killer, who presumably grew tired of pretending to be a ghost and merely frightening women, and so turned to murder. The madman killed first a reporter, making it appear to have been a fall, and then killed the famous Dr. Watson, without troubling to conceal his gunshot. I shall be an eyewitness to your death and provide a suitably colorful description. The search for the madman should divert attention from Shinford."

I tried to keep the commissioner talking as I measured the distance between us. "Will you keep Shinford's money?"

"His ill-gotten funds will be useful to me. As will some of his materials, when I find them, which I will be able to do without attracting the notice of my colleagues."

"What will the Bass excursion people say? What will talk of a crazed killer do to the future of Scarborough?"

"I really don't care. The town will always have enough money to pay their police department, and the department always requires a commissioner. But you've been a good chap, Dr. Watson. You're cleverer than I thought. I'll give you a good send-off. I'll say that the shot was meant for me. You ran valiantly at the killer and took the bullet, right in your noble heart. The madman got away while I tried to help you. You'll die a hero."

58

I said, "At least my wife won't be ashamed of me."

Then I leaped at him, diving for his ankles even as I heard his gunshot, hoping to get beneath the trajectory of his bullet and knock him over.

My shoulder collided with his legs as I tackled him. We hit the hard ground together, I on top. He cried out at the impact. I heard another shot, and then another. I was amazed to have felt no bullet, but I still expected to be hit at any moment. I reached out, flailing for his gun.

My fingers were brushed aside by a polished black boot, containing a hard, powerful leg. The boot was stamping down on the commissioner's wrist.

I scrambled to my feet.

The commissioner lay sprawled before me, writhing in pain, his pistol on the ground perhaps two feet away. There was blood on his white shirt front. It made a dark stain in the cold moonlight.

Standing over the commissioner were two young men, both dressed in uniforms of the British Army. One bent down and picked up the commissioner's pistol.

"Apologies for cutting it so closely, Dr. Watson," said one. "But we needed to hear all we could."

"Who are you?" I managed to ask.

"We're night guards from the South Steel Battery Magazine just over there. We protect the munitions. Normally it's a pretty boring job."

"But this afternoon we had a call from the office of the Secretary of War," said the other. "Gave us orders to put two more men on duty tonight and station ourselves here at the castle. Even though it's not Army property. Something to do with a special request from Mr. Sherlock Holmes."

Epilogue

Less than twenty-four hours later I was back in London, somewhat travel-weary, having hurried straight from Kings Cross Station to join Mary at a table for two in the brilliantly sparkling dining room of the magnificent Criterion Restaurant.

As we savored our Valentine's Day evening celebration, I recounted my story. I noticed how her lovely blue eyes reflected the light from the candle between us.

But as I finished my tale, those blue eyes were flashing with indignation.

"So that was his idea of being 'with you in spirit', was it?" Mary said. "Have a cabinet minister send a message to the army, and then just hope for the best?"

59

All I said was, "Fortunately, it worked."

"You might have been killed!"

"Glad I wasn't," I said.

"Even so, you've torn your best trousers and coat, and you've scraped your elbow."

"And justice was done."

"I suppose so." She paused as our waiter appeared and carefully placed our dessert orders on our table: A sorbet for her and a crème brûlée for me.

"Will you send Mr. Holmes a report?" she asked, after our waiter had departed.

"Through Mycroft, as instructed," I said.

"Where do you think he is now?"

"In Paris, I believe."

I reached out and put my hand on hers. "But wherever he is, I know one thing."

"What's that, John?" she said softly.

"I wouldn't trade places with him."

# NOTES:

1.  This is a work of fiction, and the authors make no claim whatsoever that any of the actual locations that appear in this story were even remotely connected with the adventures recounted herein. Moreover, all the characters appearing in the story, except for Sherlock Holmes, John Watson, Mary Watson, and Mrs. Hudson, are entirely the product of the imaginations of the authors. However . . . .

2.  The Scarborough Castle has been the site of many ferocious battles and assaults over two millennia and is now listed as a scheduled monument of national importance under The Ancient Monuments of Archeological Importance Act. The castle has been managed by English Heritage since 1984. The castle grounds are reputed to be haunted by numerous ghosts, including the headless spectre of Piers Gaveston, Earl of Cornwall, who reportedly leaps out of the shadows to frighten tourists into falling to their deaths from the cliffside castle ruins.

3.  1890 Scarborough parish documents describe a South Steel Battery near the main tower, and a magazine in which military stores were kept at that time. There was also an army barracks and a master gunner's house on the site, which served as an accommodation until 1920.

4.  The Bass Excursion was an annual summer railway trip provided by the famous brewing company for its employees from the 1860's through 1914. Many British vacation destinations competed for the highly lucrative business. Scarborough is listed as the destination chosen for eight of the Bass excursions, including 1890, but not 1891.

5.  Dr. Watson records that during the winter and early spring of 1891, newspapers reported that Sherlock Holmes *"had been engaged by the French government upon a matter of supreme importance"*.

# The Case for
# Which the World is
# Not Yet Prepared
## by Steven Philip Jones
### *(To Gary Reed)*

### Chapter I – Mr. Sherlock Holmes

I have on an occasion referred to my friend Mr. Sherlock Holmes as an automaton, an observation inspired as much by his curious faculties as his almost habitual callousness. His numerous accomplishments in the field of detection stand as testament to his mental talents, and on numerous occasions his iron constitution proved the equal to his brain power, but even the most inhuman two-legged calculating machine is made of clay and all mortals have limits. So, while the weakness of failure much less emotion frequently seemed impossible in Holmes, there were rare instances that revealed him to be as human as any man.

One of those instances occurred after The Great War, which I had served on the staff of Queen Alexandra's Military Hospital, primarily in London but occasionally my duties carried me elsewhere, including Malta. Holmes and I had kept in touch during those years through correspondence, but we had not seen one another since immediately before my joining the Royal Army Medical Corps, so I was delighted but surprised when he called at my rooms on Queen Anne Street on a warm September afternoon in 1920.

"I have just come from visiting Mycroft at the Diogenes Club, Watson. It's put me in a melancholy mood, which, as you know, is sure to turn my brain upon itself. Activity remains the least expedient but preferable antidote. Being a retired detective, my only recourse is recollection, so I believe the time has come to make a serious effort at that textbook on the art of detection I've been putting off."

"An excellent idea! Your book is long overdue! Can I be of any assistance? I'd be honored to put down any of your undocumented investigations, like you suggested I do with the Cornish Horror."

"You might be of invaluable assistance regarding one case, some details of which require some clearing up. I hesitate to ask, however, as it requires you breaking a confidence."

"What confidence is that?"

"Do you recall my once making mention of the *Matilda Briggs*?"

"Of course. The ship that was somehow associated with the Giant Rat of Sumatra."

"A story for which the world was not yet prepared. The repercussions from its revelation would have been catastrophic. I wonder, however, even with The Treaty of Sèvres, has the necessity for such caution passed? Perhaps it never will. Perhaps it never mattered. Man is destined to walk upon ground cursed since Adam, so it is told, on a pilgrimage through the Valley of Violence in hopes of reaching the Kingdom of Wisdom. That is the way of things, which is why, before this war, I believed our land would be stronger and better for weathering the coming storm. It is in some ways, but our destiny hasn't changed. It never does. There shall come bitter winds until God's will be done, and even the best mortal's finest efforts can only delay the inevitable. Nevertheless I believe such efforts can be noble as they do play a part in Man's destiny. So, Watson, let me suggest that we decide what we should reveal to the world after an exchange of information. I shall tell you all that I know about the Giant Rat *after* you tell me of the part you and our old comrade Inspector Lestrade of Scotland Yard played in the matter of Ivanhoe Ffriend."

I was struck dumb hearing that name, one I hadn't thought of for many years. All I could think to say was the truth. "You ask no easy thing."

"Have no doubts I appreciate the dilemma I have put you in, as revealing what I know puts me in the same predicament. Would it make it easier if I told you that the only reason I know you were ever acquainted with Mr. Ffriend is because of Mycroft?"

"Not especially. When did your brother confide this to you?"

"Soon after you and Lestrade aided me in the capture of Colonel Sebastian Moran. Mycroft agreed to clarify some points for me regarding his part in Moran's eventual arrest, which, as you'll see, also involved Mr. Ffriend, making him and my brother the sole elements residing within the intersection of the Venn Diagram of our individual adventures, Watson. In the process of clarifying those points, Mycroft felt it necessary to mention that he was indebted to you and Lestrade, but would add nothing more."

All I could do was nod as I stood at a crossroads. If anyone but Sherlock Holmes had broached this favor, I would never have considered it. Eventually I excused myself to retrieve some pages from my private papers and presented them to my friend. "I recorded the adventure while the facts were still fresh. Force of habit. My notes are rather rough, as I never had reason to go back over them."

Holmes thanked me then spent the next few minutes reading as I ran alongside with the words, replaying the events in my mind.

63

## Chapter II – The Adventure of the Wrong Gentleman

Inspector Lestrade of Scotland Yard had not had cause to call on me for several months when he visited quite late on a cool and windy night in June of 1893. Two years had passed since the death of Sherlock Holmes, and, in the interim, I moved my practice from Paddington to Kensington. My wife had also passed away, and there were many evenings when our home felt intolerably empty, so, not for the first time, I had fallen asleep reading rather than carry myself to bed. I was therefore more-or-less presentable when Lestrade arrived at half-past-twelve to request my aid in an urgent matter.

Our destination, The Photogravure, was a private museum housed in a brick three-storey villa in Belsize Park, dedicated to photographs and "modern" paintings. "A lot of West Enders like this new art," Lestrade said as he unlocked the museum to let us in. "Not my taste, I'm afraid. Place belongs to The Honorable Damon Nostrand, a member of what remains of Professor Moriarty's old organization. Nostrand's father may be a peer, but his son's a genuine toff and a regular nimmer. Buys, sells, and smuggles, all from here. Stolen art's his specialty. Not that we can prove it, so the C.I.D. has been sending rotating teams of jacks posing as patrons to drop by and look about and see what they could see. Tonight's pair didn't check in as scheduled, so we sent a bobby to pop his head in. He found the place closed before hours and all of Nostrand's men gone."

"No trace of your detectives?"

"None, Doctor. We've searched this building from shingles to cellar three times and can't find a hint of what happened. We already suspected Nostrand had lit out of the country a few days ago. We don't know why, but, if he did, it makes no sense for his men to abandon their base unless they were following orders."

"Or they had no choice."

"Either way, men's lives may be at stake. If they weren't, I would have never disturbed you so late. Could you look around and see if we missed anything?"

"Me?"

"You know Mr. Holmes's methods. He said it himself."

"Well, yes, but Holmes trained himself for things like this. It was his specialty. He not only saw things that I couldn't, but he knew things that I don't. But, yes, of course, I'll try, Inspector."

Lestrade thanked me and, as I examined the museum's first floor, I inquired if he knew where Nostrand might have gone if he had left the country.

64

"Rumor has it he's heading to India or Nepal. No idea why, at least not yet."

Nothing on the first floor seemed useful, so I moved to the second while Lestrade remained below on the chance any fresh word about the missing detectives arrived. I said nothing, but there was something about the museum which bothered me. Something that was out of place, although I had no idea what. However, ambiguous feelings had proven useful to Holmes in more than one of his investigations, so I kept a sharp watch out for any indication of what might be causing mine.

Nostrand's office was the last room that I searched, a chamber that struck me as being smaller than I had expected. As I looked around, a growing sense of nostalgia unexpectedly enveloped me. At first I suspected Nostrand's eclectic decorations were inspiring my recollections of the jumbled Baker Street rooms that I once shared with Holmes. Then I realized my wistfulness was being ignited by the sweet fragrance of a tobacco that was softening by the instant. The next moment I spotted a crumpled piece of paper in a corner behind Nostrand's desk, which turned out to be a ship's manifest. I started to call to Lestrade, then decided the wiser course was to rush downstairs to inform the Inspector that I had found something.

"What is it?" he asked.

"No time to waste! Follow me!"

I dashed to the four-wheeler that had brought us to the museum while Lestrade locked the building. Before climbing in, I loudly told the driver to turn towards the docks when he reached the end of the street. Once on our way, Lestrade asked, "What's so important at the docks?"

"Nothing. We're not going there."

"But – "

"Indulge me a moment, please, Inspector." I waited until the four-wheeler had turned before instructing the driver to pull up and park under some trees. Next I showed Lestrade the wrinkled manifest and explained how I found it.

"'Morrison, Morrison, and Dodd.' And Damon Nostrand is aboard! I can't believe we missed this."

"I don't believe you did."

"We must have."

"Not if someone dropped it there after your last search. Someone who needed to lure us away from the museum."

"Who? Nostrand?"

"I can't say. Does he smoke kreteks?"

"What's that?"

"A fairly new cigarette from Central Java. Rather uncommon in England, but Holmes studied it to update his monograph on tobacco. It blends cloves and other ingredients with tobacco to create a distinctive sweet smell that doesn't linger long. I smelled hints of it in Nostrand's office."

"Sounds a bit refined for Nostrand's indulgences. So someone's hiding in the museum. Where? We searched everywhere."

"Not the darkroom, I'd wager."

"What do you mean? We found no darkroom,"

"Neither did I, but what sort of photograph museum would be without a darkroom?"

Lestrade grimaced at this oversight, then snapped his fingers. "As a smuggler, it'd make sense for Nostrand to have a priest hole. Making it a darkroom kills two birds with one stone."

I didn't disagree.

"Whoever is hiding in there must know what happened to my missing men."

"I hope so, but remember Holmes's precaution about theorizing before possessing all the facts."

"Oh, I remember Mr. Holmes's advice, all right, but this is a leap to my liking. In any case, all we have to do is wait for our kretek smoker to show himself to find out."

We didn't wait long. After approximately fifteen minutes, a larger than average man came out of the museum. We were too far away to perceive him clearly, but even so I could tell he was dressed as a gentleman. We watched him shut the door, tack something to it, and walk away.

"That's it, then!" Lestrade ordered the driver to remain under the trees as we hurried to the museum. Our quarry was a brisk walker and around a street corner by the time we reached The Photogravure, where Lestrade motioned me to look at what was tacked on the door while he continued the chase. I found a folded piece of note paper, opened it, and saw it was blank. In the act of taking down the note I pushed the door ajar and, curious as to why the stranger would leave the museum unlocked, I went inside. It occurred to me that he had caught on to my game when I spotted a dim light emanating from the office. Following the beacon, I found the concealed door to the museum's darkroom standing open. A candle glimmered inside the darkroom, which was empty except for a stone statue carved in what I guessed was an Indonesian style and about the size of a young child. Before I could examine it, Lestrade shouted for me and followed my voice to the darkroom. "Come with me, Doctor! I found them!"

66

"You nabbed him?"

"The fellow gave me the slip, but I found James and Joe! They were dropped in a doorway!"

"Your missing men? Are they all right?"

"They're unconscious, but just look knocked about a bit."

"I'll see. Better take this along, just to be safe." With a grunt and more of an effort than I anticipated, I lifted the statue.

"What is that ruddy thing?"

Giving the statue a second look, I made my best guess. "I'd say it's a rat. Not my taste, I'm afraid."

Lestrade's diagnosis of the condition of his comrades was correct. Once revived, their injuries amounted to little more than the cuts and lacerations typical to a street brawl. As for how they ended up to in the doorway, the last thing either man could recall was overhearing a row in the museum's office, and, when they went to intervene, found themselves overpowered by a brutally large man. Lestrade set the detectives to writing this down to add to his official report mere moments before a Government messenger arrived from Whitehall with instructions for the Inspector and me to bring the statue without delay to Mr. Mycroft Holmes.

There had been some correspondence exchanged after the tragedy of the Reichenbach Falls, but my first encounter with my late friend's older brother had been the case of Mycroft's Pall Mall neighbor Mr. Melas, the Greek interpreter. That adventure began with Holmes introducing me to Mycroft in the Stranger's Room at the Diogenes Club, the only chamber in that oddest of London's clubs where anyone is permitted to speak, and it was here that Lestrade and I were told to deliver the statue. Just like on that day five years earlier, Mycroft was staring out the small chamber's bow-window overlooking Pall Mall when we entered. The elder Holmes seemed to have changed very little, still tall and portly, his deep-set grey eyes as alert as I remembered under his masterful brow. But then I noticed there was none of the subtle play of expression in his face, and his lips, characteristically firm, were tense. It appeared that Mycroft was not concentrating on anything outside the window, but rather on something inward.

"Good morning, Doctor Watson. Inspector Lestrade. How good of you to come." Mycroft shook our hands warmly before gratefully patting the head of the statue, which I had placed on a table. "Thank you for recovering this. Your actions may yet rescue our country and many others from the direst circumstances. To that end, I must beg a favor of you and ask you to call upon an acquaintance of mine named Ivanhoe Ffriend."

"Who would that be, sir?" asked Lestrade, sounding understandably confused.

"The owner of this statue. If I'm correct, he should be able to answer any questions that you may still have regarding the events at The Photogravure last night." Mycroft reached into a pocket and presented Lestrade with an official envelope. "His address is in here on a letter that I pray you read before giving to him. Under no circumstances are you ever to discuss its contents with anyone except Ffriend and myself, and anything that he confides to you is to be brought back to me under the same confidence. I would also appreciate it, Doctor Watson, if you would appraise me regarding the condition of Ffriend's health. I give you gentlemen my word that there is a good reason for such secrecy, which shall be made clear when next we meet."

The address was not so distant that Lestrade and I couldn't have walked to it in a reasonable time. However, we hired a cab to drive between Trafalgar Square and Chelsea so that we could read Mycroft's letter in privacy. Much of it made little sense to us, but to say one part of the letter upset Lestrade would have been understatement.

Ffriend's house and the man himself were remarkable in different ways. Every available space in the wondrous abode was either shelved with a library of books in a dozen different languages, or decorated with at least one artifact or piece of artwork from every tribe and culture on the globe. In contrast, the homeowner, with the exception of being somewhat larger than was common, was rather plain. His speech and dress classified him as an educated American gentleman, but he was neither ugly nor handsome, and his age could have been anywhere from late thirties to early fifties. In most ways, Ffriend appeared to be an unremarkable and impassive man, but I noted that his knuckles were bruised, there was a cut on his right ear, and, judging by the way he held his left arm while opening the envelope and removing Mycroft's letter, I suspected it was mildly sprained.

After reading the letter Ffriend said, "This appears to be in order. Understand, sirs, that up until now your government, through the office of Mr. Mycroft Holmes, asked me to keep information regarding the statue a complete secret."

"Well, like the letter says, Doctor Watson and I are here on an unofficial visit."

"That sounds like an extension of immunity."

"It is," Lestrade huffed. "Nothing said here will appear in any official police report, but Mr. Holmes feels it's essential that we tie up some loose ends regarding our recovery of your statue."

"He is also concerned about you," I added.

Ffriend paused to consider what he wanted to do, during which his expression never changed. "All right. Sit down, if you want. Would you like some brandy? Or something else?" The inspector and I declined. "Then, dispensing with pretense, I was at Mr. Nostrand's museum last night. I was invited to bring the statue there by three of his men who came here around nine."

"'Invited'?"

"That was their word, Inspector, but one man fiddled with a straight razor, the second brandished a loaded bludgeon, while the third let his bulk do his intimidating for him."

"Was Nostrand there?"

"No. A man claiming to be his assistant, a Mr. St. Clair, was there in his absence. Anyway, as long as the statue remained in my possession, I saw no harm going with the three men. As soon as we arrived, I was escorted into Damon's office. I noticed two Scotland Yarders in plain clothes were alone in the gallery, but they can tell you I kept my face turned so they couldn't see it. It's a precaution of mine. St. Clair thanked me for coming and our conversation proceeded as follows. You should write this down for Mr. Holmes, Doctor. I have a reliable memory, and assure you this is accurate word for word. St. Clair appraised the statue for a few moments before telling me, 'Like most tribal art, it's not a very pretty thing.'

"'There's more to art than beauty.'

"'Her Majesty's Government told you about its history?'

"'I was informed it belongs to Teuku Umar, leader of a guerilla campaign against the Dutch in the Sumatran sultanate of Aceh.'

"'And that it was stolen from Umar?'

"'In 1883 by a Dutch officer.'

"'Such a silly thing to do in a fit of pique. The officer was frustrated in his efforts to convince Umar to help the Dutch rescue the British ship *Nisero*, which had been captured in a part of southern Sumatra outside Dutch control. Umar had the last laugh, I suppose, when the Dutch rescue raid failed. Now, all these years later, the Dutch want the ugly thing returned to Umar as a gesture of reconciliation. The ebb and flow of politics, eh? But I guess it is a favorite of his. By the way, how did you come by the statue?'

"'I have no intention of telling you that, Mr. St. Clair.'

"'Oh? Well, it doesn't matter, so long as we have it.'

"'And I have no intention of selling it to you.'

"'We don't intend to buy it.'

"'That's irrelevant. The statue belongs to me until the British Government takes possession and returns it to Umar. I've given them my oath.'

"'And you have my oath that that statue will never be returned to Teuku Umar. We are employed by a powerful party that insists upon this. Because of your neutral reputation, Mr. Nostrand believed that stealing the statue would be unnecessary once this was explained to you. He respects you not only as a client but a collector, and wishes no harm come to you, but my instructions are quite clear regarding what to do failing your cooperation.'

"We had reached an impasse, so Mr. St. Clair and the three men attempted to take the statue. They failed."

"'Failed'?" I asked. "How so?"

"Immunity or not, all I'll say is they're in no position to attempt anything like that again. There was some commotion and those two policemen tried to step in, but the bulky man overpowered them before I could reach him."

"Mr. Ffriend," Lestrade started to ask, "are you trying to say – ?"

"I'm not trying to say anything. You wanted me to explain about the statue and I have. If you doubt me, I'm sure the doctor can verify that I am suffering from a few minor injuries consistent with close combat."

"I can see that for myself."

"Before I could attend to Damon's underlings, you and other policemen arrived and started searching the museum. I had no choice but to wait with the lot and the statue in the darkroom. After you left, and I put St. Clair and his crew in their proper place, I carried your two men around the corner where you eventually found them, and then returned for the statue. That's when you two arrived. I'm familiar with the doctor's stories, as well as many of the monographs written by the late Mr. Sherlock Holmes, and I had earlier noticed the ship's manifest on Nostrand's desk, so I tossed the manifest in the corner and smoked one of my kreteks to get you out of the museum long enough to get away."

"After all that, why leave behind the statue?"

"It seemed the simplest course of action. The doctor's reputation as a loyal servant of the Queen is well known, and I was confident that Mr. Holmes would contact the inspector to take the statue off your hands when word about it reached him."

This is the report we took back to Mycroft Holmes, who seemed to be as amazed by it as Lestrade and I. Nevertheless, when asked if he believed it, Mycroft told Lestrade, "I have no reason not to."

"Then what should we do, sir? Even if it was self-defense, Ffriend all but admitted to killing four men."

"Four of Moriarty's men," I pointed out.

"Which is relevant, but there's more to the matter, Doctor Watson," Mycroft said. "Dismantling the Professor's organization continues to be a

Herculean task, one the Moriartys are defensing by wreaking as much havoc as possible."

"And preventing the statue from returning to Umar would further that cause?"

"Quite possibly, but the scheme goes much deeper. As we speak, Damon Nostrand is on his way to Sumatra to not only tell its ruler, Sultan Alauddin Mahmud Da'ud Syah II, about our plan to return the statue, but show him stolen official Dutch articles on how to end the war in Aceh." Mycroft paused. "These articles minimize the Sultan's importance and recommend that the Dutch government concentrate recruiting efforts with the *Ulee Balang*, Sumatra's hereditary chiefs and nobles, rather than the *Ulema*, Sumatra's religious leaders – which at least one article recommends be assassinated."

"My word," was all I could think to say.

Lestrade was not so horrified. "Bad as that may be, I don't see the reason for all this worry and secrecy. What does any of it have to do with England, sir?"

"Our world sits upon a precarious point in its history, Inspector, and, as Moriarty's organization is all too aware, events in one part of the globe can cause horrible conflicts to arise in another. As example, the war in Aceh started in 1873 because of discussions in Singapore about a possible treaty between Aceh and the United States, which the Dutch claimed violated an 1871 treaty they made with Great Britain. Because of this, the Dutch frequently request our aid in this war. Meanwhile, the Sultan of Sumatra has solicited aid from nations like Italy, France, and Turkey. Our nations have rejected all these pleas so far, but doing so is becoming increasingly difficult. If it ever becomes impossible, this awful but little war on an Indonesian island could spark a multi-national conflict. That is why Nostrand is going to Sumatra and why we are currently doing our best to intercept him."

Chapter III – The Adventure of the *Matilda Briggs*

There my account ended.

Holmes looked up from his reading and asked, "Isn't there more that should be added to your notes?"

"That's everything so far as Lestrade and I played a part. I swear I've shared all that I know."

"Thank you, Watson." Holmes returned the pages then leaned back, stretched out his long legs, and pressed the fingers of both hands together to form a steeple before repeating, "Thank you. Many of the questions I've wondered about over the years have been answered. I am indebted to you."

"I presume Ffriend's statue is the Giant Rat of Sumatra."

"It is." A smile fluttered over Holmes's lips. "You and Lestrade are to be commended. If Mycroft had not seen fit to mention your having a hand in this business, I should never have suspected anything clandestine between you three, even when Mycroft brought Lestrade in tow to Baker Street when the disappearance of the Bruce-Partington Plans similarly threatened international peace only two years later. A murder like Cadogan West's necessitated that Scotland Yard be brought in, in even so delicate a matter, but, after winning Mycroft's trust with Ffriend, I believe Lestrade would have been the professional called in regardless. And *you*, Watson?"

"Me?"

"How you let me prattle on that fog-shrouded day, bragging up Mycroft's role with the British Government. Truly, I was the one in a fog."

"I am sorry, old man, but what else could I do? I had to follow my duty. Besides, I always felt that you were proud to speak of your brother and his accomplishments."

"I'd never expect anything less from you, and, yes, while Germany had its Holstein, I think history will show that even he wasn't Mycroft's equal." A mischievous twinkle kindled in his eyes. "Time now for me to hold up my end of our bargain. Perhaps I should begin by verifying that Nostrand never talked to the Sultan."

"I guessed that for myself when Mycroft's fears for Sumatra never occurred." Then, without warning, I recalled my first conversation with my friend after discovering he hadn't died with the Professor. "You told me once that you remained in contact with Mycroft during your sojourns after Reichenbach, two years of which were spent travelling in Tibet."

"I've said it before, Watson, I'll never get your limits. Age seems only to sharpen your faculties, while it incessantly dulls mine. You are correct, although my travels had carried me to neighboring Nepal by the time an agent from Mycroft's office requested my aid in finding Nostrand, who had narrowly escaped being netted in Kathmandu. With the hounds at his heels, it seemed most likely that Nostrand would head for Patna, the nearest city where a vessel to Sumatra could be chartered from Morrison, Morrison, and Dodd, the same shipping firm he did business with in London. We traveled fast, but missed our quarry by two hours. Once Mycroft's agent was able to establish that he was on Crown business, the shipping clerk wired his office in Kolkata with instructions to seize Nostrand's charter, the *Matilda Briggs*, and the man aboard when it arrived. The clerk also placed their fastest steamship, the *Czarina*, at our disposal."

"What did you do with Nostrand after you reached Kolkata?"

"I've never been to Kolkata, and we never did lay hands on Nostrand."

That seemed impossible. "You must have! If not, then what happened next?"

"While Kolkata lies upon the most expedient course from Patna to the Bay of Bengal and then Sumatra, I gave Nostrand more credit than to follow the most obvious path at such a late stage of the game. By that time the *Matilda Briggs* would have already passed Farakka, south of which the Ganges splits into the Padma tributary, which is nearly twice the distance and far more perilous, but there are no cities along the way and the tributary offers several mouths into which to enter the Bay. As our presence in Kolkata would make no difference in Nostrand's capture if he went there, I had the *Czarina* follow the Padma tributary."

Here Holmes's voice grew softer and his face took on the same faraway expression as Mycroft's when Lestrade and I met him in the Stranger's Room.

"You and your Army revolver were never missed more than on that day, I promise you, Watson. Nostrand began firing at the *Czarina* as soon as the *Matilda Briggs* came into sight. Her crew was unarmed, and we hadn't thought to bring firearms aboard the *Czarina*, but fortunately our quarry was no Colonel Moran when it came to marksmanship. Mycroft's agent would have jumped aboard with a kukri machete once we drew near enough, but her captain took matters into his own hands and ordered his crew to abandon ship and swim for shore, leaving the *Matilda Briggs* to the mercy of the river's current. A moment later, we rounded a bend and a waterfall came into view."

"Good Lord!"

"It was rather drastic, but our captain was not so willing to see the *Matilda Briggs* scarified. He ordered his crew to snare it with grappling hooks while there was a chance to haul the ship to safety. This they did as Nostrand continued firing. When his supply of ammunition was depleted and it became clear that the *Matilda Briggs* would be rescued, Nostrand flung himself into the river rather than face the penalty for failing the Professor's executors."

Holmes said nothing more, but continued to focus his attention inward. Considering his experience at the Reichenbach Falls, it was natural the memory of Nostrand's suicide would haunt my friend. Before long, however, he inhaled deeply, sat bolt straight, and pronounced, "And there you have it. My half of our story."

Chapter IV – The Mark of a Man

"You can't be finished," I protested. "Were the Dutch articles recovered? Was the statue returned to its rightful owner?"

"Ah! I warned you of my dimming faculties. My only defense is that lapses are to be expected whenever a man strays from his field of expertise. You are the gifted amateur in the telling of tales, Watson, while I shall never be more than a workman. Umar's statue was returned, and, as he'd been instructed, Mycroft's man destroyed the damning articles. Have I forgotten anything more?"

"I don't think so, except perhaps the real reason for your visit today."

Holmes barely blinked. "What do you mean?"

"There's more going on here then you're letting on."

"How could you know that, Doctor?"

"I know you, Holmes. Everything about the business of the Giant Rat has more to do with national policy, Mycroft's field of expertise, than yours, the art of detection. So why would you even consider including it in your book? The answer is, you aren't. There are also your comments before about Man's destiny and God's will. Can you blame me for suspecting that your visit to the Diogenes Club set you pondering about mortality as much as it did morality? After all, the latter isn't possible without the former, and Man's destiny since Adam, so it is told, has also been to return to the ground, which means even the best of men, including Mycroft, are mortal."

There was no reaction from Holmes until he finally permitted his shoulders to sag. "And yourself." He paused. "Mycroft is good for me, as you are. I like to think that I am a wise man, Watson, and a mark of a wise man is that he always keeps better men than himself within his circle of acquaintances." Another pause. "Think back on the glimpse you and Lestrade got that day of Mycroft's role in the government. A war was delayed. Surely, unlike the Inspector, you came away appreciating the gravity of my brother's duties."

"I did. However I don't believe you're being totally fair to Lestrade."

"Good old Watson. Fixed and reliable as always." Holmes tilted his head as he reconsidered. "Looking back over his career, perhaps I am doing Lestrade some injustice. A more courageous or tenacious man I've rarely met, or one so proficient while in his element yet so lacking whenever the problem called for more than the workmanlike skills of the professionals. Be honest now. I've just finished with your notes. Is it really a disservice to say that events outside the purview of the Metropolitan Police, say like the Mayerling incident, were likely to weigh heavier upon your mind than his? What effect did Mycroft's concerns regarding the

74

delicate balance of world events have upon Lestrade? Certainly you must have discussed it afterwards."

"We might have, if not for Ffriend."

"So there is more than you wrote in your notes?"

"Only that Ffriend perplexed me. I didn't think it merited including at the time, but I mentioned it to Lestrade."

"Perplexed you? How?"

"He reminded me of a wasp."

Holmes perked up. "An unusual statement."

"Lestrade commented how Ffriend struck him as cold, but I suspected it ran deeper than that. I still do. As a boy – I suppose that I must have been about nine – I was pulling weeds for my mother when I poked my face under a bench where a queen had built her nest. The next thing that I knew, a swarm was buzzing all around me. I was at their mercy, but not one stung me. I had meant no harm, and I think the wasps knew that because they let me be."

"Bees are more my flavor, but, based upon my limited experiences with the genus *Vespula*, I cannot deny there is some evidence to support your theory."

"Lestrade said I was lucky."

"There is some evidence that supports his theory, too."

"Ffriend behaved like those wasps. Nostrand's men made threats but, until they were actually going to harm him, he let them be, in which case they shared some of the blame for their fate."

"An intriguing hypothesis. What was Lestrade's opinion?"

"He permitted that men like Moriarty and St. Clair were evil, and it had been his experience that history generally deals with evil men in two ways. In the first, a villain confronts someone on the side of justice who refuses to acquiesce until the evil man is defeated, or both men are dead."

Holmes said nothing but slowly nodded.

"In the second, the villain crosses what Lestrade called 'the wrong man'. 'No matter how smart or big or cruel you are, there's someone who's smarter, bigger, or more cruel.' That's what Lestrade believed happened to St. Clair and his men. They crossed paths with the wrong gentleman and paid the price."

Holmes sat quietly, weighing my words, then stood, lit a cigarette, and paced. "It seems the journey from my brother's club has only brought me around again to that perennial problem that perpetually confounds all human reason. I asked you once what object is served by this circle of misery, violence, and fear?" Holmes halted. "There must be some end to it, Watson, as the alternative, a universe ruled by chance, is unthinkable."

75

"Which is what we've been talking about when, you come down to it," I said. "God's will and Man's destiny. You ask, 'What is the object?' In other words, 'What is our purpose?' Well, when a man has a purpose in his life and makes a difference in the world, isn't that proof of an underlying greater purpose is at work? How can the universe be ruled by chance when our efforts, good or ill, have some sort of outcome? You're right – there is misery, violence, and fear, but even the thorniest path has flowers, and as you observed once to a decent man at his nadir, we have much to hope from the flowers."

Holmes drew long on his cigarette. "A reasonable observation, but one predicated merely upon hope. You have no more proof than the skeptic has disproof. A skeptic can just as reasonably declare there is no meaning to be gleaned from the historical process."

"All that means is that declaring there is or isn't meaning in history comes down to faith. I won't deny that your skeptic's belief is as rooted in man's experience as mine, but no skeptic can deny that my declaring that any man's living and dying has purpose gives us what a wiser person than I calls 'point and direction to the life of man.' A moment ago you said Mycroft delayed a war. You're wrong."

"Surely not. There was no war."

"Precisely. Mycroft prevented a war that day, just as I have little doubt that he has prevented wars many of the days he has served in the British Government. But suppose Man's morality made the terrible war we just survived inevitable? I find it hard to imagine that Mycroft has ever believed Man's destiny isn't inevitable, or he wouldn't do as much as he does to give his fellow man time to try to find a different path. That is Mycroft's purpose. His mark, if you will."

"A mark very few men will ever know about, and in regards to the war we just survived, it proved futile."

"Does it matter who knows? Would it make any difference if everyone knew? And I'll never believe that helping and serving your fellow man is ever futile. Mycroft's efforts touch millions of lives, and if they never know, then it just makes his purpose nobler. Not everyone can be a police inspector or an Army doctor or the first consulting detective, and even the best of men have their limits, but within those limits is so much potential. That's always been good enough for me. I pray it may be good enough for you, Holmes."

He finished his cigarette, sat down, and leaned back in the chair. Closing his eyes and steepling his fingers again, he said, "Perhaps, so long as there are men like Mycroft and you to go with the Ffriends and St. Clairs. No, Watson, I'll never get your limits. I pray I never shall."

# The Adventure of
# the Returning Spirit
## by Arthur Hall

I will always remember a day in the spring of 1894 as one of the worst in my life. More painful, in its way, even than my experiences in Maiwand.

As I trudged up the stairs of my former lodgings in Baker Street, the cloud of gloom and depression surrounding me seemed, if anything, denser even than the night before. Sleep had eluded me, and thoughts of grief and uncertainty had proved haunting companions, so that I resolved to seek the advice and wisdom of my friend, Mr. Sherlock Holmes, immediately after my poor attempt at consuming breakfast.

"Watson!" He greeted me with apparent delight as I entered our old sitting room.

"Good morning, Holmes. You sound, if I may say so, rather cheerful. You have, perhaps, gained a new client?"

"Not so, old fellow, my mood has been elevated by a prolonged Turkish bath. I returned here not half-an-hour ago and . . . .' His eyes swept over me and he became very still. "But what is it? I perceive that you are not yourself today. Are you ill?"

I took off my hat and coat and sat down, not in my usual armchair but in the basket chair. "Holmes, I am besieged by melancholia. I apologise for visiting you in this state, but I feel a strong need for human company this morning."

He was beside me at once, lowering himself into the nearest armchair. "My dear fellow, it is usually I, not yourself, who is afflicted in this way. What is it that has brought it upon you again? When I returned to London you were still suffering from the loss of your wife, but I formed the impression that you had managed to come to terms with it, and had almost recovered."

"You were not mistaken. The pain of grief had begun to fade, and your reappearance was a welcome distraction."

"Then what is it that troubles you now?" He leaned closer, his concerned expression deepening. "Pray tell me. If anything can be done to assist, you have only to mention it."

"Thank you, Holmes, but there is nothing that any man can do."

"It is still the loss of Mrs. Watson that haunts you, then?"

"It is, but there is more." Holmes got to his feet. "You must tell me all, but first a brandy to steady your nerves."

"It is too early, I think."

"Nonsense. You are in need of a restorative. Time has nothing to do with it." He took up a crystal glass and poured from the decanter. I let the harsh spirit burn my throat and then calm me gradually. By the time I was ready to speak, I did indeed feel somewhat improved. As I prepared myself to begin, the only sounds were of passing hansoms and four-wheelers. Then raucous laughter floated up through the half-open window and faded as two young men strode by and were quickly out of earshot.

"I saw her, or so it appeared, last night as I returned to Kensington. It was late. My patient's fever did not break until early evening."

"You saw Mrs. Watson?"

"I did, Holmes, as clearly as I now see you."

"Old friend, you are a medical man and not usually given to fantasies," he said gently. "Do not torment yourself, for you know this cannot be so."

"She called to me."

"As I recall, there was a fog last evening, the thickest for weeks. Looking from this window, I was unable to see the street below. Such a setting, especially if you had allowed your mind to dwell upon your loss, could have fired your imagination."

I spent a few moments, breathing deeply in my frustration. "Holmes, I am aware of your total disbelief in the supernatural and I have usually held a similar view, but I swear to you that I saw and heard Mary last night as if she were still alive."

He sat back in his chair, now regarding me with a thoughtful expression. "Very well, Watson. Relate to me exactly the scene that you witnessed. I cannot believe that the departed, however much they are loved, can return, but I see trickery in this. As to the reason behind it I cannot yet tell, but we will see what results from a little reasoning."

"I was almost at my front door," I said when I had collected my thoughts, "as a coach appeared out of the fog. I heard the horses' hooves and then saw faintly the glow of the side-lamps. It slowed its pace, which I dismissed as a necessity because of the greatly restricted visibility, and it was then that I heard a woman's voice calling my name. She identified herself as Mary, saying that she had returned and would be with me again soon. No sooner had I taken this in, than the coach was lost to my sight."

"Was the voice that of your wife, as you remember it?"

"It could have been, allowing for some slight distortion caused by the fog."

"And the woman's appearance?"

"As far as I could tell, it was she."

78

"Because of the fog and the shock this would have been to you, I can understand that you would not have thought to take note of the coach's number although, of course, it could have been a private conveyance. But what of the coachman? Were you able to see his face clearly – perhaps recognise him?"

I shook my head. "I had an impression of a vague figure, possibly clad in a black rain-cape with the collar turned up to conceal his face. The apparition appeared and was gone, so quickly."

Holmes nodded slowly. "Is there anything more that you can tell me?"

"There is. This morning I received a note. It was in my letter-box and delivered by hand. It said simply, '*John, I will soon be with you again*'."

"Do you have it with you?"

I nodded and withdrew the crumpled sheet from my pocket.

Holmes studied it for a moment, then produced his lens. "Poor quality paper, rather pail ink, written with a well-used nib. The handwriting is indeed a woman's, but that is far as I will go with your assertions." His voice took on a softer tone. "Watson, you must know that this is some sort of cruel trick. There are no such things as ghosts or returning spirits. How many times have we been confronted with cases that appeared to be concerned with the supernatural, only to finally discover a perfectly ordinary down-to-earth solution? Ask yourself, do ghosts leave notes in your letter-box? Consider this also, would this have affected you so, were you not still grieving for your departed wife? Ordinarily, you would have immediately identified the situation for what it is, would you not?"

I allowed his words to impress themselves upon my mind. After a moment, I had collected myself sufficiently to realise the sense of his statements, and the foolishness of my gullibility. There have been times however, when I have seen things that could not be explained. I mentioned this to Holmes.

"Old fellow," he began after a pause, "you must not underestimate the power or versatility of the human imagination. Additionally, the eyes do not always reveal accurately what is before us. Light and shade, mirrors and suggestion can all play their part in deceiving us. However, that deals with past experience. What we have here is, as I have said, nothing more than human trickery. Tell me, after such a shock, do you feel you can conduct your practice today?"

I straightened my posture, feeling rather like a man emerging from a confused dream.

"You are right of course, about everything. I must take myself in hand. I have to collect myself and open my surgery." I reflected, briefly. "Sometimes it is the little things that you remember when you think of a lost loved one that are the most painful by their absence. The way she arranged my slippers, and my pipe and my book, in readiness for me to sit with her before the fire on winter evenings, are memories that I will always keep."

"I am, as you are aware, unacquainted with such emotions," Holmes said, and I wondered if I imagined the touch of sadness in his voice, "but it grieves me to see your distress." He paused, and I formed the impression that something had occurred to him. "There is at this time a case of momentous importance before me, which I expect to break within a day or two. Nevertheless, Watson, if you depart now to attend your practice, I will attempt to gain some insight into these extraordinary events. I suggest that you call here after closing your surgery this afternoon, when I hope to be able to enlighten you somewhat."

I murmured my thanks to my friend. Then, still in a troubled state, I set out to return to Kensington and what seemed to be an endless stream of patients.

The day proved to be as unremarkable as I had feared, with little to take my mind from the images that haunted me. Among the legions of influenza cases, children with measles, and the elderly suffering a myriad of complaints, were some who remarked that I seemed preoccupied or enquired about my state of health. Relief descended upon me like a cloud, as I finally closed my surgery doors in the late afternoon.

I quickly found a hansom nearby and was back in Baker Street soon after. Mrs. Hudson gave me a concerned look as she admitted me, but it was the tone of her greeting that told me how obvious my distressed state must appear.

As I ascended the stairs, the mournful wail of Holmes's Stradivarius matched my mood. I hoped that my friend had discovered something that would lift my depression.

"Ah, my dear fellow." He replaced his violin in its case and came to greet me – somewhat excessively, I thought. He seemed in a lighthearted mood, probably for my sake. "Do sit down, while I call for our good landlady to bring tea."

I was about to tell him it was unnecessary, but thought better of it. Mrs. Hudson must have been waiting for his summons, for she appeared more quickly even than usual. She avoided my eyes, but there was pain in her face. She never failed to be concerned when Holmes or I suffered injury or distress.

He said little while we drank but scrutinized me constantly. "I suppose you can think of no one who would wish you harm," he said suddenly.

"I received a letter from Doctor Bolt, yesterday. He accuses me regularly of poaching his patients and issues veiled threats, but I never take that seriously. I am afraid that his increasing absent-mindedness is the reason for his declining practice. In any event, I cannot see a man of his age arranging something of this sort."

"Most unlikely, I am certain. If you had any lingering doubts about your experiences being anything but a despicable trick, you can dispel them completely," my friend said then. "The results of my enquiries suggest that you are not the only intended victim. I fear we are both to suffer, if the perpetrator is allowed to continue."

"What can you mean? Have you discovered who is behind this?"

"Not as yet, but I suspect that our adversary is he who drove the coach that so alarmed you last night. However, I first concerned myself with the woman who impersonated Mrs. Watson. It occurred to me that she is most likely accustomed to taking on the appearance of others, since she appeared so convincing. My starting point therefore, was to investigate within the theatrical profession. You may recall that I have consulted Miss Gloriana Roland before, at the Imperial Theatre where her play is enjoying an extended run. After examining the tiny portrait of your late wife which I borrowed from where you left it in your former room, she was able to supply me with the names and whereabouts of four actresses known to her who could have assumed her identity. I spent the remainder of the morning and some of the afternoon in eliminating three from the list, leaving me with Miss Agnes Bowman, of King Alfred Square, St John's Wood."

I have long been acquainted with Holmes's methods, but I was surprised at his rapid progress and doubly appreciative of his assistance. "Have you interviewed this woman?"

"It seemed more advantageous to delay the encounter. I thought you might care to accompany me this evening, to see for yourself that she is merely flesh and blood. Miss Roland has explained that Miss Bowman is at present between parts since her last production proved unsuccessful, so we have a good chance of finding her at home."

"Holmes, I am most grateful to you."

"Think nothing of it. Incidentally, I have informed Mrs. Hudson that you will be staying for dinner. I hope I was not presumptuous?"

"Not at all," I replied, feeling suddenly in a lighter frame of mind. "At this moment, I can think of nothing I would like better."

We stood at the entrance to King Alfred Square, a small enclave in Grove End Road that was sparsely lit by the pale glow of several street-lamps. The villas were of uniform appearance, some of them brightly illuminated from within but most in darkness. After taking a moment or two to survey his surroundings, Holmes strode forward. By his side, I asked which house we were bound for.

"I believe Miss Roland gave the number as Twenty-eight," he said, peering around us. "Ah, there is Number Thirty, so this is Miss Bowman's home two houses further on."

We approached a door with an ornate knocker in the shape of an elephant's head which Holmes ignored, rapping urgently on the thick panels with his cane. There was no response. He repeated the summons and we listened for any sound of activity within.

"Either she is not inside, or she wishes us to believe that," he whispered. "Perhaps the view from the back of the house will be more enlightening."

I preceded him to the wooden gate at the side of the villa, which opened easily as I lifted the latch. We passed silently into a paved passage that led to the back of the house. Holmes stared through a small window into the shadows of the kitchen. A row of saucepans hung from a rack immediately ahead, obstructing our view. He changed his angle of observation several times, until he could see through a half-open door into the room beyond. The light was minimal, but his sharp eyes must have seen something immediately, for he turned to me urgently.

"Someone is there. We must enter, Watson."

There was apparently no further need for stealth, for he produced his pick-lock and opened the door in seconds without attempting to maintain silence. He rushed through the kitchen and into the living room and I followed close behind, but a single glance told me that the woman within was beyond my help.

"Whoever did this was particularly brutal," I observed.

Miss Agnes Bowman was sprawled across an armchair, in which she had been occupied with embroidery. Her mouth was open and her eyes bulged, adding to the terrible expression that was frozen upon her face. The cause of her death was apparent, for a thin wire had been wound around her neck and tightened to the extent that it had become embedded in the bloody flesh. Despite my long experience of death and injury, I felt myself shiver.

"How long, would you say?" Holmes asked.

I moved closer, and carefully felt the stiffened flesh. The blood had long since dried. "At least twelve hours."

"She had served her purpose and was of no further use. Doubtlessly she knew too much about her murderer, and he could not risk her divulging anything that could lead to his capture."

"You are certain that it was a man?"

"Not absolutely, but the strength required to sink the wire into this unfortunate woman's neck to this depth strongly suggests it."

"And you believe she was killed by someone of her acquaintance?"

"I will confirm that in a moment." He retraced his steps into the yard. After a short search of the single patch of coarse grass he gave a cry of satisfaction and returned holding up a key for my inspection. "He evidently entered with her consent, probably by the front door, since there is no damage anywhere. He left, locking the kitchen door and throwing away the key. That patch of grass is the only possible place of concealment at the rear of the house."

I picked up the oil lamp and turned up the wick before bringing it nearer to the body. "Holmes, this cannot be the woman who impersonated Mary. The colour of her hair is similar, but her features are quite different."

"Indeed it appears so, but notice the almost identical shape of the head and particularly the nose. I have some experience of such things, and I can tell you confidently that a skilful master of his craft would be capable of transforming her into an acceptable likeness, especially when viewed from a distance."

I exhaled deeply, feeling a strange relief despite the circumstances. "At least, there is now some explanation."

"For the simulated reappearance of your wife, yes. We must of course notify the police after leaving here, but already I have my suspicions."

"You have formed a supposition?"

"I have, but for the moment it is no more than that. However, we will inform the good inspector and he will come to his own conclusions. I am now certain that I, as well yourself, am an intended victim in this affair."

I considered, but could not fathom his reasoning. "How so?"

He began to scrutinize the room carefully. "I will tell you presently, if I am proven correct." He shook his head, appearing disappointed. "He was careful, it seems."

We did not return to Baker Street directly. Holmes requested the cabby to wait outside Scotland Yard, and vanished inside without a word. He returned shortly and we continued our journey. He spent the first few minutes peering into the passing streets ensuring, I thought, that no one followed. When he was satisfied, he spoke at last.

"Lestrade was away, Watson, but I left a message and the key. If his absence is prolonged, I expect Gregson or MacDonald will take it up."

"You are not taking an active part then, after all?"

"Oh, but I am. There is more to this than a rather clumsy attempt at persecution. I intend to discover the truth."

I stayed in my old room at Baker Street that night. When I came down the following morning, Holmes had already gone out. The remains of his breakfast lay upon the table, and the teapot was cold. On consulting our landlady, I learned that he had left more than an hour earlier.

For me, the day passed slowly. I was anxious to learn more of the curious situation that surrounded us, and I hoped that Holmes would inform me when I saw him next. At last the hour came when I could close my surgery doors. I was fortunate in finding a hansom quickly, and was soon back in Baker Street.

I must have dozed, despite myself. A loud noise woke me and I realised that the door had been slammed below. Quick footsteps on the stairs followed, and a moment later Holmes entered the room with a flourish.

"Ah, Watson, looking distinctly better, I observe."

"I find myself less distressed, thanks to your help and advice."

He struggled out of his coat and laid his hat on a side-table. "I have much to tell you, old fellow. Let us prevail upon Mrs. Hudson for coffee, after which I will reveal all."

We had finished our coffee and the tray had been retrieved by our landlady before we sat back in our chairs and he produced his old briar. During this short interval, there had been little conversation between us, and I sensed that he waited for me to calm myself of any remaining feelings of discomfort regarding the nature of this affair.

He blew a cloud of aromatic smoke into the air above him, and began.

"As you know, I have many sources of information across London. I had to visit quite a few of these today, gleaning bits and pieces as I progressed. At the end of my enquiries, I felt much as if I had spent the day retrieving pieces of a puzzle, so that only now could I see the entire picture. I must say, though, that every moment spent in this pursuit was worth the effort, for now the situation is clear to me."

"I am anxious to know how Mary is connected with this."

"And so you shall. Our adversary's intention was, as I suspected, to bring about not only your death, but mine also. Nor is that the end of it, as you will see. His first step was to make it appear that your wife had returned to life, thus causing you considerable distress and probably giving rise to new hope that could have no fulfilment. I believe his aim was to make you doubt your own senses, and to upset the balance of your mind. In addition, he knew that this would have a detrimental effect on me, because we are friends. He spent considerable time in learning about our activities by consorting with the criminal classes. This was a fatal mistake, since some of those he consulted are also my informants."

I could contain myself no longer. "Who is this, Holmes? Someone, perhaps, who we have brought to grief before now?"

"That is not entirely true." He drew on his pipe for a final time, before knocking it out on the hearth. "Do you recall those last few days before we set off for the Continent to escape Professor Moriarty?"

"I do, and they are not pleasant memories."

"Indeed. You may remember that at one point I looked down on Baker Street from this very room, and remarked that our lodgings were under observation."

"A man called Stoker, I think you said."

"You are almost correct. It was Stuker, a professional garrotter of German extraction, and one of Moriarty's most efficient henchman."

I thought back and shook my head. "He cannot be behind this, Holmes, although that would explain the method used to murder Miss Bowman, for I recall reading in *The Standard* that he had died in prison."

"There was a younger brother, a recent addition to Moriarty's organisation. He is thought to have left the country some time before Scotland Yard closed its net around the gang, and has not been heard of since."

"And you suspect this man intends to kill us?"

"From the information provided by my informants, I am forced to that conclusion. You were provoked to doubt your own sanity, before being despatched in the manner of Miss Bowman, and I was to follow soon after. These were to be acts of revenge for Stuker's capture and subsequent demise. I've said that our deaths would not be the end of this, which is apparent when we consider that Inspector Lestrade was closely involved with the capture of the gang."

"Lestrade?" I said in astonishment. "He is to be the next victim?"

"So I have concluded, from the answers to the questions I asked of my underworld contacts."

I rose from my chair. "We must inform him at once! He is in deadly danger!"

"Calm yourself, Watson. I have reason to believe that these murders were to be carried out in rotation. It was to be first you, then me, before the good inspector. As our adversary has not yet progressed beyond causing severe distress to yourself, I do not think that Lestrade is in immediate danger, though preparations for his demise may be in hand. Regarding ourselves however, I suggest we take the greatest care until this is over. I will accompany you, when dinner is concluded, back to your home in Kensington where, if you will allow me to advise you, it would be wise for you to pack a bag with enough clean shirts and whatever else you need, to last for about a week. This may be unnecessary, but I cannot ignore the likely threat."

"You are sending me out of London?"

A quick smile crept across his features. "Much to the contrary, old fellow. I am asking you to move back here for a while. Mrs. Hudson approves wholeheartedly."

"I will be glad to." A feeling of warmth and contentment swept through me, despite everything. "It will be like old times."

"Indeed. Including the early capture of our opponent, I sincerely hope."

That evening saw me move back to Baker Street without incident. Holmes had suggested that, while our lives were under threat, we should remain in each other's company at all times save while we slept, and I therefore made arrangements by telegraph for my practice to be temporarily in the care of a *locum*.

The following morning we breakfasted early and were seated in Lestrade's office before nine o'clock. We refused tea and the little detective closed the door, shutting out the protestations of a prisoner who was being marched along the corridor.

"Now then, gentlemen, I presume it is the murder of Miss Bowman that you are here to talk to me about. I can tell you that whoever did it was careful, for we have found few clues as yet. Nevertheless, he will make a slip, you mark my words, if he hasn't already. I have only just returned from Sussex on another matter – otherwise we would doubtlessly have progressed further." He paused for a moment, before directing his gaze to my friend and asking, "Can I enquire, Mr. Holmes, what it is that you have discovered, and why you and Doctor Watson visited this lady's house?"

Holmes's expression was unaltered. "To answer your questions in reverse, Lestrade, Watson and I were there in the course of an investigation in which Miss Bowman was involved. As for our discoveries, they were remarkably few because, as you have said, the killer was careful. I have, however, shed more light on this matter since then, and I can tell you without the slightest doubt that not only are our lives in danger from the same source, but yours also."

The inspector became very still for a moment. Then, to my surprise, he laughed.

"Come, Mr. Holmes, this is nothing new. We are used to this sort of threat here at the Yard. There is always some villain who wishes to get back at the force after a spell in prison." He paused, his expression changing and his eyes flitting from Holmes to me and back again. "You appear to be taking this seriously. Is there something more?"

Holmes then related the events since my encounter with the coach in the fog, and their connection with the murder of Miss Agnes Bowman. Finally, he confided his conclusions.

"We had all three better watch our steps then," Lestrade said when my friend ceased to speak, "but you need have no worries on my account. I have had a new fellow assigned to me, to learn the trade so to speak. Detective-Sergeant Cullen is a strong, reliable officer who has recently joined the force. He can serve as my bodyguard," he smiled, to indicate that this was something of a jest, "as well as learning the ropes. He volunteered to work with me, impressed by my reputation I'm sure, so now this killer of yours has to deceive two pairs of eyes instead of one. I do not think he will find it easy."

"I am certain that he will not," Holmes confirmed, "but perhaps I can request something of you."

The bulldog-like face became a mask of suspicion. "You can, Mr. Holmes, but I cannot guarantee my agreement."

Holmes glanced at me and then looked at the inspector with concern. Then to my astonishment he contradicted the intentions he had previously expressed to me. "I would be obliged if you would let Doctor Watson accompany you and the detective-sergeant for, let us say, a week as you perform your official duties. I realise that this is an irregular procedure, but I have the greatest respect for the cunning and resourcefulness of the murderer of Miss Bowman. If your precautions should fail, the presence of a medical man may well be the difference that ensures the survival of yourself and others."

Lestrade looked surprised at first, even outraged at this suggestion, and for a moment I expected him to refuse absolutely. Then his expression cleared, and he smiled cynically. "That is an unusual request as you say, but I cannot see that any harm could result from it. Who knows, Mr. Holmes? Doctor Watson might learn something from our way of doing things, to his advantage."

"There is that possibility, of course," Holmes said with a straight face. "Thank you, Inspector."

The week passed slowly. Lestrade was a methodical and persistent policeman, but appeared slow to me after Holmes. I saw my friend only at breakfast and in the evening, and he would say little of his own activities. I related to him my observations of every case where I had accompanied the inspector and Detective-Sergeant Cullen, and his invariable response was a slow nodding of his head. At no time was there any incident that could be connected with Miss Bowman's killer and, as his own investigation had halted for lack of new evidence, I believe Lestrade had dismissed the affair from his mind.

I discovered later that Holmes had followed us closely. The elderly country gentleman, the bespectacled lawyer, the plodding schoolmaster, and the coarsely-spoken groom and others were all present at some stage of Lestrade's cases. All of them were different, all of them were Holmes.

As for Detective-Sergeant Robert Cullen, he seemed an agreeable fellow. Rather reticent at first, I soon discovered that he possessed a not inconsiderable knowledge of medicine, was well-informed regarding the geography of the British Isles and, like myself, had a weakness for the fair sex. He was a tall man, as much so as Holmes, but more heavily-built. He wore a sombre expression that frequently changed to a knowing smile, and I began to suspect that he was far more acquainted with the ways of the world than his manner would suggest.

By the end of the week, I had become disenchanted with the task that Holmes had given me. On the afternoon of the last day he appeared at Scotland Yard, apparently pursuing a different matter since he requested an interview with Inspector Gregson. This was granted, and had not concluded as I left with Lestrade and Cullen. Later, at dinner, he dismissed the encounter lightly, and I knew that to pursue the subject would be futile.

However, he continued to follow Lestrade's activities through me. Reluctantly, I agreed to spend further days with the inspector, who seemed already to be aware of the arrangement when I mentioned it. I formed the impression that some change had taken place, that the situation had become more urgent, since three constables were unexpectedly added to our group. Constable Cheshire was a slow but purposeful middle-aged man who spoke unceasingly about his family. Constable Harbridge was tall and brisk, with a magnificent handlebar moustache, and Constable Curtis was short and bald with a fixed, determined expression that never varied. As the days progressed, I was no longer able to pick out individuals who might be Holmes in disguise, and I therefore concluded that he watched us from concealment.

There continued to be no incident that could be construed as an attempt on Lestrade's life, and it occurred to me that Stuker's younger brother, if indeed it was he, might be allowing us to develop a false sense of security, while he awaited his opportunity to strike. This apparent halt in the case began to concern me, as did Holmes's seemingly declining interest. I had seen little of my friend of late – when I was in our rooms he was elsewhere, and vice-versa.

I had watched Lestrade even more carefully during this time spent in his company. He had solved a burglary case and apprehended a young man who sustained himself by robbing elderly ladies, and rightly commented that he considered himself to have done well. On the last day occurred the events that I had long expected, but dreaded.

Dusk was closing in rapidly when Detective-Sergeant Cullen burst into Lestrade's office with the news that a report had been received of a sighting of George Mellor in the grounds of a house in Clapham Common. George Mellor was wanted for at least three murders, and it had long been Lestrade's ambition to capture him because, among other reasons, his colleague Mister Peter Jones had attempted to do so and failed.

By the time we reached Suttliffe Court, for so the place was called, full darkness had fallen. Our party comprised Lestrade, Cullen, the three constables, and myself. We travelled in two police wagons and the inspector ordered the drivers to take their conveyances to the end of the quiet tree-lined street to await our return. A rusty gate set in a long high wall allowed us admittance, and we found ourselves in a small wood with the house a short distance beyond.

"The house has been unoccupied for some time," Lestrade said. "The owner died leaving no heir. Mellor may be hiding inside or among the trees. Do not use your lanterns, lest he become aware of our approach, and proceed silently. Spread out across the forest, and move in a line forwards. We should reach the courtyard soon."

"I will search in this direction, with Doctor Watson." Detective-Sergeant Cullen whispered somewhat surprisingly. Lestrade murmured his assent and he and the others melted into the darkness. I peered around me, to see only the vague outlines of bare branches. Nowhere was there a glimmer of light.

"This way, Doctor." Cullen moved confidently forward and I followed, guided by the faint sounds of his passage rather than sight. We seemed to progress in a sideways direction. Possibly his intention was to approach the house from a different direction to the others, cutting off another route by which Mellor might escape. We emerged into a tiny clearing and he stopped suddenly.

"Have you seen something?" I asked in a low voice.

To my surprise, a vesta flared suddenly. By its light I could make out the revolver that Cullen had pointed in my direction. He blew out the flame, and we were again in darkness.

"Do not move," he said in a different voice. "Come no closer."

"What is happening?"

"You are about to witness the culmination of much planning, Watson. That is why Lestrade and yourself are here."

An awful realisation came to me. Fear held me in a tight grip.

"George Mellor's presence was a fabrication, I presume."

"An invention of mine. I knew that Lestrade's ambition would compel him to attend here immediately. The setting is perfect."

"For what purpose, exactly?" But I knew the answer, already.

He laughed. An eerie sound. "I do believe that Detective-Sergeant Cullen, an acquaintance who I cultivated purposefully, asked me a similar question, before I killed him. Also Miss Bowman, I think."

"Then you are . . . ." I began.

"Jonathan Stuker," he finished. "I am sure your friend Mr. Holmes has deduced that, by now. He may also have realised the reason for my actions. Together with you and Lestrade, and others who I have yet to identify, he was the cause of the death of my brother. I could not let that pass without setting myself upon a path of vengeance."

"Your brother was a murderer. Had that been proven, he would have died on the gallows."

"I prefer to think of him as one who chose a different way through life, as did his employer Professor Moriarty, and as did I. All of the hunting class, you see – the slaughterers of those who obstruct us."

"Why did you bring my deceased wife into this?"

He was silent for a moment, during which I listened in vain for sounds of the others among the trees.

"My original plan was to make both you and Holmes suffer," he said then. "You, because I was certain that you hadn't fully recovered from her death, and he as your close friend. Had this been successful, you would have known much pain and confusion before you met the fate I had in store for you. Mr. Holmes I intended to deal with later, and Lestrade after that. I regret that my strategy had less than the desired effect, but we are here now and Lestrade will meet the same fate as you are about to, before I slip away. By this time tomorrow I will be far from here, and Scotland Yard will be short of one Detective-Sergeant." I sensed a movement and concluded that he had pulled something from his pocket. "It is fitting that you should receive the death that my brother was so adept at bestowing. Turn around."

With his revolver trained on me, I had no choice but to obey. Already, I imagined the sharpness of the wire that he had drawn from his pocket, cutting into my throat and extinguishing my life. Fear I felt – yes, even terror – but even greater was the dreadful thought that I was unable to warn Holmes of what was to befall him. I had some notion of turning to face Stuker as he approached, to grapple with him in a desperate bid to survive, but this was dashed as he was behind me so rapidly and I heard the wire hiss as he swung it toward my head.

Before it could sink into my flesh, I sensed a quick movement from the nearest trees. I turned my head as the vague form of Constable

Harbridge dealt a blow to Stuker, his truncheon striking not the head but the hands that gripped the wire. I heard the breaking of bone, before the cry of agony became lost in the forest.

I carefully took the wire and threw the vile thing to the leaf-strewn earth.

"Thank you, Constable," I gasped inadequately, turning to the indistinct shape. "You appeared at just the right moment. An instant more, and I would have been a dead man."

"You surely cannot believe that I would have allowed that, Watson, after listening to Stuker's confession."

"Holmes!" I cried in astonishment, as I recognised his voice.

I detected a moment as he removed the moustache. "It is gratifying to see that I can surprise you after all these years. Are you injured, old fellow?"

"Not at all, you prevented that. But how did you know to follow us?"

I sensed his smile in the gloom. "You will recall that I was at Scotland Yard when 'Cullen' was introduced to us. When he removed his gloves, I noticed at once the marks across his hands where he had encircled the wire around them to take the strain as he murdered Miss Bowman. The marks were fresh but far from conclusive and, without proof, I could do nothing. Hence my successful attempt to persuade Gregson to allow 'Constable Harbridge' to temporarily join the force. I explained that both yourself and Lestrade were in deadly danger, and he eventually agreed after impressing upon me many times that I was engaging in a most irregular procedure. I think my past assistance to The Yard swayed his final decision."

Stuker let out a long moan as Holmes lit a lantern and handed it to me. "Let us make our way back to the road, where Lestrade and the others will be waiting. I informed them of the truth of this matter before I left to follow you." He then gripped our prisoner by the arm, with more force than I had seen him use before and disregarding his injuries. Stuker appeared to move with great difficulty, but Holmes was relentless. Not long after, he was transferred to the custody of Inspector Lestrade, and my friend and I engaged a passing four-wheeler to return to Baker Street. After a short while we were sitting comfortably in our familiar armchairs, he having resumed his normal appearance. Before a warming fire, we sipped glasses of an excellent port.

"I am glad that this business is concluded, Watson," he said as he put down his glass, "if only to see the relief to you that comes from exposing the false resurrection of your wife. Although you knew, as I have always been convinced, that such a thing is impossible, the immense emotional shock to you was evident. I cannot apologise enough for my insensitivity to your predicament."

I shook my head. "Much to the contrary, your voice of reason helped me to retain my senses. It does prove however, that Mary's death still affects me more than I had realised."

"We all need time to heal, old fellow. Some of us more than others." He was silent for a moment before retrieving his glass and draining it. "I think it best if we strive to put this affair behind us. If, as you have indicated, you wish to move back into your old room, I suggest you occupy yourself tomorrow with transferring your remaining possessions from Kensington. As for now, I think we have both earned a well-deserved rest."

With that he stood up and stretched himself before bidding me goodnight, and a moment later I was alone in our sitting room. Shortly after I sank gratefully into my bed, weary enough to expect a dreamless sleep. In fact, my dreams were vivid and very real to me. They were of Mary, clad in a long white gown, calling to me in the sweet voice that I could never forget. She told me that she knew of the strain of my recent experience and should disregard it for the falsity it had been. Reassuringly, she said that she was and always would be with me still, and would watch over me. She spoke of a sign that she would leave for me, but I knew not her meaning.

I awoke to a new day with sunlight filling the room. The dream had been curiously uplifting, though of course it was nothing more than a wishful product of my imagination. I decided not to mention it to Holmes, in order to avoid bringing down upon me another lecture of the folly of believing in the supernatural or anything that could be construed to be connected with it.

Our breakfast conversation was pleasant enough, my friend eager to embark upon the new case he had referred to before. He left early and I returned to my house in Kensington later that morning. I walked around the familiar rooms, allowing memories to return to me briefly. The cart I had engaged waited outside with the horse stamping its hooves impatiently, and two burly young fellows stood ready to enter and begin removing my possessions. I was about to call for this to begin when I hesitated, having noticed a strange thing: My slippers, my pipe, and the book I was in the midst of reading were arranged as she would have done – as she used to do. I had no memory of doing this when I was here last. I resolved to say nothing of this to Holmes, but in my mind – and indeed my heart – the conclusion was clear.

# The Adventure of the
# Bewitched Tenant
## by Michael Mallory

When I think back on the time of my having returned to Baker Street after an absence of three years, I do so with an inescapable feeling of sorrow. It was not so much what happened as a result of my renewed living situation with Sherlock Holmes, or, indeed, anything Holmes did directly. Nor was it the result of the singular case that commenced shortly after I had renewed my position as Holmes's living companion. No, the source of the dull, leaden agony that consumed my being was caused by an event that had happened before I came back to my former lodgings: The death of my wife, Mary.

It was in the latter part of May, 1894, on a Thursday morning, which promised very little difference from a week's worth of preceding days, at least for me. Holmes was endeavouring to raise my dismal spirits by offering to take me to see the new programme at the Canterbury Theatre of Varieties. While I did not feel up to patronizing a music hall, the spectacle of Holmes striving so earnestly to improve my demeanour was rather touching, and it was beginning to have an effect on my commitment to sad martyrdom. I was, in fact, on the verge of acquiescing to his entreaty when the sound of footsteps was heard on the stair outside of our rooms.

"It would appear that we are about to be consulted," Holmes said, and out of habit, I rose from my chair and went to the door, opening it.

"Oh, hello, Dr. Watson," said our landlady, Mrs. Hudson. "How are you feeling, poor dear?"

"I cannot say well, though Holmes is certainly doing his part to help in my recovery." I looked out into the hall. "Whom have you brought with you?" The good woman often escorts prospective clients from the front door to our rooms.

"Unless my hearing has become faulty, no one," Holmes interjected, "since it was only one set of footfalls I detected."

"That is right, I am alone," Mrs. Hudson said.

"And since you are not accompanied by your Ewbank, I must assume that sweeping the rug is not the purpose for your visit."

"No, though Heaven knows it needs it. Instead, I have a request."

"Pray, come in."

She stepped through the door, which I closed behind her, but she declined to take Holmes's offer of a seat. "Mr. Holmes, I'd like you to investigate someone for me" she said.

"May I ask what this person has done to warrant investigation?"

"He's done nothing, not really. But for the last several days I've seen him outside, just standing around, looking guilty. Then after a while, he starts to leave, then turns and walks back, fidgets some more, and then goes away – at least for a while. I think he might be planning a robbery."

"Would this man be a fellow of slightly less than medium height, clad in a grey suit with a *boutonnière* of Sweet William in the lapel, a dark maroon waistcoat, a tall bowler hat, and carrying a large gold watch with a hunter-case?"

Mrs. Hudson's mouth fell open in surprise. "The very one! How on earth did you know?"

"Because it is a public street on which he stands, and I, too, have seen him, through the sitting room window. I suggest, however, that robbery is not his goal. His watch is of a far too expensive make for the man to be worried about money, unless he is of the ilk to steals for the sheer pleasure of it. Were that were the case, he would have made his move by now, instead of deliberating so."

"Deliberating about what?" I asked.

"Isn't it obvious? Whether or not to come inside. Watson, do be a good fellow and go down and invite the man to come up, for based upon the timing of his appearances over the last three days, I expect him to be in front of the house at this very moment."

Holmes was, of course, correct in his assessment of the man, who appeared startled by my approach, implying nervousness as well as indecisiveness. "Mr. Holmes will see you now, if that is your intention."

"Y-yes, thank you," he stammered as I escorted him to the front door.

Mrs. Hudson was coming down the stairs as we entered, passing us without uttering a word, but casting a stern glance toward our visitor. "Follow me," I told the man, leading him up the staircase. Holmes was waiting for us at the door.

"I assure you, sir, I do not bite," he said to the stranger.

"Oh, well," the man replied. "I, uh, I did not think that you did."

"Yet you were uncertain about consulting me. Do come in and introduce yourself."

"I am Julian Harcourt, though I doubt that means anything to you," the man said, stepping inside and doffing his hat to reveal wispy hair the colour of curry, which was pasted on his pale dome to give the illusion that something was still rooted there. "I cannot say if I am doing the right thing by coming here, but I am in a quandary."

"Pray, be seated and describe to me your problem."

Julian Harcourt eyed Holmes's guest chair suspiciously, as though unable to decide whether it was safe or not. Finally he settled into it and withdrew a handkerchief from his pocket, using it to dab at his upper lip. "This has to do with a tenant of mine. I own a house in Barnes village that is rented to a Mr. Gabriel Pembroke and his wife, and I'm afraid that payments for it have ceased. Mr. Pembroke is some two months in arrears."

"Surely this is a matter better suited to a solicitor than a detective," Holmes said.

"My solicitor has, of course, delivered communiqués to Mr. Pembroke, but each time he ignores the entreaty, claiming he is putting his money to better use elsewhere."

"By which you mean that Pembroke is not without the means to pay you – he is merely refusing."

"Quite so. He is indeed a man of means, having inherited a veritable fortune and a fine house from his late father – or so I have been told."

"Told by whom?"

"Well, Pembroke himself has told as much to my solicitor. Yet he refuses to part with any of it. After long deliberation, I decided to take matters into my own hands and visit the man at home and put the proposition of payment directly before him. It was frankly difficult to communicate with him, since he was already holding a communication – with his father."

"Just a moment," I broke in. "Did you not just state that his father was *dead*?"

"Indeed I did. He was communicating with the elder Pembroke's spirit through a witch-board."

"Through a *what*?"

"A witch-board. It is a flat plank of wood with letters printed on it. He places his fingers on a small, triangular device he calls a 'planchette', and the device moves to point out certain letters which, when combined together, form messages. He claims the planchette is moving through the efforts of a spirit guide which, in this case, is his late sire, Ambrose Pembroke."

"As a man of science, I cannot accept that," I muttered.

"As a man of commerce, I find it incredible, too," Harcourt rejoined. "But the fact is the spirit guide . . . or whatever it is . . . has already provided the names of horses upon which to bet at the races, and he has won each time. It has recommended investments to Pembroke, each of which has paid off. This is why he devotedly follows the entity's advice and continues risking his wealth in such arcane ways. He is convinced he will

95

soon be the richest man in England, and it is all because of the ghost of his father."

After lighting a cigarette and blowing out a great gust of smoke, Holmes asked, "Do you believe he is actually communicating with this entity from beyond the grave?"

"I do not know what to believe, Mr. Holmes. I have never been a man for table rappings or manifestations of ghosts, but neither do I know how to explain that the witch-board continues to provide him with information that proves to be uncannily accurate. I have witnessed him do it. I have seen with my own eyes the planchette spell out a cogent message. All I know is that I am owed money that is not forthcoming, and as long as my tenant keeps successfully redoubling his wealth, he will not give up the endeavour. In fact, he has become as dependent on his spirit board as an opium addict is to the pipe." Harcourt once more mopped his lip with his handkerchief. "His wife Margaret is even more alarmed by his behaviour as I, because she fears this otherworldly force might in reality be is a malevolent spirit disguising itself as Pembroke's father in order to set him up to lose everything."

"I take it she fully shares his belief in the board's powers?"

"She believes in the money that is delivered to them by a man at their bank, the result of their winnings and investments."

"Have you spoken with this banker?"

"I have not, though I understand his name is Cooper."

"I am not quite certain what it is you expect me to do."

"Well . . . I don't know – Hence my hesitation to approach you. My goal is to be recompensed for the two months in arrears, and then to continue being paid the money I am owed. After that, I suppose I do not much care if he is hobnobbing with the spirits. If you can convince him to adhere to his financial obligations, Mr. Holmes, I would be most appreciative."

"Does either one of the Pembrokes know that you were planning to consult with me?"

"No. He is too taken up with this witch-board to know much of anything, while she was frankly too upset by my appearance at the house, and my questions, to provide more than the basic information I have told you."

"We shall keep them in the dark, then. I shall take your case, Mr. Harcourt. Please provide all the pertinent information regarding your property, chiefly its location."

"I told you, it is in Barnes Village."

"Indeed, though a specific street and number would be helpful as well."

After jotting down the address, Julian Harcourt reiterated, "All I desire, Mr. Holmes, is remittance of the money owed me. Please do whatever you can." He then scurried out of our rooms, as though late for an appointment.

"What did you make of that fellow, Watson?" Holmes asked, taking another draw on his cigarette.

"Most curious chap," I said. "Based on his information, however, I concur that he would have been better off consulting a lawyer and going through the courts. Honestly, Holmes, I cannot imagine why you would be interested in such a fanciful proposition."

"Shall we say for reasons of professional curiosity? I think we can agree that Mr. Pembroke is not communicating with the dead in any literal sense, though I am interested in how the trick is being done, and to what end. I will, however, understand fully if you do not wish to accompany me in this investigation."

"Of course I shall go with you," I said, thinking that sharing another case with Holmes might be more conducive to taking my mind off of my sorrows than the Canterbury Theatre of Vanities. I was, however, forced to wait for any such relief, since Holmes left the premises very shortly after securing my participation and did not return until some five hours had passed. "Where have you been?" I asked as he strode back into the flat. "I thought you wished me to accompany you."

"I had a series of stops to make first," he replied. "Among them was Sandown Park, where I inquired after Gabriel Pembroke's wins at the track."

"What did you learn?"

"Nothing, Watson. No one connected with the racing season could recall hearing his name."

"Perhaps he places his wagers through the banker, Cooper."

"An excellent, deduction, Watson. Wrong, as it turns out, since I inquired after him as well, but excellent nevertheless. After that I went to consult with the management at the Canterbury Theatre of Vanities."

"Holmes, I am overwhelmed by your attempts to elevate my mood."

"I did not go there to inspect the bill. I asked the management to put me in touch with a professional stage magician."

"What on earth for?"

"In the hopes that a man whose livelihood lies in creating illusions designed to fool others might have an opinion as to how a so-called witch-board works."

"Once you put it that way, it is sound reasoning."

97

"I do not traffic in unsound reasoning. Unfortunately, the man with whom I sought information, Grimoire the Great, was not able to answer my question."

"A wasted journey, then."

"Not entirely so, since I learned how to do this," Holmes replied, suddenly producing a deck of playing cards out of thin air. "Grimoire referred me to another, who may be able to provide more help. In the meantime, there is something that I would like you to do."

Depositing the cards on a table, Holmes handed me the scrap of paper upon which Harcourt wrote the address for his rented house. "Please pay a call on Pembroke this evening, if you would."

"For what reason?" I asked.

"To witness the alleged ghostly communication for yourself. In particular, I wish to know if the spirit guide recommends a winning horse in tomorrow's race, so that I may check it for accuracy."

"And what if the betting tip proves to be accurate?"

"That would certainly add a level of mystery to this case, would it not?"

"How am I supposed to accomplish this?" I asked. "Do I simply walk up and say, 'Hello, I hear you are conversing with your deceased father, and I felt the urge to come and watch?'"

"Use your imagination, Watson. Present yourself as a solicitor for the estate. Perhaps by doing so you will also learn why Pembroke is so reluctant to leave his rented abode and move into the house he has inherited."

"You wish me to purport myself as something I am not?"

"Do not then. If you are so satisfied with your life at present that you do not wish a respite from it, however momentary, go to him as a medical man."

I opened my mouth to protest, but found the words would not emerge. Holmes, in his blunt way, was absolutely right. My situation at present was weighing heavily upon me, and the opportunity to don the persona of someone else, much in the way I mentally inhabit a character in my writings, was not an abhorrent thought. I only hope that I was as accomplished an actor as Holmes, who could transform himself at will into anything, from dockside ruffian to a wizened beldame. "Are you certain that I am up to the task?" I queried.

"I wouldn't have proposed it if I did not think so," he replied. "Please go this evening. I must attend to other matters."

A quick check of the *Bradshaw* informed me that there was a rail station in Barnes, which was in proximity of Richmond, though I decided that simply hiring a carriage to take me there directly would save time and reduce uncertainty. The journey, though, would offer me time to prepare the manner in which I was to make my unannounced presence known to Gabriel Pembroke. In the past when Holmes sent me off on my own in a case, as in the instance of the matter of the hound in Dartmoor, it was with the full knowledge of the client. This was different.

I arrived at the address in Barnes just as the sun was contemplating its descent into the horizon and paid the driver. The brick house owned by Julian Harcourt was not large but was handsome, even if its grounds were rather untended. Going to the door, I took the knocker and rapped briskly. Within seconds a woman answered the door. She was of thirty or so years, dark-haired and very comely, though an expression of worry appeared to have been steam-pressed into her face. "Yes?" she said.

"Pardon the intrusion, madam, but my name is Dr. Watson, and – "

"Yes, I was foretold of your coming."

"You were what?"

"Come in, please."

She held the door open widely enough for both me and my confusion to pass through.

"I will take you to my husband."

"Are you certain I am not intruding?"

"If only you were," Mrs. Pembroke sighed. "If only you could pry him away from that . . . *thing*."

She led me to the living room where I saw Gabriel Pembroke kneeling in front of a table on which was the spirit board. Dressed in shirtsleeves and a waistcoat, his neck unencumbered by a collar and tie, his reddish face glistening with perspiration, he focused his entire attention on the wooden plank containing ornate letters, over which device described by Harcourt appeared to move across of its own volition, seemingly unaided by Pembroke's resting fingertips!

"Gabriel, this is Dr. Watson," Mrs. Pembroke said, and then turned and left.

"How do you do, sir," I began. "I have been sent . . . that is, I am here because . . . well . . . ."

"I know why you are here," he interrupted, his deep voice coming in quick breaths. "Your coming was foretold."

"What are you talking about?"

"Father," Pembroke said to the board, "what do you wish to convey to our visitor?"

I watched as the planchette moved quickly from letter to letter, with Pembroke calling out each one. "*N . . . O . . . T . . . F . . . A . . . T . . . H . . . E . . . R . . . .*" Only then did the man look up. "This is most peculiar," he declared. "It is not my father communicating." Turning his attention back

99

to the witch-board, he asked, "Who are you then? *M . . . A . . . R . . . Y . . .* Mary."

I suddenly tensed.

"Mary who? *W . . . A . . . T . . . S . . . O . . . .*"

"What is this?" I shouted, but Pembroke ignored me.

The planchette was moving even faster now, and instead of calling each letter, Pembroke now spoke the words being formed: "*Don't . . . grieve . . . so . . . my . . . darling . . . sea . . . no . . . seam . . . us . . . Seamus.*"

"What did you say?" I whispered, my body instantly chilled.

Now the planchette stopped moving. After a moment, Pembroke removed his fingers from it. "I presume you to be Seamus," he said. "Mary asks that you not grieve."

"This is – !" I cried, but was unable to finish the thought. I wanted to say *outrageous*, but the word would not come.

"Why are you upset?" Pembroke asked, staring at me with a wide-eyed gaze. "If she is a loved one, you should be happy that she is at peace and content on the other side."

My legs weakened and I staggered to a nearby chair.

"Margaret, our guest appears to have fainted," Pembroke called.

"I have not fainted," I began, but Mrs. Pembroke rushed back into the room.

"Dr. Watson, you are the colour of ash," Margaret Pembroke said to me. "Do you require something to drink?"

I did not answer. My mind remained fixed on that one word: *Seamus.*

That was the name Mary, and only Mary, used for me. It was a private jest between us that acknowledged Holmes's comment to the effect that I was his "Boswell." She playfully would call me *James*, which was Boswell's given name, but in time adopted the Irish equivalent *Seamus.* That was known only to Mary and me – so how could a man I had only just met, and that in the broadest sense of the term, possibly know? Did a portal through which one could reach beyond the grave actually exist?

"Doctor, are you all right?" Mrs. Pembroke asked again.

"Yes. At least I think so. But I wish to examine that board."

I rose unsteadily and walked toward Pembroke, taking the witch-board and planchette from him. I found no strings, magnets, or any other rational means of propulsion that would explain the triangle moving across the board. Neither did I find any hidden pivots in the wood that would allow the planchette to shift direction in a subtle or even unperceivable manner. The only possible explanation was also the most obvious: That Pembroke was moving the triangle himself to spell out a message of his own creation. That, however, could not explain the business of referring to me as *Seamus.*

100

"Why are you doing this?" I demanded of the man. "Have I not suffered enough?"

"I do not understand. Doing what?" Pembroke responded. "My father speaks to me in order to help me out financially. I already conversed with him today, and he told me you would be coming to receive a message. I merely assumed it would be from him, not someone named Mary."

I struggled to maintain my composure, and was only able to do so upon remembering why I was here. "If you wish to convince me of your veracity and sincerity," I said, "tell me the tip that was given to you by your father today."

"For what reason?"

"I seek verification of your story. If you tell me the name of the horse and it wins tomorrow, then I will know you are speaking the truth."

"Sorry, my good man, but race is already over, and my horse won. It paid off quite handsomely, did it not, Margaret?"

"It did," she replied. "The man from the bank picked up the winnings and delivered them this afternoon."

"The name of the pony, madam, if you please."

"Winged Mercury." Yet her face betrayed an emotion less than elation at having a winner at the races.

"Mrs. Pembroke, might we have a word?" I asked. I was about to excuse myself to her husband, but he had already taken up his spirit board again, and for all intents and purposes, had forgotten I was there. The woman led me to the foyer of the house. "I sense that you do not believe in this business of your husband's late father looking out for him."

"Doctor, no longer know what to think," she said. "I fear no lasting good can come of this."

"Is it true that he is predicting winners at the racetrack?"

Looking aggrieved, she nodded, and said, "But for how long?"

"Can you not simply take the board away from him?"

"I have tried. I managed to hide it from him one time. He simply created one of his own on a bare floor with chalk, used a wine glass for the planchette, and continued to communicate. I am at my wit's end, Doctor. I'm haunted by a prediction of my own, which is that Gabriel's devotion to that thing will bring ruin down on us. I've gone so far as to threaten to leave him if he doesn't stop. You say you are a doctor. Is there any way you can help?"

"I am a medical doctor. Were he ill or injured physically, I could treat him, but I know nothing of problems of the mind. Outside of shallow breathing, which is a sign of excitement, I saw nothing that would alarm me as a physician. Has he reported anyone other than his father speaking through that board before tonight?"

101

"Not that I'm aware of," she sighed.

There was little more I could do here. I had obtained the specific bit of information that Holmes requested, the name of the winning horse. I had also been shaken to my core by the events of this evening. I decided to take my leave.

Hailing another cab, I spent the journey back to Baker Street with the echo of Holmes's frequent exhortation rolling around in my mind: *When one eliminates the impossible, whatever remains, no matter how improbable, is the truth.* What was the truth of this situation?

Holmes was not in when I returned, and I went to see Mrs. Hudson about possibly getting a bite of supper. I carried the remnants of a cold joint, mustard, and wedge of stilton up to our rooms. It was hardly lavish, but it was enough. Holmes returned about an hour later and helped himself to a bit of the cheese.

"How fared you with Pembroke?" he asked, taking up his pipe and tamping tobacco into the bowl as he seated himself in his chair, which creaked under his weight.

"I do not know how to describe it," I said. "I am completely puzzled by the entire matter."

"You did see the man, though."

"Yes, I saw him, and I saw the so-called witch-board. His wife referred to it as a 'plaything'."

"You spoke with her?"

"I did. She asked me for help."

"What sort of help?"

"As Harcourt had indicated, she is worried his placing bets based on the information gleaned from the alleged 'other side'."

"She talked freely?"

"She did, describing her situation and even asking if I might be able to help. I believe she fears for his health, though all I could detect was a quickness of breath and a wide-eyed stare, due most likely to excitement. The woman appears desperate, Holmes. She even confessed to me that she had threatened to leave if he didn't dispense with the board." I then recognized the expression on his face as the one that usually accompanies a realization. "Is any of that somehow meaningful?" I asked.

"All of it," he replied, sitting back and closing his eyes. "What of today's horse? You did ask after that, I trust."

"Yes, I did. Pembroke – or rather, his wife – said the winning pick in today's race was called Winged Mercury."

A smile broke out on Holmes's lean face. "Excellent. Have you anything else to report?"

"There was another matter, though I do not even know how to describe it."

"You are normally quite facile with words."

"Yes, but . . . very well. Pembroke received a message for me through that damnable board of his, Holmes. A personal message . . . from Mary. *My* Mary."

His eyes opened wide. "How personal?"

"Through that infernal plank of his, he spelled out a name that only Mary ever called me. A name he had absolutely no way of knowing, unless he had been told either by me, or by her. I assure you I did not mention it, and I refuse to believe it was really her communicating from . . . beyond."

"Dare I ask what it was?"

"Seamus. It was her pet name for me. How could he possibly have known that?"

"I daresay we will know what is behind this matter soon enough," Holmes said. "Perhaps even by tomorrow. Until then, there is little we can do, and so good night, Watson." Getting up from his chair, Holmes retreated to his bedroom, closing the door behind him."

While my mind was desperate for answers, it was clear that none would be forthcoming tonight. With nothing to keep me company except my confusion, I attempted to read the newspaper, but had a hard time following any of the stories. By eleven-half I decided to throw in the towel of consciousness and prepared for bed.

I dreamt of Mary that night. In the dream, I was unable to coerce her into speaking to me, though the expression on her face was one of such undying love that it did not require words. I awoke immediately, the moisture from my eyes having dampened my pillow. I knew better than to believe she was actually coming to me from the beyond – this was nothing more than a phantasm conjured up by my own mind, as were all dreams. As likely as not, it was prompted by the episode at the Pembroke's home, and should be relegated to the same repository as all dream-stories, to be forgotten upon the morrow. Yet I could not. Seeing her so vividly caused my battered heart to ache even more.

I did manage to get back to sleep and dreamt no more, though I remained in a melancholy mood the next morning. Holmes, on the other hand, appeared quite chipper. "Are you up to the rigours of investigating?" he asked.

"Yes. I could use the distraction."

"Splendid. Our first stop is the Pembroke home."

"Do you plan to confront the man?"

"Not at all. Our task will merely be to watch."

"Watch for what?"

103

"Not *what*, Watson. *Who*."

My confusion had in no way abated when we arrived at the house in Barnes an hour later, via hansom cab. I was about to open the door when Holmes prevented me.

"We must wait here," he said.

"For how long?"

"As long as it takes." He then recommended that the driver, whom he was recompensing very well for his time, jump down and tend to his horse to make our presence there look natural. But after forty minutes, the driver poked his head into the cab and said, "Guv, I've done everything for ol' Silas here except brush 'is teeth. 'Ow much longer 'ave we got to stand 'ere?"

"Perhaps not long at all," Holmes replied, looking past the man to a figure walking down the street. It was a tall, slender, well-dressed man whose face I hadn't before seen. He stopped in front of the Pembroke home, pulled his watch from his waistcoat pocket and glanced at the time, then stepped up to the door and lightly knocked. A moment later Mrs. Pembroke opened the door and then stepped back to allow him in. "Return to your seat, driver, and wait for my command," Holmes said.

"Do you suppose he is Cooper the banker?" I asked.

"His name may very well be Cooper, Watson, though I doubt he is in the banking profession – not wearing a soft hat in place of the requisite bowler."

The horse was becoming restless when the man finally emerged from the house about twenty minutes later and started walking back from whence he came. "Follow that man, but at a distance," Holmes instructed the driver, and we slowly pulled away from the kerb to being pursuit. At the end of the street, the man turned the corner and stopped, as did our cab.

"Do you suppose he's seen us?" I asked Holmes.

"No, I believe he has stopped for another reason."

He was, of course, right, as only a few moments later a brougham appeared, which the man engaged, and the pursuit continued. Our driver never lost sight of the other cab, though at one point the distance between us became so great that the danger of losing our prey – whomever he was – registered as distinctly possible, at least in my mind. We followed him all the way back to the city, and watched as the brougham came to a stop in front of the Alhambra Theatre in Leicester Square. After examining the poster announcing the bill, Holmes began laughing heartily. "That is it!" he cried. "The last piece has fallen into place. It would appear our mystery man is too clever by half. Driver, we are no longer in pursuit. Please return us to 221 Baker Street."

Holmes said maddeningly little throughout the day, even when I entreated him to allow me in on his deductions. "All in good time," he smiled. "This evening, in fact, after the performance."

"Performance?"

"We are attending the music hall this evening – but not the Canterbury. Instead, the Alhambra. It should be very illuminating."

"Will you at least tell me who is performing?"

"The Amazing Barrelli, Master of the Mind."

"I have never heard of him."

"He, however, has heard of you."

Holmes elaborated no more and, as was often the case, I would merely have to be patient and trust him. As we were preparing for our outing later that evening, he surprised me by asking me to bring along my service revolver. "Are we really walking into that much danger in a music hall?" I asked.

"It would behove us to prepare for a little drama of our own. Hopefully there will be no need to actually fire it, though its very presence could have an effect."

After arriving at the Alhambra, we took our seats and sat through the first part of the bill, which included a pantomime artist, a young woman who sang rather well, a man who imitated birdcalls on a violin (which appeared to fascinate Holmes), and another who was able to contort his body in a variety of incredible ways. Being well versed on the physiology of the human body, I could only assume he possessed the condition known as double-jointedness. Finally The Amazing Barrelli came onto the stage, accompanied by a chair.

To my surprise, I recognized him immediately.

"Ladies and gentlemen," he called in a strong voice, "tonight you shall witness one of the most astounding achievements in mesmerism ever presented to the public on any stage. I assure you that what you are about to see is not trickery in any form. I leave such common jiggery-pokery to my competitors. Instead you shall witness a genuine demonstration of mind control."

The man's delivery was such that he created a hush among the crowded theatre.

"I shall require a volunteer from the audience, anyone who would care to participate in the extraordinary realm of mesmerism." Holmes was already out of his seat and heading toward the stage, his eagerness drawing scattered laughter from others in the crowd, and encouraging less adamant would-be volunteers to drop their hands.

"I see we have a brave participant making his way up here even as I speak," Barrelli said. "Come up, sir, and welcome,"

Stepped onto the stage, Holmes transformed into another person, not through his usual application of cosmetics and costume, but through his expression and body position. To anyone who did not previously know him, the man standing beside the Amazing Barrelli was awkward, nervous, maybe even a little slow-witted, but nevertheless relishing the excitement of being in the spotlight. His eager manner and gaping smile drew laughter from members of the audience.

"Have you been on stage before, sir?" Barrelli asked.

"Me. No, no, no, no, no . . . ." Holmes replied, eliciting another chuckle from the crowd.

"What is your name?"

"William Scott," Holmes said, which caused me to smile. I did not know what his game was, but clearly he was up to something.

"Thank you, Mr. Scott, for volunteering this evening. If you would, sir, please take a seat in this chair." Holmes did, and Barrelli withdrew from his pocket what appeared to be a clear crystal orb. "I would like you to relax and empty your mind of all thoughts. Can you do that?"

"Most people I know say so," Holmes replied earnestly, prompting another rolling wave of laughter.

"Very well, then Mr. Scott, look into this globe. Watch the point of light at its centre. Do you see it?"

"Yes," Holmes said.

"Concentrate on that point of light." The mesmerist slowly moved the crystal around, and Holmes gaze remained steadfastly on it. "You hear nothing by my voice. We two are the only people in this room, do you understand?"

"I understand," Holmes said, his voice now dull.

"Excellent. Keep watching the globe. You are becoming weightless. You are floating in the air. Can you feel it?"

"I . . . feel it."

"You are approaching a state that is like slumber, yet is not. In a moment I will remove this globe from your view, yet the spot of light at its centre will remain in your vision. Do you understand?"

"I . . . understand."

"Look at the centre of light. Now, close your eyes." Barrelli slipped the crystal orb back into his pocket. "Now, slowly open your eyes."

Holmes did so.

"Do you still see the centre of light?"

"Yes."

Turning to the crowd, the mesmerist said, "Mr. Scott is now completely under my power. Whatever action I suggest he do, he will carry out." Facing Holmes again, Barrelli said, "Mr. Scott, can you stand upside-down?"

"No."

"I say that you can. Try it."

With some uncertainty, Holmes rose from the chair, turned around, and placing his hands on the sides of the seat, lifted his legs upward until he was standing upside-down on the chair! The audience reacted with applause.

"Excellent, come down now," Barrelli said, and Holmes righted himself. "Do you dance?"

"No."

"I say you do. I say you are the finest principal dancer from the finest ballet in Europe. Please show us."

Without hesitation, Holmes leapt into the air and upon landing, spun around, again and again and again, until he had covered the entire stage. The audience applauded heartily. I was uncertain as to exactly what I was watching. While I had never known Holmes to frequent the ballet, let alone perform in one, he was proving remarkably proficient at it.

Had he indeed fallen into a trance and was not responsible for his actions?

When Barrelli finally bade him stop, Holmes did instantly, earning another smattering of applause.

"Now then, Mr. Scott . . . or should I say, Jumbo the elephant," the mesmerist went on. "For that is who you are, the late star attraction of the London Zoo. Place your foot on the stand, Jumbo."

Barrelli gestured toward the chair, but Holmes remained still. "Jumbo, we are waiting."

"Not . . . Jumbo," Holmes uttered, his voice strangely pitched and hollow.

"You are not Jumbo?"

"No."

"Oh, dear. Who are you then?"

"Am . . . brose . . . Pem . . . broke."

That appeared to catch the Amazing Barrelli by surprise. "Who?" he asked.

"Ambrose Pembroke . . . at least I was . . . once. Now . . . I have gone . . . into the beyond."

A murmur rolled through the audience.

"I do not understand – " Barrelli said.

"I . . . am . . . dead."

The murmur now turned into a collective gasp.

"You know my son . . . Gabriel . . . you mesmerize him . . . for your own gain."

"I . . . I . . . I – " Barrelli stammered, before stating, "I do not know what you mean!"

"You do."

"I think we have had enough entertainment from Mr. Scott," the mesmerist said. "Mr. Scott, when I clap my hands, you will awaken." Barrelli did so, but Holmes remained ostensibly possessed by the spirit of another.

"Not . . . Mr . . . Scott," he said. "*Pembroke*. Why are you cheating my son?"

Rushing toward the wings, Barrelli shouted, "Something's gone wrong! Take this man away!" Two stagehands appeared, but neither seemed to know what to do.

Holmes was now pointing at the mesmerist. "Why are you cheating my son?" he intoned. "Why? You must tell me . . . you must admit your crime. You have summoned me . . . I will never leave you unless you tell me . . . ."

"Your money, of course!" Barrelli screamed. "Leave me alone!"

"Does Mar . . . garet know?"

"Pembroke's wife? Of course! It was her idea!"

In the next instant Holmes stopped shuffling and lowered his arm. Then turning briskly to the audience, he said, "Ladies and gentlemen, if you have enjoyed this little presentation, please watch for the full production of *The Haunted Mesmerist*, which will be playing here in London next month. Thank you for your rapt attention!"

This received the most heartfelt applause of all, and even garnered some cheers from the attendees. The Amazing Barrelli seemed not to hear it, since he had collapsed and was being pulled into the wings by the stagehands. Turning back, Holmes shouted, "Watson, up here, quickly!" and I dashed toward the stage. When I joined him, he said, "It appears we will not need your revolver after all. In his present state, he will put up no resistance." Then turning to one of the stagehands, he instructed that the police be summoned to the theatre.

"What's he done?" the man asked.

"It is what he was *going* to do that will concern the authorities," Holmes said.

Unaware of the truth behind the drama that had just unfolded before them, the audience began to call for the next act. Holmes and I repaired backstage with the still-prone body of the Amazing Barrelli, who was the man we had witnessed earlier entering the Pembroke home, and then had followed to the theatre – the presumed banker Cooper. At that moment I realized what had given Holmes such delight while reviewing the bill posted in front of the theatre. *Cooper*, the archaic term for a barrel-maker, billed as The Amazing *Barrelli*.

Too clever by half indeed!

When the police arrived, Holmes had a word with the officer in charge, after which we left the theatre through the stage door. Once ensconced in the cab that was returning us to Baker Street, I said, "I find it hard to believe that Mrs. Pembroke was part of this scheme. She appeared so genuinely worried about her husband."

"It was an excellent performance, no question," he said. "But I suspected her from the beginning. Your visit with her confirmed my suspicions. Her statement that she was considering leaving her husband I am convinced is absolutely true, but she was planning to leave with Cooper, accompanied by her husband's inheritance."

"So this entire affair was a means of obtaining his money?"

"It was."

"For heaven's sake, Holmes, please tell me, how they were able to make the thing work?"

"If your forbearance can withstand one more evening in the dark, I shall reveal everything tomorrow in front of Mr. Harcourt. There is yet another stop I must make in the morning before I will be satisfied that I know every detail of this remarkable case."

"My forbearance is beginning to growl!" I commented, knowing that further argument was futile. I was, in fact, nearly in a state of outrage at Holmes's cavalier attitude toward keeping me informed, though I have since come to understand his rationale, for that night – for the first time in weeks – I went to bed consumed by an emotion other than grief over Mary.

After a restful, dreamless night, I awoke the next morning to an empty apartment. Holmes arrived about a half-hour later, having completed his tasks, one of which sending a telegram to Julian Harcourt to request his presence at Baker Street that afternoon, while the other was a visit to Scotland Yard to learn what had been revealed through their interrogations of The Amazing Barrelli and Margaret Pembroke.

Harcourt arrived at the appointed time looking measurably more at ease. "Does this mean I am to be paid what is owed?" he asked.

"It means Mr. Pembroke indeed has the money to pay you," Holmes replied. "How soon that occurs, however, is a matter for you and your solicitor."

"Pray, Mr. Holmes, tell me what was behind these bizarre matters."

"Yes, Holmes. Pray do," I echoed, perhaps even more eager to learn the truth than our guest."

"I must first state that I make it a practise not to believe in the supernatural," Holmes began, leaning back in his chair. "What is dreamt of in my philosophy, Mr. Harcourt, is confined to this earth only. I knew from the onset that trickery must be involved. I therefore consulted a professional magician named The Great Grimoire, who assured me that there is nothing supernatural about a spirit board. He confirmed my suspicion that the hands unconsciously move the planchette to achieve the desired response, usually based on what the person holds as a deep-seated desire, or else a deep-seated fear. Either way, the player, if you will, is not aware he is actually moving the planchette. The question then became what if someone else wished to influence the player so as to control the responses that emerged? Grimoire informed me that the easiest way to produce such a desired result was through hypnotism, or mesmerism, as Barrelli seems to prefer. He then referred me to a performer whose specialty is mentalism, a man who goes by the name The Baffling Borgus, who, with some encouragement, explained how it might be done. Cooper, or Barrelli, would hypnotize Pembroke and give him certain information, which would later emerge through his unconscious manipulation of the planchette over the so-called witch-board. Pembroke would be fully awakened before using the device, and would have no conscious memory of the implanted information. He genuinely believed he was communicating with the prescient spirit of his late father. Your testimony regarding the man's wide-eyed stare, Watson, confirmed my theory, since I am told that is a characteristic of one under hypnosis."

"But that still does not explain the prediction of the winning horses," I argued.

Holmes smiled. "That was simplicity itself," he said. "They were not predictions at all. The names of horses that were fed to Pembroke under hypnosis were the winners of *previous races*. I confirmed that by comparing the information I received through my visit to Sandown Park with the information you provided, Watson, after you called upon the Pembroke. Winged Mercury was indeed the winner, but for the race held the *previous* day."

"How, then, could he receiving winnings on a race already won?" Harcourt asked.

"He did not. The truth was, no money exchanged hands at any time during this charade. Cooper merely *pretended* to retrieve the winnings, while Mrs. Pembroke went along with the ruse. With her husband's attention so consumed by his presumed successes through bewitchment, he simply believed whatever he was told. He also, quite foolishly, trusted his wife."

"What was the purpose of all this?"

110

"Mrs. Pembroke had fallen in love with Cooper. How and where they met I do not know, though it hardly matters. The two planned to leave together, and they desired Pembroke's inheritance to finance their new life. The game's end would have come soon had you not intervened, Mr. Harcourt. The plan was to convince Pembroke to gamble his every pence on a risky investment, which he would have done without a second thought, since he believed his father's ghost had served him so well up to that point. Still acting the role of the distraught wife, Mrs. Pembroke would deliver an ultimatum: If he took the risk, and ruined them, she would have no choice but to leave him. That final presumed investment, however, would be a ruse set up by Cooper himself, which would, of course, fail spectacularly. The now bankrupt Pembroke would be without his fortune, his wife, and, I am quite certain, further advice from his father."

"So much trouble," Harcourt uttered. "Why not simply abscond with the money?"

"Because the sudden disappearance of his wife and his money at the same time would certainly have forced Pembroke to deduce what had happened," Holmes explained. "The realization that he had been deceived would almost certainly have prompted him to report the matter to Scotland Yard, which would begin searching for the wife. This way, Pembroke would be left a shattered man, but one convinced that there was no one to blame for his misfortune but himself, since I doubt he would have reported to the Yard that a ghost had been the cause of his downfall. The personality of The Amazing Barrelli was a contributing factor as well. How much more satisfying would it be for him to use his unique skill to commit this fraud then simply resort to common thievery?"

"Incredible," Harcourt murmured.

Holmes went on. "Like a good stage illusion, everything had been worked out – everything except your appearance at the house, Mr. Harcourt, which Mrs. Pembroke had not anticipated. Attempting to make the best of an unexpected development, I believe she quickly realized that a third party's knowledge of Pembroke's activities with the spirit board could ultimately be beneficial to the scheme, since if the police were to be called in, you could testify to her husband's erratic behaviour. By the time of your visit, Watson, she was so confident of that tactic that she came close to over-playing her hand."

While Holmes was on the subject of my visit to the house, there remained one mystery I needed to have explained, but before I could raise the question, Harcourt asked, "What will happen to them?"

"That will be up to the police and the courts," he replied. "If there is any mercy left in either of them, however, The Amazing Barrelli will hypnotize Pembroke one last time to erase the memory of this entire incident."

"That is it, then," the client said, checking the time in his watch. "Mr. Holmes, I cannot thank you enough. Please send me your invoice."

"In the meantime, be sure to consult with your lawyer," Holmes said, rising up and leading the nervous man to the door, then bidding him goodbye.

"That is not all there is, Holmes," I said, when he closed the door and turned back. "What about the business of Pembroke knowing of Mary and her personal name for me? Surely he did not get that information from Cooper."

"On the contrary, Pembroke *did* receive the information from Cooper, as well as the fact that your appearance was imminent. It was implanted through hypnosis along with that day's other instructions."

"But how could he have known I would be coming?"

"Margaret Pembroke told him."

"How on earth did she know?"

"Because I told her."

"You *what*?"

"As I have already stated, from the beginning I had a suspicion that the wife was involved in this matter, but I needed proof. I made one more stop while I was out yesterday which I did not reveal to you. I went to see Mrs. Pembroke in the guise of Harcourt's solicitor. She tried to keep me from seeing her husband, but I insisted, and saw him playing with his board. I pretended to be torn between belief and disbelief, but said that I had a colleague who was a man of science, but who leaned toward otherworldly matters since the death of his wife. At one point I pulled her free of her husband's hearing and casually asked if she went by the name of Meg or Maggie, or some other diminutive of Margaret, which she did not. But that was simply a way to introduce the fact that Mary called you 'Seamus' affectionately. It was the only means by which to impart that necessary knowledge, since I presumed you would later introduce yourself as John. But the fact that Pembroke knew that, and unconsciously spelled it out on his board, meant that he had been given the information by Collins, who could only have gotten it from Mrs. Pembroke, which conclusively proved they were working together."

"Very well, then, Holmes. How did *you* know of the name? I never told you."

"No, but Mary did."

"Mary did?"

"We did speak on occasion," Holmes said with a smile. "Boswell, indeed."

"I do not appreciate being used so," I declared. "I do not appreciate it at all."

"My abject apologies, Watson. It was, however, the most efficacious way to obtain a bit of evidence that was vital to the case."

"The case. Always the case."

"Always. You know that. Am I to be forgiven, then?"

"I shall think on it," I said, retreating to my room.

I dreamt of Mary again that night, more vividly than before. This time she spoke, and the very sound of her voice was like a visitation from an angel. *You must forgive, my darling*, she said.

"You mean Holmes?" I replied in the dream.

*No, Seamus, me – You must forgive me.*

"For what?" I asked her.

*For leaving you.*

I awoke then, perspiring, but with a sudden insight into what my subconscious mind was telling me: My deep and terrible sorrow, while genuine, had also been a mask for unfocused, irrational anger at having been abandoned in such fashion. That realization having forced to my level of consciousness was like having a ten-stone weight lifted off of my heart. "I forgive you, my love, if you will forgive me in return," I whispered to the silent, empty bedroom. While my soul was not fully healed, I now felt as though I might be able to function once more in normal fashion.

While I revealed none of this the next morning at the breakfast table, I did announce to Holmes that he was forgiven. I even agreed to his offer of an evening at the Canterbury Theatre of Varieties.

"Splendid," he said.

"Unless," I added, "you would rather stay in this evening and regale me with more of your prowess as a ballet dancer. You know, Mrs. Hudson might even enjoy that."

# The Misadventure of the Bonny Boy
## by Will Murray

$T$he passenger locomotive was wheezing through the Cheshire countryside, stirring up clouds of newly-fallen leaves. But I had no eye for their warmly enchanting autumn hues. We were bound north for Manchester, Sherlock Holmes and I. An urgent telegram had summoned us. The yellow flimsy had lacked all but the essential details of the matter.

*Sherlock Holmes*, (it began)

*Come to Manchester at once. My bonny boy is alive. You must help recover him safe and sound.*

The message was signed, *Ronald Talbert*.

The name meant nothing to Sherlock Holmes, for he had been out of England until comparatively recently, and mistakenly believed lost to this world.

"What do you make of this?" he asked me upon its receipt.

I glanced at the telegram and gave a start.

"I recognize the name. It was in all the papers during your European *interregnum*, as it were. Ronald Talbert's only son Allister had disappeared after an argument with his father. Something about running away to sea. Ronald Talbert put his foot down and the son rebelled. He went out into the cold night, and was never heard of again. At least, not directly."

"This is news to me," replied Holmes. "Pray continue, Watson."

"Less than a month after all hope had been given up, the parents received a demand letter asking for ransom. A photograph of the boy was enclosed, but it was taken in a room that was dimly lit. Moreover, the picture was blurred by an unsteady hand holding the camera. Nevertheless, the camera study convinced the parents to pay the ransom. This was done. But nothing more was heard of the laddie, nor did the extortionist make any further demand. The case was never resolved."

This was sufficient to pique Sherlock Holmes's interest. Without further consideration, he bustled me out of the sitting room and we were on our way to Euston Station, where Holmes dispatched a telegram to Manchester, promising an early arrival.

During our picturesque journey, my good friend plied me with many questions. I did the best I could, but my memory for details failed me in many respects

"There were some peculiarities attending the lad's disappearance," I offered. "Mad talk of him having been spirited away by fairies and the like. Circumstantial stuff, amounting to not very much. The particulars have faded from memory."

"No matter," reassured Holmes. "We will soon plunge into the matter."

"Have you any preliminary deductions?" I inquired.

"I would not think the boy was still alive, based on the data you have provided me, Watson. Except for one particular."

"The fact that he threatened to go to sea?"

"Precisely."

"I believe inquiries were made at all the shipping concerns, as well as of the Royal Navy. No boy matching that description had secured passage on any vessel departing Manchester in that December month. All of this was before the Manchester Ship Canal was completed, of course."

Holmes nodded. "This would not preclude a nipper from stowing away and being discovered days after shipping out. I would suggest a clever boy might successfully secrete himself for upwards of a week, possibly a week-and-a-half. By which time, there would be no practical way to return him home until the voyage was concluded."

"It was such a sensational case that I rather doubt any ship's master would have failed to deliver the boy at the completion of his round. Then there was the strangeness."

"You alluded to this before, Watson. Kindly elaborate."

"The authorities in Manchester dismissed these reports as the workings of local imaginations heated up by the mysterious disappearance. For several days after the boy disappeared, his cries for help were heard less than a mile from his home."

"I imagine that a thorough search was conducted."

"Quite thorough. Alas, it came to naught. Those who heard those cries, heard them distinctly, yet swore that they issued from the open sky. I believe there were other oddities surrounding the disappearance, but here my memory fails me utterly."

Holmes settled back in his seat, his features relaxing. "No doubt the parents will have better recall of these details than you have retained, Watson."

"I wish it were in my power to more reliably supply you with additional facts, my dear Holmes, the better for you to work your remarkable powers upon the mystery."

115

Holmes nodded distractedly. "Had I more to go on, I might well arrive at a theory before we arrive at our destination. But without sufficient data, I have threads, but an insufficient quantity with which to weave a skein."

"My apologies."

"Tut-tut, Watson. Three years is a long time. No matter how sensational the case, memory naturally fades. Experience shows that the longer the interval between the time an event is impressed upon the brain and the need to recall it, significant and understandable distortion in the details follows. Indeed, even in the order of the details. But I agree with you upon one point."

"And what is that?"

"My remarkable powers, as you call them, will get to the root of the matter sooner than later."

"Is that a boast, my good fellow?"

"Not at all. Nearly a prediction supported by past successes. This sounds like a simple enough matter, complicated by unusual circumstances."

"Kidnappings are not often complicated crimes," I allowed.

"I am not yet convinced that this is a kidnapping."

"Is it because the child was not returned?"

"No. Kidnappers are rogues of the first water and rogues cannot be counted on to live up to their promises. Simply because a ransom is paid does not automatically lead to the release of the ransomed party. Especially when the perpetrator is known to the victim. Remember the case of Martha Roberts. Abducted, ransomed, and later found strangled in her own bed, having been placed there by the criminal who lived up to his part of the bargain for her return, but neglected to honor the portion that stipulated a *safe* return. He was caught, of course."

"Were you involved, Holmes?

"Only insofar as I wrote a letter to the authorities in Brighton, pointing out the obvious."

"Which I confess escapes me completely."

"Surely you can puzzle it out, Watson. No? Ask yourself what motive would compel a kidnapper to risk discovery and capture while in the brazen act of restoring a strangled woman to her own bed?"

"As I recall, her unfaithful husband did the deed."

"Precisely. Mrs. Roberts had never left her own home. Lured into her attic, she was dispatched there and placed into a steamer trunk. The parents paid the greater part of the ransom, with the husband contributing a mere third. A sum he soon recouped, since he was the ransoming party."

"Which he forfeited upon his arrest, as I recall."

"Mr. Roberts forfeited a price far dearer than that tidy sum," Holmes reminded. "I understand they were buried side by side, despite everything."

A slowing of the train, accompanied by blasts of its steam whistle, signified that we were nearing Manchester London Road station. Soon we were within its capacious confines.

"Halloa, we have arrived," remarked Holmes, gathering up his coat.

Disembarking, I took notice of the magnificent iron-and-glass train-shed that distinguished the modern station from all others. The air was more chilly than it had been in London a few hours previous, but the advancing hour no doubt explained the abrupt change in atmosphere.

A man rushed up to greet us, his face red with excitement. "I am Ronald Talbert," he said, clasping Holmes's hand eagerly.

"Good to meet you," said Holmes diffidently. "My esteemed associate, Dr. Watson, has given me as many essentials in the case as his memory would disgorge. But I am lacking many of the fine details. If we could repair to a quiet spot, I would like to hear your story and ask pertinent questions. I am confident that we can get to the bottom of this if we approach the problem systematically."

Mr. Talbert escorted us to a cab stand and we availed ourselves of a handsome four-wheeler. Soon we were rattling along to their modest home not a mile distant.

A fair-haired woman with a care-worn face greeted us at the door. There was no maid in evidence.

"This is my wife, Melissa," said Talbert, closing the door behind us.

The woman wrung her hands strenuously. "Oh, it is so good of you to come, Mr. Holmes, so good." Her pale blue eyes were bright with an eager anticipation.

A cold supper was served, and we addressed it properly while Holmes listened to the couple's tale.

It was much as I remembered it. Allister Talbert was nine years old in the year in which he disappeared. A reader of nautical books, he aspired to go to sea, but his father, an accountant, had other aspirations he considered to be paramount.

"I forbade him from going to sea," the man said firmly. "And I have never regretted it. It was the right way to deal with the laddie, for he was dreamy of mind and awkward of manner. He was not fit for shipboard life – at least not at his tender age."

"Allister was a bonny boy," chimed in Mrs. Talbot. "Fair to look upon, he was, and gentle in his manners. I agreed with my husband. The sea was not for him."

117

At that juncture, Mrs. Talbert left the table and returned with the framed photograph of the boy. He appeared younger than nine in the photograph, a point on which Sherlock Holmes immediately remarked.

"Taken when he was seven, I should judge," remarked Holmes.

"Very perceptive, Mr. Holmes," said Ronald Talbert. "He was seven years and three months old at the time of that sitting."

"You can see that he was a bonny boy," added the mother. "A very bonny boy."

"Indeed," said Holmes agreeably, sharp eyes studying the lad's features as if seeking some arcane sign that he yet lived.

After committed the features to memory, Holmes looked up.

"Watson informs me that the boy was heard calling for help some time after his disappearance."

The mother responded instantly. "Yes, he was! I did not personally hear it, but those living around the old crematorium in the fairy burying ground said that it was a boy's voice, calling faintly for help. I am certain that it was young Allister."

The father interjected, "We went to the old burying ground and searched endlessly. No sign of Allister did we find. Nor did we hear any calls for aid."

"Were there any open tombs?" asked Holmes.

The mother responded. "None. All were sealed. The burying ground has been shunned for more than a generation, ever since the fairy rings started to sprout." She paused. "Mr, Holmes, they were in full cry then. Rings of mushroom chaps, with the sward all around them dead as if blackened by fire!"

Ronald Talbert noted, "The old bricked-up crematorium was forced open by police order and it, too, was searched, but to no avail. It would have been impossible for the lad to have sought shelter within, had he a mind to do so, for the old iron door was padlocked and the windows sealed with brick."

"I see," said Holmes thoughtfully.

"One thing was found, however," added the father. "A crow landed upon a hawthorne branch during the time of our search. In its beak was a fragment of white cloth. Curiously, the bird happened to drop the fragment, and out of curiosity, or perhaps desperation, I fetched it. It was a bit of shirt cuff, and written on it was a single word: *Flew*! *F-L-E-W*, all in capital letters."

"I will never forget it!" wailed the mother. "For hawthornes are the fairy's favorite trees!"

The father went on in a grave voice. "I could not make oath upon it, Mr. Holmes, but I believe that it was a fragment of Allister's shirt cuff.

And the word was inscribed in dried blood, in thick strokes taking up the entire patch."

"My word!" I cried.

The mother looked to Sherlock Holmes with widening eyes.

"Do you think that the fairies carried him off, Mr. Holmes?"

"I do not," returned Holmes in a restrained tone of voice. I had no doubt but that under less delicate circumstances, Sherlock Holmes's response would have been coldly dismissive. But he restrained himself, out of respect for the aggrieved mother of Allister Talbert.

Mrs. Talbert then launched into a teary soliloquy.

"You must understand that as Allister's mother, I possess a sympathetic bond with my son. During that horrible day of searching, I felt that he was alive, and nearby. In my heart, I still feel it to be so. But with the passing years, it is harder, much harder to hold onto that feeling. Can you understand a mother's heart, Mr. Holmes?"

"I believe, as do you, that Allister was alive at the time of the search. In fact, I have little doubt about it."

The woman's right hand flew to Holmes's coat sleeve and squeezed it mightily.

"Oh, thank you, kind sir! Thank you from the bottom of a mother's broken heart."

Sherlock Holmes looked as uncomfortable as I have ever seen him. Mrs. Talbert withdrew her hand and her handkerchief came out, blotting her moist eyes.

"Now what new evidence convinces you that your son is alive?" Holmes asked suddenly.

The father brought a manila envelope, and from it extracted a candid photograph. It showed a blond shaver about twelve years old, seated before what appeared to be a bedsheet hung behind him in order to disguise the room in which he stood. It was impossible to determine the eye colour, of course. Yet Holmes astonished us all by stating, "Your son Allister's eyes were a pale blue, I perceive."

"Very pale," said the mother excitedly. "But however did you know this, Mr. Holmes?"

"I have made a close study of photographs," replied Holmes. "While it is sometimes challenging to do so, sifting out the eye colour in black-and-white photographs is a skill in which I take justifiable pride. Your husband is brown-eyed. I see that your eyes are a pale blue and they suggested to me that the eyes of the seven-year-old boy in the studio portrait were much the same."

"Oh, yes, yes," replied the father excitedly. "Allister took after his mother more than he did me."

"He was a very bonny boy," repeated the mother.

"Yet this recent photograph I now hold in my hand," continued Holmes, "shows a boy whose hair is undoubtedly a combed but clumsy wig and whose eyes I would judge to be grey."

"But Holmes!" I exclaimed. "How can you be certain of this fact?"

"The gradation in tone tells me that this young man is grey of eye, not blue of iris."

I observed the parents closely as Holmes spoke in his neutral tone of voice. He was entirely unemotional. The father's shoulders sank, while the mother brought her delicate hands up to her open mouth.

"Moreover," continued Holmes, "the shape of the ears are dissimilar. This recent photo shows the young man with pendulous ear lobes, while your son has rather truncated lobes. There are other configurations which inform to someone who has studied the various configuration of the human ear that the nine-year-old in the older photograph could not have grown to be this twelve-year-old. In short, this photograph is a cruel hoax."

"Oh, and I so wanted it to be my bonny boy!" cried the mother in despair.

Stealing himself against the understandable emotional onrush, Sherlock Holmes asked politely, "Did it come with a note?"

The father produced a sheet from the manila envelope.

Holmes took this and read it silently, and then read it again aloud:

*To the Talberts:*

*Your son Allister lives. I am quite done with him. As I find myself to be hard up at present, I am prepared to return him to you if you are able to pay the second half of the ransom you so kindly surrendered all these years ago."*

*If you agree to this, your Allister will be restored to you. But not before. And certainly not ever, if you fail to complete the payment in full. I need not state the amount in pounds. No doubt the sum is branded into your brains. Kindly surrender an equal amount and there will be no further difficulties. I promise you. Place an advert in* The Manchester Guardian *saying the following:*

*"We are grateful to a merciful God for what He has restored to us."*

*Once I read this in printed form, instructions will be posted to you. Do not under any circumstances contact the authorities, and all will shortly be squared away, and Allister will come through with flying colours, I promise you."*

The letter was not signed.

"Do you have in your possession the original ransom note?" asked Holmes, laying aside the sheet of paper

"No longer," replied the husband. "The authorities took it."

Holmes frowned. "And if I request a look at it, it would arouse police suspicions, and could well cause the culprits to flee."

Holmes studied the letter again and squeezed the bridge of his nose between two fingers. I didn't recognize the gesture, but I knew it signified something. My friend's mannerisms were well-known to me, so I deduced that he was struggling with an unaccustomed emotion.

"As difficult as this is to convey to you, Mr. and Mrs. Talbert," Sherlock Holmes began. "I do not recommend paying any ransom to this rogue, whomever he may be. It will not result in the return of your son, Allister. I would stake my modest fortune upon it."

"That is exactly why we summoned you, Mr. Holmes," Ronald Talbert explained. "We do not possess the required sum, and have no means by which to raise it – certainly not without arousing sharp interest in our financial activities to that end. So we beseech you, how can our son be restored to us under such impossible circumstances?"

Holmes's reply was immediate. It did not show that he gave the question any extended consideration. But when I heard his next words, I knew that he had already formulated a plan.

"You may place the required advertisement in the newspaper. That will do no harm, and may accomplish some good. Place it tonight. We will not worry about raising the required funds until we have our response."

The mother clapped her hands together, tears starting from the corners of her eyes. Her care-worn face was all but glorified by some inner in motion that was suffused by a rising hope.

"So there is a chance that our bonny boy may be restored to the bosom of his loving family?"

Sherlock Holmes said solemnly, "If it is within my powers to do so, rest assured did that the fate of your son will no longer endure as an open wound in your hearts. For all mysteries have solutions, and I have solved more than my fair share of mysteries in my career."

"Did you hear, Ronald?" cried the mother. "Our son is coming home. Our bonny boy will belong to us again."

The father had been in charge of his emotions up until this point. But hearing these words, his shoulders commenced shaking and his face was received by his upraised hands. We did not see his tears, for his manly pride refused to permit us to behold them.

Excusing ourselves from the supper table, Sherlock Holmes and I went out into the night air in order to give the couple their privacy.

As we walked along, I asked my friend, "Have you true hope of the restoration of the lad?"

"If he has not gone to sea, I do," Sherlock Holmes said quietly. Again, he pinched the bridge of his nose between elongated fingers and his expression was unreadable to me. "But I fear the worst," he added in a low voice.

Sherlock Holmes and I walked the streets of Manchester as dusk grew deeper and a freshening wind made the trees rustle with their dying leaves of autumn, like tiny decaying hands.

Holmes walked with his chin tucked into his chest, his somber eyes raking the cobbles before him. I knew him to be in deep thought, so forbore to speak. My friend's powers of concentration were such that it was as if he were immersed in another world than the one through which we strolled – a world of thought in which logic, data, and the myriad connections thereof substituted for the familiar pathways of Manchester.

I did not think that Holmes's promenade possessed a definite destination, for he seemed to wander, lost in thought. Withal, we found ourselves at the gates of the old burying ground, all but abandoned, according to local legend, due to the fairy rings that came and went with the changing seasons.

The iron gate was ajar and Holmes slipped in without inviting me to follow. Naturally, I did follow.

The ancient burial ground was a dreary spot, the grass more dead than any sward I had ever personally beheld. Necrotic grass, I have heard such dead spots termed. Some of the leaning stones were centuries old, so worn by the elements that they were all but unreadable. Once, we passed a headstone whose surface was pocked by musket balls, no doubt fired into it approximately during the reign of George III. Or so the deceased's date of the death suggested.

A brilliant moon illuminated all. It made the waving trees spectral, for night was upon us. It has crept up steadily, but now it had arrived in full force.

The moon substituting for his lantern, Holmes wended his careful way through the grassy paths. Amid the rustle of dead and dying leaves there came an intermittent creaking, as if the rigging of a sailing ship was stirred.

Apparently drawn to that sound, Holmes padded along, his feet strikingly silent in their methodical tread. I knew my friend to be capable of the stealth of an American Indian when necessary, but here his quiet tread seemed inexplicable to me. I did not think it was respect for the long

122

interred, but I could imagine no other reason. Holmes didn't subscribe to the existence of fairy folk.

I wasn't surprised when we arrived at the door of the old crematorium, for its leaning chimney stood out strongly in the moonlight, prominent as the mainmast of a sailing ship.

Holmes paused at the door, noted the heavy iron padlock was in firmly place, and made a circuit of the building. The vertical windows had been sealed with brick, as reported. The building was not so old that it appeared to have fallen into disuse from age, but it showed signs of being unsound. That the structure was settling was undeniable. Perhaps the foundation was faulty.

Arriving at the rear of the forbidding building, Holmes stopped and turned his attention to a spreading hawthorne tree growing several yards distant. It threw out amazingly gnarled yet sturdy branches, and it was one of these which produced the creaking sound. The outstretched branch had reached out over the roof of the crematorium and was rubbing up against the tilting brick flue, its terminus passing beyond the brick face, as if a woodsy hand with spindly fingers had attempted to grasp the chimney, but failed to do so.

This towering chimney appeared unsound to my eyes. Missing and crumbling bricks lent it the semblance of a mouth with vacant teeth, and the rectangular structure teetered alarmingly. Here, thought I, was another possible reason why the crematorium was abandoned.

Holmes studied the chimney for some minutes in absorbed silence. Then to my surprise he doffed his coat and started scaling the hoary hawthorne, causing its dying yellow-green leaves to tremble.

Reaching the crown with the agility of a monkey, he clambered around and thrust his hands into an orifice that he discovered in the upper reaches of the trunk. Extracting something, he examined it in the moonlight, then placed his discovery in a pocket. I couldn't see what it was.

After that, he climbed higher and studied the roof of the crematorium at great length, paying particular attention to the tottering chimney.

Where at last he returned to solid ground, Holmes's expression was an unreadable etching in the stony planes of his countenance.

"Come, Watson," he said glumly. "Let us find lodgings for the night."

"What did you discover?" I inquired.

"I discovered that a mother's sympathy for her son's welfare is unerring. The boy was indeed alive at the time of the search."

But that was all he would say about the matter.

We found a public house that would take us in and retired for the night. I, for one, slept soundly. I cannot speak for Sherlock Holmes. I could hear him rattling about in the adjoining room, a certain indication that he was immersed in the unsettling case before us.

Morning found us at the bustling and rejuvenated Manchester docks, which threatened to take so much sea-trade from old Liverpool. Cranes were hoisting bails of Alabama cotton, cargoes of Cuban sugar, and what-not from the decks of steamer ships that had worked their way inland along that marvel of Victorian engineering, the stupendous Manchester Ship Channel, and which were fast transforming the formerly landlocked city into one of England's most formidable ports.

Sherlock Holmes lead me to Trafford Wharf, his chin low, eyes downcast, countenance doleful, the very picture of the so-called "brown study". He seemed to have no eye for anything we encountered until we were dockside. Then he took special notice of the boys who were naturally congregating about, the day not being a school day, watching the still-novel activity along of quays.

"You aren't searching for the boy among these scruffy ruffians, are you?" I inquired when I perceived the pattern of his attentions.

"I am looking for one boy in particular, Watson," replied he. "I will settle for no substitutes."

That cryptic utterance gave me hope for the life of young Allister Talbert.

The boys congregating about the busy wharves were naturally varied as to their ages, but Holmes didn't seem to discriminate against any one, regardless of their station of youth.

To my immense disappointment, none seem to capture his attention beyond the immediate glance. It was clear that he was classifying them, sorting them out in his mind as it were, and casting them aside when they didn't meet his measure.

At a news agency on the Salford side of the canal, he purchased a newspaper and, after glancing at the front page, turned immediately to the advertisements.

"Ah, the advertisement has been published. We may not see any results for some hours yet. I should like to stroll the quays in order to pass the time, if you don't mind, Watson."

"If it you think it will advance your cause," I responded heartily, "I offer no objections. The day is pleasant, and the westerly breezes invigorating without being excessively bracing. And I do not look forward to treating with the Talberts unless it is with their long-lost son in tow."

"Fear not on that score, my dear Watson. Allister will be restored to his family in the proper order through events that are now unfolding."

124

I confess that my heart gave a violent leap of hopeful anticipation upon hearing these electrifying words, but I didn't press Holmes further on the point. I knew that it would do no good and might only evoke an example of the terseness that comes over him when he is engrossed in a case. Sometimes I wonder why I am invited along, since Holmes's mental machinery, as it were, operates best when lubricated by solitude and sustained through silence.

At the same time, I full well understood that even an eccentric fellow such as Sherlock Holmes oft times craves companionship – although I sometimes detected a tart tinge of ego suggesting that he enjoyed my expressions of astonishment whenever he produced one of his miracles of ratiocination.

We whiled away the next few hours in absorbed silence, at one juncture mesmerized by the Barton Road swing bridge which revolved majestically in order to permit a steamer to make its way back to the Mersey Estuary and thence to the Irish Sea. I wondered why Holmes took so little notice of the dockers and stevedores bustling about. If Allister had been kidnapped so many years ago, and his abductor had resurfaced once more to claim his pound of flesh, in exchange for the many pounds of Allister Talbert, I would have thought my friend to have gleaned at least an inkling of his nature, if not his identity. I have in the past witnessed feats of deduction that would have passed on the stage as examples of a magician's legerdemain.

Noon had come and gone without result. Holmes laconically suggested lunch. I was more than happy to join him in a meal, my breakfast having been limited to excellent India tea and a single scone.

Instead of turning back to the heart of town, Holmes found a dockside pub that served food. Into this we entered.

Over a simple but satisfying repast, Holmes ruminated at length. To my disappointment, almost all of it was in silence. I understood that I was often a sounding board for his theories, even if my own musings seldom rose to the level of excellence that marked the work of my superlative friend. Yet I was disappointed in the prolonged silence.

When lunch was almost fully consumed, I ventured to break into his unfathomable thoughts.

"Do you suppose that Allister Talbert has returned from the sea?"

Holmes was uncharacteristically slow in replying. "I do not."

"How odd. I had assumed that was the reason for our scouring of these docks."

"Never assume," said Holmes. "Always seek certain knowledge. Assumptions are dangerous. They lead one astray, and down dark alleys and byways that should never be plumbed."

"I do not possess your powers, Holmes. My mind tends to leap to assumptions and conclusions, no matter how I discipline it through your example. As I have said so often, there is only one Sherlock Holmes."

"And there is only one Dr. John H. Watson. Just as there is only one Allister Talbert. Your statement is as vacuous as it is obvious."

I must admit to being slightly stung by my friends soft yet sharp words. Had we not shared so many adventures, I might have taken offense. And I knew that his moods shifted with his mental tides, from calm to turbulent and back again. Peaceful waters were never far off.

"I apologize for my vacuousness," I replied, keeping the stiffness from my tone.

"It is of no consequence," returned Holmes dismissively. I had seen him sink into gloom before, but this brown study seemed to be of a distinctly darker hue.

"You confuse me, Holmes," I burst out, unable to keep my emotions in check. "On the one hand, you show signs of having solved the case. On the other, you appear to be in a quandary. It is as if no progress has been made whatsoever."

Holmes's eyes were dark and reflective.

"The progress I have made," he said slowly, "manages to be both excellent and entirely unsatisfactory."

"Well, is that not half the battle?"

"It is not the battle that concerns me, for the outcome is all but certain. It is the aftermath."

After that, he would not speak again.

Another hour mingling with the rough denizens of the Salford and Manchesters wharves produced no manifest consequence, whether good or bad. Abruptly, Sherlock Holmes spun about and stalked back towards the Talbot residence, head lowered, his outward demeanor that of a man consumed by an accompanying cloud of gloom.

Ronald Talbert greeted us at the door in a state of mingled agitation and anticipation.

"Mr. Holmes! We have received our instructions. This note was found in the jamb of the front door. We do not know who put it there. It was not the postman."

Eagerly, Holmes snatched a sheet of paper from the man's hand. Swiftly, he perused it. Then he handed it to me. It was disappointing in its brevity, and seemed devoid of clues.

*At first light tomorrow give the one who calls for it the funds.*
*Do not follow him. If you do this, we will all be in the clear,*
*you and I and young Allister.*

"This tells me nothing," said I, returning the ransom note. "Do you glean anything from these few lines, Holmes?"

"No more than I did from the first communication," he snapped. "The writer of that note is a knave and a seaman, for he employs common nautical phrases. Beyond that, the details do not matter. It is the boy who will call for the ransom money who is of interest to me."

"How the devil did you know a boy was involved?" I exclaimed.

"Do not be so dense, Watson. A boy has been involved since the beginning of this affair. Do you not recall the first photograph of the supposed Allister?"

Holmes's tone was so sharp that no doubt the expression on my face betrayed my what was in my heart.

Seeing this, Holmes's stiff countenance at once softened. He turned and clapped me on the shoulder, saying, "Buck up, Watson. This is a difficult matter. It has been fretting upon my nerves since last night. I meant you no offense. Please do not take the sharpness of my words to heart, for they have nothing to do with your question, I assure you."

Mrs. Talbert was standing nearby, and commenced wringing her hands once again. "Oh, Mr. Holmes. Do you truly in your heart believe that our Allister will be restored to us very soon?"

Sherlock Holmes did not turn to address her, and in fact studiously avoided her beseeching gaze, but spoke to the room at large. "I have no doubt up on the score, madam. It will be as I have held it to be from the beginning."

Ronald Talbert raised his voice, which quavered with uncontrolled emotions.

"Do you believe that the scamp who is coming for the ransom money to be Allister himself?"

"It would be foolish of the villain to send the object of the ransom to call for the ransom, would it not?"

"Yes, I suppose it would. Surely we would recognize her own son."

Holmes's mouth drooped glumly. "No, you might not recognize your own son. The hardships of sea might have changed him significantly. Allister would have aged three years, and grown accordingly."

"Do you now think that, contrary to your previous understanding, Allister has been at sea all these years?"

"At this time, I prefer not to put forth theories when facts are all that matter. Your son will be restored to you, such as he is."

No more could any of us get out of Sherlock Holmes.

Declining the Talbert's kind offer of hospitality, Holmes said that he would return to the docks and continue his search, but that he could be counted upon to return before daybreak and lie in wait for the boy who was expected. "If he isn't discovered before that fateful hour," he concluded.

"You propose to capture the boy?"

"I would prefer to hand him a ransom and follow him to his confederate, but we must make do with the resources available to us. When he knocks upon the door, we will pounce upon him."

The boy came at the announced hour.

We were crouching amid the privet hedges adjacent to the house, Holmes and I. The morning sun was peeping over the rooftops and dawn was breaking with its customary autumn clarity. Morning birds were flitting about here and there. All was otherwise quiet.

In the diminishing darkness of the incipient dawn, a young urchin came striding up the street, silent as a mouse, but showing no furtiveness. His clothes were of the sort common about the wharves. I took him to be about twelve years of age. In the dusky dawn, I couldn't discern his features. The color of his hair was concealed by a cloth cap.

He walked up to the front door of the Talbert dwelling, took the iron knocker firmly in hand, and banged it smartly.

At once, Ronald Talbert threw the door open and looked down upon the stripling who had presented himself upon his threshold with the boldness of fearless youth.

"What is it you want?"

"Nothing more than what I have come for," replied the gamin in a breezy tone.

"Well, here it is," snapped the father, surrendering a fat envelope stuffed fat with paper. Eager fingers clutched the parcel. The loose flap fell open, disgorging only newspaper cuttings.

"Here now! What's this?" the boy exclaimed.

It was at that point then Sherlock Holmes and I sprang out of our concealment and rushed in.

Being fleeter of foot than I, my friend reached the young fellow first, took him by the shoulders, and spun him around.

"The game is up, my fine young imp! Give us your name for a start."

"Why, it's Allister. Allister Talbert."

With that announcement, Mrs. Talbert flew out of the doorway, and confronted the boy.

She searched his face, his unkempt hair and clothing in turn, then took him up in an irresistible embrace, exclaiming, "My bonny boy! My son has come home to us!"

128

Looking uncomfortable of countenance, Sherlock Holmes said in a strict tone of voice, "That is not your son. His ears are all wrong. His hair is darker than your son's fair locks."

"I know my only son when I behold him, sir!" she cried out. "Yes, his face is older and more bony. His hair has darkened. But these are the clothes Allister was wearing the very day he vanished."

"Nonsense!" retorted Holmes firmly. "Look at his eyes. They are grey."

"It was the fairies! They wrought these strange alterations upon him. But this is Allister! He admits to it. Why would he say such a thing if you were not my own son?"

"Because he is a willing accomplice to the crime of extortion. And he will lead us to his confederate, if I have anything to say about it."

But the mother was adamant. She refused all facts and all logic. "I birthed only one son, and it is he!"

Ronald Talbert had stepped out and was examining the boy's face in the ever-warming light. He yanked off the cloth cap, studying the shock of light brown hair.

"Melissa," he said gently. "I do not believe this is Allister."

"He *is* Allister. He admits it! The rest is the work of the fairies."

Now faith in fairy folk remains common throughout the British Isles. even in this day and age. It was pointless to argue against such closely held beliefs. But the evidence of my senses told me that this was not Allister Talbert.

Then the youth gave himself away. "Where is the ransom money? Quick, if you want to see your son again!" His words were strikingly bold for one of his callow years.

Blue eyes mirroring sudden horror, the mother recoiled from the twisted mouth from which emerged those cutting words.

"Ransom!" she cried. "What need is there for ransom when you have delivered yourself back to our very doorstep, Allister?"

The woman's confusion was pitiful to behold. Clinging to the fading belief that this was her long-lost son, Melissa Talbert was struggling with the boy's cruel words.

"I must take the ransom money back to him," the lad insisted. "He will beat me if I don't. Worse, he will beat Allister. Mark my words. He is a cruel man, cruel and unyielding."

"You are not Allister!" she shrieked.

"I have admitted it," the brat returned in his surly tone.

"But your clothes!"

Sherlock Holmes said gently, "Those could not be Allister's garments. They would hardly fit him after three years of growth."

"Fairies could have worked their will upon him," the distraught woman insisted.

"This is no changeling," Holmes insisted, "but rather the urchin who impersonated your son in the false photograph. The ears match perfectly."

A low moan as if produced by a banshee escaped Melissa Talbert's throat. Climbing in pitch and volume, it became an inconsolable wail. Her lank form seemed to shrink into her simple dress.

"You promised that Allister would be restored to us, Mr. Holmes!" she cried out weepingly. "You gave your word of honor!"

"And I shall keep it, I assure you," Holmes said stiffly.

His own features collapsing in misery, Ronald Talbert took his wife by the shoulders and led her back into the house, her shoulders shaking with her sobs. The truth of Holmes's words, combined with the young man's manner, had collapsed her fragile bubble of belief.

Once the front door was shut, Holmes grasped the boy by one arm and squeezed him so hard his entire beardless face winced. My friend's strength was not to be countenanced.

"Name the man behind this outrage!" Holmes demanded. "Is he on shipboard, or dwelling at a sailor's inn?"

"Damn you, I'll not tell!"

Holmes squeezed again and the young man's face clenched like an arthritic fist. The pressure was not gentle.

"Give me his name before I turn you into the authorities."

"If you do so, young Allister will never be seen again. Mark me!"

In a low voice Holmes said, "I think otherwise. Your words ring hollow as a cracked bell. Now, I will ask you only one more time: Who is your confederate in this foul crime?"

Fingers that were scarred and stained by chemicals squeezed once more, this time with less restraint. The nipper gave a wretched cry, and tears fled his eyes.

"Neil! Neil Nelligan. You'll find him at the Sailors Inn, waiting for me."

"Describe the culprit."

"He's fifty, if he's a day. Thick neck. Weight about thirteen stone. Scraggly hair as grey and dirty as an old mop. You'll know him by his missing ear."

"The right ear," prompted Holmes.

"Yes. However did you know?"

"I spied a sailor by the docks missing his right ear and made a mental note of it. But there was nothing otherwise suspicious about him. Now, your name."

"Alec McGuiness."

"Very well, young McGuiness. You must be surrendered to the authorities."

"But Holmes," I interrupted. "What of poor Allister?"

"The fate of Allister Talbert is known to me," murmured Holmes. Taking out a silver whistle, he blew upon it shrilly. Before long a constable came bounding up.

"I am Sherlock Holmes. Take this boy into custody."

"What is the charge?"

"Aiding and abetting an extortion for ransom fraud. I will have more to say about it later today. Allow me the freedom to seek out his confederate, the actual extortionist."

"It is highly irregular."

"Not in London. Ask Inspector Lestrade of Scotland Yard. And if it is good enough for London, it should go in Manchester. Do you not agree?"

The constable took the unresisting boy in hand well in hand, and he scratched his head for a moment before speaking. "I expect I will see you at headquarters before very long, Mr. Holmes."

"You may count on it, Constable. Thank you."

Without further ado, we strolled to the waterfront quays, walking because there were no cabs or carriages about. Holmes appeared to be in no great hurry to reach his destination. Again his chin was sunk upon his chest and he seemed deep in thought. Once he pinched the thin bridge of his nose, and again I failed to detect the significance of the gesture.

We arrived at the docks forthwith. Dawn illuminated the usual bustle of dockside life. Seagulls wheeled about, crying raucously as is as their way.

Going straight to the Sailors Inn, we at once spied a sailorly ruffian pacing Trafford Wharf, just short of the graving dock and with view of the Mode Wheel locks beyond. As he promenaded about, it could be perceived that the impatient fellow lacked a right ear. Beneath his woolly cap, this dirty grey mop of hair grew down, concealing whatever orifice remained, but otherwise not hiding the fact that he lacked the aural organ's natural cartilage.

Quickening his pace, Sherlock Holmes strode up to the fellow and accosted him in a manner less artful and more rude than was his normal demeanor.

"Your name is Nelligan, I take it?" he demanded.

The fellow turned, his voice and expression becoming surly. "What if it is? And who the devil are you?"

"Sherlock Holmes. I imagine you have heard of me."

Holmes might have introduced himself as Satan incarnate, for the reaction of Sailor Nelligan was virtually identical.

Spinning about, he attempted to flee.

But my friend was too quick for him. The same steely fingers that had squeezed the truth out of Alec McGuinnis took hold of the man's collar and jerked him almost off his feet.

"The game is undone, sir. Your cabin boy – for that is what I assume him to be – is in police custody."

"I have done nothing!"

"On the contrary," Holmes returned coldly. "You have callously excavated a mother's grief and laid her sorrows bare like a fresh wound. At the same time, your dastardly scheme has brought me to this city, and the truth about Allister Talbert has come out. So I will give you a measure of credit for that result – even though it was largely my doing and certainly not your intention."

"Your talk is nonsense. Unhand me, or I will have a constable on you!"

To my surprise, Sherlock Holmes released the man's collar. Then in an example of pugilistic skill that was breathtaking in its speed and accuracy, his hard right fist came up and struck the point of the unshaven chin, rocking the sailor's head back so sharply I feared the man's thick neck would snap.

To his credit, Sailor Nelligan did not lose his feet. He stepped backwards several paces, his burly arms waving aimlessly. Shaking his head, he struggled to clear his stupefied brain. Seeing Holmes produce the silver police whistle, he turned with every intention of taking blind flight – and plunged into the water.

I imagine he had been intending to mount a gang plank and flee into the bowels of the merchant ship that was docked there, but he was so addled by Holmes's unexpected blow that he missed it entirely.

Nelligan floundered about in the filthy water.

"Is this your ship?" Holmes called down to him.

"What if it is, ye stinkard?"

"Thank you. I will have your captain place you in irons, pending a police inquiry."

"Who the devil are you to think that you can do such a thing to a sailor of Her Majesty's merchant fleet!"

"Have you forgotten? I am Sherlock Holmes."

Once matters were explained to the captain of the steamer *Finsbury*, the cruel scoundrel was lodged irretrievably in the ship's brig, and after Holmes made his explanations to the police, I found myself once more standing before the old crematorium in the ancient burial ground shunned because of its fairy reputation.

The police were there in numbers, as were several local labourers who had been summoned.

Mr. and Mrs. Talbert were standing by the gate, looking anxious and bewildered.

As the workmen climbed onto the roof and set ladders all around the tottering brick chimney, Holmes recited his conclusions.

"Allister Talbert was never kidnapped. Neil Nelligan and his cabin boy took advantage of newspaper reports of the young boy's disappearance, and knowing that their ship was about the sail, taking them out of reach of the authorities, he endeavored to extort ransom money, which he did successfully."

Climbing their ladders, the workers commenced chipping away at the chimney pot with their steel hammers, knocking it off and going to work on the loose and crumbling mortar.

"In time, Nelligan no doubt squandered that handsome sum in various unsavory ports. Finding himself once again back in the Port of Manchester, he decided to prey upon the grieving couple anew. In both cases, Alec McGuinnis, for that is his true name, posed for the absent Allister. But this time the conspirators took the game too far, Watson. Worse for them, not being content to leave well enough alone, he inadvertently drew me into the affair."

"That much I comprehend." I asserted. "But I fail to understand why we are here, and what became of the poor missing boy."

Precariously balanced workmen were now employing wooden mallets to knock the bricks out and away. They clattered to the roof and slid down to the dead grass surrounding the old crematorium. With each section reduced, they descended another rung or two, continuing their painstakingly destructive toil.

"Surely you have an idea as to Allister's fate by now," murmured my friend in a morose tone.

"I fear that I do," I replied, watching the workmen chip away at the tottering chimney with the single-minded industry of termites at an old tree stump.

"You will recall that Allister vanished on a late December evening. No doubt the weather was inclement, and hostile to sleeping in the rough. Whether Allister intended to run away to sea, or was afraid to return home to his father's wrath is immaterial at this point. He found his way to the cemetery grounds and, seeking shelter, was thwarted by the padlock on the front door of this structure and the fact that the windows are all bricked up. Yet the solidity of this impermissible building promised comfort. So

133

he climbed the old hawthorne tree, and crawled his way across the stout branch that scrapes against the chimney. For someone that young, it was not difficult to scale the last few feet of the chimney and slip down the flue."

"So he did gain entry to the place?"

Holmes shook his head solemnly. "Watson, do you recall the word written in blood upon the young man's torn shirt cuff?"

"Yes. It spelt '*Flew*'! Curious message, if it was a message in truth."

"That it was. It was curious only because it was misspelled. Allister was attempting to communicate that he was stuck in the *chimney flue*, whose base had also been sealed against the elements. His forlorn cries for aid availed him little, for the chimney flue carried them skyward, where they resounded untraceably. Strength flagging, the trapped youth eventually abandoned that tack. Lacking a pencil, he managed to break his skin and trace four letters on his torn shirt cuff in blood and send it to skyward. Had he more material to work with, he might have inscribed a more complete message, but by the time desperation had birthed this idea, he was no doubt far gone from thirst and hunger, as well as numbed by the bitter cold."

"But however did he get the fragment of cloth out of the chimney flue?"

"By wrapping it up about a rubber ball carried in his pocket. The weight of this allowed him to throw the ball high enough that it escaped the chimney top and landed on the sloping roof, where it rolled to the ground, apparently becoming dislodged. A canny crow happened to pick up the note and deposit it where the parents could see it. By that time, Allister was far gone. Otherwise, the eerie and untraceable cries for help that had preceded the discovery of the fragmentary note would have been heard."

"How can you be certain of this?"

From a pocket, Holmes drew a small rubber ball. Etched in flaking dried blood onto the surface were the initials *A. T.* Wrapped tightly around this was a faded elastic band, which no doubt had kept the note in place.

"A squirrel happened to pick up this ball and secrete it in his drey, which was a cavity in the hoary hawthorne, where I discovered it. When I recognized the initials, everything fell into place. I made my way to the chimney and peered downward, confirming my suspicions. Wedged in the blocked chimney and unable to climb out again, the unfortunate boy had succumbed to exposure, if not privation."

At that moment, the methodical workmen had successfully reduced the chimney by one-fourth. Visible in the noon daylight was revealed a small immobile head, distinguishable by its faded locks of yellow hair, which breezes stirred to a sad semblance of life.

From the old iron gate, Mrs. Talbert gave out a keening cry. "My boy! My bonny, bonny boy. I have you back!"

"It is as I promised," said Sherlock Holmes solemnly. "Alas, this is not the outcome that I desired."

My friend took the bridge of his nose between finger and thumb, and at last I understood the significance of the gesture. Holmes had put off breaking the unimpartible news as long as he could, and it had pained him to do so to the last.

We took our leave without saying our goodbyes, Sherlock Holmes because a mother's inconsolable grief was something that he could not bear to confront, and I because I had no comfort that I could offer in this terrible hour of desolation.

But I shall never forget to my dying day, the weird timbre of Mrs. Talbert's voice as she repeated, "My bonny boy! My poor, poor bonny boy!"

# The Adventure of the
## *Danse Macabre*
### by Paul D. Gilbert

It is a well-documented fact that when actively involved with a particularly challenging case, my friend Sherlock Holmes was prone to disappear for days on end, without leaving either a word or indication as to his location or circumstance.

As frustrating as this trait of his undoubtedly was, after many years of having to endure this thoughtless behaviour, it was something that I had eventually become rather used to and grown to accept. The affair of "The Treasure of The Poison King", however, took this to new extremes, for he had neither been seen nor heard of in over a week!

Notwithstanding the most singular nature of this adventure, at Holmes's earnest request, I must consign my account of this to another time and concentrate instead upon the unique problem brought to us immediately afterwards by Lady Roberta Wakeham.

She had presented herself and her predicament to us on a particularly wet and windy morning towards the end of October. The trees that had lined Baker Street had been twisted and contorted into grotesque caricatures of their usual stately selves and the gales had howled through every crack and crevice.

We had been assured of the gravity of her situation by virtue of the fierceness of the conditions that she must have endured in reaching us in the first place. She had clearly dispensed with the convenience and shelter of a carriage, for her hooded cape was soaked through and her hair, once it had been finally revealed, was bedraggled and dripping profusely onto our rug.

Holmes was on to his feet in an instant and he draped the lady's outer garment over the back of a chair close to our fire before showing her to a seat adjacent to his own. An instant later Mrs. Hudson arrived bearing a tray of steaming coffee and some feminine care and comfort. We allowed the poor woman a moment or two of warm indulgence before gently inquiring as to the nature of her predicament.

Lady Roberta Wakeham was a slim statuesque woman in her early sixties to whom time had dealt most kindly. It had not been hard to visualise her as very attractive in her youth, and she had lost neither her poise nor posture with the passing of the years. She spoke with a light, modulated tone and her smile was a soft and gentle one. She passed a card over to my friend and he smiled at its sodden condition and the lady's strict adherence to protocol.

"You have endured much in your efforts at reaching our door on such a day and I observe that your right hand still shakes, despite it having been warmed by the fire and Mrs. Hudson's coffee. Pray, explain to me how I might be able to aid you at this trying time. Remember that you should exclude nothing, no matter how trivial it might appear, and you can rest assured that the discretion of my colleague, Dr. Watson, may be relied upon as surely as my own." Holmes was leaning forward, with his elbows resting upon his knees. However his tone was invitingly modulated as opposed to his usual authoritative pitch.

"You are very kind, Mr. Holmes, although I do hesitate in setting this matter before you, such is the somewhat *outré* nature of my distress."

"Lady Wakeham, you should have no concerns on that score," I smiled as I brought out my notebook and pencil, "for Mr. Holmes positively rebels at the very notion of the commonplace."

"Well said, Watson. Please begin, Lady Wakeham." Holmes sat back into his chair, clasped his hands together, and closed his eyes in a deep, meditative state of concentration.

"You should know at the outset, Mr. Holmes that my late husband and I fell in love and were married at a very early age, and that we remained as such throughout our forty years, right up to the moment of his untimely death last Halloween. That is not to say that we enjoyed forty years of continuous, unbridled bliss. Of course, that is not only impossible, but I am not even sure if that is desirable.

"My husband, Henry, inherited his fortune and estate, and therefore had neither the need nor the inclination to do a day's work in his life. Naturally he had an excellent education, but he used this to hone his undoubted talent as a poet, a passion for which he had enjoyed since his early childhood. His talent and energy have been rewarded with the publication of many of his collections, and he has even enjoyed a form of celebrity as a result of this."

"Ah, of course, I am very familiar with his work!" I exclaimed, much to my friend's obvious annoyance. Lady Wakeham gently tilted her head in appreciation before continuing.

"Mr. Holmes, you should know that my late husband had his demons, as is quite often the case amongst those great romantic poets, of which my husband certainly was one.

"On those not uncommon occasions when the words refused to reveal themselves to him and his inspiration had failed to motivate him, he was prone to drown his angst and frustrations in a frenzied orgy of drinking. He was never abusive or violent during these Bacchanalias, you

137

understand, but he did take himself off to the far wing of the house, where he felt that he would cease to be the cause of any distress. In that he was correct and successful. However, during the course of these excesses he was also liable to abscond to a small, exclusive gentlemen's club, whose name escapes me, where he would quite often gamble away a considerable sum of money." Lady Roberta was clearly distressed by these horrendous recollections – quite understandably I should say – and she paused to delicately blow her nose and draw a deep breath or two before quietly apologising for her protracted pause.

"Although I had not realised this at the time, Henry had almost drained the coffers dry. Indeed, what should I have done? He had always been most discreet in all of his indulgences, and all matters of business and finance had remained within his exclusive domain. It was only several months after his passing that his creditors began arriving at my door."

"Calm yourself, Lady Wakeham, for you are surely amongst friends here." I offered. She smiled gratefully and continued.

"My ignorance regarding our affairs prompted me to seek the advice of one of our oldest friends and Henry's solicitor of long standing, sir. Cecil Blanding. It was only now that the full horror of my situation revealed itself. Blanding searched through each and every one of Henry's books and papers and finally came to the deplorable conclusion that my only hope of staying out of the courts and avoiding public ruin was to sell up the estate and pay off Henry's debts with the proceeds of the sale!"

Despite the stoic comportment of those of her creed, this last revelation proved to be too much for her Ladyship, and Holmes waved me impatiently towards her, that I might calm and comfort her. Meanwhile, he had leapt up from his chair and hurriedly lit a cigarette by the window.

"Lady Wakeham, as distressing and unfortunate as your predicament surely is, I fail to see how any crime has been committed, save for your late husband's reckless disregard for your future well-being," Holmes pointed out with an unnecessarily acidic air. "I am afraid that my humble practice has no means of paying off his debts for you."

Lady Wakeham suddenly stood up and raised herself to her full and not inconsiderable height.

"Mr. Holmes, I shall disregard your discourteous manner, in the hope that even now you might prove to be of use to me. I shall tell you something now that I hope you will regard with an open mind, rather than that of the pragmatic sceptic that I would normally have expected of you.

"You see, I am well acquainted with Dr. Watson's accounts of some of your adventures and I am aware that you regard matters of the heart with a derisory distain."

"I cannot deny it." Holmes admitted apologetically and he suggested that her Ladyship return to her chair with a wave of his hand.

"Henry and I were unashamedly romantic, Mr. Holmes, and had been from the moment that we first met all those years ago. That is why I know that he would never have left me in this predicament without having first made provision for such an eventuality. He made three pledges to me, Mr. Holmes, the nature of which might seem absurd to a man of logic like you, but they meant everything to me."

"Three pledges?" Holmes repeated impatiently, and Lady Wakeham nodded her head defiantly and emphatically.

"In his darker moments, Henry's thoughts and quite often his work turned to the nature of death and its aftermath. He believed that should we two remain in love and faithful to the other, it would transcend even death itself. I have remained true to this pledge and despite all that has befallen, my love for him has kept him alive, in my heart at least – or so I thought."

"Lady Wakeham, please!" Holmes was clearly becoming exasperated by her Ladyship's most extraordinary declarations.

To her credit, she ignored Holmes's ire and persisted with her explanation.

"Henry further pledged that should anything happen to him, he would ensure that adequate provision would be made for every eventuality that might befall me. Obviously Cecil Blanding's revelations caused me to believe that Henry had sadly failed me, but I had not allowed for the results of our third pledge."

Holmes's impatience and irritation had, by now, transformed into a marked indifference. Consequently, it was I who inquired further into her Ladyship's true meaning.

"What exactly did you mean when you said 'or so I thought' when referring to your enduring love?"

"I used that phrase, Dr. Watson, because I now have good reason to believe that Henry has not really left me at all! Before you admonish me further, Mr. Homes, for your refusal to accept a supernatural explanation is well known to me, I must tell you that I am not a young girl prone to flights of fancy. I have good reason for my doubts. Let me explain." Holmes eyed her quizzically with knitted brows.

"Henry and I first became acquainted at a recital held at the home of a mutual friend in Holland Park. Our eyes met as they began to play a passage of music that we subsequently discovered to be our favourite piece: *Danse Macabre* by the French composer, Camille Saint-Saens. From that moment, the music became forever embodied within the soul of our romance, so much so in fact that Henry wrote a poetic accompaniment to the piece.

"I loved the poem as surely as I did the music, and subsequently we both pledged that it should remain within our private domain for all of time. Indeed, we further vowed that it should remain so, even after death and that the survivor would place the poem within the coffin of the other, sealed forever from public gaze. The dire consequences of his compulsions left poor Henry a broken man, and his health suffered and deteriorated beyond repair. Mercifully, his end was brief and without pain and with his final breath he thrust the poem into my trembling hand.

"I kept my promise, Mr. Holmes, and the poem of *Danse Macabre* has resided within my husband's coffin since his passing, a year ago today."

"Madam, you have yet to explain why you hold the belief that your husband has somehow managed to defy man's ultimate destiny" Holmes stated simply, although now clearly intrigued by our client's tale.

"Not surprisingly, my belief is beyond your realm of understanding, Mr. Holmes. Nevertheless, I would appreciate your logical explanation for the fact that this envelope came through my letter box this very morning!"

Lady Wakeham offered Holmes a plain, unmarked buff envelope, but he directed it in my direction. Somewhat hesitantly, I pulled out two folded sheets of foolscap paper. However, they nearly fell from my grasp when I saw the heading at the top of the first sheet.

"*Danse Macabre*," I read in a hushed deferent tone.

At once Holmes returned to his seat and pursed his lips with his left forefinger.

"Read it, Dr. Watson. Please read," Lady Wakeham implored, and Holmes nodded his acquiescence.

> On an unholy night such as this,
> Two lovers glow in eternal bliss
> And so they dance
>
> Turning to each other they exchange a kiss
> And swear to the other a lovers Trist,
> And still they dance
>
> The night of the spirits closes in,
> And soon their wailing creates a dreadful din,
> They will dance for evermore, evermore.
>
> So still the night, starry bright night
>
> The flying clouds betray a lustrous moon,

140

*The lovers start to sway and swoon,*
*And still they dance.*

*They are drawn towards the unearthly sky,*
*And feel as if they can truly fly*
*As they dance.*

*The music of the spirits calls to their soul,*
*But still they meld and closer hold*
*And still they dance.*

*The demons sing and the night grows cold*
*Lovers shuddering not so bold*
*Their swirling slows as the cockerel crows,*
*Their spirit fades.*

*Their skin turns white as the spirits fall*
*They fade to naught as the gravestones call*
*The dawn is king and they dance no more, no more . . . .*
*Nevermore*

It seemed an age before another word was uttered and it fell to me to break the silence.

"What a truly remarkable and evocative piece of work."

Holmes dismissed my remark with an impatient wave of his hand. He reached out hungrily for the envelope, surprisingly ignoring the sheets of poetry that had been folded within, and then began to examine it meticulously with his smallest glass.

"Lady Wakeham, as you so correctly observed, I have no truck with ghosts and the like, so I will ask you to dispassionately explain to me how this envelope happened to come into your possession. There are no letters or markings upon it, so it had obviously been delivered by hand before you awoke, by someone wearing a meticulously clean pair of gloves. The stationary is of the very finest quality and bears a water mark that is unique in my experience."

"I have no theory, Mr. Holmes, other than the one that I have already presented to you. I believe that my husband has never truly left me, just as he pledged. However, I must tell you that the word '*Nevermore*' did not appear upon the version of *Danse Macabre* that had been buried with him! Nevertheless it is impossible that anyone else had ever seen the original, much less be able to add to it." By now, Lady Wakeham had worked

141

herself up into a frenzy of utter confusion and she glared imploringly towards my friend for help.

I too looked to my friend for any sign of sympathy or compassion. After all, he had surely been presented with a case that under normal circumstances that he would unhesitatingly dismiss out of hand. Yet, when the distracted lady had mentioned *"Nevermore"*, my friend's countenance had suddenly altered and he had disappeared into one of his protracted, contemplative dispositions.

Holmes turned away from us both and as he lit his pipe he murmured, "Please leave your address and that of your solicitor with Dr. Watson. We shall be with you within the hour."

Clearly Lady Wakeham had not taken kindly to being so dismissed, but she allowed me to hold the door open for her with good grace and paused long enough to ask me for an explanation. My enigmatic friend had left me no wiser than her Ladyship, and I merely answered her entreaties with a woeful shrug.

Anticipating my pent-up barrage of questions, Holmes turned towards me with a winning smile.

"Watson, we must not allow ourselves to be beguiled by her Ladyship's wild tales of eternal love and poems of the supernatural. If we are to be any use to her at all, we have to examine her conundrum with calm and dispassionate logic. I am certain that you would concur with the probability that Lord Henry Wakeham did *not* resurrect himself and leave his coffin merely to add one word to the end of a poem, even to one as special as *Danse Macabre?*"

"Well, of course I would! However, she does hold her beliefs with such heartfelt conviction that it would be a travesty to break that spell before we have discovered another resolution. Why would her husband have left her in such a financial dilemma, especially after having made so sincere a pledge?" I asked.

"I take it that you have heard of C. Auguste Dupin?" Holmes's surprising response had been such a departure from the nature of our discussion that I became totally nonplussed and incapable of a coherent reply.

Holmes continued as if my answer, had there been one, would have been a total irrelevance.

"Dupin has been my entrance into the world of Edgar Allan Poe. Although an acquired read, Poe has achieved a form of notoriety for his tales and poems that test the nerves of those brave enough to delve into the darker realms. Poe also introduced the world to the notion of an amateur consulting detective – namely C. Auguste Dupin, who featured in his tale 'The Murders of the Rue Morgue'."

"I certainly understand your interest in the man," I admitted.

"Judging by Lady Wakeham's reaction to the word '*Nevermore*', I would wager that she has never sampled Poe's work either. Now, however, I suggest that we hasten to Farringdon!"

"You must mean Holland Park, surely?" I queried, but my friend was already dressed for the harsh elements beyond our door and halfway down the stairs by the time that I had realised that no reply was to be forthcoming.

We had stepped outside into an unrelenting sheet of the type of fine and insidious rain that permeates every pore and sinew. Yet my friend seemed to be singularly unaffected by and indifferent to this meteorological inconvenience, and he sat perched on the edge of his seat while leaning upon his still furled umbrella

Holmes had been as good as his word and, upon reaching a small but discreet address in Farringdon, he alighted from our cab and dashed off without even an indication of his purpose. He returned, a few short minutes later, flushed with excitement and success, while holding aloft a blank sheet of paper as if in a moment of great triumph.

"I think that we can safely say that we now know the source of Lady Wakeham's resurrected poem!" he beamed.

"No doubt you hold a sample of Cecil Blanding's stationary and that it bears the same water mark as does the poem?"

"Oh Watson, you absolutely radiate insightfulness today!" my friend declared with a jovial sarcasm.

"I suppose that Lord Wakeham had entrusted a copy of his poem into the care of his solicitor, with the instruction that it should only be delivered to his wife at a time of crisis. However, apart from its otherworldly significance to Lady Wakeham, I fail to see how we are any closer to delivering the poor woman from her awful plight," I declared quietly, but my friend remained in a thoughtful silence until the moment of our arrival at the Wakeham's address in Holland Park.

A long, beech-lined driveway soon revealed a spectacular white-marble mansion, whose grand entrance was flanked by a magnificent set of Ionian pillars. On other nights one could easily have imagined each of the large undraped windows illuminated by a festoon of crystal chandeliers while the sound of gaiety and music filled the air outside.

Tonight, however, each of the many rooms were shrouded in a melancholy darkness, save for one, and our wheels churning through the ever enlarging puddles was the only recognisable sound. A grave sadness seemed to have been hanging over the entire edifice, and a cheerless butler met us at the door.

Tyler, this faithful servant, tried to present us with a smile of greeting, yet even his sparkling, bespectacled eyes could not disguise the gloom of the household. On our way to the drawing room, where her Ladyship pensively awaited us, Tyler offered us a warming glass of cognac, which we eagerly accepted.

Despite the blaze of a large roaring fire, there had been no escaping a surprising and voracious chill that seemed to fill the entire room. We soon discovered its source when a violent gust of wind blew the drapes into a wild billow and a cascade of rain and leaves sprayed onto the floor in front of us. Lady Wakeham scolded her servant harshly for his oversight, although he had assured her that he had left the window securely locked when last in the room.

Ignoring this disruption, Holmes readily accepted a seat by the fire and he smoked a cigarette while he sipped upon his brandy. Suddenly he turned towards our hostess.

"Lady Wakeham," he stated simply and without explanation, "I can tell that you did not share your husband's enthusiasm for the works of Edgar Allan Poe."

"Although true, that is a somewhat unusual assertion for you to have made. Mr. Holmes." Her Ladyship had been clearly put out by my friend's statement, as if she had been expecting something more illuminating from her reluctant ally. Then she noticed something in my friend's manner that suggested to her that there had been an unforeseen significance to his claim.

"Mr. Holmes, throughout our marriage I had always made a point of trying to appreciate and share in my husband's passions, save of course for those destructive indulgences that he reserved for his club. In most instances, this was something that I found hard to do. Our tastes in music and literature seemed to run along similar paths, and we obtained great pleasure and satisfaction in each other's company, regardless of the chosen activity.

"In the case of Edgar Allan Poe, however, I did find it difficult to understand my husband's enthusiasm. Undeniably I tried to appreciate Poe's work. Indeed, at times I would lock myself away with one of his stories, in the hope that an epiphany would soon come upon me. Sadly this did not happen, I found his style unbearably dark and morbid, if not disturbingly psychotic at times, but I was at least successful in constructing a convincing facade that my husband never breached. However, I do fail to see how you came to that conclusion."

"That does explain his use of the word '*Nevermore*'?" Holmes said self-indulgently under his breath. "Madam, would you be so kind as to

144

show me through to the library?" Holmes requested whilst rising hurriedly from his chair.

Lady Wakeham appeared to have been as taken off guard, as confused by this request as I was. Nevertheless, she immediately pulled upon a bell rope and a moment later Tyler appeared, bearing a bright oil lamp before him. We climbed slowly to the first floor and all the while Tyler's flame flickered and occasionally ebbed as the gathering storm outside forced its way through the tiniest fissures, thereby creating a series of broad dancing shadows upon the walls.

The library proved to be a large elegant room, laid out in the spacious, Romanesque-style of the Georgian era. On Holmes's demand, Tyler turned up the gas and Holmes immediately began a frantic but thorough search through the section predominated by books of poetry. Not surprisingly, it did not take my friend long in finding a selection devoted to the works of Poe, but he seemed to concentrate upon those volumes devoted to "The Raven".

Again, I could not offer her Ladyship a single word of explanation for my friend's unfathomable behavior, and this took a further turn when he began to flip the pages of each book back and forth in the most fierce and urgent manner imaginable. Finally, with a pronounced grunt of disappointment, Holmes sank slowly to the floor upon his haunches, as if bereft of energy and ideas.

We three exchanged glances of bewilderment while my friend continued to crouch there, in a breathless silence. Then another idea occurred to him and he rose slowly with a languid elegance and something akin to a suppressed smile upon his inscrutable face.

"Lady Wakeham, did your husband keep a smaller, more personal library, wherein he might have also done his writing?" Holmes asked expectantly.

"Indeed he did, Mr. Holmes, although I cannot for the life of me understand your obsession with the books of Edgar Allan Poe." She was clearly becoming exasperated by my friend's inexplicable conduct, whereas I knew from experience that there was a logical purpose behind each one of his actions

"Very likely not. However, it is your husband's devotion to the works of Mr. Poe that holds the key to your salvation. Did he by any chance refer to this room as his 'chamber'?"

Lady Wakeham's open mouthed incredulousness proved to be the only confirmation that Holmes had required.

"Tyler, kindly show me to the chamber, and would you also be good enough to bring with you a ladder?"

145

"A ladder, sir?" The butler asked, but without another word Holmes fled from the room, bounded up the stairs, and began a speculative exploration of the darkened corridors of the floor above.

By the time that Tyler had arrived with his light and ladder, Holmes had already found the object of his search. He had been staring up at the arch above a small solid doorway and the statues that adorned the columns on either side of the arch. On the left I could recognise a marble bust of the Titan Pallas, while on the other rested a fierce-looking, jet-black raven.

The wind outside howled raucously as we gazed up at this fearsome bird, and the flickering flames seemed to imbue a fiery, spectral light to the creature's eyes. Holmes bade the butler to focus the flames upon the plinth beneath the raven's claws, and we all drew gasps of wonder when we recognised the words that had been engraved into the base: "*Nevermore*"!

In a thrice, Holmes had unfolded the ladder and was soon face-to-face with the raven's menacing beak. Despite my entreaties that he should take care, Holmes wrapped his arms about the creature and began to grapple with the cement that bound it to the plinth. Despite almost losing his balance on more than one occasion, Holmes soon had the raven loose, and he handed it down carefully to me before making his descent.

"It is deceptively heavy," I stately simply, while my friend could barely suppress a triumphal smile.

He led us back down the stairs to the drawing room and placed the raven in the middle of the table before sending Tyler for the "sharpest knife in the house". As we waited for the tireless butler once again, Holmes lit a cigarette and gazed at his mournful prize.

In anticipation of a myriad of questions from both her Ladyship and me, Holmes began his explanation through a plume of slowly exhaled smoke.

"Lady Wakeham, I fear that had you not sought my consultation, your deceit would have rendered your husband's subtle clue as worthless."

"My deceit, Mr. Holmes? Whatever do you mean?"

Holmes diverted his gaze from the bird to her Ladyship.

"Your pretence for a love of Poe led your husband to believe that you would understand in a trice his addition of the word '*Nevermore*' to his poem. For that is the name of the raven in his most famous work. '*Perched upon a bust of Pallas above his chamber door*', I believe is an approximate quote, and one that Lord Wakeham would have expected you to recognise at once. By the way, that envelope had not been delivered from beyond the grave, but from the offices of Blanding and Blanding of Farringdon," Holmes concluded.

"As usual, Holmes, your reasoning is quite flawless," I said, no doubt echoing the thoughts of our bemused client, "but I still fail to see how the statue of a bird will prove to be her Ladyship's salvation."

At that moment, Tyler returned with a most sturdy and fearsome looking instrument. Holmes snatched it from his grasp without warning. He raised it to the raven's left wing and gently scratched away a slither of thin black paint.

"Good heavens, Holmes, it is only paint! What does this all mean?"

"It means, Watson, that despite Lord Wakeham's other flaws and weaknesses, he did keep his final pledge. Unless I am very much mistaken, this imposing bird is made of nothing other than solid gold, and Lady Wakeham's future has been secured!" Holmes pronounced while grabbing his hat and gloves from the astounded butler.

By now, Lady Wakeham, who had hitherto remained enwrapped in a stunned silence, sank into a chair and held out her hand that Tyler might fill it with a glass of cognac.

"How will I ever thank you, Mr. Holmes?" she asked with a breathless smile before taking a sip.

Holmes dismissed this with a smile and a wave of his hand. "Lady Wakeham, your gratitude should be directed towards your husband and Mr. Edgar Allan Poe! Come, Watson!" I followed in my friend's wake, and a moment later we were sheltering from the equinoctial storm in our cab.

As we reached a bend in the driveway I had been afforded a brief glimpse of the brightly lit drawing room, wherein I had imagined Lady Wakeham, still seated in a state of elated exhaustion. However, she had since moved to the window and I could see her endlessly and rhythmically twirling in time – no doubt, to the imagined strains of the *Danse Macabre*.

Had it been my imagination, or perhaps the distorted movements of the bare twisted branches of the beech? Or was someone with her, locked in a timeless embrace, *"while they danced"*?

*"Quoth the raven: Nevermore."*

# The Strange Persecution of John Vincent Harden

## by S. Subramanian

*On referring to my notebook for the year 1895, I find that it was upon Saturday, the 23rd of April, that we first heard of Miss Violet Smith. Her visit was, I remember, extremely unwelcome to Holmes, for he was immersed at the moment in a very abstruse and complicated problem concerning the peculiar persecution to which John Vincent Harden, the well-known tobacco millionaire, had been subjected.*

"The Adventure of the Solitary Cyclist"
(*The Return of Sherlock Holmes*)

In chronicling the circumstances associated with the singular affair of John Vincent Harden, widely known by the sobriquet of "The Tobacco King", I find myself at a strange disadvantage. It is perhaps the only case from among the countless ones in which I was associated with Mr. Sherlock Holmes that had the peculiar feature that I was present at its commencement but absent at its *dénouement*. Those readers who have been kind enough to bestow some attention upon my memoirs of the great detective may recall that Holmes's engagement with the Harden case was interrupted by the intrusion of another one, which I have recorded elsewhere under the heading of "The Adventure of the Solitary Cyclist".

In vain did Holmes plead his prior preoccupation with another case. But our beautiful client, Miss Violet Smith, was not to be put off, and eventually Holmes capitulated, with that mixture of grace, humour, and chivalry which was characteristic of the man. However, in view of his being detained in the matter of the Harden affair, Holmes deputed me to undertake some preliminary investigations on Miss Smith's behalf, in Chiltern Grange, about six miles from Farnham on the borders of Surrey.

It was during my absence in Farnham that Holmes prosecuted and concluded the Harden case. In recording this affair, therefore, I have had to rely on Holmes's patchy accounts of its latter parts in which I was not myself directly involved. I have tried my best to fill in the gaps, from a combination of Holmes's laconic testimony and my own imagination, and if the effort should prove to be wanting in complete satisfactoriness, I trust

I may nevertheless count upon the indulgence of my readers to view the chronicler's predicament with a modicum of sympathy and understanding.

I choose to record the Harden case not for any intrinsic worth it may have from the point of view of criminal interest – which it assuredly does not possess – but because of those aspects of the eternal human condition which my friend encountered in so many of the cases that he investigated, and which are so integrally a feature of the present affair. For the sheer combination of the apparently esoteric and actually commonplace, the Gothic and the comedic, this affair must stand out in the annals of Sherlock Holmes.

We received our first intimation of the case on an April morning. The winter of '94 was slow in fading, and even late April of the year '95 retained enough frost and chill in the air to warrant a fire in the grate of our modest sitting room in 221b Baker Street. Mrs. Hudson had just cleared away the remains of our late breakfast, I had lit a cigarette and settled down in my armchair with the latest issue of *The Lancet,* and Holmes, lounging on his armchair in his favourite mouse-coloured dressing gown, had just lighted his first pipe of the morning, composed from the dottles of the previous day's smokes, when he looked up from his correspondence and tossed across a note to me, with the words, "I gather the impression, Watson, that we are expected to feel honoured by the impending visit of a client to our humble quarters."

The communication read as follows:

*11, Cadogan Square, Knightsbridge*

*Re: Professional Consultation*

*Sir:*

*I write on behalf of my employer, Mr. Paul Sebastian Harden, in order to seek your professional advice in a matter concerning his older brother, Mr. John Vincent Harden. I am directed by the junior Mr. Harden to inform you that he, accompanied by me, will call on you for a consultation at 11 a.m. on Friday. He wishes to impress on you that you will be rewarded generously for any light you may shed on the matter in question.*

*I am, sir,*
*Faithfully yours,*

*Stephen Meade,*
*(Private Secretary)*
*for*
*Paul Sebastian Harden, Esq., of*
*Harden Tobacco Enterprises*

"The note is indeed peremptory in tone," said I. "I see that no attempt has been made to ascertain your own convenience as to date and time, and the suggestion also is that your willingness to accept the case can be secured entirely by the promise of adequate monetary compensation!"

"Ah, that, Watson, is the way of the very rich, is it not?" remarked Holmes. "And 'very rich' should be a just description of any man who has his residence in Cadogan Square – not least when the man in question happens to be John Vincent Harden, the tobacco millionaire. Let us see what the Index under '*H*' has on our man. What have we here? Hampton, the coiner, Hannay, of deplorable memory, who poisoned three wives to death . . . hmm . . . here we are!

"John Vincent Harden: An Englishman who, as a youth of twenty-five in 1870, made his way to the New World in quest of a fortune – and found it in the 'black' tobacco plantations of Kentucky. Clearly a man of great daring and enterprise. In a matter of a decade he seems to have made his millions, invested his wealth wisely, and consolidated his tobacco empire, gradually relinquishing his complete control over it to his two brothers Mathew Jerome and Paul Sebastian Harden. In 1888, he seems to have largely retired from his earlier consuming interest in his business, leaving its day-to-day management to his two brothers.

"In the same year, and after a whirlwind courtship, he was married to Miss Mary Byrne, a young school-teacher who had been brought up in St. Vincent's Orphanage in Louisville and educated at the Nazareth Academy. The childless couple lived in Louisville for a period of six years, until August 1894 when, in response to the call of the home country, John Vincent Harden returned to England with his wife and the youngest of his brothers, Paul Sebastian, leaving the administration of his commercial interests in Kentucky largely to the care of the other brother, Mathew Jerome. Upon his return, the millionaire purchased the palatial mansion which he now occupies, with his family, in one of the wealthiest neighbourhoods of Knightsbridge. Thus are lives of even the richest and most powerful of men swiftly encapsulated in a few words that take not quite three minutes in the telling."

"Well, will you see the man's brother and his private secretary?" asked I.

"I have no case on hand, Watson, and would greatly welcome the diversion of an investigation. And my curiosity is aroused. What can John Vincent Harden, tobacco millionaire of Knightsbridge, want of Sherlock Holmes, indigent consulting detective of Baker Street? Let us await eleven o'clock, Watson, and I will be grateful for your presence at the consultation."

"Nothing would give me greater pleasure than to be of service," I said warmly.

Sharp upon the hour there was a peal of the bell, followed by steps upon the stair, and in a moment, Mrs. Hudson had ushered in our clients Mr. Paul Sebastian Harden and his private secretary, Mr. Stephen Meade. The former was a very tall, wiry, muscular individual with a handsome face that was marred only by more than a slight suggestion about it of arrogance and dissipation. The secretary was a small, fidgety man who gave every appearance of being a fussy, nervous, and essentially daunted character. It was impossible to resist identifying him with the actor Penley's portrayal of the Rev. Robert Spalding in Charles Hawtrey's *The Private Secretary*, the play that had rocked London about a decade earlier.

Holmes welcomed his clients in his usual quiet and restrained fashion and, directing them to seat themselves, invited them to present their case.

Mr. Meade, the private secretary, cleared his throat and, in a high-pitched, timorous voice, addressed himself to my friend. "Mr. Holmes, we are grateful to you for agreeing to see us at such short notice. We are, of course, seized of your considerable reputation for your forensic acumen and skills of deduction – "

"Say," said his companion, interrupting his secretary without ceremony. "Reputations have to be earned, and cannot simply be assumed." In an accent marked strongly by the twang typical of our American cousins' spoken word, he continued, in tones that could only be interpreted as being gratuitously offensive and provocative, "If you are such a clever fellow as you are made out to be, perhaps you will tell me what you can deduce about the owner of this pair of gloves from an examination of the objects. Here, Holmes – Catch!" And with that, the man stripped the gloves off his hands and hurled them rudely at Holmes's face.

Sherlock Holmes caught the gloves unhurriedly in his hand in front of his eyes and favoured the tobacco millionaire with a look that was a compound of contempt and amusement. "I am not, sir," said he, "given to establishing my credentials before my clients by offering them little tricks of inferential logic for their entertainment. However, and as Watson here will testify, I find it hard to resist the temptation of deducing the man from his possessions. Besides which, a challenge is a challenge!"

151

With that, Holmes subjected the gloves in his hand to a minute examination under his magnifying glass, while Meade fidgeted uneasily in his chair and Harden looked on from under his hooded eyes with a faint and arrogant smile upon his face. In a few moments, Holmes straightened up from his scrutiny of the gloves, and said in a bored voice, "I thought for a moment that there might actually be some intellectual trial involved in this, but, as it has turned out, it has been a mentally trivial exercise to deduce from an examination of these gloves that their owner is a tall, wiry, muscular man who is also a bachelor, a gambler, an alcoholic, a bully, and a womanizer. Pray advise me on any other vices on which I might have missed."

Paul Harden's face slowly darkened as it composed itself in a mask of fury, suffused with the blood of injured pride and insulted honour. With a crass muttered ejaculation and before we knew what was happening, he had hurled himself upon the detective and grabbed him by the lapels of his coat. As Meade and I made to separate the man from his apparent victim, Holmes's voice rang out loud and clear. "Pray do not discommode yourselves, gentlemen. I believe I can handle this perfectly well on my own." In a moment, Holmes's left hand was upon Harden's right. His fingers fastened themselves around the millionaire's wrist in a grip of vice-like hardness that tightened with each passing moment until Harden was forced to release his hand from Holmes's coat, and fell back on his chair with a muttered curse, nursing his injured right wrist in his left hand. "Damn you, Holmes!" he cried out petulantly, with an almost tearful resentment against the injuries to his spirit and his body. "Damn you, that really hurt!"

"Well," said Holmes drily, "you are advised that that was only my left, or subordinate, hand, and I was not really trying, you know. But one more exhibition of ill-mannered schoolboy behaviour, Mr. Harden, and I shall have no hesitation in *really* hurting you. Is that quite well understood? Do you wish to continue this consultation, or would you rather retire while the retiring is still good?"

The little secretary went into a huddled and whispered conversation with his employer, and in a few moments the latter appeared to signal sullen acquiescence with the former's suggestions. Meade turned to Holmes and said, "My client apologises for his behaviour, Mr. Holmes. If you will permit, and since we do wish to seek your opinion and advice, may I lay out our case for your consideration?"

"Pray do so," said Holmes, adding, with a half-smile, "and without any further dramatic interruptions, please!"

What follows, in substance, is the content of Stephen Meade's narrative.

Six months earlier, John Vincent Harden and his wife Mary had moved from Louisville to London, where they established their home in one of the most impressively manorial houses in the fashionable Knightsbridge neighbourhood of Cadogan Square. Having made a massive fortune from the cultivation, processing, and sale of tobacco in the south-central American State of Kentucky, Harden had decided that he would like to return to his home country with his wife and his youngest brother, Paul Sebastian, leaving the administration of his business in the capable hands of the middle brother, Mathew Jerome, who would be assisted by Paul on the latter's frequent visits from London to Kentucky. While his tobacco business continued to thrive, John Harden intended, with his wife, to lead a life that would be devoted to the pursuit of leisure, society, and culture – and perhaps, in time, politics.

The first couple of months were taken up in establishing the household and recruiting the full complement of the servants and staff that would be required to attend to the maintenance and upkeep of the millionaire's manorial home. Among the higher ranks of the staff was a young lady by the name of Constance Sutherland, who had been hired from an agency to assist Mrs. Harden with her social commitments and charitable work. Harden was known to have a heart condition, and on his wife's insistence a resident physician – a young man called Patrick Flaherty – was hired to oversee his employer's health while having the freedom to pursue his own practice from a room in the sprawling premises of 11, Cadogan Square. Stephen Meade, a bachelor in his late thirties, was appointed as a private secretary to the brothers Harden. He was tasked with performing secretarial duties that included taking dictation, handling the brothers' business correspondence, and generally overseeing the daily affairs of the household and its staff. Meade also lived on the premises at Knightsbridge. A frequent visitor to the house was a newly ordained Jesuit priest from the Brompton Oratory in Knightsbridge. His name was Brown, and he ministered to the spiritual needs of Mrs. Harden.

The affair which had brought our clients to Baker Street had apparently had its origin about a month ago. John Vincent Harden had begun, increasingly, to display signs of withdrawal, silence and – above all – fear. His reluctance to engage in conversation with anyone had eventually hardened into a virtually complete dumbness, from which could only be gathered some intimation of vampyric visitations to which the millionaire would allude from time to time, in whimpered whispers of the word "vampire", or gibberings about "hounds from hell", or mimes involving bared teeth and hooked fingers, or ducking retreats of a fearful face behind a hand thrown up in defence as against some frightening vision invisible to others. The symptoms were particularly well-marked after a

153

relatively peaceful night and, during the day, were reflected in displays of fear, anxiety, and facial twitches.

Dr. Flaherty, the resident physician, put the symptoms down to some underlying mental pathology of delusional fantasy. Not being an expert in diseases of the mind, he recommended that the matter should be referred to a qualified alienist, such as the celebrated Harley Street specialist Dr. Moore Agar, who was himself was not able to do much more than confirm Dr. Flaherty's diagnosis. In his opinion, Harden's condition did not lend itself to easy detection as to its aetiology, though it suggested a strong strain of inherited insanity. It was confirmed by the younger Harden that a great-grandfather on the paternal side was indeed known to have suffered from delusions of persecution. Dr. Agar's professional knowledge of the affliction suggested that it was typical of certain strains of what we commonly call madness that can skip two generations before reappearing in a descendant. The alienist's prognosis was essentially pessimistic. His assessment was that John Vincent Harden would slip into deeper and deeper recesses of fear, melancholia, and withdrawal from the ordinary processes and interests of life and, indeed, living. In the expert's estimation, John Harden was not for long upon this earth, and all that could be done was to ensure a restful and peaceable existence for the remainder of his time. This information was shared only with Paul Harden, Flaherty, and Meade. In particular, it was kept from Mrs. Harden, as knowledge that would be needlessly hard for her to bear.

At this point in his narrative, Meade arrived at what was perhaps the most macabre and perplexing feature of John Vincent Harden's persecution, a feature which cast doubt on whether the millionaire's predicament was entirely the product of a sick man's hallucinations and his fevered imagination. The event in question had occurred just two days prior to our clients' visit and proved to be a compelling reason for their decision to consult Sherlock Holmes in the matter.

Meade gave us to understand that the daily routine in the Harden household was something along the following lines: Mary Harden would spend the bulk of the day with her husband, who was largely confined to his bed, in between attending to the quotidian tasks of running a household and performing duties of service to the community and her church, which she had taken upon herself as a responsibility to discharge. Every night, before settling her husband in bed, she would read to him from the Bible, and before retiring she would administer to him his nightly medication, as prescribed by the physician.

Miss Sutherland, the secretary, would visit the sick-room whenever Mrs. Harden required her assistance with her correspondence or other chores, and when not so occupied, the young lady would attend to her other

154

duties under the direction of Meade. The physician, Dr. Flaherty, made at least two regular calls on his employer, once in the morning and once in the evening, apart from being on call through the day. Paul Harden would visit his brother daily, often several times, and with no fixed frequency. On some of these visits, Meade would accompany Harden.

On the day in question, Paul Harden and the private secretary happened to accompany Dr. Flaherty when he called on his employer for his regular evening visit at six o'clock. John Harden was in bed, Mrs. Harden had just been called away on some domestic chore, and Paul Harden and Stephen Meade were standing behind Dr. Flaherty as the latter bent down to take his patient's pulse. At that moment, all three men noted that the patient was staring fixedly at the window on the wall on the other side of the room from his bed. The doctor noted to his dismay, as did Paul Harden and Stephen Meade, that the tobacco magnate's face was contorted in a look of indescribably frozen horror.

Turning round to look at the window which seemed to hold the man in such thrall, the three men themselves became witness to a terrifying spectacle. Framed dimly in the gloaming outside the window pane and looking in was the malevolent visage of a man with red-rimmed eyes and teeth, bared in a savage grimace which revealed two pronounced fangs where there should have been a pair of canines on any normally constituted human's upper jaw. In a moment, the face had vanished, before reappearing. Meade walked quickly but unobtrusively to the window and flung it open, but he could discern nothing of significance in the dim light outside. The doctor, meanwhile, walked out of the house to investigate, only to return shortly thereafter and report that he had found no trace of any presence outside the window or its environs.

After his return to the sick-room, the three men tacitly agreed not to mention anything of what had just transpired to Mrs. Harden, save to inform her that her husband had undergone another episode of nervous debilitation. Dr. Flaherty administered a sedative to soothe the nerves of the shaken millionaire, and after posting a guard to keep an eye on the area outside the bedroom window, the three men retired. Mrs. Harden stayed on, holding her husband's hand until he gradually recovered something like a measure of composure. She then gave him his supper, read the Bible to him, administered his medication, and made sure that he slept under the influence of Dr. Flaherty's sedative, before leaving his room for the night.

"Tell me, Mr. Holmes," said Paul Harden, in a chastened tone very different from the hectoring one he had employed at the beginning of the consultation, "tell me who or what is behind my brother's persecution, and we will be indebted to you."

"I take it that your decision to consult me is not common knowledge?" enquired Holmes.

"That is correct," said the private secretary. "I must take responsibility for the suggestion to seek your advice, with which Mr. Harden acquiesced. Nobody else knows of our visit to you."

"It would be best for things to remain that way," said Holmes. "Before we proceed, let me ask you if there is anything – apart from the episode of the face in the window – which it occurs to you might be playing a role in causing, or at least promoting, Mr. Harden's affliction."

"It is hardly for one in my position, Mr. Holmes" said Meade nervously, "to hazard any conjecture in the matter – "

"Oh, quit being coy, Meade," interrupted Harden tersely. "The gentleman needs all the information we can supply if he is to get to the bottom of this affair. So why not tell him of your suspicions regarding the possible drugging of poor John?"

"I trust you will not think it presumptuous on my part to advance a view, Mr. Holmes, but it seemed to me quite compatible with the observed symptoms of restful nights and irritable, disordered days experienced by Mr. Harden to entertain the suspicion of opium being administered before sleep. That would explain the relatively quiet nights and the unquiet days of confusion, disorientation, fear, and anger caused by the wearing away of the calming effect of the opium. I read a good deal, Mr. Holmes. It is part of my effort to keep myself educated," said the little man earnestly.

"A splendid ambition, Mr. Meade," cried Holmes approvingly. "But surely, if Mr. Harden's condition is induced or exacerbated by drugs, it should be possible to medically test for the presence of opium in his bloodstream? What say you, Watson?"

"As Mr. Meade has probably discovered from his reading," said I, "it is difficult to detect opium in the bloodstream after five or six hours of its ingestion or injection. If administered before sleep, and assuming seven to eight hours of sleep during the night, the opium is unlikely to leave behind its traces in the bloodstream on the following morning."

"Ah," said Holmes, "so that is not a promising line of enquiry, and we might have to content ourselves with the findings available from signs and symptoms. A risky enterprise at the best of times. Now tell me, how are the various members of the family and staff disposed toward each other? I understand that Mr. Harden is both mentally and emotionally impaired now, but that Mrs. Harden continues to be devoted to him?"

"As completely devoted and committed as ever a wife could be to a husband, Mr. Holmes," cried Stephen Meade.

Observing a look that passed between the private secretary and his employer, Holmes said drily, "But – ?"

"Come, Meade," said Paul Harden. "Out with it! You did tell me, did you not, that you have the impression that the doctor is sweet on Mary?"

It was amusing to watch the little man blushing and bridling in embarrassment and annoyance. "It is not my place," said he, "to seem to be gossiping about my employers and my colleagues. However, since you insist, yes, I believe it is common knowledge that Dr. Flaherty admires Mrs. Harden – with an intensity that some may hold to be more than entirely natural in an employee's estimation of his employer. Indeed, he seems to exert a great influence upon the lady and to have her unqualified and implicit trust in his skill, judgement, and wisdom. This is not for a moment to suggest any slightest conscious impropriety in her conduct or intent toward the young man – " And here Meade stopped abruptly, in some confusion and unease.

"Very, well, I understand," said Holmes. "And now, gentlemen, I would beg you to return to Knightsbridge, and to continue to keep the fact of your consultation with me confidential. Today is Friday. The earliest that Watson and I will be able to see you again is on Monday morning. I trust you can receive us by eleven in the morning on the twenty-fifth. To anyone that might care to ask, Watson and I may be described as business clients. I would like you to ensure that Dr. Flaherty is called away upon some errand that will keep him occupied for the entire day on Monday. I am afraid we shall have to take advantage of his absence to undertake a search of his personal effects, and I should be very surprised if the search does not yield some conclusive discoveries that should help in clearing up this little matter. Rest assured that the affair is under my consideration, and that matters should be amenable to explanation along lines which I should not be surprised have already occurred to you."

With that, Holmes dismissed our clients and also – to all intents and purposes – any further deliberation upon the case they had brought to his attention.

As I have mentioned at the beginning of this narrative, Holmes's attention was distracted the following day by the visit of Miss Violet Smith, in whose cause he dispatched me to undertake some investigations on my own, near Farnham, on Monday. From this point on, my account, as earlier detailed, is based entirely on hearsay. At eleven o'clock on that Monday morning, Holmes presented himself at John Vincent Harden's sprawling mansion in Knightsbridge, where, to explain my absence, he made some excuse to Paul Harden and Stephen Meade of my being called away on a medical case.

Present on the premises was the young Roman priest Brown, of whom I have earlier alluded. A diminutive man with a large and shabby umbrella, the prelate presented the picture of a cheerful, if somewhat vague, individual, given to blinking in an absent sort of way through a pair of comically rounded glasses. Holmes, who was a master in the swift assessment of human character, took an instant liking to Father Brown, and formed the quick impression of a man who, contrary to his appearance of a 'chump', was in fact an extraordinarily sharp-witted person.

In accordance with the plan outlined by Holmes in Baker Street, Meade had arranged to send Dr. Flaherty out on an errand which would keep him away from Knightsbridge for the rest of the day, leaving it open for his room to be investigated. Summoning Father Brown to his aid, and leaving the younger Harden brother and his secretary to their business, Holmes gained access to Flaherty's room. A picklock from his burglar's kit which would leave behind no traces was sufficient for Holmes to enter Flaherty's chamber and to search the drawers of the physician's cupboard. It did not take Holmes and Brown long to recover, from under a pile of the doctor's clothes, the mask of a grinning demon, and in his medicine cabinet was a large stock of Dover's Powder, the popular compound of ipecacuanha and opium that was available with most pharmacists.

Thrusting the mask and the powder in his capacious pocket, Holmes turned to Father Brown. "Well, Reverend," said he. "You know what I am here for, and you have now seen what I have seen. I should be greatly interested in having from you an account that would cover the facts of the case."

"Mr. Holmes, you place your confidence in my intellectual abilities at your own risk," said the priest, blinking.

"Pray let me be the judge of that," said Holmes good humouredly. "And now, if you will provide me with an explanation of the known facts – "

"Very well," said Father Brown dully. "Here is an explanation that should account for the facts as they have been presented to us. I suppose the most direct explanation should revolve around that old, old story of a young man of ambition grasping beyond his reach – and sometimes succeeding. Dr. Flaherty is one of only three men in the immediate environment with an intimate knowledge of John Vincent Harden's medical condition, and of the man's impending demise. He cannot deny to himself the attraction that Mrs. Harden has for him, nor is he able to entirely discount the power and influence which he fancies he himself wields over the lady. What should prevent an ambitious man in his position from doing what he can to expedite his employer's end through nightly infusions of opium administered (unwittingly, one hopes, dear Lord!) by the man's wife?

"What would surely also help is to bribe one of the minions in the establishment to suspend a fearsome mask from the balcony above, on a length of string outside the patient's window, and to have it hauled up in a trice again when the window is opened, leaving no trace of any presence outside . . . The unexpected presence of two other witnesses is troublesome, but not quite fatal. With shocks and interventions such as these, designed to hasten the millionaire's end, an enterprising and attractive young man may be forgiven for believing that upon allowing for a decent efflux of time after his employer's death, it should be possible for him to make a marriage with the vulnerable – and wealthy – widow."

"I believe your account would largely confirm the sorts of suspicions which the younger Harden and his secretary have already conveyed to me. And how do you suppose they will deal with Flaherty's villainy when I have conveyed the Brown Theory to them?"

"I would expect that they will not confront Flaherty. The effort would be to minimise all suggestion of sensation, in a bid to spare Mrs. Harden's feelings, and also in the general interests of avoiding a scandal. The private secretary, it is to be hoped, will succeed in getting his hot-headed employer to handle the situation with discretion and circumspection. Having convinced himself, on your authority, of Flaherty's guilt, I suppose Paul Harden will simply relieve the doctor of his responsibilities. He will be asked to leave quietly. The very rich among us do not owe others, nor apparently themselves, explanations for their actions. By the way, you allude to my explanation as the *Brown Theory*. Am I to understand, Mr. Holmes, that there is a different, or *Holmes Theory* available?"

"Let us just say, shall we, that I should be able to vest more faith in the Brown Theory if the Reverend Brown himself backed it. Does he now? Tell me, Father Brown, do you believe the explanation you have furnished to be the true one?"

"You asked me only for an explanation that would fit the facts. That, I believe, I have supplied. I have not said it is the *true* explanation."

"Well then, do you believe it is?"

"I would, Mr. Holmes, if I were as much of a turnip as I might seem. But God has gifted, or at least burdened, me with a brain which appears to have the ability to delve directly into the truth, as distinct from shadowy constructions which are merely compatible with it. To uncover a crime, or at any rate a wrong-doing, requires one to be on intimate terms with the failings of man. I am a man, and I hope a self-conscious man, so I have no particular difficulty in possessing the required intimacy. In this case, it is not even particularly clear if it is vice or virtue that has led to wrong-doing. Do I make myself clear, Mr. Holmes?"

"Yes, though it is for no reason of your failing to speak in riddles, Reverend," said Holmes drily. "I gather that the vice (or virtue) you speak of is love, and the wrong-doing in question is that of bearing false witness."

"It is a queer world, Mr. Holmes," said the priest, "in which a confirmed misogynist and a celibate simpleton find themselves speaking of *love*. But you are perfectly right, you know. I am in a position to testify to the absolute accuracy of your observation. You see, there is nothing wrong with my eye-sight once it has been corrected with glasses. And God presumably gives a priest ears like mine that stick out of the head in order to facilitate the business of listening. That is as good a case as any for Aquinas' Argument from Design. As a priest, and in a largely Catholic environment, I am frequently the recipient of whispered confessions – intended or unintended. Briefly, I see things and I hear things. I cannot help it.

"Among the things I could not help observing is that Stephen Meade has fallen hopelessly in love with Miss Constance Sutherland, who is as blissfully unaware of this fact, as she is happily aware of being the object of Dr. Flaherty's attentions. When love comes to a man at a time of his life in which he has just reconciled himself to remaining a bachelor for the rest of his natural existence, it comes with a particularly smiting force. And Meade has been forcefully smitten. The virtue of a gentle and other-regarding love has turned into the vice of a distorted, possessive, jealous passion, such as will not let him be unless he removes from the scene the man he sees as his rival. Hence the apparently diffident but constantly poisonous insinuations about Flaherty's allegedly guilty ambitions, aimed at influencing Paul Harden, who strikes one as being an unimaginative and therefore easily impressionable man. And, of course, it was Meade who had bribed some hireling to manipulate that mask on a string outside the window from the upper floor, and to snatch it up upon the pre-arranged signal of Meade's opening the window and looking out. The master stroke was to get Sherlock Holmes involved in the case, and arrange for him, with the aid of some trumped-up 'evidence', to corroborate the picture that he, Meade, had created."

"Quite," said Sherlock Holmes. "I virtually asked for the evidence to be planted, by hinting broadly to my clients at a theory of Flaherty's guilt such as you had initially furnished, and which Meade was working on my buying. I am afraid the man is in for a deep and unpleasant shock. This situation would be a comic one if it were not also so tragic. Come, let us try to do the best we can under the circumstances. The planted 'evidence' must, of course, be suppressed. I am carrying all of it in my pocket, and it will be disposed of on my way back to Baker Street.

"Paul Harden must be told that his brother's condition is a product of nature, not of sinister human intervention, and that there is no cause for

160

entertaining any suspicion that goes beyond Dr. Moore Agar's expert opinion. The only thing that needs to be explained is the face in the window. I have come prepared for it. In my brief-case here I have a kite I purchased at a shop in Oxford Street, with the picture of a gargoyle on it, which should pass muster as the face at the window from the dark without. The official story will be that the kite was blown by the wind that evening, that it rested briefly against the window, and was then blown away again, and that you found it, and picked it up, in the adjoining field on your walk to Knightsbridge this morning.

"I hear footsteps approaching – ah, I see that it is Meade, coming in to verify if his scheme has gone according to plan. I'll have to leave you to deal with him, Reverend. This is your department. I must also leave it to you to speak to Paul Harden. I have no appetite for a conversation with that brash young man. Please just convey my 'findings' to him, and make any excuse you like for my leaving without taking his leave. If he should speak of payment, kindly let him know that inasmuch as there was no mystery to solve, there is also no charge. I have not the heart to make money out of this sad business.

"For the rest, it has been a real pleasure to meet you and to get to know you. Farewell, Father Brown, and, as the Good Book enjoins: Be of good cheer!"

Sherlock Holmes and Father Brown clasped hands, and Meade, who had just wandered in, could not fail to see the light of mutual respect and affection in the two men's eyes.

After Holmes's departure, Father Brown had a very long conversation with Stephen Meade. What they said to each other must remain a secret between them. But there was every indication that Mr. Meade came out of that conversation, and several further ones which he had with Father Brown, a wiser if sadder man. Brown also spoke briefly to Paul Sebastian Harden, delivering to him the script agreed on with Sherlock Holmes. Within a week, Meade resigned, "for personal reasons", his position as private secretary to the Hardens, and began a new life as a librarian in a small grammar school.

This narrative can now be wound up with a few final words. Paul Harden sent a handsome cheque to Sherlock Holmes, which Sherlock Holmes endorsed in favour of the Reverend Father Brown, who in turn found excellent use for it in the orphanage with which he was associated. Within three months of the case having been brought to our attention, John Vincent Harden died from the persecution of his illness and a failed heart. Dr. Flaherty and Miss Sutherland were married, and the former went on to

161

have a successful medical career at Guy's. Mrs. Mary Harden returned to the States, she associated herself with the Sisters of Charity, and became one of the principal patrons of Spalding University, that fine centre for women's learning in Kentucky.

Father Brown devoted himself to his work, which still takes him through the streets of London, on ha'penny omnibuses, or clumping along in his disgraceful shoes, hat on head, umbrella in hand, and spectacles on nose. And Mr. Sherlock Holmes of Baker Street diverts himself from time to time with a dreamy air on his violin, lights his pipe, and continues to receive those people, with problems large or small, who turn up at his humble quarters to seek the help of the foremost consulting detective in Europe.

# The Dead Quiet Library
## by Roger Riccard

### Chapter I

In early May of 1895, not long after our cycling adventure with Miss Violet Smith [1] and her notorious suitors, my friend, the consulting detective Sherlock Holmes, and I were enjoying a leisurely lunch at the lodgings we shared at 221b Baker Street in northwest London. I was just pouring myself a second cup of tea when we heard the doorbell ring and, soon after, the tread of footsteps ascending to our rooms.

"A case, Watson," declared Holmes. "Unless I'm much mistaken, for surely that is young Stanley Hopkins."

No sooner had the words left him than a quick knock and opened door revealed the recently promoted Scotland Yard Inspector. Approaching thirty years of age, Hopkins reminded me a little of Holmes in appearance from when we first met back in '81. Tall and lean with a thin face. Like me, however, he sported a moustache, which almost gave him a military air. Unlike his counterpart, Inspector Lestrade, he was far more eager and amiable to Holmes's assistance on his more confounding cases.

The exertion of climbing the seventeen steps to our rooms was certainly no great effort for the fit young man. The pained expression on his face was that of a troubled soul and I insisted that he sit immediately. I motioned him to the chair where I knew Holmes preferred to observe his potential clients and poured him a cup of tea.

Holmes left the dining table and sat across from our visitor. He leaned back in that casual posture of his, meant to put guests at ease, and spoke in a conversational tone.

"Good afternoon, Inspector. What troubles have the citizens of Chadwell Heath laid at your feet on this fine spring day?"

"How do you do that, Mr. Holmes? Yes, I was called out to St. Chad's College first thing this morning."

"There are burrs of a plant which is prominent in St. Chad's Park attached to your trouser cuffs," answered the detective, "and a train ticket stub in your hatband is quite obvious. Has another mysterious death intruded upon that bucolic institution?"

"I see you are aware of the incident which occurred two months ago," responded Hopkins. "It was ruled accidental, but the circumstances have left a shadow of doubt among those of us at the Yard. Now a second death has occurred, and I'm not so sure we don't have a calculating murderer on our hands."

Being unfamiliar with the previous incident, I queried Hopkins. "I hadn't heard of any mysterious deaths out in Chadwell Heath. What has aroused your suspicion?"

Holmes chimed in as well, "Yes, Hopkins, please refresh our memory, and I beg you, tell us all, and not just what the newspapers reported."

The young man set down his teacup and leaned back in his seat to settle himself as he began his tale. "Two months ago, on Friday, March eighth, a student named Aloysius Bass was in the Lansbury Library on St. Chad's campus. His reasons for being there were never confirmed. He was not a studious sort, and rumours were told about his assignations with young ladies. As you should be aware, St. Chad's has followed the example of University College, Bristol [2] and admits women to its student population. At any rate, somehow he remained in the building after the nine o'clock closing. Avoiding the librarian wouldn't have been difficult if it was intentional, for it was assumed that all visitors would wish to be reminded of how late it was and leave voluntarily when the closing bell was sounded.

"The next morning being a Saturday, the library didn't open until ten o'clock. The librarian, one Orson O'Hare, is an elderly gentleman of nearly sixty years. With his bifocal glasses, however, his vision is quite normal, though his hearing is weak in one ear. His mind is sharp and memory superb. When he opened the doors for the day, he took up his post at the front desk and waited on visiting students and professors as usual. It wasn't until around ten-forty-five that someone had occasion to visit the third floor, which is the uppermost of the building, and found the body of Mr. Bass."

"Good Lord!" I exclaimed.

Holmes added, "As I recall, it was reported that he died of a broken neck. Did the coroner pinpoint a time of death?"

"He believed it to be between nine and ten o'clock the previous evening," Hopkins continued. "He was found at the base of a book ladder and a volume from the top shelf was on the floor next to him, so it was believed that he simply slipped and fell."

"But you aren't convinced it was accidental," stated Holmes.

"Even the coroner was reluctant to state so," replied Hopkins. "But there was no conclusive evidence to the contrary, so it was ruled a 'Death by Misadventure'."

"Pray tell us, what was nagging at your mind back then?" requested the detective.

"As I said, Bass was not the studious type. His being there on a Friday night was totally out of character, so what was the reason? Also, the break to his neck. It was not a snapping, horizontal break as one might assume from landing on his head. It was a violent twist that one would expect from a human agent – especially if someone had combat training. Finally, there's the reputation of the library itself."

"Reputation?" I queried. "How do you mean, Inspector?"

He shifted uncomfortably and leaned forward with his elbows on his knees. "The library was once the ancestral home of Sir Osbert Lansbury, and legend has it that he still haunts the place."

"Poppycock!" declared Holmes in disgust at such a suggestion.

"And this relates to your case in some way?" I asked, attempting to be more civil to Hopkins predicament.

"Not that I believe in ghosts, Doctor," he said. "But, there have been occasional sightings of a cloaked figure and unusual sounds heard, in what otherwise is an extremely quiet building due to its thick walls and heavy doors. Now that there has been a second suspicious death, I cannot merely dismiss such evidence out of hand."

"Tell us about this new victim and the circumstances of his demise," asked Holmes, impatiently.

Hopkins leaned back again and took a notepad from his breast pocket, referring to it as he reported. "Clifton Douglas, age forty-two, Dean of Athletics and Rugby coach. Married, no children. Has been in his position for eleven years. Found in the library this morning, again on the third floor. Coroner puts time of death at roughly between nine and ten last night, just like Bass. This time, however, cause of death appears to be a trip and fall. There was a rug rumpled at his feet and a gash along his left temple as he apparently tripped and hit his head on the corner of a reading table."

The young inspector snapped his notebook shut and put it into his pocket saying, "I don't like it one bit, Mr. Holmes. Two violent accidents resulting in death this close together in such a peaceful location are much too coincidental for me. Also, whether it means anything or not, Bass was a Fullback on Douglas' rugby team. One of his star players, in fact."

Holmes leaned back and steepled his fingers, head toward the ceiling but eyes closed in thought. He held this position for nearly a minute and I could see Hopkins patience wearing thin. Just as the inspector opened his mouth to speak, Holmes suddenly stood and said, "We must go to Chadwell Heath immediately. I presume the coroner has the body?"

"Yes, Mr. Holmes," replied Hopkins.

The detective strode over to the writing table and jotted out a quick note. This he dropped at the telegraph office on our way to the railway station. When questioned by the inspector, he merely stated he had wired a request to the coroner's office, hoping to preserve evidence until we arrived.

The trip to Chadwell Heath was fairly quick, being a mere twenty-two miles away, but Holmes chafed at the roundabout route which the train took to get there, as the tracks are not laid as the crow flies, but instead as a wide arc, rounding about north of London and coming back eastward into the more rural area. The three of us crowded into a cab upon arrival at the isolated red-brick station and were in the coroner's office shortly after two o'clock.

The coroner, a rather young fellow named Dr. Palmer, greeted us with enthusiasm, "Mr. Holmes, Dr. Watson, a pleasure to meet you, sirs. I hope you can prove to the Magistrate that we have a killer on our hands."

He spoke thus as he led us to the autopsy room and pointed out the latest victim on the examining table. "His death was no accident, just like that of Aloysius Bass. No mere trip and fall would have delivered sufficient force to cause this head wound and death. He had help."

Holmes questioned the young man, "If you are sure of Bass' cause of death, why did it get reported as an accident?"

Palmer leaned in conspiratorially and spoke softly, "The Magistrate, Robert Caldwell, is an alumnus of St. Chad's, and is adamant about avoiding adverse publicity. The old stories of the haunted library had faded into ancient history and he wants nothing stirred up that would affect future enrollment. It's rumoured that the school is in financial straits, and any significant reduction in student population could cause it to shut down."

"Surely," I exclaimed, "he cannot condone letting a murderer get away – especially now that he's apparently struck again!"

"There was no proof of a second party in the room the first time," chimed in Hopkins. "With just the twisted neck theory, there were no supporting facts for a murder."

Palmer fumed, "It's no 'theory', Inspector. No matter how he landed from that fall off the ladder – if he even fell – hitting his head on the floor would not have resulted in that twisting break of his vertebrae. There was also just a light bump above his left ear and no other contusions or bruising. How did he hit his head hard enough to break his neck without leaving a more significant mark? No, sir! Bass was murdered, and I'll wager that this fellow was too – for his neck was twisted as well!"

Holmes stared down at the body of Clifton Douglas, but instead of taking a closer look, made a request of Dr. Palmer. "I'd like to examine his effects. Where are they?"

The coroner led us over to a nearby shelf and pulled out a box that he set on a table. Hopkins and I observed as Holmes methodically went

166

through Douglas' clothing, paying special attention to his coat and shirt. He also gave a cursory look at the soles of his shoes before returning all the items to the box.

"There is certainly nothing about his shoes that would explain a misstep or trip," began Holmes. "However, he is missing the second button off his shirt and the shirt itself is quite wrinkled at that point. Almost as if someone had grabbed it with a fist."

He gave a telling look to Hopkins as he made this statement and then requested to take a closer look at the body. Magnifying lens in hand, my old friend made minute observations of the victim's hand, even going so far as to borrow some tweezers to extract something from beneath the fingernails. He then proceeded to examine the legs, feet, chest, back, arms, and finally the head wound itself.

When he finished, Palmer spoke without even waiting for Holmes's conclusion. "I'm right, aren't I, Mr. Holmes?" It was more statement than question.

The tall detective leaned back against a post, tapping his lens to his lips as he stared down at the lifeless form of the former academic. At last he put his glass back into his pocket and replied, "You are, Dr. Palmer, without a doubt. Gentlemen, we have a murder to solve."

## Chapter II

"You're sure, Mr. Holmes?" asked Hopkins. "There's no evidence of anyone else being there."

"We shall take a look for ourselves, Inspector. Douglas here has fibers from some clothing other than what he was wearing under his fingernails where he likely grabbed his attacker in self-defense. They appear to be from a blue coat or cloak, possibly a collegiate sports jacket. There are also hairs pulled from his chest where he was grabbed in the motion that undoubtedly caused his shirt button to be torn off. In addition, there is bruising to the body, arms, and legs where he would have been grabbed, punched, and kicked in a struggle that ended with his head being slammed against the tabletop as his feet were swept out from under him."

"Surely someone would have heard such a confrontation, Holmes," I said.

"From the time of death, Watson, it was likely after hours" he replied. "Even if it were right at closing time, a strong, athletic man like Douglas may have been over-confident in his ability against his opponent and chosen not to use energy or break his concentration by crying out. The struggle itself was on the top floor and the noise may have been

167

insufficient to carry to the floors below – especially in a building that has a reputation for being so quiet."

Palmer spoke up, "If it means anything, Mr. Holmes, St. Chad College's biggest rival is Ashlyn College over in Basildon, and their school color is blue, whereas St. Chad's is green."

Holmes nodded at this information and commanded, "Come gentlemen," as he swept out of the room. "We must examine the scene of the crime before crucial evidence is lost."

We reacquired a cab and made the short trip to St. Chad's campus and the Lansbury Library in mere minutes. Before we went in, Holmes insisted on investigating the grounds around the outside of the building. There was no moat, but the walls were guarded by a thick hedge that couldn't easily be penetrated. The only break in this greenery was along the windows on the east and west sides of the ground floor. My companion made careful observation of the dirt beneath each one. When he had completed his rounds, we entered the facility and I was struck by the absolute silence, such as I've only experienced at the Diogenes Club. [3]

The foyer included tapestries, coats of arms of the Lansburys and other related families, and a suit of armor, labeled as belonging to Sir Osbert Lansbury himself. I noted it's size and commented, "Sir Osbert wasn't a very large fellow for a knight. This looks like it was made for a fellow only about five-foot-six, perhaps shorter."

"Three-hundred years ago, that wasn't short, Watson," observed my companion. "The average height of mankind creeps ever upward as healthier foods and lifestyles enable more conducive conditions for growth. You and I are certainly tall for our times, but I imagine that a hundred years from now we would find ourselves merely average." [4]

We proceeded inside and found that, to ensure the quiet, the librarian's desk was enclosed by wood and glass walls so that conversation could be held behind closed doors. Fortunately, it was quite roomy, as it had to accommodate students lining up to check out materials.

Orson O'Hare sat on a tall stool behind a counter as he waited on students. When he stood to greet us, I judged him to be about five-foot-eight and a stocky two-hundred pounds. His brown hair was parted in the middle and flowed back in waves until it curled over his collar. There were grey streaks along the temples and his short beard and moustache were completely grey with just slight streaks of brown stubbornly showing through. He wore gold-rimmed bifocal eyeglasses and spoke in a pleasant baritone voice as he addressed us.

"Hello again, Inspector. Are these the gentlemen from London of whom you spoke this morning?"

"Yes, Mr. O'Hare," answered Hopkins. "This is Mr. Sherlock Holmes and Dr. John Watson. I wanted you to meet them before we went upstairs to examine the scene."

"A pleasure, gentlemen," he replied as he shook our hands in turn, with a strong grip for a man of his age. "I will be happy to answer any questions you may have, but in the meantime, feel free to look around."

We took our leave and proceeded up the staircase to the top floor. Hopkins had taken the precaution to surround the area where the body had been found with chairs. A handwritten note was fastened to one, stating that the area was to remain undisturbed, so that any students on that floor would not contaminate the scene. Holmes congratulated the young man on his foresight.

Immediately my old friend set to work. He removed the chairs and carefully studied the floor. Except for the rugs under the tables to reduce the noise of chairs being pulled in and out, the flooring was of polished oak planks. The bookshelves, which wound around most of the perimeter, included four long, free-standing aisles, taking up two-thirds of the room. They were likewise of thick oak to support the weight of volumes residing there, and stretched all the way to the ten-foot ceiling. Each row had a rolling ladder suspended from the top shelf for students to reach the highest levels. The rest of the room was set up as a study area of six rectangular tables, with two chairs on each side.

"Why is this room so large?" I pondered. "You would think this floor would be devoted to bedrooms."

"You're thinking of it as a home, Doctor," answered Holmes. "While not a castle in the true sense, it was meant to be a fortified structure. This floor was likely an armory, with access to the roof for archers defending against the enemy."

We continued our examination and, at one point, Holmes laid down on the floor, positioning himself so the spot where the body fell caught the light of the windows on the west side of the room as it filtered down the long aisles formed by the bookshelves. Then he took up the curled-over corner of the rug and laid in flat again. There lay the missing button from Douglas' shirt.

A satisfied "A-ha!" escaped his lips as he rose to his knees. He handed the button to the inspector and bid him to get down and observe what else he had seen. Hopkins complied, then stood again shaking his head. "I don't know how I could have missed that."

"What is it?" I asked, not deigning to test the limits of my old war wound by attempting to lower and then raise myself from the floor.

"Footmarks, Doctor, and *not* those of Mr. Douglas," answered Holmes. "These have a rubber sole, all the more suitable for sneaking up behind someone. As for missing them, Hopkins," he continued, addressing the young man, "do not fault yourself. Your examination was made this morning, long before the advantage of having the afternoon sun streaming through the windows."

"Then there *was* a second person here," I said. "Very likely the killer."

Holmes stood and brushed off his trouser knees. "A distinct possibility. Although, the button could have just fallen off and Douglas tripped attempting to retrieve it. However, given the condition of his shirt, I find that unlikely. Unfortunately, there is no way to know for certain when those shoe marks were made. They are fairly fresh, but it's still possible they were made by someone who helped remove the body. Do you have knowledge of who that was, Hopkins?"

"Palmer will know the name of the men who assisted him. I'll find out for you, Mr. Holmes."

"So," I commented with a wry grin, "you haven't completely eliminated the ghost yet."

Holmes gave me a surly look and replied, "Watson, please. The only ghost here was the departing spirit of Clifton Douglas."

Having finished his examination of the floor, he then began a perimeter search of the room, starting with the windows. The bottom of the sills were about three feet up from the floor and extended six feet up toward the ceiling. There were four of them, each about three feet wide and capable of being opened by sliding the bottom half up. It was quite obvious that these were modern additions to the building, as structures of this style in the late sixteenth century wouldn't have had windows of that type. Holmes checked each one, looking for footmarks on the sill and observing the outside, to determine if anyone could have climbed up from the ground or descended on a rope from the roof. Satisfied that these were not the approach of the killer, he then began inspecting the walls.

Curiosity got the better of Hopkins, who asked, "Couldn't the killer merely have walked in like any other visitor and laid in wait for his victim? Perhaps he lured Douglas here by some message, struck at the opportune moment, and then walked out with everyone else when the library closed, or even afterward."

Holmes replied over his shoulder as he examined the bookshelves along the wall. "Certainly plausible, but I believe unlikely. Our killer would desire to keep his presence in the library unknown, if possible – especially if someone could connect him with a motive for killing these men. If you noticed the lock on the front door, you would know that once it is locked, no one can get in or out without a key. As a Dean, I had surmised that Douglas would be one of those entrusted with one, and there was a key of that type among his personal belongings at the morgue. That also confirms that the killer didn't take it. He wasn't afraid of being locked in the building after closing. Therefore, since he did not need Douglas' key to leave, and yet he wished to not be noticed among the visitors going in and out, we have two possibilities."

Hopkins snapped his fingers and exclaimed, "He had a key of his own!"

Holmes gave that brief flash of a smile of his and turned toward the young Scotland Yarder. "A possibility that we must explore. While we are here, it is conducive to investigate the only other option available: That the killer has intimate knowledge of this ancient structure, and is familiar with some secret passage, which were quite common in those turbulent times."

"Like a priest's hole?" I queried.

"Exactly, Watson. Somewhere in which our culprit could hide for the night and then slip out at any time the next day when the library was re-opened. Or, more likely, leave by way of a tunnel that exits far away from the building."

## Chapter III

I noticed, as Holmes crept along the wall in search of such an exit, that he concentrated his observation only on two areas. One between three-and-a-half and four feet above the floor, and the other along the baseboards. Hopkins also took note and questioned his mentor.

"Why are you concentrating on the wall at that particular height, Mr. Holmes? Couldn't a secret locking mechanism be anywhere?"

"I will certainly expand the search parameters if necessary, Hopkins. However, I'm attempting to save time by observing the two likeliest locations. Somewhere along the base of the wall could be a catch that is operated by one's foot. There is a disadvantage as such a device could be accidentally tripped by someone cleaning the floor, but mechanically it is a sound placement. This particular area along the wall," he said, waving his hand in a sideways motion, "is based upon Sir Osbert's height of roughly five-foot-six-inches. There would likely be a manual release somewhere between his waist and chest where he would have the most leverage to operate it.

"May I suggest, gentlemen, that you also pay particular attention to the floor and note any signs of disturbed dust, or scratches from a swinging door. Although I believe it far more likely that such a door will swing *into* the wall, one cannot discount other directions. You should also keep an eye out for any type of peephole or movable slot where someone inside the wall could observe the interior of this room before opening the door."

Hopkins and I took these instructions to heart and chose other sections to assist in the search where the walls appeared thick enough to admit human passage. As Holmes neared the corner, I saw him suddenly stop and study an ancient shield on display on the wall between the windows and the bookshelves. It was a ceremonial shield showing no wear nor indentations from use, and it was shined to a high silver gloss, obviously a result of the current era's cleaning crew. It bore the crest of the Lansburys: A knight's helmet with red plume atop a standard shield with a red rose, yellow lion, brown oak tree, and a blue lyre within the four quadrants created by a red cross upon it.

Holmes walked up to it, studiously looking back and forth from it to the perpendicular shelf that formed the corner of the room. Holding his hands up with splayed fingers, he began to study the bookshelf at roughly the height of his own shoulder, which I realized must be about eye level for Sir Osbert.

Suddenly, he reached forth and grasped a vertical support for that particular shelf and manipulated it until it turned about forty-five degrees. The empty space behind aligned perfectly with the shining shield. Peering in with the help of a lit match, one could see the space where someone could hide. The three of us excitedly examined the edges around the shelving until Holmes found a catch that enabled that section of the bookcase to swivel on a central post. It slowly swung open, ingeniously suspended by the smallest fraction of an inch above the floor, so as to be unnoticeable by anyone standing in front of the shelf.

Within the thick wall was a landing where one could stand and observe the reflection of the room in that shining shield. There were wall sconces for ancient torches and stone stairs leading downward. The light of the windows with the door opened was sufficient for us to see to the next landing and we descended the steps to the second floor.

There, Holmes found another "peephole" and gazed about the room before opening the door. This appeared to be a bedroom that had been converted to an unoccupied meeting room. We entered, and this floor featured a central open space where the stairwell passed through and a landing spread all the way around it. Then we saw a mannequin of what was ostensibly a likeness of Sir Osbert Lansbury in court dress. This turned out to be on a wheeled platform. along the east wall, facing toward the campus. Holmes took a quick glance around and seemed to take great interest in Sir Osbert's attire. Then he ordered us back into the passage where we went down to another landing. This looked out upon the first floor, but Holmes was on the scent. By now we had descended beyond the daylight from our original ingress and Holmes pulled a candle from his coat.

"How did you happen to have a candle with you, Mr. Holmes?" Hopkins declared. "I swear, sometimes watching you work seems like witchcraft!"

The detective responded over his shoulder as he continued to lead the way, "I anticipated a secret passage, Inspector, given the scene of the crime. Had we not been informed of this location, it's likely we would be attempting this descent by the light of whatever materials were at hand, if any were available. Watch your step!"

That warning came as the stone step beneath his feet rocked from imbalance at the loss of ancient mortar. We navigated it safely and stopped briefly at the ground floor. Again, Holmes peeped out to note our location, which was at the rear of a pantry that was part of a kitchen. He slid a panel aside and found a kerosene lantern on a nearby shelf. He inspected it briefly. It was about half-full and in working order. He extinguished his candle, lit the mantle of the lantern, and we continued our descent as the secret passage steps continued downward.

"As I suspected, there is an underground tunnel trailing off to the west. Look here, Hopkins. There are traces of fresh footprints, and the cobwebs have been swept away. This tunnel has seen recent use, no doubt. Let us see where it leads."

The inspector hesitated, and I noted some physical symptoms which concerned me. "Are you all right, Hopkins?" I enquired. Holmes looked back and spoke before the young man answered. "It may not be wise for the three of us to journey forth, since no one knows where we are. You should remain here, Hopkins, and keep an ear out for any sounds of distress, should the tunnel prove unstable. We will return shortly. Here, take the candle for yourself."

I could see a visible wave of relief pass over Hopkins face as his colour returned and he replied, "A sensible precaution, Mr. Holmes," he said, lighting the candle. "I shall remain here on guard. Good luck, gentleman."

We walked on slowly with Holmes in the lead, as the passage was just a bit narrow for the two of us to traverse it side by side. Once we were beyond the inspector's earshot, I spoke to my companion. "You obviously recognized Hopkins' symptoms, Holmes. It was kind of you to offer him a plausible excuse to avoid a claustrophobic attack."

"I remembered hearing of the French discoveries of such a condition when I was a student back in the seventies. As I know Hopkins is not normally a man given to fear, I quickly surmised he had the condition. I do wonder that it didn't manifest itself as we were descending the narrow passage between the walls."

This was one of those rare occasions when my medical knowledge complemented Holmes's memory of facts, and I replied, "Often it is the *type* of enclosed space that affects the patient. Passing within man-made walls where there was a lit avenue of retreat was obviously tolerable. An earthen tunnel, which could prove unstable, and with only one light source, was obviously too much for him. Also, there may have been an incident in his past where such conditions first triggered his fears."

Holmes merely hummed in reply and pointed ahead. The tunnel was coming to an end. This area was wider, possibly used to store weapons or foodstuffs, and there was a framework of what may have been for a bed at some time in the past. There were more kerosene lanterns on a shelf, which my companion checked for dust and signs of recent use. A ladder in good repair rose about ten feet to some sort of trap door. Holmes went first and threw open the door easily and silently, with nary a squeak to its hinges. I followed and we had emerged in a thick grove of oak trees and ground covered in sparse bracken along the eastern edge of St. Chad's Park.

Holmes examined the ground around the trap door, which, itself, was covered with bracken. While there were signs of disturbance, there were no readable footprints or any other trace of evidence.

I looked back toward the library and saw that we had gone perhaps fifty yards to the west. Holmes requested that I go back for Hopkins while he explored the ground between our exit and the building. We would meet up back at the pantry on the ground floor. I took the lantern and made my way back through the tunnel, shouting out a "Hello" as soon as I saw the flicker of the inspector's candle in the distance, knowing that he must be getting anxious by now. Relieved to see me, I further distracted his anxiety by explaining to him where we had come out and what Holmes's plan was. I gave him the lantern and he led the way back up to the landing that opened into the pantry. The pantry itself was a large storage area at the back of a kitchen that had seen little use in recent times, judging by the layer of dust on the counters. We brushed off a couple of chairs at a small table and awaited the detective's arrival.

We struck up a conversation, as we knew Holmes's thorough methods of search might take a while. Hopkins volunteered that he'd had a traumatic experience as a child while exploring a cave with cousins near his grandparents' farm. They were almost out of sight of the entrance, proceeding by candlelight, when one of his cousins thought he heard something up ahead. He threw a rock that bounced off the walls and set up a roar as hundreds of batwings began flapping and screaming past them. The boy holding the candle dropped it and it went out. The cloud of bats briefly blocked the daylight from the entrance and for several seconds young Stanley was plunged into total blackness with only screeches of both bats and boys to accompany him.

I sympathized with his plight. Such a traumatic experience could easily affect someone for life, I reassured him. I explained the intricacies of claustrophobia and it seemed to make him feel better, knowing that it was a medical condition and not an expression of cowardice.

Holmes arrived at that point and took up the now extinguished lantern, advising us not to mention it as we returned to O'Hare's office. The librarian was just finishing with a student as we entered and waved us to some seats off to one side. Holmes set the lantern on a small table and crossed his legs nonchalantly. When he was free, O'Hare walked out from behind his counter and asked if we'd found anything.

"Indeed, we have, sir," declared Holmes, almost jovially. "We've discovered a secret passage that leads down through the wall from the top floor clear to an underground tunnel, which would take someone wishing to get away out to the edge of St. Chad's Park."

"Extraordinary!" exclaimed the elderly gentleman. "Are you convinced then that Bass and Douglas were murdered, and the killer got out that way?"

Holmes raised a forefinger, as if in caution, and replied, "Not as yet *convinced* as you say, but it confirms the possibility that someone other than a keyholder to the library could have been involved."

O'Hare seemed taken aback, "You thought someone with a key killed them?"

"It was a highly probable explanation," said Holmes. "Considering that once you lock the door for the night, no one can get in or out without a key. Douglas had one, but it's still with his effects. Who else has a key?"

O'Hare tilted his head in thought, then answered, "The Chancellor, of course. All of the deans. The groundskeeper and the head of the custodial crew. I believe that is all."

I had written these facts down at Holmes's instruction and then he said, "We shall have to determine if anyone of them had motives against both these individuals – which I admit, does not seem likely on the surface. The odds favor some connection with their participation in the Rugby program. Do students from other schools come to use this library?"

O'Hare seemed to beam with pride, "Why, yes, Mr. Holmes. All the local academy and college students from Stratford to Brentwood have been known to come here for various types of research."

"So it wouldn't be uncommon for students from Ashlyn College over in Basildon to be here?"

"I've noticed a few of their blue blazers from time to time, yes."

"Anyone on the day Douglas was killed?"

O'Hare thought a moment, "I believe there were two Ashlyn students here together that afternoon."

Holmes brightened a bit at that, "Do you recall what time they left, or if they left at all?"

The librarian shook his head, "If they didn't check anything out, Mr. Holmes, they could have walked right out the front door without my seeing them."

"Well," said Holmes as he stood, "it appears we have our work cut out for us. Good day, Mr. O'Hare. I've no doubt we'll speak again."

I noticed, as we followed Holmes out, that he left the lantern behind. However, we hadn't made it halfway to the exit when O'Hare appeared in his doorway, holding the object in his hand and, due to the atmosphere of the facility, emitting a stage whisper to inform us that we had forgotten it.

Holmes retreated a few steps, so as not to have to raise his voice, and replied, "Oh, that is yours, or rather, the library's. You do not recognize it?"

O'Hare looked at it curiously and replied, "We have gas lighting throughout the building. There's no need for this. Where did you find it?"

"It was in the pantry of the old kitchen," said Holmes, pointing in that direction.

"Really?" the elderly man commented. "Well, I suppose I'll just put it back there for now. Thank you, Mr. Holmes."

He turned off in that direction and we continued our exit. Once outside I asked my companion, "What was that all about with the light?"

"Just trying to see how truthful our librarian was. If he had been able to return the lantern without our help, it would be almost certain that he knew about the passage and its exit into the pantry where the lantern was kept."

Hopkins interjected, "Come, Mr. Holmes. You surely can't suspect that old man capable of dispatching a youthful athlete like Bass, or a man of Douglas stature."

"As Watson will tell you, Inspector, I always attempt to eliminate the impossible until I am left with the most likely solution, no matter how improbable. It seemed a convenient time to test Mr. O'Hare, and now we can move on to more probable avenues."


Chapter IV


Hopkins suggested our next stop should be the Chancellor's office. He had already spoken with the man that morning, having called him in when the death was reported. Now he deemed that a conversation with Holmes might prove more revealing.

176

My friend was in agreement. We were soon granted access to the office of Randolph Stockton-York, a wizened old man of seventy years, short, stocky, bald with a half-circle of white fringe about his head and mutton-chop whiskers to match. An older-fashioned black suit featuring a tailcoat and dark green brocaded waistcoat, undoubtedly a bow to the school colors, completed the picture.

Behind him, as he sat in a high-backed ornately tapestried chair, hung a picture of Richard III, last king of the House of York – a nod, no doubt to his ancestry. There were four guest chairs facing his expansive desk. I sat between Holmes and Hopkins, which left my flatmate almost directly across from our host. I discreetly took out my notebook and prepared to record anything significant.

"Gentleman," began the man, in a grandfatherly tone, "I do hope you are not going to go about spreading rumours of *college killers* or a *haunted library*. Surely these were unfortunate, if coincidental, accidents that can be put to rest."

Holmes took control of the conversation, "I do not indulge in rumours, Chancellor, only in facts. At this point, the *facts* indicate you have had two people murdered in your library. I will not bandy this information about until I have absolute proof, mind you. Once that proof is in hand, justice must be served. Surely you wouldn't wish to taint the college's reputation by rumours of conspiracies or cover-ups? Who would entrust their children to an institution that puts the safety of its student body below a false reputation?"

The old man sat back, hands grasping the edge of his desk as he took this in. He twice started to speak and thought better of it, as the implication of Holmes's words swirled about in his mind. Finally, he conceded. Raising his right hand in conciliation, he spoke, "Ah, very well then, Mr. Holmes. As the Bard said, '*Truth will out*'. I suppose it's better that we are seen as champions of justice than have our name sullied in the mud as deceivers of the public trust. King Richard would not approve." He pointed back over his shoulder at the painting and winked. Then he asked, "What can I do to help?"

Hopkins answered in his official capacity, "All we ask is permission to speak with any staff or student whom we may deem of interest in this matter. We also need access to school records."

"What records?" asked the Chancellor, cautiously.

Holmes answered. "Student records that may indicate disciplinary actions or low grades. Employment records of staff. Anything that might shine a light on who, if anyone, may have been involved. I should also explain that we will be looking at external sources as well – rival schools and the like."

Stockton-York raised his eyebrows at that suggestion and almost smiled as he considered it, "Yes, yes, that would certainly be a more likely explanation. Very well, gentlemen. I shall put the word out to the staff, who will also inform their students that you are exploring the deaths in the library to ensure everyone's safety. Will that be satisfactory?"

Hopkins replied, "That is all we ask, Chancellor. Thank you. If you could call in your clerk to take us to your file room?"

The old academic rang a bell on his desk and a young woman appeared in the doorway at his summons. "Miss Tomkins, please show these gentlemen to the records room and assist them with whatever they need. Long live the King!"

The woman who responded was attractive with short brown hair that curled up just above her shoulders. She was also quite tall, perhaps five-foot-nine. She wore eyeglasses, but didn't seem in the least self-conscious about them, as so many young women are. I assumed from her age that she was either a senior student or a recent graduate. I presumed that, this being a Saturday, the Chancellor had called her in to assist when he learned of Douglas' death and the police investigation.

As we walked down the hall, I posed a medical concern to the young lady. "If I may, miss, is the Chancellor quite all right? He seems a bit lost in time."

She looked about and, once sure we could not be overheard, replied, "He has good days and bad ones, Doctor. He takes great pride in his York family roots, and used to teach history before his went into administration full-time. They say his lectures on The Hundred Years War were quite emphatic. Lately he's been slipping away into the past more and more. It's not for me to say, but I believe he may be forced into retirement at the end of the term."

I nodded in sympathy and noted that Holmes also took an interest in this little tidbit. Arriving at the records room, she unlocked it with a key on a ring containing several keys hooked to the belt of her skirt. Inside, we found that the walls were lined with wooden file cabinets, each labeled and dating back to the very beginnings of the school, over a century before. There was a table in the middle with six chairs around it. I noted that the older records took up far less drawer space than those of the last few decades. Hopkins immediately opened the current year's student file. I sought and found the faculty records. Holmes, however, chose to question the young woman who had escorted us.

"If I may, Miss Tomkins: Did you know the student who died recently, Aloysius Bass?"

She crossed her arms and almost sneered, "Not as well as he would have liked, Mr. Holmes. I've never been one to fraternize with younger men, let alone muscle-bound, dim-witted egotists like Bass."

"It sounds like he may have desired to change that," commented Holmes.

"I believe he may have seen me as a mere challenge, thinking that he would be irresistible to someone like me. I represented a conquest he could not make."

"But he tried?" enquired the detective.

"Only once," she responded. "He attempted to corner me in my office one day after the Chancellor had left. When he reached for me, I grabbed his wrist, twisted his arm behind his back, and kicked his feet out from under him. He hit his head on the desk and was too dizzy to stand right away. That was when my fiancé', Alan – that is, Professor Muncy – came by to pick me up. Alan took the situation in hand, lifted Bass up by the front of his shirt, threatened to expel him if he ever heard of him approaching me or any other girl on campus in such a manner again. Then threw him out the door, where he fell on his backside in the hallway in front of a handful of students who were walking out for the day. His embarrassment was complete and he ran out of the building."

"And he never bothered you again?"

"I never saw him again, Mr. Holmes. He obviously took my fiancé's threat to heart and kept his distance. That was a year ago now."

I spoke up and asked, "How did you manage to overpower him, Miss Tomkins? I understand he was quite an athlete."

She smiled and replied, "I grew up with three older brothers, Doctor, holding my own against them in our youth and learning from them as we aged."

Holmes thanked her and advised her that we would be awhile and would let her know when we finished, so that she could lock up again. Holmes had me pull Muncy's file while he retrieved that of Clifton Douglas. In the meantime, Hopkins was looking over Bass' file, and also those of other students. I queried his research.

"These are the students whose names show up in Bass' file as having had run-ins with him. There are three boys and four girls who've made complaints against him, including Miss Tomkins. There also a written reprimand from Professor Muncy."

Holmes remarked, "With such a volatile personality and so many public complaints, one wonders how many victims remained silent out of fear? Our suspect pool grows significantly. We shall have to do something about that. Make sure you note all the contact information about these complainants, Inspector."

We spent the better part of an hour referencing and cross-checking anyone who may have held a grudge against Bass or Douglas, looking for someone that each victim had in common. In several cases, Douglas came to Bass' defense, either as a witness or to supply an alibi. There was also a report of an altercation between Douglas and Muncy, shortly after the incident which Miss Tomkins had related to us.

Hopkins suddenly had another thought and left us in order to question Miss Tomkins again. When he returned, he sought out the files of two other students to add to those he had already pulled.

"What have you found, Inspector?" queried Holmes.

"These are the students known for their practical jokes," answered the inspector, "according to Miss Tomkins. There have been several recent 'ghost sightings', and since we are not entertaining that possibility, there must be some human element involved. Practical jokers would be the most likely to perpetuate the ghost story, and it may well be that somehow their paths crossed our victims."

"You're not suggesting that they would kill to keep their secret if they were caught in the act?" I asked.

"Just on the chance that the deaths are unrelated to each other," responded Hopkins. "It may be that Bass threatened to expose them. He may have confronted them with blackmail, a fight ensued, and got out of hand. In the other case, if it was Douglas who caught them, he may have charged them with expulsion and they over-reacted, accidentally causing his fall against the table."

"That would not explain the twisted necks," observed Holmes.

Hopkins turned to me, "Doctor, would it be possible for Douglas to have fallen in such a way that his weight overcame the inertia of his head hitting the table edge and caused his neck to twist from the momentum?"

I thought back to the scene of the latest death and considered, then replied, "A mere fall from a standing position would not be sufficient, Inspector."

"What if he were pushed or thrown against the table?"

"It's not a likely outcome, but not impossible," I speculated.

Holmes spoke up. "So, you've added three more suspects to our pool, Inspector."

Hopkins shrugged his shoulders, "At the very least, we can talk to them and see what they may know about our victims. Men of that stripe are usually well-informed."

"Oh, I quite agree," nodded Holmes. "As for myself, I believe a talk with Professor Muncy is in order, as well as with Douglas' widow. Watson, I shall require your expertise on women for that interview."

I harrumphed, "You give me too much credit, Holmes, and not enough to yourself. You are quite capable of interviewing women successfully when you put your mind to it."

"Nevertheless . . . ." he implored.

"I shall be happy to accompany you, as always. What about the possibility of rival rugby players from Ashlyn?"

"I would prefer to play close to home for now. The passion required for these murders seems far beyond that of winning a mere sporting cup."

Working with Miss Tomkins, we scheduled to meet with the students in question on Monday when they returned to school. She also consented to having us join her and Professor Muncy later that afternoon, before their dinner plans. Holmes desired to question the widow Douglas that evening as well, but Hopkins and I both prevailed upon him, out of common courtesy, to give lady time to grieve and put off his questions until the next day.

Our interview with Professor Muncy took place in the lobby of the ladies' lodge where Miss Tomkins resided. Muncy was a barrel-chested fellow in his late twenties, clean-shaven with light brown hair worn slightly long, as is the fashion with some academics.

As Holmes, Hopkins, and I sat down with him and his fiancée, the professor jumped right to the heart of the matter. "From what I'm hearing, gentlemen, it sounds like you don't accept the 'accident' theory of Bass' death, which leads you to suspect Dean Douglas' death as well. I admit, had the order of their demise been reversed, I would have been less surprised. Bass had a temper and an ego far beyond his actual value. I could more readily accept his killing of a teacher who threatened his grades and eligibility to play ball."

I was taken aback by this frankness and replied, "Do you know of any threats he made to the faculty?"

"I am not personally aware of any direct threats, though he made no secret of his displeasure at certain teachers, present company included."

Holmes spoke up and enquired, "After your altercation, did he ever confront you again?"

Muncy grinned, "He knew better, Mr. Holmes. I know it may not be my place to say it, but every once in a while a student comes along who needs to have his ears boxed. He was well aware that I was not afraid of him and gave me a wide birth."

Holmes nodded in appreciation at his honesty and continued, "Were there any other staff members who felt as you do?"

The professor shook his head, "Not to the extent that they would kill him. Douglas did his best to keep him under control because of his skill on the rugby field, but if you ask me, that skill was overrated. He was selfish with the ball, and not really a team player. That will only take you so far. Against the better schools he was more hindrance than help."

"Could Douglas have confronted him and the argument have escalated into a killing in self-defence?" asked Holmes.

"Douglas would certainly have had the advantage in a fair fight," replied Muncy. "I doubt Bass would ever fight fair. I suppose, if it came to that, Douglas could have done it. I could only imagine it would have been an extreme circumstance, like putting down a wild animal. Even then, I would expect him to come forward and explain himself and not stage an accident."

"One never knows how a person will react when confronted with a traumatic situation," said the detective. "The most rational and intelligent man may succumb to any number of emotions and perform incredibly out of character when controlled by fear and panic.

"Tell me, do you have any thoughts on who might wish Professor Douglas dead?"

Miss Tomkins spoke up at that, "Clifton was well-liked by his students. Perhaps too much so by some of the girls. There were some rumors but nothing substantiated. The only complaints I've heard about him have been from parents of athletes who thought their boys weren't getting enough playing time."

"Interesting," commented Holmes. "Was he the flirtatious sort, in spite of his marriage?"

"Not exactly, Mr. Holmes. I never saw any overt action on his part. I never witnessed any discouragement either. I think he welcomed the attention. However, I don't believe that he ever acted upon it. Not to my knowledge anyway."

Muncy chimed in, "He's certainly never been caught at any inappropriate behavior. He would have been sacked immediately. The Chancellor and Board of Trustees would never have stood for it."

We then changed the course of the discussion toward any students who might have had grudges with either Bass or Douglas. The most notable revelation was that all of the practical jokers we had discovered had had fights with Bass.

We took our leave of the young couple and decided to arrange lodgings for the night at the same hotel where Hopkins was staying during the investigation. First however, Holmes expressed a need to return to Baker Street, so the two of us caught the next train back to Euston Station. We packed a few clothes and informed Mrs. Hudson we would be gone for two or three days. I grabbed my medical bag and my old Webley revolver, just in case. Holmes had a second carpet bag to complement his overnight suitcase. As we walked out, our kind landlady handed me some sandwiches wrapped in paper, knowing Holmes penchant for forgetting to eat – something of which I took advantage on the return train. We were back at the Bentley Hotel by eight-thirty and agreed to a plan that Holmes had outlined for us for the evening.

## Chapter V

Chadwell Heath, being a much more respectable village on the outskirts of the capital rather than some of the seedier parts of London down by the Thames, did not have an overabundance of pubs or other drinking establishments. Holmes suggested that Hopkins and I go off together, while he, in one of his disguises from his carpet bag, went about in the other direction. Our goal was to discreetly infiltrate the gossip-mongers and see what the locals thought about the death of the college professor, and their theories on what may have happened.

It was after eleven p.m. when we returned to our hotel. Hopkins and I had heard numerous opinions. Many believed it was accidental as reported, while others were convinced it was the ghost of Sir Osbert. Some thought it was an argument with one of his players that escalated into violence and an unintentional death. One old wag, for the price of a drink, offered the opinion that it was one of Douglas' jilted female students and decried the fact that women should not be attending the same school as men.

After we shared these with Holmes, he added some additional viewpoints that he had gleaned. These included: Friends of Bass exacting revenge on the coach for killing Bass; Douglas' wife did it, after finding out about her husband's affair with a student; the boyfriend, brother, or father of some female Douglas had wronged, killed him in revenge.

The interesting thing about all of the theories we had heard was that, except for the one about Douglas killing Bass, everyone seemed to accept Bass' death as accidental. The local populous seemed to agree with the official report that he fell off the ladder, in spite of his reputation. The general feeling was that someone out to kill Bass would use a more tried-and-true method.

At this Holmes invoked one of his adages, "There is nothing more deceptive than an obvious fact. [5] We've gleaned many points to ponder, gentlemen. Tomorrow we shall – "

A sharp knock on the door interrupted his conclusion and Hopkins answered it. It was Professor Muncy.

"Gentlemen, I think you should come with me. There is something I'm sure you'll want to investigate."

"What is it?" asked Holmes.

"The ghost of Sir Osbert is wandering the library. Alice and I saw him through the windows as I walked her home."

We all looked at each other skeptically. Hopkins was the first to move. As a sworn officer of the law, he was duty bound to investigate any possibility of foul play. I followed out of curiosity, and Holmes looked forward to debunking this superstition once and for all.

We arrived at the Library in mere minutes. As we approached, we could see a candlelit figure on the second floor, passing back and forth across the windows in medieval dress and wearing the blue mantle of a knight of the Order of the Garter. We also noted that the Librarian was just about to enter the front door. Holmes had Muncy wait outside and keep observing the actions of the figure in the window while Hopkins ran to join O'Hare in hopes of apprehending whoever or whatever that apparition on the top floor turned out to be.

In the meantime, Holmes motioned me to follow him to where we knew the tunnel exit was located. We lay in wait upon the hinge side where we wouldn't be visible until our prey was up and out of the hole. Fortunately, a three-quarter moon provided enough light through the trees that, being this close, allowed us to see. My companion had me draw my revolver, just to dissuade any objections to our trap.

It was just as well that I did so. When the first man out of the tunnel realized that we were there, he started to yell for his companion to go back. My order to "halt or be shot" dissuaded the second fellow from retreating, and they both raised their hands in submission. Holmes looked down the tunnel. Seeing no light, he determined that these were the only two and ordered them back to the library, through the front door this time.

The two culprits were young, likely students in their late teen-aged years. Both were of average build and clean-shaven. One, a redhead with freckled face and hazel eyes, was doing well at hiding his anxiety. He exuded a confidence that seemed determined he could talk his way out of trouble. The other fellow, with short black hair and fearful brown eyes, was shaking with nerves. Holmes sat them down in O'Hare's office and sent me up to get the rest of our party.

When we came back down, Professor Muncy immediately confronted the boys by name, "Colm. Walter. What have you two been up to? Was Frederick with you?"

Colm, the redhead and obvious leader of this little pack, replied, "Just the two of us Professor. Freddy didn't have the stomach for it tonight."

"The stomach for what?" ordered Hopkins, after introducing himself as an Inspector from Scotland Yard. Walter, the timid fellow, buried his head in his hands at this revelation, then looked up and blurted out at his companion, "I told you it was too soon! Freddy was right! We should have waited until the heat died down."

"We didn't mean no harm, sir," he said, answering Hopkins. "It was just a joke."

"You broke into my library to play a joke!" cried out O'Hare, incensed at the gall of the two youngsters. "The night after a murder?"

"Murder!" cried Walter. "Oh my God! Colm, what did you drag me into?"

Colm, not quite so cocky now, tried to be defiant, but his voice betrayed his fear at this revelation. "We didn't know anything about a murder! We thought Coach Douglas had a heart attack or tripped and hit his head. We just wanted to give the superstitious folk more gossip by moving around old Osbert's mannequin. You know, pretending the ghost was still out and about and maybe responsible."

Holmes, who had been oddly quiet, had been observing the scene and finally spoke up, "Just where were you boys last night, around ten, when the library closed."

Walter rushed to speak, "I was at home, sir! You can ask my parents. I didn't have anything to do with what happened to Dean Douglas."

The detective turned his steel grey eyes on Colm and the boy answered, a little more confidently now, "I was over at Freddy's house 'til near eleven. His parents can vouch for that. His father talked me into joining a family card game."

"And after that?"

"Straight home, sir. I live right next door to Freddy. It's over on Southern Way near St. Edward's Church, about a mile east of here."

Holmes ascertained that the boys had been pulling this prank for two years now, ever since they started attending the school. Then he asked, "How did you find the secret panel and the tunnel?"

Walter started to answer, but Colm jumped in and confessed, "I did it. I snuck into the kitchen one day to see if I could find something to eat and went into the pantry. I went to light the lantern and when I lit my match it flickered like there was some bit of wind. I checked around and found the passage."

The look on Walter's face indicated that this was not at all the truth, but a glare from his companion dissuaded him from contradicting the story. Holmes let it pass and finally asked, "Does anyone else know about it, besides you two and your friend Frederick? Have you seen signs of anyone else using it?"

"Just the three of us is all," replied the redhead. "We swore each other to secrecy. I've never seen anything that looked like anyone else had been in there for a long time."

"Is that right, Walter?" asked the detective. "How about you? Have you seen signs of anyone else using it?"

The lad cocked his head to one side and said, "No, sir. I wasn't looking for any such signs, so there may have been. But, if so, it weren't obvious."

"*Wasn't* obvious," corrected O'Hare. The librarian side of him automatically reacting to improper grammar.

Holmes asked a few more questions, then turned the boys over to Hopkins, who enlisted Professor Muncy's help to take the boys to their respective homes and verify their alibis. My companion and I stayed with O'Hare to discuss the matter.

He broke into a coughing fit and we retreated to the pantry for some water. Sitting at the table there, Holmes waited for the elderly man to settle and then asked, "Does Colm, or any of the others, have older brothers who attended here?"

"Why, yes. Colm's older brother, Devon, graduated from here about four years ago. Why?"

"Were there any incidents or ghost sightings during the time that he was in attendance?" asked the detective.

O'Hare raised his eyes to the ceiling in thought as he searched his memory, then lowered his head to face us, "Actually there were, as I recall. During Devon's graduation year, there were a handful of incidents. A few times there were books piled on the tables with Sir Osbert's mantle thrown over them. At least twice it was reported that someone had seen a ghostly figure in the second floor windows late at night. One time all the old Latin bibles were laid out upon a table, every one turned to the 23rd Psalm, and Osbert's shield had been taken off the wall and laid atop them, as if protecting them from something."

Holmes nodded, "Any activity of that sort recently?"

O'Hare shook his head, "Just the movement of the mannequin on some nights, like tonight. Though I did find Sir Osbert's broadsword on the floor one time. Next to his shield on the third floor. Between the shield and the wall. Usually it's on the first floor, with his armor."

Holmes pondered that a moment, "Just out of curiosity, which direction was the sword pointing?"

"It was perpendicular to the shield, aimed at the wall with the point right up against the paneling."

"Odd, but not impossible. When was this?"

"It was there on the Monday morning, after the Saturday we found Bass' body."

Holmes made a note of that, then declared as he rose to leave, "I believe we've gleaned enough for one evening, Watson. Just one more thing, Mr. O'Hare. Where did Mr. Douglas go to church?"

## Chapter VI

The next morning, Holmes insisted that I join him for Sunday services at St. Chad's Church. We arrived early and found many parishioners outside, discussing one of two subjects: The death of Clifton Douglas, or the celebration preparations for the dedication of St. Chad's as a parish church. Apparently the following month there was to be an official recognition as a parish in its own right, and no longer the daughter church of Dagenborn Parish of The Church of England.

Naturally our interests lay in the discussions and theories regarding the latest victim in the library. To obtain as much information as possible, we split up and attempted to overhear as many conversations as feasible. In an effort not to be inundated with questions, Holmes had continued his disguise from the previous night and told anyone who spoke to him that he was just a businessman passing through.

In this manner, he was able to circulate rather freely. I, on the other hand, concentrated my efforts around those folks who were comforting the widow Douglas who, in spite of her mourning attire and veil, seemed quite attractive and a bit younger than her husband. I heard many condolences, but also whispered remarks behind her back that seemed to reinforce what we had gleaned about her husband's reputation. Some even went so far as to speculate that it was a male relative or friend of a spurned student who had done him in.

When the bell tolled for everyone to enter, Holmes and I drifted back toward each other and happened upon Orson O'Hare. He greeted me warmly, but didn't recognize my companion until Holmes spoke and requested that he not use his name. The Librarian followed suit and merely said, "I did not recognize you, sir. Welcome to St. Chad's." As they shook hands, I saw Holmes inspecting the man in that surreptitious manner of his and I followed suit, though I am not nearly so observant as my friend. The only difference I saw in O'Hare was him being in his Sunday best clothes and wearing a fine gold watch with some sort of medallion on the fob and an ornate ring on his finger. We entered together and Holmes, in spite of the circumstances, was in fine voice for the hymns. Afterward we bid O'Hare farewell and went off to a nearby pub, where we had agreed to meet Hopkins for lunch.

The inspector had not accompanied us to church that morning, having to report to the Yard. Now he was back and anxious to hear if we had learned anything. I repeated what I had shared with Holmes about rumours of infidelity and revenge, and then my companion spoke.

"As a general consensus, Dean Douglas was treated with respect for his office and his record as the rugby coach. However, the man himself seemed to have fallen short of being held in esteem. Many appear to feel sorry for Mrs. Douglas, more for putting up with his philandering all these years than for losing her husband. Some exhibited happiness that she is now free to pursue a more worthy spouse, for she is well-liked among the parishioners."

"What does that do for your theory of the crime, Mr. Holmes?" asked Hopkins.

"Certainly it presents a possible motive," answered the detective. "Not one that connects this killing with Bass, and I am loathe to separate the two as yet. I should like to call upon the widow this afternoon and would prefer to do so in an official capacity, rather than appear as some interloper upon her mourning. Would you be amenable to come with us at three o'clock, Inspector?"

It was agreed upon, and at three we were at a neat Tudor home in Portland Gardens, just north of St. Chad's Park. We were greeted at the door by a strapping fellow of nearly six feet in height. We recognized him as the man who had escorted the widow Douglas to church that morning. From what we had overheard, we knew this to be her brother.

"Yes, gentlemen? May I help you?" he asked, in a tone that clearly conveyed he would brook no superfluous intrusion upon his sister's mourning. This, being an official visit, caused Hopkins to speak for us as he held up his identification.

"Good day, sir. I am Inspector Hopkins of Scotland Yard. This is Sherlock Holmes and Dr. Watson. We would like to ask Mrs. Douglas a few questions so that we might complete the official report on her husband's death."

"Can't this wait, Inspector? My sister has had a very trying day."

Before Hopkins could answer, Holmes spoke up, "Perhaps you could answer the majority of our questions, sir? Then the intrusion upon your sister would be minimal."

The brother looked back over his shoulder, then acquiesced, "Very well. We can talk in the dining room." He let us in, showed us the way, then left us momentarily to inform his sister what he was doing so she could rest. When he returned, he sat at the head of the table with Holmes and me on one side and Hopkins on the other. "My wife is seeing to Helen's needs for now, but I'd like to hurry this along. The undertaker is coming by at four to go over funeral arrangements."

The inspector had his notebook out, as did I, and he asked, "First of all, what is your name, sir?"

"Sherman. Calvin Sherman."

"And where do you live?"

"Enfield. I'm a design engineer for the Royal Small Arms Factory there in Lea Valley."

"When did you arrive in town?"

"I received a telegram from Helen around noon yesterday. My wife and I arrived on the four o'clock train. Why all these questions about me? What do you really want to know?"

"Just being thorough, Mr. Sherman. We need to account for everyone's whereabouts at the time of the death."

"You're making this sound like a murder investigation. Are you saying Cliff didn't die by accident?"

Holmes answered that in a soft voice, "The Coroner's Report leaves some room for interpretation. Are you aware of any enemies that your brother-in-law may have cultivated?"

Sherman leaned back in his chair, his hands on the edge of the table, then looked up at the ceiling momentarily. Finally he bent forward, hands clasped in front him as his chin hovered above them. Keeping his voice low he replied, "If you've been investigating a possible crime, then I'm sure you have heard rumours of infidelity. I confronted Cliff on this very matter some months ago. He assured me that, while there have been some female students exhibiting infatuations toward him over the years, he had never responded and was absolutely faithful to Helen. I believed he was sincere. I also made it plain to him that, should it prove otherwise, he would answer to me."

"Was there a reason for your skepticism?" asked Holmes.

He looked toward the door and then back to us before he replied, "Helen was one of those students fifteen years ago."

In my mind, that solved the reason for her youthful appearance. She must have been at least ten years younger than Douglas.

Hopkins, without judgement, took up the official inquiry and enquired, "For the record, Mr. Sherman, where were you on Friday night?"

Our host stared at the inspector, "I understand you must ask the question, sir. However, I assure you, I would not make my sister a widow. Cliff may have found himself requiring substantial medical attention after the thrashing I would have given him, but he would still be alive. As to my whereabouts, my wife and I were visiting neighbors for dinner and an evening of whist."

Hopkins took that down, then asked one more question, "Are you aware of any dealings that Douglas' may have had with the student who died in the library two months ago, Aloysius Bass?"

"I don't know if I ever heard the name. I just heard that one of the rugby players had died from a fall off a book ladder. Do you think there's a connection?"

"Just an odd coincidence, and I detest coincidence," replied the inspector, who then looked at Holmes. My friend merely nodded and then said, "I believe that's all we require from you. Mr. Sherman. If we could just ask your sister one or two questions, we'll wrap this up."

"I would ask that you not bring up any questions of infidelity, Inspector. This is hardly the time to make her face that cruel inference."

Holmes spoke up, "If I may, Inspector? Mr. Sherman, I merely have two questions for your sister and I assure you that neither will infer any misbehavior on her husband's part."

Sherman agreed, and when we were led to the parlour where the widow and her sister-in-law were quietly drinking tea, Holmes took the lead, after introductions.

"Mrs. Douglas, I assure you that we do not wish to intrude upon your troubles. We have two questions that will assist the doctor in his final report, to enable your husband to be released for burial."

She sat up a little straighter and dabbed her tear-streaked cheek. With a sniffle she bravely replied, "Yes, Mr. Holmes, what is it?"

"Firstly, has your husband seemed unduly worried about anything lately – any nervousness, or has he seemed distracted?"

"No, sir. Just the opposite. He has been quite cheerful. His team is doing well and he was looking forward to the summer recess and a trip we were planning to the Continent."

"Very good, madam. Just one other point: Has his health been quite regular? No dizzy spells or incidents showing a lack of coordination? Dropping things, tripping, or losing his balance?"

"He was in the peak of health, Mr. Holmes. He was quite vigorous and of good stamina."

Here her voice broke, and she could not help but let out a sob. I spoke up, knowing that Holmes had his answers. "Thank you, Mrs. Douglas. We just needed to rule out the possibility of any medical symptoms of his brain or heart. I am confident now that tripping on the rug would have been accidental and not due to any medical condition. With your permission, we shall take our leave. You have our deepest condolences, madam."

In her state, she merely waved us away and we left. Holmes suggested another trip to the library to re-examine the scene of each crime. Hopkins said we could pick up Douglas' keys from the Coroner, but Holmes waved aside the suggestion. "No need to bother the man on a Sunday afternoon. I suggest we enter by way of the secret tunnel." Noting the look on the inspector's face, he amended his statement, "That is, I shall enter through the tunnel, and let you and Watson in by the front door."

When Holmes let us in, the first thing I noticed was that the suit of armor had been moved to the opposite side of the foyer. I queried Holmes, who speculated that it had likely been moved by the boys as part of their prank to continue the legend of the ghost of Sir Osbert. Then I pointed out that the sword was missing. "Remember, O'Hare told us the sword had been moved before. Up to the top floor next to the shield."

"It's not upstairs," said Holmes.

"How can you know that?" asked Hopkins

Holmes pointed across the room, "Look there!"

We followed his gesture and there, in front of the door to the Librarian's office, was Sir Osbert's broadsword, driven into the floor like a stake. We walked over and Holmes knelt to examine it. The blade was facing the doorway and the handle was angled at about twenty degrees toward the front door. The blade itself was clean and polished bright. Holmes judged that it was sunk about two inches into the floorboards. It had struck about a foot in front of O'Hare's door, directly in the center between the jambs.

"It would require someone of considerable strength to drive the sword that deep, especially at that angle," noted Hopkins.

"Not necessarily," responded Holmes. "The angle actually points to the method. This was not held in two hands and thrust straight downward, as one might expect. The fact that it is on an angle indicates the wielder circled it around in a throwing motion and built up momentum so its's own weight would add to the centrifugal force and allow for deeper penetration. The culprit could have added even more momentum by getting a running start."

"But why? And why here, at the Librarian's door?" asked the inspector.

Holmes responded as he yanked the broadsword from the oak floor, which took considerable effort, I might add. "At the moment, my primary concern is *who*. Certainly knowing *why* could help us narrow that down, but, speculating upon motive for such an unusual act would be too time-consuming without further data. Let us consider what we do know. Besides the three of us, and now O'Hare and Muncy, we know that Colm, Walter, and Frederick know about the passage and could have gotten in here."

I spoke up and offered, "I'm sure Colm and Walter are being kept under strict observation by their parents after last night. So that leaves Frederick."

Holmes tilted his head, "That we know of. I'm convinced that Colm was lying about discovering the passage himself. I think it much more plausible that the secret has been passed down from form to form, and that Colm's brother, Devon, likely told him about it."

"That would certainly account for all the reported sightings over the years," said Hopkins.

"Yes, and the fact that the tunnel seems well-maintained, unlike some passages that have lain unused for centuries. For now, however, Frederick is our primary suspect for this act. But that does not address the larger crime. Who is our killer – or killers?"

That piqued my interest, for I had only been thinking in the singular, "You think the boys may have ganged up on Bass and Douglas, Holmes?"

"A consideration we cannot discount at this time. I believe a visit to this Frederick fellow is in order."

The three of us, after checking the notes that we had taken from the student files, made our way to the home of Frederick Grayson. His parents bore out his alibi as having been home with them and his friend Colm on the night Douglas was killed. Still, Inspector Hopkins used his authority to insist that we be allowed to speak with the lad alone.

Freddy, as he was referred to by his friends and parents, was very tall. I would put him at six-feet-and-four-inches. He was very thin and seemingly non-athletic. I should say he was still growing into his height, like a young colt awkwardly finding it's footing before developing into a thoroughbred.

We met with the lad in his room, where he folded his spindly arms and legs into a chair while we stood above him. Hopkins opened the questioning.

"We have heard from your parents and witnesses that you were here last Friday evening and didn't go to the library. Correct?"

The lad's Adam's apple bobbed as he nodded and put great effort into not wringing his hands – which was only partially successful. Hopkins continued.

"But you have been in the library at times when it was not open to the public by way of the secret tunnel."

His eyes widened at the fact that we were aware of the tunnel, then he bowed his head and quietly said, "Yes, sir."

"Have you ever gone into the library through the tunnel on your own, or were you always in the company of Colm and Walter?"

"Oh, I'd never go in there by myself, sir. Not with the ghost of Sir Osbert walkin' about."

Holmes jumped in, "Come now, Master Frederick. Surely you've never seen such an apparition?"

The boy cocked his head and thought before answering, "Well, no, I haven't actually seen him. But there have been plenty of times when he made his presence known. Moving things about and such. One time, when we went to leave, his shield was on the floor leaning up against the passage door, like it was trying to block our way."

Holmes pursed his lips and asked, "When you made these little jaunts into the library, did you always stay together, or did you separate from each other to perform different mischiefs?"

"Usually we stayed together, but sometimes we split up, though I always stayed with Wally while Colm went off by himself."

"How long have you been engaged in these little mischiefs?"

"Since we met up in our first year. Once we got to be friends, Colm showed me and Wally the tunnel, and we would sneak in and just move things around or put books out of order. We never damaged anything."

The detective nodded and then stated, "And it was Colm's brother, Devon, who told him about the tunnel. Does anyone else know?"

The lad seemed a bit taken aback by that. "Colm told you that? He made us swear an oath that we would never reveal who told us and we would have to all agree who we would pass that knowledge on to after we graduated." He seemed crestfallen, "Well, now that you know, I guess the game is up."

"Just one more question," said Holmes. "Do you have any opinion as to who might wish to kill Aloysius Bass or Dean Douglas?"

"Kill!" exclaimed the young student. "I thought they both died in accidental falls. You don't think we had anything to do with that do you? Oh, my God! No!"

He started to stand as if he needed to be upright to defend himself, but Holmes placed his hands on the lad's shoulders and kept him seated.

"It's all right, my boy. Calm down. We are not accusing you. I just wish your opinion, if you have one."

After a few deep breaths, Frederick put his head in his hands as he thought. After several seconds he looked up at us and spoke. "I don't know about Dean Douglas, but there were rumours about Bass and some girl. She left the school in the middle of the term last year, and I think I heard that she died. Maybe someone was getting revenge?"

The three of us looked at each other at this revelation. Holmes nodded at Hopkins, and the inspector told the young fellow that we were finished for now, but he was not to discuss our conversation with anyone.

After we left the Grayson home, we decided to split up as we did the previous evening and see what gossip mongers had to say about this tidbit of information. When we rendezvoused back at the hotel, we gathered in Holmes's room to share our findings.

Conflicting testimony seemed to rule the evening, including a few theories about the ghost and other parties who may have had a motive. One thing that we had heard in common was about the death the previous year of "the Lancaster girl". The first name varied from Abbey to Angel to Virginia, all religious connotations, but no confirmation as to the fact. Some blamed Bass, while others thought Douglas was involved. After we had discussed our findings, Holmes suggested we look into her school records in the morning after he "smoked a pipe or two upon it tonight".

However, the next morning brought an early message from O'Hare. He wished to see Holmes and me, in the Library immediately – without Inspector Hopkins.

## Chapter VII

Holmes made no mention of this message to the inspector, as Hopkins received a telegram that morning, requiring him to return to Scotland Yard immediately regarding another, more urgent, case.

"Let me know if you find anything, Mr. Holmes," he stated as he bid us goodbye on his way to the train station. Holmes and I then proceeded to the Library, instead of the college records room as planned, to see what was so urgent in the elderly gentleman's mind.

Entering the library, we were surprised to see that the sword had been returned to the position where we had found it the day before, impaled into the floor at O'Hare's office door. We walked around it and looked in upon the man.

O'Hare leaned back in the chair behind his desk and bid us enter. There was no panic on his face, as he simply took off his spectacles and nonchalantly cleaned them. He placed them back on his face and looked at my companion, "What took you so long, Mr. Holmes, and was it really necessary to impale a sword at my door?" Then he added, "Please, both of you, do sit down."

I was certainly confused at that statement. Holmes, however, immediately took a seat and I followed suit. Holmes replied to the librarian in a conversational tone.

"To answer your second question first, Mr. O'Hare, I did not plant the sword in the floor at your door. We and the inspector found it that way yesterday afternoon. I believe Colm's older brother, Devon, may be responsible, but I have not had the time to test that theory.

"Secondly, I do not make accusations until my deductions leave me no choice. While I did not eliminate you completely, I did not consider

194

you a strong suspect at first, due to your age difference with the victims. You also passed my little test with the lantern from the pantry. However, you did slip and say 'murder' when we confronted the boys Saturday night. Even now, while I have no doubt as to your involvement in these killings, I have been only able to speculate on your motives. It is for this reason that I am glad that Inspector Hopkins was unable to join us. I should like you to speak freely, sir, without fear of the official police taking down what you say to use against you."

The elderly gentleman gazed toward the ceiling and took a deep breath, followed by a vicious cough, which took some time to recover from before answering. "So, the sword wasn't your doing? I thought it a message meant to warn me you were on to me. That's why I sent for you, to tell my story before it was too late. I didn't think Devon was in town, but I suppose he may have come home for the weekend." He stopped and then gave a snort of laughter, which set off a long drawn out coughing fit.

Finally, he was able to speak again, "Hah! 'Tis probably the ghost of old Osbert telling me he's coming for me. It matters little what you do, Mr. Holmes. My time on this mortal coil will likely be at an end long before a trial and sentence can be carried out."

"Tuberculosis?" I speculated sympathetically, as I observed him from a medical viewpoint.

His Irish heritage slipped through his speech as he answered, "Aye, Dr. Watson. Six months, maybe less they tell me, is all I have. T'was time for me to act, while I still had the strength for it."

Holmes had crossed his legs and steepled his fingers beneath his chin during this exchange. Now he folded his hands across his waistcoat and quietly spoke. "You have taken on the role of vigilante, meting out punishment where others have failed to act. But were their deaths fit for their crimes?"

"Death was too good for them!" said the librarian in a cold, measured voice that belied his normal demeanor. "But I didn't have the power to sentence them to long living deaths in prison, and Caldwell would never bring shame upon his alma mater by even investigating a student or faculty member."

"We've heard rumours about Bass, but why Douglas?" I queried, fearing the answer even as I asked, for O'Hare's wrath even now seemed to ooze from his pores like heat from a fever.

"You've discovered Bass' reputation among the maidens of our fair hamlet, no doubt. While most have suffered his ultimate rejection in silence after being courted by him for a time, there was one lass, a poor innocent creature, whom he could not win over by his winning looks and smooth tongue. Angelina Lancaster was her name, and a fitting one it was, for she had the looks and gracious heart of an Angel of God. Her father had died when she was quite young and she had no brothers. I was probably the closest thing she had to a male protector, for she spent hours each week here in the library. Not only was she learning on her own, but also reading to younger children and helping them. I've no doubt she would have become a fine teacher.

"But that bastard Bass would not take 'no' for an answer. One day, last spring, he cornered her alone after school, overpowered the poor creature, and dragged her to a cloakroom to have his way with her. She was too delicate to have left any mark upon him of her struggles to get away, and when she reported it, not only did Bass deny it, but Douglas swore that his star player was practicing with him on the other side of the campus at the time. He was just as guilty as that smug bastard, Bass. Caldwell completed the travesty when he refused to press charges and admonished her for her lies.

"Well, gentlemen, you can imagine how she felt. She could not return to school to face her attacker in the halls every day. There wasn't money enough from her mother's meager income to go away to another school. Then, the cruelest blow of all hit her. She found herself to be with child."

"The poor girl!" I exclaimed.

The elderly gentleman closed his eyes and bowed his head upon his hand propped up by the arm of his chair, his thumb and fingers pressed to his eyes. It was several seconds before he could speak. At last he looked up, eyes on the verge of tears.

"It was too much for her. The thought of bearing that monster's child was more than she could take. They found her body, three miles from here, drowned in Fairlop Waters. A suicide note was left in her bedroom, again accusing Bass, and again it was ignored by the Magistrate."

"So, you took matters into your own hands," suggested Holmes.

"Something had to be done!" cried O'Hare, slamming his fist on the arm of his chair. Another coughing fit hit him and it was several seconds before he regained his composure and continued, "Had I still owned my old service revolver, I would have shot the beast on sight! Instead, I concentrated on seeing to the needs of Angelina's mother, who was so distraught she eventually needed to be admitted to an asylum."

"Yes," commented Holmes. "I had discerned that you were former military by your bearing, and the academy ring you wear on Sundays. Your watch fob indicates some time spent in the Orient. I presume that is where you learned your hand-to-hand combat skills?"

"Correct, Mr. Holmes, I was stationed in Hong Kong for two years and was able to incorporate Chinese fighting skills into my training. It has always helped me to triumph over larger opponents. I was hoping the

196

'accidents' I staged would cover up that fact, but you were too persistent. You and that Inspector Hopkins."

"Why kill them in the library?" I asked. "Surely that was your greatest risk."

Holmes replied to that, "You should know the answer to that, Watson. How many times have you brought up the ghost of Sir Osbert? Even among skeptics like myself, the reputation of a location can effect perception. Accidents can happen due to an as-yet to be explained condition, other than the ghosts who get blamed for it. Tricks of the light or uneven surfaces or the like. Tell me, Mr. O'Hare – at least some of the recent sightings of Sir Osbert's ghost were the result of your doing, were they not?"

The librarian allowed himself a faint smirk as he answered. "Not at first, Mr. Holmes. There have been unexplained phenomena over the centuries, of course, but when Colm and his gang started the latest rash of events. I merely took up the mantle, so to speak, and perpetuated the myth."

"Appropriate," responded Holmes, "as the blue velvet mantle of The Order of the Garter is a key piece of the wardrobe on the mannequin of Sir Osbert's likeness. Its placement on a rolling stand must have made it quite easy to move it past the windows with strategically placed candlelight to fool observers outside the building. If anyone who had a key passed by, you could merely duck into the secret passage, emerge outside, and appear to arrive with all the other curiosity seekers."

The old man shook his head, "Only once, sir. On all other occasions I merely went home and waited to be called upon, thus establishing my alibi. Finally, the time came when conditions were right to strike. I took note of Bass' struggles as he studied for upcoming examinations that would keep him off the rugby team if he failed. He was oblivious of my knowledge of Angelina and his crime, and was eager to accept my offer of assistance to help him prepare for the exams. We agreed to meet one night at closing time, so that he could maintain his reputation as being non-studious. I had placed books he needed on the top shelf, requiring him to ascend the ladder. As I stood beneath, I could barely contain my anxiety as he came down, step by step, until he reached that fateful rung where my hands could wrench his feet away and make him fall. He cried out on his way down, but this library is deadly quiet, as you know. He hit his head on the floor, though still conscious when I fell upon him, driving my knee into his kidney to knock the wind from him. I wrapped my hands around his skull and whispered Angelina's name into his ear. It was the last thing he heard before the fatal twist was applied to his neck."

197

"I presume you used a similar pretense with Douglas," commented my companion. "I would wager that you also incorporated the use of Sir Osbert's blue mantle in your attack, and that was how the threads came to be under his fingernails."

"Yes," answered the librarian. "I suggested meeting at the end of the day, and I made sure that everyone was gone and the doors locked. I told him I thought I knew the real killer of Bass and hinted it was one of his other players. I arranged to meet him on the third floor where I could expound my theory at the scene of the crime. He was sitting at the table when I arrived, carrying the cloth, thinking it could give me an advantage over his greater size. He had turned to greet me when I tossed a book onto the table as I came up from behind his shoulder. When he turned back to look at the volume, I threw the mantle over his head and jumped on his back with all my weight, using my hands to force his head onto the table's edge and repeated my cry of Angelina's name as I finished him off.

"I spoke her name, so that they would have that flash of memory as their last before death. The final thought that would be ever present as they stood before Heaven's Judgement Seat."

I chose not to question him regarding his own thoughts of his position on that looming day, for I was sure he saw himself as God's instrument of justice. To be honest, I'm not so sure I wouldn't have done the same in his shoes.

Holmes and I sat in silence. I felt as if I had just sat through a moving performance of the Scottish Play [6]. O'Hare, himself, seemed likewise emotionally drained. My friend sat perfectly still, deep in thought as he closed his eyes.

At last he opened his eyes, stared grimly at the elder man and spoke, "There are yet two more people on your list."

The librarian lowered his head in a slow nod, "Just one, Mr. Holmes. The Chancellor is a senile old fool who thinks The War of the Roses is still going on, and that his Yorkist background automatically condemns all Lancasters as the enemy. He needs to be removed from office, but his mind is too deteriorated to hold responsible. I do wish, however, that I could have remained at liberty long enough to exact justice on that scoundrel of a Magistrate, Caldwell."

Holmes then stood and made an extraordinary statement, "If I may elicit your word of honour not to take any more vigilante actions, Mr. O'Hare, will you allow me to handle the matter?"

"Holmes!" I cried in protest as I also rose.

The detective turned to me, "Watson, dear fellow, do you not agree that this poor man is not a danger to society? That his only 'crime' has been to render justice where none had been served?"

"But, *murder*, Holmes?" I questioned.

He placed his hand upon my shoulder, "Put yourself in his place, my friend. What if the victim had been your poor Mary?"

My right hand automatically stole to my left ring finger, where I could still feel the indentations left by my wedding band, now a cherished keepsake in my jewelry box. The pain of her illness and death of but two years before, still lingered strong in my memories. His suggestion wrenched at my heart and I could not deny my empathy for O'Hare's plight.

"What are you proposing, Holmes?" I sighed.

He clapped my shoulder and turned back toward the librarian, "We do not mention this conversation to anyone. If Hopkins gets there on his own, then you will be left to your own defence, sir. At present my deductions are based on conjecture, with little physical evidence to prove them as fact – merely as a possible scenario, which is hardly worth reporting, as it would not be enough for a court case. Consider also, Magistrate Caldwell is highly unlikely to bring any matter to court that would taint the reputation of the college. Under current conditions, our accusations would fall on deaf ears.

"However, if you will trust me, I have connections with no little influence in governmental affairs. If Caldwell is as corrupt as you make him out to be, I am sure that investigations will prove that and be the ruin of him. He will not likely be put to death, unless there is some heinous act of which we are not aware, but he will be disgraced and quite likely imprisoned. A more suitable lingering punishment than a quick death, would you agree?"

"If only I could live to see it," rasped O'Hare, as another coughing fit overtook him.

"I cannot promise that," replied Holmes. "The wheels of justice often turn slowly. But even if not swift, I can guarantee they will be sure."

The gentleman stood and shook the detective's hand, "Then I will take you at your word, Mr. Holmes. Frankly, I'm not sure I have the strength for another confrontation, so I will leave it in your capable hands."

## Chapter VIII

O'Hare's rapidly declining health, with its increasingly violent coughing fits, served to eliminate him from even crossing Inspector Hopkins mind as a possible suspect in the two deaths. Holmes steered him away from consideration of other suspects, citing insufficient evidence to make a case.

Finally, much to Hopkins' and Dr. Palmer's chagrin, the cases were left to stand as "Death by Misadventure", but were not officially closed, in case more evidence came to fore.

By the following October, Holmes and his government sources, (I suspect his brother Mycroft played no small part), had obtained enough evidence for Robert Cadlwell's arrest on charges of both receiving bribes and judicial misconduct. I arranged an ambulance to be present at the scene, so that Orson O'Hare could witness the Magistrate being hauled away in handcuffs to a police van and driven back to London to await trial.

The Librarian passed away a few days later. Content in knowing Holmes had kept his promise, his last words were a quote from Sir Francis Bacon: "*Revenge triumphs over death*". Caldwell was found guilty and sentenced to ten years in Newgate Prison.

It was less than six months later when Holmes and I read of the former magistrate's death at the hands of another prisoner – someone whom he had sentenced to that same institution years before.

The justice which O'Hare had sought for Angelina had come full circle.

## Postscript

As to the ghost of Sir Osbert Lansbury, there are still sightings from time to time, even though the tunnel has been sealed. While Holmes was satisfied his case was complete, once we had the Librarian's confession, I did a bit more investigating on my own and found that Colm's older brother, Devon, was *not* in town on the day the sword was planted in front of O'Hare's door. There is always the possibility that, like Colm, Devon had associates who may have done the deed. I, however, having grown up with ghost stories in my Scottish youth and witnessing mysteries of the Middle East during my army days, am inclined to a more open mind than my friend, the scientifically logical, Sherlock Holmes.

*"There are more things in heaven and earth, Horatio, than are dreamt of in your philosophy."*
– Hamlet to Horatio, *Hamlet* (1.5.167-8),

# NOTES

1 – "The Solitary Cyclist" (published in 1903)

2 – University College, Bristol was the first higher education college in England to allow mixed education for men and women in 1876

3 – The Diogenes Club was founded by Sherlock Holmes's elder brother Mycroft. Speaking was absolutely forbidden, except in the Stranger's Room, where the two brothers would occasionally meet to discuss a case.

4 – Watson describes Holmes as "rather over six feet" in *A Study in Scarlet*. Based on the Sidney Paget drawings of Holmes and Watson, the doctor was not much shorter, perhaps five-foot-ten or eleven.

5 – The quote appears in the "The Boscombe Valley Mystery" (published in 1891)

6 – Shakespeare's *MacBeth* is often referred to in this fashion, due to superstitions surrounding the play and fear of a curse coming upon anyone who speaks its name aloud.

# The Adventure of the Sugar Merchant
## by Stephen Herczeg

It was early one cold autumn morning that Holmes and I were dragged into one of our strangest cases ever, an adventure involving Haitian voodoo and, of all things, zombies.

I was in the sitting room of 221b Baker Street on that cold morning, the fire ablaze to strip the chill from the air. I had finished off a wonderful breakfast provided by our landlady, Mrs. Hudson, and was relaxing with a second cup of coffee and the morning papers when I came across a late article, slotted in between the international affairs and finance sections. It detailed the account of a fire in a warehouse down in Canary Wharf. Many of the city's fire brigades were called, but their efforts were to no avail. The warehouse succumbed and crumbled under its own weight in the late hours of the previous evening. The article had been included so late that there was no more than the scarcest of details.

It was at that point that my erstwhile associate Sherlock Holmes arose from his slumber and sauntered into the sitting room, resplendent in a smoking jacket and looking quite awake for one who had arrived home in the early hours.

"Ah, Holmes," I said, "finally joining the living, I see."

Holmes smiled and helped himself to a coffee. "Obviously you are aware that I was home late."

I nodded.

"I was on the trail of someone that I had presumed to be involved in the affair of the disappearance of the eldest son of Lord Langley. Sadly, the trail went cold sometime in the wee hours of the morning. I returned home to re-invigorate myself for another long night ahead."

"A shame," I said. "Any other clews?"

He looked off into the distance through the window and absent-mindedly replied, "A few, but nothing substantial. The boy has simply disappeared from the face of the Earth."

He sipped his coffee and turned. Spying the open newspaper, he asked, "Anything exciting to relieve my mind of my disappointment?"

"A warehouse fire in Canary Wharf. Scant details. Could be arson. Could be an accident. Could be nothing really."

Holmes harrumphed, pursed his lips, sipped his coffee, and sat down in his easy chair. "Then I will cogitate further over the Lord's son." He placed the cup down, clasped his hands on his chest, and sat back, eyes closed. This was a natural meditative pose for him, or as I soon noticed, a comfortable pose where he could quickly drift off to sleep.

I smiled to myself and quietly finished the paper.

I snapped awake as the doorbell downstairs rang. I glanced across and saw that Holmes had left his chair and was nowhere to be seen. The clock on the mantel told me it had been an hour since I watched Holmes fall asleep.

I started to rise when Mrs. Hudson appeared at the doorway with Inspector Lestrade in tow. I shook the inspector's hand and thanked Mrs. Hudson. I also asked if she'd seen Holmes at all. She denied any knowledge of his leaving, so I hoped he was still on the premises. I led Lestrade into the sitting room, where it was a tad warmer. He shed his overcoat and gloves and placed them over the back of a chair.

"What brings you on this miserably cold day," I asked.

He looked a little embarrassed but went on with his request. "There's been a fire," he started.

"The warehouse?" I asked.

His eyes opened wide in surprise. I indicated the discarded paper on the settee. "There was a brief article in *The Times* this morning," I said, a wry smile on my lips.

"Ah, that would explain it," he said.

"What about the fire requires Holmes's involvement?" I queried, just as the man himself entered the room.

"Did I hear something about a fire?" he asked, "Not the warehouse fire that you mentioned, Watson?"

I nodded. "Seems to be."

Holmes indicated the seats and took his favourite chair. He sat back and looked at Lestrade across his steepled fingers. Lestrade sat and I made my way to the door to call down for coffee from Mrs. Hudson. I returned just as Lestrade began and sat down myself, a little flush of excitement within me. I always hoped that Lestrade would bring some case that piqued Holmes's interest.

He began to relate the events of the previous night. "You're quite right, it was a warehouse fire – a big one, down in Canary Wharf. Arson as far as we can tell. It burnt the entire place to the ground. The brigade got it under control quickly. We were lucky it didn't spread any further."

"Any suspects," I asked.

"Just one."

"Oh, well do you need us to help track him down?"

"No," he said. "No need for that."

203

"Why?" I responded.

"He's dead. They found him in the fire."

"Oh."

Holmes unsteepled his fingers as a question formed on his lips. "What makes him so remarkable that you needed to come here?"

Lestrade wiped his brow with a handkerchief. "It's two things. The first is we know he was the arsonist, because the flint box he used to light the fire was lying nearby."

"How very strange," I said.

"The other thing is, the Coroner reckons he's been dead for at least three days."

Lestrade's final comment urged the three of us to travel to the city morgue. There we found the coroner, Smithers, working away on the desiccated corpse of the poor unfortunate that had been found in the burnt-out warehouse. The poor man's hair had all but burnt off, and his face was blackened and slightly blistered. His hands were blackened, but the rest of his body was virtually untouched. From this observation, I assumed his clothing had taken the brunt of the flames.

The smell was horrendous, but Smithers had tried to temper it by placing small piles of rose petals around the room to release their fragrance. Holmes held any disgust at the smell in check and began to examine the corpse. He moved in a complete circle around the body, viewing it without touching. He hummed and murmured to himself, an indication that he was finding interesting observations.

"What's your opinion, Smithers?" he asked.

The coroner stood upright and thought for a moment. "He was in here three days ago," he said. "Same body, at the time he was in good condition, but now he's as you see him."

"How do you know it was the same body?" I asked.

Smithers moved around to the head. He pointed at a few wisps of unburned hair. "It's a male. The hair colour is the same. The height is the same. Weight is about the same, give or take what the fire took with it." He pointed at the corpse's mouth. A gold tooth gleamed dully from within the rictus grin. "Second upper pre-molar on the left has a gold cap. Not rare, but given the other features, it points to the same man." He nodded to a pile of scorched and burnt clothing on a nearby chair. "He's was also wearing the same clothing that he was when previously here."

Holmes was impressed. He peered at the gold tooth and the hair. "If this body was here three days ago, how did it get up and leave?"

Smithers turned to face him, his eyes glancing across to Lestrade who had obviously already asked this question. "He didn't. He wasn't here at the time. He was found down at the river's edge last Tuesday. The constables that brought him in said he was just another homeless person. His clothing said as much too. He was part of a group of men all found dead. Four in all. It was a very busy night."

He folded his arms and leaned against the autopsy table. "We've had recent instructions from the Health Ministry and Scotland Yard to process any vagrants as quickly as possible. The cold weather has started to run through the city's homeless population like the plague. Those in charge are worried that we don't have the resources to spend time on each homeless death."

His face grew grim. "I'm neither impressed or in favour of such actions, but I have my orders." He waved a hand over the dead man. "I performed a cursory examination – heartbeat, temperature, and ligature resistance – to make sure I could pronounce him dead. He was then taken to a local funeral parlour in preparation for cremation. How he was taken from there is a matter for them to explain."

"And you have no reason to suspect the man was still alive?" I asked.

Smithers gave me a withering look. "Doctor, you as well as anybody should know that someone presenting with no heartbeat, a sixty-degree body temperature, and *post mortem* ligature stiffness shows all the hallmarks of a dead man."

Holmes smiled. "I think he has you there, Watson."

I kept my mouth shut at the rebuke.

Holmes continued. "I think your assessment is quite correct, Smithers, and I must commend you for it. The man is obviously dead now. Whether he was dead previously is down to your observations and, given we were not present, we must accept them." He moved around the corpse, his hand on his chin as he contemplated. "The main problem is that I believe this man to be Dominic Langley, the son of Lord Byron Langley, fourth Earl of Northbridge."

"Good God!" I exclaimed. "How do you come to that?" I knew that Holmes had been on the trail of Dominic Langley for a number of days and had been frustrated at every turn.

"Same height, weight, hair, and eye colour. The evidence of the gold tooth seals the deal. Plus . . . ." He moved over to the pile of charred clothing and leafed through the items. "Dominic Langley had a strange compunction to eschew the trappings of his wealth and station and to seek the excitement of the lower classes. He would often wear the clothes of the street and reside amongst the vagrants down at the river bank."

Holmes turned back to stare at the corpse. "Though there is something that troubles me," he said. "Do you object, Smithers, if I conduct my own examination?"

Smithers turned towards Lestrade who nodded. "Not if the inspector doesn't mind," he replied.

Holmes moved around the body and gently picked up its right hand. He bent down and sniffed it. His nose wrinkled at whatever odour wafted from the digits. He repeated with the left hand then placed both at the body's side. He then moved across to a nearby table covered with instruments and picked up two pairs of forceps, a pair of cotton swabs, and a small ceramic bowl. He moved back to the corpse's head and gently prized the man's jaw apart. A sickening cracking sound issued. I assumed it was the tendons stretching beyond their current capabilities.

Holmes placed a swab between the tines of the forceps and pushed it deep into the poor man's mouth. He moved it about then pulled it out again. He withdrew his magnifying glass and examined the swab. "Hmm," he murmured. "Most interesting."

I moved over and stared through the glass at the swab. It was relatively clean, except for the last vestiges of saliva from the corpse. "Clean?" I posited.

"Yes. I had half-expected it to have traces of ash and soot on it."

"A natural assumption if the man was still alive during the blaze," he said. "He would have inhaled the soot as he drew his final breaths."

"Exactly, but there is no evidence."

"So he *was* dead?"

"One would presume such, but I smelt traces of turpentine on his fingers – a powerful accelerant used recently in other cases of arson around the city."

"Perhaps the arsonist was sending a message. Trying to lay blame on the dead man."

"That is one line of thought. There's also this." Holmes pointed out some more observations to me. "Watson, if you would notice: The skin that was covered by clothing is virtually untouched. A little dirty, probably from the fire, but not burnt or scorched in any meaningful way."

He picked up the other swab, dipped it in some water, and ran it across the corpse's cheek. It left a bright area of unblemished skin. "The skin on the man's face is likewise relatively untouched by the fire. There is a little blistering on his scalp where, I assume, burning embers settled to ignite some of his hair, but the rest was only discoloured by the falling ash." He picked up the corpse's right hand and examined the fingertips, murmuring to himself as well.

"What does it all mean?" I asked.

"His fingertips are damaged and scorched, as well as smelling of turpentine, but the rest of him is relatively unharmed. In my opinion, this man, Dominic Langley, simply set fire to part of the warehouse, then lay down in a clear area of the floor and awaited his fate."

I was taken aback. "But he was supposedly dead. How, and why, would anybody in their right mind do such a thing?"

"That is what we need to find out. It is sad to think that young Langley died in this way, and I feel that there is something more to his fate. He was a healthy young man, not one prone to die of exposure, so why did he present as dead in the first place? And then why was his body stolen from the crematory, if indeed he didn't walk out on his own? Then, how did he end up in the middle of a burning warehouse? I am perplexed, and these questions pose the next part of the mystery that we shall address," he finished.

The carriage dropped Holmes, Lestrade, and me outside of a wonderfully appointed four-storey Georgian mansion nestled in a quiet street near Grosvenor Square in Mayfair. Holmes made his way to the front door while I paid the cabbie. Lestrade looked a little out of sorts at the opulence of the area. I admit I felt a little awkward as well.

A well-dressed butler in full formal dress answered. Holmes murmured something that I failed to hear, and we were shown into the immaculately presented main foyer where the man took our hats and coats. He showed us into a nearby reception room to wait until our introductions were made to the master of the house. I moved around the room, relishing the richness of the furnishings and decorations.

"Remarkable," said Holmes looking over my shoulder, "how much wealth a simple thing as sugar can produce, isn't it?"

"What do you mean?"

"Lord Byron Langley is the single largest importer of sugar to the United Kingdom. His father, the third Earl of Northbridge, was ambassador to Jamaica during Lord Byron's childhood. He grew up amongst the rich West Indian culture and decided to stay once his father returned to England. He married Myra, a missionary's daughter, who sadly died during the birth of Dominic Langley."

"How sad," I remarked.

"Yes. Dominic was sent to England to be educated while Lord Byron grew the industry that his grandfather had bought into, and expanded it to include the importation of sugar to the United Kingdom. He returned only a couple of years ago. My understanding is that was to be with his son during his final years of college, with the intent that Dominic would eventually take over the business. All this will be a bit of a shock to him, I imagine," he added.

As I was about to ask further questions, the butler returned and spoke. "Lord Byron will see you now. If you would follow me."

All three of us duly followed and were let into an ornately furnished study, with bookshelves lining all four walls and a massive oak desk in the centre. Lord Byron was a rather tall and rotund man, with a large beard and the look of someone that enjoyed life to the fullest. He walked around his desk and took Holmes's hand in both of his own.

"Mr. Holmes!" he said. "Welcome, welcome," He turned towards Lestrade and me. "And these gentlemen would be?"

Holmes introduced the both of us, then his face turned grave. "I suggest you take a seat Lord Byron," he said. "I do not bring pleasant news."

Lord Byron's face dropped, a touch of fear flushed across his visage. "It's Dominic, isn't it?" he asked as he took a seat.

Holmes nodded. "Yes, I'm afraid it is," he said. "Very early this morning, your son was found in the remains of a burnt-out warehouse. I'm afraid that he had passed."

Lord Byron's face turned to shock and dismay. "Oh, my," he said. "How?"

"We are unsure at this stage, but it appears to be smoke inhalation from the fire."

Lord Byron looked off into the distance for a moment and murmured to himself. "Silly boy," he murmured. "What have you been up to?"

"I beg your pardon, sir," Holmes asked. "I didn't quite catch the question."

Lord Byron looked up in surprise. "Sorry. Nothing. Just thinking out loud. Do you have any clews as to why he was there?"

"None. I was hoping you might know, but didn't want to press, as I assumed the news would be upsetting enough for you."

Lord Byron took a deep breath to calm himself. He let it out in a relaxed and controlled way before speaking. "I won't lie. It is distressing, though part of me believed that Dominic's wild behaviour might result in such an eventuality." He stood up and strode around the room, waving his arms as he spoke. "I gave him everything. The best schools. The riches of Croesus. He has never wanted for anything, but he preferred to turn his back on all that at times to live with the down-and-outs in the slums. To learn what it was like to have nought, he would tell me."

He looked out a side window for a moment, gathering his thoughts. "I had assumed it would be in one of these slums that he would meet his end. Was it at the waterfront down Southwark way?" he said, turning back to face us and pressing up against the desk.

"No," Holmes said. "Actually, it was a warehouse in Canary Wharf."

208

Lord Byron's eyes lit up. "Where in Canary Wharf, exactly?"

Lestrade pulled out a small pad of paper. "20 Bank Street, on the South Dock."

Lord Byron's face dropped in shock. He sat heavily in his seat, deflated, as if he had been struck in the face.

Holmes stood and moved to the desk. "Lord Byron?" he asked. "Is something wrong?"

"That's *my* warehouse," he replied.

Lord Byron insisted on joining our little excursion to his destroyed warehouse, explaining that he would have already gone there sooner, except that he was awaiting word about his son. He ordered his own carriage brought around, and within several minutes his driver had us wending our way through the centre of London, Whitechapel, Shadwell, and finally Canary Wharf. The driver pulled up before the awful sight of the devastated warehouse. We exited the cab and Lord Byron's face fell in a shock greater than the news of the death of his son.

The warehouse was beyond salvage. Three sides had been gutted, the wooden walls burnt to the ground. Only the fourth wall, made primarily of red brick, had survived. The contents, large bales filled with refined sugar, had been reduced to large puddles of thick, black sludge. The location of Dominic's body was evident from the lighter-coloured patch in the middle of the scorched cobbled floor. Holmes went straight towards it and began examining the area.

The remains of a wooden fire-lighting kit lay nearby. He bent down and ran a finger over the stones next to it and rubbed two fingers together. He scanned the rest of the area and stood as something in the far corner piqued his interest. He walked to the corner and bent down again. A small lumpy object lay in the soot. Holmes picked it up to examine it. He sniffed, and then pulled away in disgust.

"Something, Holmes?" I asked.

"I think I've found the source of the blaze," he said holding up the object. It appeared to be glass or ceramic, but was blackened by the fire. "This was once a small glass vessel and held turpentine. Whoever set the fire, and sadly I believe it to have been Dominic, lit it near this part of the wall. As the liquid burned and became hotter, the surrounding wall ignited and the glass eventually melted. The rest is fairly obvious." He stood and wiped his hands on a handkerchief pulled from his coat pocket.

Lord Byron was flummoxed. He moved across, peering around the warehouse as he did. "Mr. Holmes, you said that you think Dominic lit this fire."

Holmes nodded.

209

"But why? Why would he do this? This was part of his legacy."

Holmes nodded again. "I must admit, Lord Byron, that I am at a loss as to the reason behind his possible actions. You mentioned he eschewed the high life to spend time with the lower levels of society. Perhaps that clouded his mind and led to this. He may have also fallen in with the wrong crowd, one that sees you as an enemy of society, and convinced him to act in this way. At this stage, I have no evidence, and no clews, so I have only conjecture."

Lord Byron dropped his head in defeat. He made his way back to the carriage, turning back before entering. "I thank you for your service Mr. Holmes. Please forward a letter of request to my accountant with your fee attached. You did as asked and found my son. His state of being was not part of the bargain. I will retire back to my residence for now and make the arrangements for his burial. Again, I thank you."

I could tell that he was on the verge of a breakdown and understood fully. In one fell swoop he had not only lost his son, but had found out that he had betrayed him and destroyed one of his greatest assets.

Holmes walked quickly to the carriage and placed a hand on Lord Byron's shoulder. "I will find out the reason, your Lordship. Until then, I would not even consider any recompense. There is something here that does not make sense, so I am just as invested in finding the solution as you are. I promise I will not let you, or the memory of your son, down."

Lord Byron patted Holmes's hand and nodded. "Thank you, sir. You are a true gentleman."

I noticed his Lordship stare off into the distance over Holmes's right shoulder for a moment before he turned and boarded the carriage. A moment later, with a snap of the reigns, the driver led them away from the desolation.

Holmes watched them go, and then he turned back and walked towards Lestrade and me. I was about to ask him whether he had noticed the Lord's last action, but he swept past the both of us and continued on in the direction of Lord Byron's gaze. I followed in his wake, intrigued as always.

On the far side of the warehouse, in a corner near the brick wall, was a large set of crates. They were scorched, but relatively unscathed from the fire. The contents not so much, however. They held a large collection of small glass vials with cork stoppers. The majority had cracked from the heat and spilled their contents, which had vaporised in the heat. Holmes reached out and moved the top crate aside, spilling a mass of broken glass and residual liquid. I noticed immediately a strong sweet odour wafting up from the spilt fluid.

Holmes found that the contents of the crate below were in much better condition and extracted an unmarked vial. He held it up to the light and showed that it contained a pale, clear yellow liquid. He popped the cork and sniffed at the contents.

"Any idea, Holmes?"

"Yes, Watson, some idea. It's certainly not sugar, that's for sure." He placed the vial into a pocket inside his coat and turned away from the crates, a look of excitement had crossed his face. "I will need to return to Baker Street. I have a long night ahead."

That evening I was called out on a late emergency and didn't return until the wee hours of the morning. I went straight to bed and awoke later that day. Still slightly bleary-eyed, I stumbled into the sitting room to find Holmes busily working away at some chemistry experiment. Coloured liquids boiled in beakers and piped up through a series of distillation tubes.

I stepped closer and spied a beaker of fresh blood sitting on the end of the table. "I'm sure you could ask Mrs. Hudson to fix you something more suited to sustaining yourself," I said pointing at it.

Holmes looked at the beaker and then at me. A wry smile came to his face. "How very droll, Watson," he said, "but regardless of what you think, I'm not a vampire. That is our young Dominic Langley's blood. I stopped by the morgue early this morning and convinced Smithers to withdraw some for me. I believe it may contain some vital answers."

"Have you managed to determine what the yellow, fragrant liquid is?"

He stopped. A look of excitement came across his face. He motioned to the bench and a large volume on botany. I read the entry aloud:

"Chrysopogon zizanioides, or common vetiver. A long-stemmed grass that produces a fragrant oil when crushed in quantity."

"Yes," said Holmes. "It is used widely in perfumes and cosmetics. The liquid we found is the oil of the plant. On the current market, a single vial of one fluid ounce would be worth the same as about ten tons of sugar."

"A very valuable commodity, then," I said. "I thought that Lord Byron was purely an importer of sugar."

Holmes smiled. "Like any good entrepreneur, he has a diverse range of investments and means to derive profit. It seems, as my research has yielded, that two years ago, Lord Byron bought out a vetiver plantation and refining plant in the southwestern region of Haiti."

"Haiti?" I asked.

"Yes. It makes sense. The vetiver can be extracted, packaged, and shipped quite simply and quickly from Haiti to Lord Byron's sugar refining factory in Jamaica, and from there to be transported to the United Kingdom or Europe along with the sugar."

"All right, a good investment then. What of it?"

He held up the vial with the remains of the liquid inside. "At this stage, not much, but given Lord Byron's distant look in its direction yesterday, I think this means a great deal to him."

"What of the blood, then?"

Holmes placed the vial down and put on some thick leather gloves. He picked up a beaker full of a cloudy yellow liquid that had been heating over a Bunsen burner. He placed it down on an asbestos mat and, pulling off the gloves, withdrew a small dropper from a glass bottle. "Let's hope this works," he said, displaying the huge grin on his face that I had seen so often when some experiment had piqued his fascination for obscure chemistry.

He gently squeezed the dispenser's bulb and two drops of a transparent liquid fell into the beaker. The result was immediate. The cloudy liquid went completely clear. "Fascinating."

I leaned in closer to the beaker. He placed a hand on my chest. "Probably not a good idea, Watson. Best to stay a little back."

I stood up and moved back. Holmes wasn't usually the most careful man during his chemistry experiments, so anything that had him cautious was obviously far more dangerous than desired.

"What is it, Holmes?" I asked.

"*Tetrodotoxin*," he replied. "Rather quite deadly."

I was shocked. This was even more reckless than normal for Holmes. "Why in blue blazes are you messing around with that?"

The poison was a highly potent neurotoxin, occurring naturally in several deadly species of fish. It would attack the central nervous system and paralyse any person or animal that came in contact with it, within moments. "I found it in young Dominic Langley's blood."

"Is that what killed him?"

"It's incredibly potent. A tiny amount can disable, and larger amounts can kill. I can't reliably tell what concentration he had in his body, but there's a good chance it was the cause of death."

"Good Lord!" I said.

"And that's not all, Watson. I also found that our Dominic had a large dose of a hallucinogenic drug or a deliriant in his blood stream. I haven't isolated it as yet, but it seems to be akin to that extracted from the common Devil's Trumpet, or datura plant."

"Strange," I said. "Where would that have come from?"

"Well, funny enough, the datura plant is quite common across Central America and the West Indies."

"Haiti?"

"Possibly."

Holmes paused in thought for a moment, his hand beneath his chin, his forefinger braced against this cheek. Finally, he moved towards his room. "I believe," said Holmes, "that we need to visit the last known location for young Dominic – the river front."

A hansom dropped us off on the high street in Shadwell. I paid the driver, who had eyed us with suspicion from the moment he had picked us up. I couldn't blame him, really. Holmes had delved into his extensive collection of costumes and was dressed in the manner of a common street beggar, complete with makeup.

I didn't have the same level of costumery available to me. I sported my oldest pair of pants, complete with several small tears, a stained shirt and vest, plus my oldest coat. I found some dust, a remarkable feat given Mrs. Hudson's predilection for cleanliness, and mussed up the shoulders a little. I located an old pair of boots and dirtied them up in a small mud puddle on Baker Street.

As we made our way towards the river bank, I felt very self-conscious, but Holmes took it in his stride. He slumped his shoulders to affect the caricature of an elderly street denizen. I tried to follow suit, but felt even more uncomfortable. We reached a small alleyway that led to the river and my hackles were raised straight away. It felt very much like a perfect place for an ambush, and soon enough shadows appeared at both ends of the lane.

A tall man shuffled towards us. The light filtering through showed me his scarred face and a sneer full of blackened teeth. "What do we have here?" he asked. "If you want to use this pathway, you have to pay the tax."

I began to speak, but Holmes shut me up. "I'm looking for Snivellin' Pete," he said in his best East End accent.

"Who?" the man returned.

"Snivellin' Pete. 'E controls this area, I'm told. An 'e don't like it when others try to take over."

The man's face grew red with anger. He stepped forward, grabbed Holmes by the shirt front, and pushed him against the wall. "I'm in charge now," he said. "This Snivelling Pete is gone. Dead."

I went to move, but Holmes was much quicker. He grabbed the man's arms, twisted to one side, stepped forward, and slammed the taller man to the ground. All but one of the other shadows disappeared.

Holmes stared down at the man and spoke in his normal voice. "Are you telling me that Snivelling Pete is dead? How would you know that?" he asked.

The man stared up with incredulous eyes. It was obvious he hadn't been bested in this way for quite a while.

"I . . . I . . . ." he stammered.

A quieter voice piped up from behind us. "Is that you, Mr. 'Olmes?"

I turned and saw a diminutive little man. He stared wide-eyed in disbelief. Holmes looked up and smiled. "Tommy the Rat, isn't it?"

"Yes, Mr. 'Olmes, yes. I know what 'appened to Pete, I does."

Holmes looked down at the man on the ground. "If I were you, I'd find another area of the river to command, or else I might be forced to come back another day. Are we clear?"

The taller man, his eyes still wide in fear, nodded. Without looking back, Holmes stepped away and the man scampered to his feet and disappeared around the corner. Holmes turned to Tommy. "Let's get out of here in case he decides to disobey my advice."

We retired to The White Swan, two streets over, where our clothing and appearance fit, and we knew we were on neutral ground in case of any reprisals. It turned out that Tommy the Rat was a long-time cohort of Snivelling Pete, whom Holmes confessed was both the local tough who controlled this part of Shadwell, and, by chance, was also a member of the Baker Street Irregulars. Holmes had hoped to catch up with him to see if he had any information about Dominic Langley's demise. He had co-opted Pete into keeping an eye out for Langley two weeks earlier.

I brought three pints of local ale back to the table. Tommy took his and downed half of it without taking a breath. I sat, mildly amused, and took a draw from my own. Holmes waited until Tommy paused before asking him about Pete's disappearance. "You mentioned that you knew what happened to Snivelling Pete."

"That I do, Mr. 'Olmes, that I do," he said taking another sip of beer.

"Well?" I asked, growing a little impatient.

"Oh, yes, sorry. Is good beer this," he said. "It all happened about three nights ago. We was just 'angin' around down at the bank. There'd been a rumour of some roughs coming down from Whitby and trying to muscle into Pete's territory. 'E was going over a plan to find them and teach 'em a lesson." He stopped and took another sip of beer.

"Was there a young man in your group that didn't quite fit?" Holmes asked.

"The toff?" Tommy countered.

"I assume, yes," Holmes answered.

"Yeah. Pete 'ad brought 'im along a week before. Said 'e would be useful to us. I didn't like 'im one bit. Seemed a bit soft if you ask me."

"Fair call. What happened to Pete and the toff?"

"Right. Well, on that night, we was making plans and getting ready for a bit of a rumble, if it came to that, an then it all goes to 'ell."

"How?"

"Pete's standing there, talking away, 'is 'and goes to 'is neck and 'e collapses. Pretty soon the other three, including the toff do the same."

"How is it that you escaped?"

"I was in the shadows, like always. I don't like the spotlight, me. Anyways, I waits for a bit then creeps out to check on 'em. I couldn't find no breath. They was dead as doornails. I got outta there as quick as like. Next day I comes back and they's gone. Don't know if the plods got 'em or what."

"You didn't take long to find another gang to run with," I said.

"It's a dog-eat-dog world out there. Man's got to do what a man's got to do."

"Quite so," said Holmes.

The next morning, I was awakened by Holmes rapping on the door to my bedroom. "Come, Watson," he said. "Time is wasting. We have far to go today."

Moments later I shuffled down to the sitting room, dressed and ready for the day. Holmes was already at the door, waiting to depart. My stomach rumbled, but I spied a basket of fresh scones that Mrs. Hudson had made on Holmes's orders. I loaded some into a tea-towel and hurried after him. "What in blazes is the rush?" I asked as we stepped into a waiting hansom.

"Our first stop," he said, "will be at the funeral parlour, the use of which has been seconded by the coroner. I wish to ask the proprietor some questions, and your presence will help in two areas: One to provide a numerical advantage, and two because of your medical knowledge."

I munched on a scone, spilling crumbs across my front, and pondered his words. I hated to admit it, but on a number of occasions Holmes's medical knowledge had outshone my own, but I hoped for my own sake that I could help.

We stopped outside of a building with *"Richard's Funeral Parlour"* emblazoned above the door. I brushed a good number of scone crumbs to the street and shook out the flour dust from the tea-towel before pocketing it. I made a mental note to return it to Mrs. Hudson when we arrived home.

Meanwhile, Holmes was examining a small window to the side of the double doors. There was a crack extending across the length of it. As I joined him, he reached out towards the doors and turned the handles. Even at this early hour the business was open. We let ourselves in to a small but well-adorned reception area. A sideboard held a jug of water and several glasses. I shrugged off my manners and headed for the water. The three scones that I had ingested had left my mouth rather dry.

As I drank, I watched Holmes examine the door through which we had just entered. I was about to ask why when a rather tall and gaunt man appeared in a doorway leading to a service room. He had a surprised but inquisitive look on his face.

"Gentlemen, I am Mr. Richard," he said, "the owner of this establishment. My condolences to you at this time."

Holmes smiled. "Oh, that won't be necessary. We aren't customers. My name is Sherlock Holmes, and this is my associate, Dr. John Watson. I am a consulting detective in the employ of Lord Byron Langley. We merely have some questions regarding a recent visitor to your establishment."

Richard's face changed slightly to suspicion. "Yes?"

"We are under the impression that you have been receiving the bodies of unidentified street denizens who have succumbed to the cold during this unseasonal weather. One such victim arrived three days ago, but we believe he may have not been disposed of properly and was taken away once more."

Mr. Richard look surprised at that last statement. "I assure you, all unfortunates that arrive here are accounted for on receipt, through to their final destination."

"In fact, it was only three nights ago," Holmes added. "The person in whom we are interested arrived at the city morgue with three others. They were quickly dispatched to your establishment."

"We tend to prepare the victims very quickly," said Richard. "He must have been cremated later that day. I could check the files if you like."

He turned to leave, but Holmes stopped him. "That won't be necessary, as we know that the man we are interested in was not cremated. He turned up at the city morgue again, yesterday morning."

Mr. Richard turned, a shocked look on his face. "Impossible. A theft of a body from this establishment has never happened. Not in the hundred years that my family has been running it."

"And I believe that to be the case. However, some evidence may contradict your assertion. If I may be so bold, where were you, exactly, last Tuesday evening?"

Without thought, Richard's hand rose to a small bandage on his neck as he thought up an answer. "I was here," he said. "All night."

"I believe you," said Holmes.

"What?" I asked.

"Quite so, Watson. I believe that Mr. Richard is telling the truth. He was here all-night last Thursday. In body, but perhaps not in spirit."

"I don't follow," said Mr. Richard.

"That wound on your neck," questioned Holmes. "Have you had it since Tuesday evening?"

Richard was shocked. He nodded dumbly.

"Perhaps, you were leaving last week and felt a sharp pain in your neck? The last thing you probably remember before waking up the next morning?"

He nodded.

"How?"

"The pane of glass outside the main doors is cracked," he said. "I propose that you stumbled, put your hand out to brace yourself, and broke the glass." Richard raised his right hand. A small cut was visible on the edge of his hand.

"I believe that you were actually attacked as you left," Holmes said. "Where did you wake up?"

"In here," Richards replied, "but I have no idea how. I had locked the doors."

"And the lock," said Holmes, "as I observed earlier, has been broken, but from the inside."

Richard again nodded in agreement.

"From the inside?" I asked.

"Yes." Holmes said.

"By whom?" I was feeling very frustrated.

"Possibly by Dominic Langley. Possibly by Snivelling Pete. Possibly by one of the bodies brought here," said Holmes.

"But," I countered, "but, they were dead."

"And that is the pertinent fact, isn't it."

That afternoon, we bought tickets and departed Paddington on the train to Windsor. Holmes had explained that we had an appointment at Lord Byron Langley's country residence. He had gone there to prepare for Dominic's funeral. I felt that there was something that Lord Byron was keeping from us. Holmes was of the same opinion, although I believed that he knew more than he was letting on. I hoped that he did. The whole question about corpses walking out of funeral homes was causing my doctor's brain to have palpitations.

We disembarked and found a hansom to take us out to Dorney Court, a beautifully presented Tudor house about seven miles from Windsor Station. Holmes remarked that Lord Byron had purchased the manor house before he returned from Jamaica.

217

"I'm flabbergasted," I said. "I didn't think that the importation of sugar could be so lucrative."

"I think it might be that, and also the other investments that Lord Byron has made over the years – especially the one located in Haiti."

"Haiti?" I asked. "There's that country again. You mentioned Haiti the other day. What about it?"

Holmes smiled. "This is one of the reasons we need to meet with Lord Byron again."

We stepped out of the hansom, crunching gravel underfoot as we made our way to the main doors. I looked up as we walked and noticed the sun setting in the west. The night was going to be clear and I presumed very cold. I was glad I'd worn one of my thickest coats. The same butler met our knocking and, after taking our coats and hats, showed us the way to Lord Byron's study.

The sugar merchant was seated behind an enormous carved oak desk with a pile of paperwork to one side. The desk sat in front of a large window which showed the last vestiges of light as the evening intruded onto the day. Lord Byron's face was grave. I put it down to the arrangements he was undertaking to bury his son. We took seats before his desk and I sat back in the comfortable folds of the well-padded chair. Holmes looked at Lord Byron through his steepled fingers.

"Again," Holmes said, "we are very sorry to intrude on you in your time of grief, but we have come across some very troubling clews and I believe that I need more information from you before I can make sense of everything that has happened."

"Anything at my disposal is yours," said the Lord as he leaned forward, "I just wish to bring the culprits for my son's demise to justice."

"Thank you. Many of the avenues of our inquiry seem to stem from the small Caribbean nation of Haiti."

At the mention of that country, Lord Byron stiffened. Holmes stood and moved across to a nearby cabinet displaying a variety of artefacts. He picked out one and studied it as he began to speak. It seemed to be a bottle made of a translucent glass with a small cork stopper. It seemed old, and an inner feeling intruded on my consciousness that urged Holmes to put it back lest it be dropped and broken.

"Your son was in fact killed by a poison called *Tetrodotoxin* – a very rare chemical in this country, but one which is extracted from the common pufferfish found across the world – including the waters of the Caribbean. Another substance was found in his bloodstream that also seemed very curious, a hallucinogen or deliriant derived from the datura plant, or what you may know from your previous homeland as The Devil's Trumpet. Incredibly rare in England, and only a few specimens exist within the hot

218

house of the botanical gardens in London. The presence of the datura deliriant once again brings up the name of that West Indian country, Haiti. The plant occurs in abundance on the entire island."

"How would my son come into contact with such chemicals here in Britain?" Lord Byron asked.

Holmes turned and smiled at him. "Indeed. A very valid question that I have been pondering for some time."

He uncorked the little bottle and brought it up to his nose. Lord Byron's eyes grew wide. Holmes took the bottle away and studied it. "This is a very old artefact," he said as he turned to look back at Lord Byron. "I place it as mid-eighteenth century, by the looks of it. A perfume bottle I would say, possibly used by a lady of some standing. Perhaps it was one of your ancestors. Your mother, or even your grandmother perhaps? Your grandparents were residents of Jamaica well before your father became the High Commissioner. Isn't that right?"

"Yes. Yes. That is right. My family resided in Jamaica for well over a hundred years. We established the sugar plantations in the central hinterlands at that time and have been importing sugar to Britain and Europe since. How does that have anything to do with all this?"

Holmes put the bottle back then turned and moved closer to the desk. "It's not the sugar that is the primary matter in this case. It's the perfume."

Now I was confused, but then Holmes brought out the glass vial he had found at the warehouse. He held it up. Lord Byron's face went pale.

"You recently procured a plantation on the island of Haiti, did you not?" Holmes asked. "Just before you returned to England."

"Yes," Lord Byron replied. "What of it?"

"The plantation," he said, "grows a special type of grass called *Chrysopogon zizanioides*, commonly called *vetiver*. The plant's oil can be extracted and used in perfumes. From what I understand, the value of the oil is over one-hundred times that of sugar by weight. For someone in the export business, this would have been worth its weight in gold. I also understand that in a short time, you have set up a very lucrative arrangement with Yardley and Statham here in London and *Houbigant Parfum* in Paris."

Lord Byron sat staring at Holmes. His face had become impassive as he listened to Holmes explain. "As you said, I'm a businessman. It was a great opportunity, so I jumped at the chance."

Holmes moved a step forward and placed his hands on the edge of the desk. His imposing height allowed him to stare down into Lord Byron's eyes with an intensity that I had always found quite disturbing. "How great was the opportunity?" he asked. "How far were you willing to go to complete the deal?"

Holmes let the question hang. The room became suddenly very quiet. The evening outside was incredibly still with no hint of wind or breeze.

Lord Byron finally broke eye contact with Holmes. He rose unsteadily to his feet and turned away to look through the window, out at the darkening night. "I only did it to ensure the future of my business and safeguard my legacy for Dominic," he said turning back to face Holmes, "The damned Government set up the British Sugar Company four years ago. They grow beets of all things and extract the sugar that way. It was becoming cheaper than importing the real thing. I had to find a way of expanding my operations. When I became aware of the plantation on Haiti, I acted on it."

"But something went wrong, didn't it?" asked Holmes.

Lord Byron's face went grim. "Yes. The local farmers weren't willing to sell. They revered the vetiver plants for some reason. They only farmed what they needed. Had no concept of industrial farming. Something about their heathen religion. I employed local militia to takeover and expand the plantations. I offered recompense to the local chieftains, but there was trouble," he said as he turned back to look out the window letting the last statement hang. His head dropped as he fought his conscience.

"Trouble?" I prompted.

He peered back then dropped his eyes. Even a man this resolute in his station in life was disturbed by what he was about to say. "The militia that I employed overplayed their hand," he explained. "They virtually wiped out a local town. Killed the chieftains and members of the council. Any men that took up arms were killed."

He turned back to us. Tears had formed and ran down his cheeks. He was truly distressed by the events undertaken in his name. "By the time I found out, it was too late," he said, "I had travelled to the plantation and made what restitution I could with the locals. I dismissed the militia and employed as many of the townsfolk that would work for me. I tried – honestly I did – but they had lost all hope. Their men were dead. Their women left as widows, their children orphans. I returned to Jamaica and started preparations to leave. My heart wasn't in it anymore. I left a manager to continue the operation, but I decided it was time to retire. I vowed to bring Dominic in to take over."

He was weeping profusely by now. "I was almost too late. One night they attacked."

"Who?" Holmes asked.

"*Zombies!*" Lord Byron whispered, his face now a wasteland of fear and trepidation.

"Zombies?" I blurted out in disbelief, "Dead people? Re-animated?"

220

He nodded slowly. "Yes. The townsfolk on Haiti had employed a *caplata*. A dark witch of the Voodoo religion. Capable of raising the dead to do her bidding. That last night, before I set sail, the plantation was attacked. My staff were slaughtered where they stood. My only saving grace was that I was in Kingston awaiting the ship that brought me back to London. I found out after I arrived. That was two years ago. I haven't returned."

He pulled out a handkerchief and blotted the tears from his eyes. A strange resolve seemed to come over him. I'm still not sure if it was an acceptance of fate or a shimmer of courage to face the unknown. He stood to his full height and spoke one last time.

"I feel that she's here," he said. "I now believe that she killed my son, turned him into a zombie and bade him to set fire to the warehouse. I know that I cannot fight her plague of dead men, but I will not go down meekly. I ran before, but now I must face my accuser and plead my case."

I was impressed but confused at his stance. He was, of course, guilty of the deaths of many people, if not by his word at least by his deed.

Suddenly, Lord Byron's guilt was no longer a factor in this case. I started to form a question on my lips when all hell broke loose, and it was forever forgotten in the maelstrom that followed.

A scream issued from deep in the house. All heads turned towards the cry. The sound of glass breaking made Holmes and me turn back to face the sugar merchant.

Several panes on the window behind him imploded inwards. Pairs of arms reached in through the broken glass. My doctor's mind noticed the long gashes form down their length as the jagged glass shards bit deep into their flesh. Blood flowed as they reached for Lord Byron. He screamed as he was grabbed by many hands and wrenched off his feet.

I remarked in my mind's eye that the owners of the arms were incredibly strong, as Lord Byron was by no means a small man. He was dragged bodily through the broken window and disappeared, leaving only a scream hanging in the tumult.

I sprang to my feet, ready to run to Lord Byron's aid. Holmes had already vaulted the desk and was peering into the gloom beyond the window.

"What in blazes happened?" escaped my lips as I ran. Holmes continued to peer into the dark grounds outside.

"Zombies, it seems, Watson," he said, matter-of-factly.

"What?" I asked.

Before he could answer, the door into the study burst open. We both turned.

Standing in the doorway was a black woman. She wore richly coloured robes and had strange designs painted across her face in light colours. She stepped into the room and was followed by two slack jawed men. They stood well over six feet tall, their arms hung by their sides and their eyes were glazed and unable to focus.

As I turned to look at Holmes, something struck my neck. It stung like an insect bite. I raised my hand and pulled the offending item from my throat. It was a small feathered dart.

My mind became clouded, my vision blurred. I managed to turn and stare at the woman once more. She held a long hollow tube to her mouth. A small sound of expelled air followed. Something flew past my face and the tiny grunt I heard could only have been Holmes.

Darkness began to cover my eyes. I fought to maintain control, but gravity won, and I fell to my knees. The wooden floor was the last thing that I saw before the shadows drew a close to my consciousness.

My eyes blinked open and drew focus on a white tiled ceiling. I lay for a moment gathering my thoughts and trying to determine where I was when a figure passed into my view. He wore a blood-stained white coat and mask and held a pair of forceps in one hand and a scalpel in the other. As the scalpel hand came closer, I thrust up my right hand up and stopped its descent.

He yelped and jumped back slightly. "Good Lord! Dr. Watson – You're alive!" he said, dragging the mask from his face.

I immediately recognised Smithers. I tried to sit up. Smithers aided me, and I realised I was sitting on an autopsy table in the morgue.

I looked around and saw Holmes lying on the table next to me. Thankfully he hadn't been the object of Smithers's occupation yet. The table beyond held a larger body, covered in a blood-soaked sheet.

Smithers noticed where I was looking.

"Lord Byron Langley," he said. "The constables said he was mauled by a wild animal or . . . something. I'm still trying to determine by what."

"Holmes?" I managed to croak.

"Dead. Like you – " he said, before rushing over to where Holmes lay.

He bent down and listened. He then stood and lightly slapped Holmes on the cheeks. A harder slap brought a groan from the recumbent form of my associate. His eyes flickered and opened. Within moments he sat up and looked around. The fog lifting quickly from his drugged mind. He focused on me and a wry smile came to his face.

"We survived," he said. "She mustn't have wanted us to join her zombie army."

"What?" Smithers and I both asked.

"The *caplata*," said Holmes. I sat staring at him with a confused expression.

"The *caplata*. The black woman. A female voodoo witch, hired by the townsfolk on Haiti. It all makes sense now."

I didn't share his feeling of completion. "In what way?"

He took a deep breath, closed his eyes for a moment then continued. "Dominic Langley was hunted down and turned into a zombie by a voodoo priestess. Under the influence of *datari*, she was able to coerce him into lighting a fire in Lord Byron's warehouse. Not only did she want him dead, but she wanted to destroy his life as well. Very vindictive, but I suppose it sent a message. In the end, she led her zombies to Lord Byron's estate and finished what she had been employed to do."

I was still confused but had to know. "What about us?"

He smiled. "We were poisoned with *tetrodotoxin*. Not enough to kill, just enough to disable us. We were lucky. Any more poison and Smithers here would have needed to conduct real autopsies. As it is, we survive to fight another day."

"The zombies?" I asked, "What about the zombies?"

"Ah, similar to us, I suppose," he said, looking around the morgue. "The *caplata* poisons them with enough to disable and incapacitate. They appear to be dead, but are in reality alive. She then administers the *datari* and bends their will to do her bidding. I wouldn't be surprised if Smithers receives several more clients over the next couple of days as the zombies are found. They will either recover, or to cover her tracks, the *caplata* will probably administer more poison to finish the job."

I contemplated what Holmes had said, but one question remained. "Dominic Langley," I said. "He was dead *before* he entered the warehouse. You established that as there was no soot in his throat."

"Yes?"

"So . . . how did he set fire to the place?"

Holmes stared at me blankly as his mind tried to determine the answer.

# The Adventure of the Undertaker's Fetch

## by Tracy J. Revels

A ghost settled onto the sofa in our sitting room at Baker Street and accepted Holmes's offer of a drink with a polite nod. I had never seen a young man so pale, his skin so white as to be almost translucent, his gray eyes milky to the point of colorlessness, his hair a disheveled bank of newly fallen snow. The effect was exaggerated by his attire, for he was dressed entirely in black, relived only by the hint of a white shirt and collar beneath his heavy coat and broad black tie. Even the cloak he had surrendered to a wary Mrs. Hudson had been of that same shade, without any touch of red in the lining or gold in the buttons. Our guest was a singularly memorable individual, one at which even a polite person might gawk.

My medical curiosity was quickly getting the better of me, and the man sensed it. He offered a thin, tired smile.

"You are no doubt wondering, Doctor Watson, if I suffer from albinism. I do not, though I suspect I missed it by whatever slim degree those blessings are granted. My late father was remarkably pale, and to this day my mother does not dare step outside without veil and gloves." He gestured to the dark glasses he had placed beside him on the sofa. "I find that even on foggy afternoons like this one, my eyes ache, and I must wear my protective lens. Admittedly, it makes me somewhat dismal in appearance. However, considering my profession, I would be a grim and foreboding individual to most people, even if I were a ruddy-face man with a sparkling personality."

Holmes passed me the gentleman's card. Written upon it in gothic script was "*Joseph Brackenhall, Brackenhall and Brackenhall, Undertakers and Dealers in Mourning Accoutrements, Regent Street*".

"You certainly never lack for business," Holmes said, in a waspish humor. Mr. Brackenhall chuckled.

"Indeed, though I must tell you that people no longer mourn as they once did. Twenty years ago, when I was a lad, every corpse required a hearse and four mutes, five carriages for the pallbearers and mourners, and a hundred years of black crepe for the household. I can recall whole families arriving to be properly outfitted for a year of grief – even the children and the servants. I used to have a large market in jet beads and mahogany frames to display memorial etchings, not to mention orders for

224

tombstones as large as imperial monuments. But I fear the day of such excess is past – even death has its fashions, gentlemen. Mr. Holmes, if you were to die today, I doubt your friend here would order more than an armband."

"He already has some experience in preparing for my passing," Holmes said. He rarely lost an opportunity to playfully tweak me about what he considered the inadequacies of my mourning for him during the three years he was presumed dead from his peril at the Reichenbach Falls. "But what brings you to us, Mr. Brackenhall – seeing as how our rude health makes us unlikely customers for your emporium?"

"I wish I could say the same about myself. You see, Mr. Holmes, I fear I am a dead man. I have seen death himself following me."

Holmes scowled. I imagined that he had suddenly lost interest in the case. "The reaper trails us all, I fear."

"But does he wear your exact countenance and stalk you in the streets? Have you seen him through a shop window or captured him in a photograph?"

Holmes flipped his coattails back and settled into his chair. "Now you begin to interest me."

"Allow me to provide you with some context, sir. I was born in London and grew up within the shadow of Highgate Cemetery. From my childhood I was fascinated by the dignity of funerals and burial. It seemed to me that death was the great equalizer, and I was taken by how even people of the lowest orders would go to great pains to give a departed loved one that last measure of dignity and regard. At twelve I left school, much to my widowed mother's dismay, and apprenticed myself to a local undertaker. I learned the trade quickly and well. By the age of twenty-five I had my own establishment in London. Only Black Peter's and Jay's are larger than my store. A client who comes to me to have his friend or relative put away properly has no further steps to make, for at my sizable shop he can not only arrange all aspects of the funeral, but purchase clothes, stationery, and any other item that might help him cherish the memory of the departed.

"I am thirty-five years of age, and my business has prospered to the point that I could be retired, but I have nothing to interest me beyond my work: No wife, no children, no close friends, no clubs or social connections. My sole hobby is the study of death and of mortuary customs from around the world. I am by no means a superstitious fellow – I could hardly have lasted at my task if I were – but I confess that stories of banshees and omens have always been my obsession. There is a German tale of the *doppelgänger* – do you know it?"

Holmes shook his head. I spoke up.

225

"It is a spirit, is it not? One that appears before a man when his days are numbered?"

"You are correct, Doctor. It always comes in the guise of its victim. A more common English term is '*fetch*', as the spirit arrives to escort its double to the land of the dead. More than once I have stood in a dying man's chamber and heard him mutter about watching himself move along the wall or hover over the foot of the bed. This I have always dismissed as the last flicker of a mind shutting down, for I could clearly see that there was no spirit twin in the room. But a week ago, I too began to see a *doppelgänger*, my own, and I have proof that he exists."

Mr. Brackenhall had become somewhat agitated. He pulled out a handkerchief and wiped the sudden perspiration from his face. "Mr. Holmes, I know that I cannot escape death, but if you can prove to me that I am not insane, I will reward you generously. I do not believe in spirits and ghosts. I look upon them as manifestations of our human need to solve the one mystery that will always go unraveled, embodiments of our desire to rip apart the veil between worlds. This thing that follows me cannot be real, yet I know what I see, what I have physical proof of. If you can reveal it as hoax I will be grateful, and if you can expose the ghost for a true phantom, then the spiritualists will hail you as a prophet."

"I care nothing for their regard," Holmes said, "I have no time for phantasms. But I remain intrigued by your statement. How many times have you seen this vision?"

"Three times, Mr. Holmes. The first was Saturday morning. My mother resides in Oxford, and I was boarding the train to visit her. I had just settled into my carriage and the whistle had been blown when I looked out across the platform and saw myself. I was standing beside a pile of luggage, clad in black, looking around as if I had never been in such a magnificent setting before. I confess that for a moment I merely gaped, unable to speak or move. Then something like an electric charge ran through me and I leapt from my seat. At just that moment, the train lurched into motion and I was thrown backward into the lap of my companion in the compartment. By the time I managed to right myself and mutter profuse apologies, the train was out of the station and I was unable to disembark."

Holmes raised a finger. "How much detail could you perceive about your double's attire?"

"I confess that I was more taken with his face than his clothes, but he was all in black and he wore the same dark glasses that I do. I recall that his hat was off, so that I saw our shared hair – as unruly as it is," he added, with a wry twist of his mouth. "His hat was in one hand, and I could tell only that it was short and rounded, not the high style that I favor."

226

"Did you mention it to anyone?"

"Only to my mother, as a curious incident, but it upset her greatly and she quickly changed the subject. My mother, I fear, is a very nervous woman who has never shared my fascination for such grim topics."

Holmes signaled for him to continue. Mr. Brackenhall's thin fingers traced the rim of his glass.

"The second time was on Tuesday evening, just as the lamps were being lit. I was moving about the shop, rearranging some items on the shelves, when I felt an odd tingling at the base of my neck. Surely you know it, sirs – that feeling that you are being watched? There is a large window at the front of the store, beautifully etched with our company name and our motto – '*Dignity and Memory*'. There is a line of cabinets in this window which display merchandise to passers-by, but they are low and can be peered over for a view into the depths of the store. My sensation of being watched did not go away – it would be common enough, I suppose, with potential customers doing their window-shopping of our wares, but I tell you that something felt different. Slowly, I turned.

"It was a foggy evening, and the lamplight was throwing queer, bobbing circles, like great golden haloes. Within one of these glowing illuminations rested my own face. This time the image was even clearer, and I could, in an instant, take in all the details that are so intimate to me: My marble-like brow, my thin lips, my high cheekbones, and the black glasses, hat, and coat that frame all of my pale features. I stared at my double, my twin, and then I gave a shout. I ran for the door, causing half-a-dozen ladies to think that I was quite mad, but when I reached the door and galloped onto the sidewalk, the fetch had disappeared. People were streaming in and out of the fog, and there was no way to know even in what direction the apparition had fled. I stepped into the spot that he had occupied. I could clearly see a clerk standing within the store, so I understood how easy it had been for the double to obtain a glance of me. A coldness washed over my limbs, followed by a sudden sweat. This was exactly what dying men had described to me, yet like them, I had no proof that the *doppelgänger* had ever existed.

"Or did I? For at that instant, as I dropped my head in dismay, I spotted an item on the sidewalk. It was a man's handkerchief, white with a black mourning band and the initials '*JB*' worked into one corner. I reached into my hip pocket and drew out its perfect mate." He pulled two cloths from his jacket, laying them before us side by side. "Judge for yourself – are they not perfectly identical?"

I shivered at this revelation. The line between Holmes's brows grew deeper.

"And there was one last appearance?" Holmes asked.

"Yes, there was. Yesterday, I accompanied Mrs. Morrow, my photographer, to the house of Sir Russel Morgan, the late hero of the Crimean War. His home, as you may know, is in Cheslea, a lovely red house with a delightful garden in which the old soldier took great pride. He had passed away only the day before, and my people had laid him in repose in the large, airy room that faced his garden, prepared to receive legions of admirers who would pay their respects. His lady wished a memorial portrait taken before the crowds descended, and of course in this we were most willing to oblige her. Olympia Morrow is an artist of some repute – her pictures of the dead are said to be the best in London. I assisted her in setting up her equipment, then moved aside to offer words of comfort to the widow. For just an instant, I thought I saw someone in the window behind the corpse, but then my attention was diverted. Mrs. Morrow made her images, and we retired to the shop, where she has a special darkroom for developing her photographs.

"I had just settled down to tea when she brought the pictures to me. She was most disturbed by the results, for while one of the photographs was perfect, another was marred by the presence of a shadowy figure in the background. A sudden movement had blurred his lines, half-wiped away his features. Still, I recognized the phantom. You will as well."

Mr. Brackenhall removed a small, framed picture from his coat, placing it in Holmes's hands. I hurried to stand over my friend's shoulder.

There was no question. Just behind the bier, turning as if startled and about to flee, was Joseph Brackenhall.

"Mrs. Morrow said that she had not even noticed the man in the background, so obsessed she was with recording the details of the departed hero's noble face. But then, as the picture developed, she saw me within it – even as she distinctly recalled that I was in the room behind her at the time the photograph was taken. It was all too much for her, and I fear that I have lost my finest employee, for she has turned in her notice." Brackenhall's laugh was almost a sob. "I have given you enough evidence, I hope. Now, Mr. Holmes, what is the answer? Is this some bizarre form of persecution? Or proof that a spirit world exists, and that I should be prepared to enter it very shortly?"

Holmes placed the photograph on the table beside him. "Mr. Brackenhall, your case is rather singular, yet I can solve it without ever leaving this armchair. The solution is obvious. You have a twin brother."

"No, I do not."

Holmes raised a palm. "You think you do not, but you do. The man is solid enough – there is the dropped handkerchief retrieved, the image captured. You have never known this twin. Your mother's distress proves it. For some reason he was kept from you and now seeks to make contact."

228

If possible, our guest grew even paler. He shook his head vigorously. "Mr. Holmes, I do not have a twin. Or – to be more proper – I no longer have a twin, for Jethro Brackenhall died a year ago, in my arms."

"Brackenhall and Brackenhall," Holmes said, the words as sharp as a curse. "You may write me up as an ass, Watson. I assumed the second Brackenhall in the business's name was in honor of his father." He struck a match and drew deeply as he lit his pipe. His client had begged a moment's patience as he availed himself of our washroom. Clearly the memory of his tragedy, compounded with his fear, was causing him great anxiety. Holmes and I stood by the window as we waited for his return. "Perhaps I am growing too old for this occupation," my friend muttered.

"It was a mistake anyone could make," I said, realizing an instant too late that those were not words Holmes would wish to hear. "But if not a family member, who could it be? It seems a cruel prank to impersonate his dead brother."

"Cruel and pointless, so far as we know," Holmes agreed. "But here is the gentleman now, to finish his tale." Holmes waved away his client's apologies and asked him to be seated, but Brackenhall was far to agitated to perch on the sofa as we settled into our chairs.

"No, I must remain upright. Some strange energy has overtaken me. My brother – poor Jethro – yes, we were as physically alike as two peas in a pod. Even Mother and Father struggled to tell us apart as young boys. Jethro never shared my fascination with death. He stayed in school, later becoming a teacher in Devonshire. The moors proved dangerous to his health, however. He sank into melancholy and listlessness, took to drink, and eventually lost his position. I convinced him to come to London, to live and work with me – his long face and grave demeanor was, perhaps, more suited to my profession than his. I even renamed my business to include him, and soon he was sober and respectable again. But our satisfaction in being reunited did not last long.

"You probably read of his death, even if you do not recall it. Some of the more sensational papers had a field day with the sad event. The rain was falling in torrents while we were carrying a body to its tomb. My brother walked just before the casket, leading the pallbearers. The ground was slick, the ancient cemetery riddled with holes and collapsed graves. Suddenly two of the pallbearers lost their footing and the coffin – a massive thing, with a sizable occupant – tipped from their hands and plunged forward. My brother was struck down under the terrible weight of the casket. His shoulders and ribcage were crushed, and he died in my embrace, long before any doctor could arrive to help him. Of course, because of the macabre nature of the story, it was lavishly illustrated when it appeared in every cheap newspaper in the nation. It infuriated me, but what could I do? I had lost my dear twin."

"Do you think that this visitation, the spirit that you are seeing, could be your brother?" I asked.

"Ghosts have no need for handkerchiefs," Holmes reminded me.

"I – I asked myself that question, a dozen times," Brackenhall confessed. He drifted toward the window, toying with the curtain. "But I am certain that the man I saw was *not* Jethro. It is difficult to explain why. As much as Jethro and I shared our distinctive features, there was something different about the *doppelgänger*. Jethro, bless his memory, had no sense of wonder – I cannot imagine him gaping on a train platform or pressing against the glass of a shop window like a child. Jethro lived his life as a dead man, while this spirit of death is – how do I say it? – lively and quick."

"Let us be more practical, Mr. Brackenhall," Holmes said. "Do you know of anyone who bears you ill will? Who carries a grudge?"

The man shrugged his shoulders. "I can think of no one. I have never dismissed an employee in anger, or sent a collector after an overdue bill. I have no close friends, but no enemies either, to my knowledge. The idea of some kind of lark or jape has occurred to me, but there is not a boy or man in my store would could pull off such a credible impression. I am not an easy man to mimic."

"That is true," Holmes said. "However, if – "

Mr. Brackenhall let out a cry. His hand left hand curled in the drapery, tearing it down from the curtain rod, while his right hand closed into a fist over his chest. I was on my feet in an instant, recognizing – I thought – the signs of a stroke. Holmes was only a heartbeat behind me, but as we reached the man Brackenhall suddenly jabbed a finger toward the window and Baker Street beyond its pane.

"There! You see? You see him?"

My breath left me in a rush. Just across the thoroughfare, standing beneath a lamp, in a swirl of yellow fog, was Joseph Brackenhall. He was so complete, so exact a replica that I reached out and shook the man beside me. Holmes saw it too, and his mouth popped open in surprise. The spirit – or fetch, or *doppelgänger* – was an exact match in every way, down to the cape and coat and dark glasses, all of it in sharp and eerie contrast to his pearly white skin. Brackenhall lurched forward, banging against the window three times before his eyes rolled back in his head and he pitched sideways into my grasp.

"See to your patient!" Holmes barked as he sped for the door. I hauled the man over to the sofa, made him comfortable, loosened his collar, and sought out some restorative brandy. Before I had completed my ministrations, Holmes returned, tugging at his own collar for air and dropping down with his hands on his knees.

"Did you see him?"

"I thought I did – I chased him as far as Regent's Park, and had him in hand, but it turned out to be a rather alarmed older gentleman and not our prey. He must have gone the other way and slipped off into this damnable fog." Holmes straightened himself and moved to the sofa. "I hope Mr. Brackenhall's shock was not too extreme. It would hardly do to have a client expire on my divan."

The man was still insensible, but his pulse was calmer. Holmes drew me away, back to the window.

"You saw it too?" he whispered.

"As clearly as I see you before me. A pity there is no more proof than our eyes."

"Ah, but there is. Look what I found beneath the lamp."

Holmes held out a pair of dark glasses, the exact shape and style of Brackenhall's. One of the lens had been broken.

"I confess this puzzles me, Watson. It is too complex for a mere prank, and I refuse to accept the idea of a spirit or fetch. The world is big enough for us. No ghosts need apply."

"Yes," I said, "but is the world big enough for *two* Brackenhalls?"

Holmes's client was weak and it was unwise to move him. Even as Mr. Brackenhall began to recover his senses, Holmes insisted that he remain with us and ordered a mild supper for us to share. A short time later, Brackenhall was once again asleep on the sofa, his breathing short and shallow. I knew, as a physician, that I had a long night ahead of me.

Holmes perched in his armchair, his legs curled inward like some Hindoo god. Out of respect for my patient, I forbid Holmes to smoke, which did nothing to improve his mood. At times I assumed Holmes had drifted into slumber, but then I would look across and find his eyes burning, serving as bright points of light in an otherwise subdued chamber.

Just as the clock struck eight, Holmes made a startled sound. He began to mutter rapidly to himself, then uncoiled and went to the bookshelf, pulling down one of his heavy city directories. I asked what he was about, but got no answer. Instead, he slammed the book shut and hurried to his room. Five minutes later, he emerged in his traveling clothes.

"No, Watson, duty commands you to stay with the sufferer. I hope to be back by mid-morning, and to have an answer to this troubling case by tea time."

"You have solved it?"

Holmes looked troubled. "I have had an idea that is either brilliant or one of the most ridiculous in my entire career. Perhaps I should discover which it is before I say any more about it. Whatever happens, do not allow Mr. Brackenhall to leave these premises. His life may depend upon our protection."

I assured Holmes that I would follow his orders. A short time later, my patient began to show signs of improvement, so much that I steered him to a more comfortable nap in my chamber, while I caught snatches of sleep in a chair. By sunrise, there was still no sign of Holmes. Mrs. Hudson brought up a hearty breakfast, and I was delighted to see that Mr. Brackenhall had awoken with an improved appetite. A telegram arrived an hour later, but it was Holmes at his most cryptic:

*Hope arises. Admit no one. Rehang drapes.*

Mr. Brackenhall and I passed the morning in pleasant conversation. Though an undertaker by trade, there was nothing innately morose or gloomy about him, and as we chatted I understood his current sadness sprang from his newfound loneliness. His success in the funerary business kept him very busy, and he saw no one socially except his mother, whom he visited once a month. Even those visits, he admitted, had become somewhat perfunctory.

"There is a great melancholy about her," Brackenhall told me. "I suppose she and Jethro were akin. My father, as much as I can recall, enjoyed life thoroughly and was rarely grim. Sometimes Mother will simply look at me and burst into tears, for no reason. I suppose it is ironic, I can tolerate tears on a daily basis from my customers, but with my mother I find them almost unbearable."

Mrs. Hudson had just cleared away the luncheon plates when the door to the suite opened and Holmes appeared, ushering in a short, squat woman all wrapped in black bombazine and a heavy cloth veil. There was no mystery as to her identity, however. Before I could rise, Brackenhall was on his feet, speaking with a startled passion.

"Mother! What on earth?"

"Watson, do allow me to present Mrs. Miriam Brackenhall, of Oxford," Holmes said. "She held the key to this conundrum all along."

"The key?"

The lady was trembling in her son's embrace. "Oh, Joseph, I did wrong not to tell you. So wrong, yet what could I say? What hope could I raise that would not be crushed?"

He guided her to sit, crouching down on one knee beside her. "Mother, what are you talking about?"

232

The lady had begun to weep copiously. Holmes rolled his eyes, but spoke softly.

"Mr. Brackenhall, Watson has made my maxim famous – whenever you eliminate the impossible, whatever remains, however improbable, must be the truth. It is impossible that you are being stalked by a spirit, for such things do not exist. It is impossible that you are being followed by your twin brother Jethro, for as much as it grieves you, he is dead and buried. It is also impossible that you are being hunted by an enemy, for you have none. Therefore, only one answer remains – the man who shadows you is not your twin, but your *triplet*."

I stared at Holmes, as shocked as his client. The lady on the sofa pulled her hands away from her tear-stained face.

"It is true. Yes, Joseph, there were three of you."

He shook his head. "How?"

"On that September morning, thirty-five years ago, I gave birth to two tiny, sickly babies, then to one who was vigorous. All three looked alike, except for the third one's size. You and Jethro were so small, so fretful, it took all I could do to nurse you. We had no money, your father and I – we could not afford any assistance. We lived in a tenement house and across the hall from us was Mrs. Garcia, whose husband had died that June, killed in a terrible factory accident. He had left her in a delicate condition, and just a week before your birth, Mrs. Garcia had a baby, a little boy, who died after only an hour of life. She was so stricken, poor thing, but she was a robust woman and she offered to help me. She took the stronger of my boys – Josiah – and nursed him."

"Then where was he when I was a child? Why didn't I know him?"

The lady began to weep again. Holmes came around and sat beside her, taking up her story.

"Mrs. Garcia proved to be a false friend to your parents. She craved an infant to replace the one she had lost. A month after your birth, just as your mother felt well enough to take on the rigors of caring for three babies, Mrs. Garcia disappeared – with your brother."

"We did everything we could think of," the lady sniffed. "We told the police, we made reports, but she was gone. There was a rumor she'd boarded a ship. If we had been wealthy, perhaps we could have hired someone like Mr. Holmes to find her. But we were poor, and after a year we gave up hope. Your father said it would be best if you and Jethro never knew you had another brother. He worried that knowing it would haunt you in some way, or maybe make you crave revenge. After he died, it was my secret to keep, to carry – until this gentleman came to my door late last night and told me that the son I had given up for dead was haunting my boy who lived."

233

"Why?" Brackenhall demanded. "Why, if Josiah exists, does he choose to stalk me, to frighten me and not speak?"

"I do not believe that he means you harm," Holmes said, "but often our most innocent actions have rather unexpected consequences. Let us ask him his reasons – for that is surely his tread I hear upon the stairs."

We all turned. Mrs. Hudson opened the door. She was white as the proverbial sheet, and kept looking back and forth between our client and someone behind her, a shadow in the gloom of the hallway.

"There's a gentleman here, Mr. Holmes. But . . . he's already here, isn't he? A Mr. Brackenhall?"

"He has come in answer to my advertisement in the morning newspapers," Holmes said. "I placed a message in the agony column, alerting a certain '*Mr. B*' that if he desired a meeting with his brother Joseph – an encounter with '*dignity and memory*' – he should present himself at 221 Baker Street at three p.m. It appears that he is early for his appointment."

It was the strangest of family reunions. The lady gave a cry and fainted, while the brothers gazed at each other as if looking into a mirror. For an instant Mr. Brackenhall bristled, as if he might strike the newcomer, who only hung his head and whispered, "I never meant to alarm you – I only wanted to see, if it was true, the things I'd been told." Then, in a joyous moment, Joseph threw his arms around his brother and embraced him as if three decades did not stand between them.

The story, as Josiah told it, was indeed remarkable. The only way in which he did not resemble his brother was his accent, which was slow and full, rich with the long vowels of the American southland. His "mother" – Mrs. Garcia – had taken an insurance settlement from her husband's tragic accident and fled with her purloined "son" to distant relatives in Savannah. Gossip increased as the boy grew, for he looked nothing like his mother – a black-haired, swarthy woman, nor his purported father, who had been of Spanish descent. Mrs. Garcia was eventually shunned by her people, but later married a kindly man named Bruxton, who gave the boy his name and taught him the bookselling trade.

"Mother made me promise her, upon a Bible, that I would never go to England while she lived," Josiah told us. "I could not understand her prohibition, especially as Father did a great deal of business here, but I was a dutiful son and so I made that vow. Then, a year ago, I saw a strange item in Mr. Pulitzer's newspaper. The headline was *Undertaker Killed By Coffin*" and it was accompanied by a series of sketches, including one of the unfortunate man who was killed and a portrait of his twin brother. I could not get it out of my head how much the men in the pictures resembled myself. Several accounts mentioned the pale complexions of the twins, as well as their age. The more I thought about it, the more I needed answers. I showed it to my mother, and from that day she began to sicken. Six months later, upon her deathbed, she revealed the truth to me – how I had been stolen from the Brackenhall family. I had grown up as an only child, and to now learn that I had a brother, and a twin at that, it was almost more than I could believe."

"Why did you not open a correspondence?" I asked.

"I assumed this family, with its success in business and its prestige in London, must be constantly annoyed by pretenders, men claiming to be the long lost Brackenhall son. I did not want to cause them any pain, especially if – by some monstrosity – the story was not true. And so I came to London to try to see my brother first from a distance. I did not know you spotted me upon the train platform, Joseph, but I saw your astonishment when you spied me through the window of the shop. I have no good excuse for fleeing, other than cowardice. You cannot imagine how it affected me, to see my own face staring back at me. As for my costume, I have always needed dark glasses to cover my eyes, the black-banded handkerchief that I dropped was made while I was in mourning for Mother, and I was informed by Father that a true gentleman in London does not sport the flashy clothes of an American, so I assumed that black, somber attire would be an effective disguise. I am glad you find that so amusing, Mr. Holmes."

My friend waved a hand. "I am not mocking you, sir – only finding humor in the strangeness of the human experience. What lured you to the bier of Sir Russel Morgan?"

Josiah Brackenhall blinked. "Who?"

"The war hero," Joseph said. "My photographer captured your image in the garden, while she was making a memorial photograph."

"That was not me," Josiah insisted. "I followed you at a distance, but I swear I never intruded upon any private property."

"It doesn't matter," their mother cried. "God has blessed me! I have two boys again!"

It was a sweet ending to one of the strangest stories I had ever heard. In due time, Josiah Brackenhall moved to London, along with his adoptive father. He took up a partnership with his sibling, expanding their business to include a bookshop that specialized in grim legends and fantastic tales, as well as professional volumes on the mortician's art. Holmes laughed out loud when, some three years later, I found a wedding announcement in the newspaper. Mr. Ambrose Buxton, widower, late of Savannah, Georgia, had married Mrs. Miriam Brackenhall, widow, of Oxford.

Neither Joseph or Josiah chose to wed, and thus London was perhaps spared of a tribe of ghostly children.

There was one other strange incident in connection with the case, which occurred only a month after the brothers had been reunited.

That night, I could not sleep. I rose and went to the sitting room, looking for a book I had left behind, in hopes that I would be able to read myself into some repose. Holmes was sitting at his desk with his lamp lit, studying the memorial photograph that Mr. Brackenhall had forgotten and left in our apartment.

"What are you doing?" I asked.

"Who is this man?" Holmes said, holding out the photograph to me. "He is not Josiah Brackenhall, nor is he Joseph. Yet his features are so similar. Do we see them only because that is what we have told ourselves to see, within the blurred image?" He tapped the picture insistently. "I have tried to duplicate this effect. It occurred to me that perhaps what we are seeing is a reflection upon the glass of the window – that it is actually Mr. Joseph Brackenhall himself, whom we know stood behind the photographer. If the photographer has merely captured his reflection, it would explain the distortions. However, I have been singularly unsuccessful in replicating this photograph."

I found myself yawning. "Does it really matter?"

"Watson – without this third piece of the puzzle, Joseph Brackenhall would not have sought my aid. But he might have seen his fetch again, in some other context, and died of shock. Instead, he came to me and my efforts led to a renewed life, instead of an early death. So was it a strange coincidence . . . or something else?"

I took up the image. "Perhaps, Holmes, you must concede that there are things you will never know. You must permit a limit to your reasoning ability, a finite quality to your deductions. Some things must be taken on faith."

My friend rose and snatched the picture from my hands. With a swift, deft movement, he tossed it onto the fire.

"I refuse to accept limits to mankind's reason. Goodnight."

236

# The Holloway Ghosts
## by Hugh Ashton

*Author's Note: This has been written as an audio play,
hence the lack of stage directions other than sound effects.*

This script is protected by copyright.

## CHARACTERS

- Sherlock Holmes
- Dr. John H. Watson
- Mrs. Hudson
- Inspector Lestrade
- Police Constable
- Mrs. Baxter
- PC Ruddock
- Otto Sussbinder

## SCENE 1: BAKER STREET

## SOUND EFFECT: BAKER STREET. SOUND OF VIOLIN BEING PLAYED COMPETENTLY BUT TUNELESSLY

WATSON: Holmes, will you stop that infernal scraping? You have been at it for some fifteen minutes now.

## SOUND EFFECT: VIOLIN STOPS PLAYING

HOLMES: My apologies. I was considering the case of The Countess of Westmererland's rubies. The only possible explanation remaining is that the maid, Laforge, passed them out of the window to the chimney-sweep, her accomplice.

WATSON: But he was taken up by the police later that afternoon, and his person and his equipment were searched most minutely. Nothing was found.

HOLMES: What the police failed to remember was that in the hours between his work on the chimneys at Westmereland House, and his

237

subsequent detention, he had visited several other houses, in which he had ample opportunity to secrete the jewels in locations where he knew they would remain undisturbed until his next visit. Possibly he was intending to leave them there for up to a year. Where the police, and, I confess, I myself, were in error, was in the assumption that the gems were purloined for immediate disposal. Those directing the operation were obviously playing a long game, allowing the scent to grow cold.

WATSON: Then you do not suspect the maid of being the instigator of the theft?

HOLMES: By no means. Despite her chequered past, with which my friend le Villard of the *Sûreté* has been kind enough to provide me, her history shows her to have been more of a catspaw than a cat, if you will forgive the expression. The sweep himself was no doubt offered a considerable inducement to play his part. I shall send a telegram to Lestrade and inform him of my – (BREAKS OFF) Halloa! I see the man himself arriving at our front door.

SOUND EFFECT: PAUSE. KNOCK AT THE DOOR

MRS. HUDSON: (OFF) Inspector Lestrade to see you, Mr. Holmes.

HOLMES: Show him in, Mrs. Hudson.

SOUND EFFECT: DOOR OPENS. FOOTSTEPS

HOLMES: Ah, Inspector. Come in. Take a seat. Cigar?

LESTRADE: Good day to you, Mr. Holmes, and to you, Doctor. Thank you, but not so early in the morning. I have come to you today, because we at the Yard are faced with a mystery, and I have to admit to you, sir, that we are baffled.

HOLMES: (LOW) Not for the first time.

LESTRADE: Have you read the newspapers today, Mr. Holmes?

HOLMES: I am afraid not. I have, however, solved the problem of the Westmoreland House robbery. There is no urgency, however.

238

WATSON: Inspector, are you referring to the incident in Holloway that was reported in *The Morning Post*?

LESTRADE: Indeed so, Doctor. The facts of the matter are, briefly, Mr. Holmes, that at half-past-eleven the night before last, our constable on the beat was approached by a man who claimed to have heard screams and the sound of blows issuing from a house opposite his in Lowman Road, which is a quiet residential street –

HOLMES: – off the Hornsey Road. I am familiar with the area. (BEAT) Pray, proceed.

LESTRADE: Our man was further informed that this house was apparently unoccupied, and had been so for several months. However, he was told that a light was visible through the windows and, as I mentioned, sounds of an altercation could be heard.

HOLMES: I take it that he did not enter the house?

LESTRADE: He reported that all means of entry were locked. The man who originally informed the constable –

HOLMES: He has a name, I take it?

LESTRADE: Allow me to consult my notebook. (BEAT) The constable recorded his details as Mr. Josef Meyer, widower, originally from Bohemia, aged fifty-four, clerk, resident of Number 18 Lowman Road, which is almost immediately opposite Number 46, which is where the alleged incident took place.

HOLMES: Thank you. "Alleged", you say?

LESTRADE: Indeed. Upon visiting the address in question, the constable observed that the house appeared to be deserted, and all doors and windows were securely fastened, as he had been told. No sound issued from the house, and there were no lights visible. Meyer, as I was saying, had previously informed our man that this was not the first time he had seen lights in the house from his room in the house opposite, but had assumed that it was the result of tramps having broken into the house and set up camp there for the night. On this occasion, the sound of shouts and screams, and what sounded to his ears to be some sort of fight, was sufficient to send him out into the street to seek assistance from our man.

HOLMES: And I take it that there has been no evidence of tramps using the house in the way suggested by this Josef Meyer?

LESTRADE: We have yet to enter the house to determine the truth or otherwise of this assertion.

SOUND EFFECT: HOLMES LIGHTING AND DRAWING ON PIPE

HOLMES: Tell me. What was this Josef Meyer wearing when he approached your constable?

LESTRADE: I have no idea. You would have to ask Constable Ruddock for the answer to that question.

HOLMES: I intend to do so, if you wish my assistance in this matter. I also intend speaking to Mr. Meyer and to visit Number 46, in company with you and your men.

LESTRADE: Thank you, Mr. Holmes.

HOLMES: There is no time like the present. Come, Watson. Lestrade, let me while away the time on our journey to Holloway by informing you of the location of the Westmereland rubies.

(FADE)

SCENE 2: LOWMAN ROAD

SOUND EFFECT: LOWMAN ROAD OUTSIDE NUMBER 46. HORSE-DRAWN TRAFFIC

LESTRADE: So here we are, Mr. Holmes. Number 46, where the ghostly lights and sounds were observed is just over there.

WATSON: You surely do not believe in ghosts, Inspector?

LESTRADE: In cases like this, I do not know what to believe. As Mr. Holmes has remarked to us on more than one occasion, when you

240

have eliminated the impossible, whatever remains, however improbable, must be the truth.

HOLMES: Ghosts, my dear fellow, are impossible. Therefore we may eliminate them from our enquiries from the start. I have neither the time nor the patience to provide you with my reasoning on the subject. Come.

SOUND EFFECT: DOOR HANDLE RATTLES

HOLMES: As you said, Lestrade, it is locked. And the windows all appear to be securely fastened. There is no sign of entry from the front. Let us proceed to the rear of the house.

SOUND EFFECT: THREE SETS OF FOOTSTEPS ON PAVEMENT AND GRAVEL. DOOR HANDLE RATTLES

HOLMES: Again, locked. Lestrade, you have no objection to my picking the lock, I take it? Excellent. (GRUNTS)

SOUND EFFECT: LOCK SNAPS. DOOR OPENS

HOLMES: Enter, gentlemen.

SOUND EFFECT: THREE SETS OF FOOTSTEPS ON WOODEN FLOOR

LESTRADE: I am glad you are on the side of law and order, Mr. Holmes. I believe that even the most skilful housebreaker in London could not match you in this matter of opening locked doors.

WATSON: Lestrade, you said that this house is reported to have been unoccupied for several months?

LESTRADE: That is correct.

WATSON: The floor seems suspiciously free of dust and grime for a building that has been empty for so long.

HOLMES: Very well observed, Watson. Indeed, there is a little dust, but it has been swept, and recently, by a broom, almost certainly that which is standing in that corner.

WATSON: I do not believe tramps would be so fastidious when it came to the place where they sleep.

HOLMES: Indeed so. Nor ghosts, Inspector. I have never heard of ghosts that keep their surroundings clean.

LESTRADE: I confess that the idea of spirits seems more unlikely, given this fact.

HOLMES: And what of the light that was observed? Let us see if the gas is still connected. (PAUSE) No, there is no gas here. Did Meyer mention what kind of light he had seen? No? We must interview Mr. Josef Meyer soon, before his memory fades.

LESTRADE: Indeed so. (PAUSE) There is a spot of candle-grease on this table, Mr. Holmes.

HOLMES: And the table has also been cleared of dust, which means that the candle, wherever it might be now, was lit and placed here relatively recently. I am guessing that it would be visible from the street if the door to the hallway was open as it is now. Shall we move into the front room?

SOUND EFFECT: THREE SETS OF FOOTSTEPS ON WOODEN FLOOR. THEY SUDDENLY STOP

WATSON: (GASPS) My God, Holmes! Look there, in the corner!

LESTRADE: Is he dead?

SOUND EFFECT: ONE SET OF FOOTSTEPS ON WOODEN FLOOR

WATSON: (OFF) Garrotted, poor soul. The ligature, some sort of leather whip or lash, is still embedded in the flesh of his neck. You can see it just below the beard. He is a big man. I cannot see that it would be easy to beat him in a fair fight, but with a weapon such as this . . . .

HOLMES: There is the argument that was reported to your man, Lestrade.

LESTRADE: Aye. I must call in the constables.

242

HOLMES: Quick, Watson, who is he? Let us search his pockets before Lestrade and his myrmidons come in with their boots and disturb whatever evidence remains. A-ha! A letter, in German, no less, addressed to Tómaš Kiska. A Bohemian name, if I am not mistaken. Let us see his boots. Ah yes, from that part of Europe, to be sure. The little distinctive touches, Watson, that help determine a man's origin. A man may change his clothes in order to appear as a native of another nation – see how this man's coat and trousers are distinctively English – but he will invariably fail to change his boots, which will always bear the mark of his native country.

WATSON: See here, Holmes. Look. Below the right ear, where the beard stops.

HOLMES: Your powers of observation are coming on apace, Watson. That star-shaped tattoo is the mark that allows members of one of the most vicious and depraved group of European anarchists to identify each other. We seem to have stumbled upon a deep mystery, Watson, very deep.

SOUND EFFECT: FOOTSTEPS ENTERING THE ROOM

LESTRADE: Here he is, constable. Discovered anything more, Mr. Holmes?

HOLMES: For your ears alone, Inspector. First, though, we should examine the rest of the house before we go over the road and visit Josef Meyer.

POLICEMAN: What are we looking for, sir?

HOLMES: Anything that strikes you as being unusual.

POLICEMAN: The whole blooming thing seems a bit queer, sir, if you don't mind me saying so. This is my beat, and I know this house has been empty for several months now. Never seen or heard anything, and then this turns up.

LESTRADE: Any idea how long he's been dead, Doctor?

WATSON: Rigor is passing. Given the recent weather, I would say that death occurred sometime within the past forty-eight hours. However, I cannot say with certainty. However, I can be reasonably sure that this is the place where death occurred, as can be judged by the lividity of the body, and the fact that the garrote drew blood, which has dripped into the beard onto the body, and not onto the floor below it.

LESTRADE: So this man was killed here, at the time that Grimsley reports that he saw the lights and heard the noises? Who is he?

HOLMES: A letter in his pocket is addressed to Tomáš Kiska, and I have reason to believe, thanks to Watson's observation of a distinctive tattoo, that he is a member of an anarchist gang, sworn to exterminate the aristocracy and royalty of Europe.

LESTRADE: I admit that you sometimes see things that escape my notice, Mr. Holmes, but I would very much prefer it if you were not to meddle with the evidence before the police have examined it. Constable, you are to forget anything that you hear today between Mr. Holmes and Doctor Watson here and myself.

POLICEMAN: Very good, sir.

HOLMES: (SNORTS) Come, let us search the rest of the house.

SOUND EFFECT: DEPARTING FOOTSTEPS. (FADE OUT. FADE UP) FOOTSTEPS ARRIVING

LESTRADE: Nothing. The whole place is clean as a whistle.

HOLMES: Really, Inspector? You failed to mark this?

LESTRADE: A minute speck of cigarette ash? Hardly of importance.

HOLMES: On the contrary, my dear Lestrade. You are aware, are you not, of my monograph on the subject of the different types of tobacco ash? This is the ash of a certain type of German tobacco, of the kind generally rolled into cigarettes. To the best of my knowledge, it is unobtainable in this country, meaning that the person who smoked this tobacco brought it into England.

LESTRADE: We are dealing with foreigners, then, it would appear.

HOLMES: Indeed so. And let us recall that His Imperial Highness the Grand Duke of Hohe-Saxburg is due to visit this country in the next week. Any attempt on his life made here could seriously damage the relations between this country and the other great powers.

LESTRADE: It seems that we must interview Meyer now, as a matter of some urgency, in that case.

HOLMES: Precisely. Come.

LESTRADE: Constable, you are to remain here and to admit no-one, do you understand, without my permission, other than myself, or Mr. Holmes and Doctor Watson here.

POLICEMAN: Very good, sir.

SOUND EFFECT: FOOTSTEPS LEAVE. FADE TO FOOTSTEPS OUTDOORS. DOORBELL RINGS, FOLLOWED BY VIGOROUS KNOCKING ON DOOR

HOLMES: (CHUCKLES) Enough to wake the dead, Lestrade.

SOUND EFFECT: DOOR OPENS

MRS. BAXTER: Yes? Who are you, then, and what do you want?

LESTRADE: My name is Inspector Lestrade of Scotland Yard, and my friends and I wish to speak to a Mr. Josef Meyer, who we believe lives here. You are Mrs. Meyer, I take it?

MRS. BAXTER: Certainly not! My name is Elizabeth Baxter, and Josef Meyer is one of my lodgers.

LESTRADE: I beg your pardon, Miss Baxter.

MRS. BAXTER: Mrs.

LESTRADE: Sorry?

MRS. BAXTER: *Mrs.* Baxter, not *Miss*.

245

HOLMES: Be that as it may, Mrs. Baxter, we would like to speak to Mr. Meyer.

MRS. BAXTER: Well, you can't.

LESTRADE: Why not?

MRS. BAXTER: Because he's not here, Mr. Clever-dick Scotland Yard.

HOLMES: He's at work?

MRS. BAXTER: I don't know where he is. He went out two nights ago and hasn't come back. Leastways, his bed hasn't been slept in last night, or the night before, as I could see when I went in there this morning. And he hasn't been taking his meals with the other lodgers. And he likes his food, he does. He's a big man. He'd have all the eggs in the dish at breakfast and leave none for anyone else if I didn't put a stop to it.

LESTRADE: I see. Then may we see his room?

MRS. BAXTER: Not without a warrant, you can't. I know my rights – and his, even if he is a foreigner who can hardly speak English. You've no right to go poking your noses into his business. If he's done something wrong, I want to know what it is, first.

HOLMES: I'm afraid we can't answer that question at the moment, Mrs. Baxter. Can you tell me if Mr. Meyer smoked? A pipe, maybe, or cigarettes?

MRS. BAXTER: Not in this house, he didn't. And not out of it, as far as I know.

HOLMES: Thank you for your help, anyway.

MRS. BAXTER: I won't say you're welcome, because you're not. Now clear off, and come back with your warrants if you want any more out of me.

SOUND EFFECT: DOOR SLAMS

246

HOLMES: Charming! Will you make arrangements for the body to be removed?

LESTRADE: I have already done so, when I summoned the constable. Indeed, I believe this is the hearse coming towards us now.

SOUND EFFECT: HORSE-DRAWN WAGON APPROACHES AND STOPS

WATSON: There is no coffin.

LESTRADE: I requested none. Let me inform the constable on duty of their arrival and allow them to be admitted.

SOUND EFFECT: DEPARTING FOOTSTEPS

HOLMES: This is a strange business, Watson. Who is this Josef Meyer? Where has he disappeared to after informing the policeman of the disturbance in the house last night? As for the letter we discovered on the body . . . .

SOUND EFFECT: PAPER RUSTLES

WATSON: You retained it after removing it from his pocket?

HOLMES: To be sure I did. Lestrade may have it when I am done with it. My German is a trifle out of practice, Watson, so you must bear with my impromptu translation. Hmm . . . Yes, here we are. *"Be prepared for the visit next week. Ample supplies will be provided via the usual source. Visit Abigail from Hamburg. Three then four and reply with three."* Signed *"Gustav"*.

WATSON: And who in the world is this *"Abigail"*?

HOLMES: I do not know at present, but she may prove to be the answer to this riddle. Ah, they are bringing the body now.

WATSON: I fail to see why Lestrade didn't order a coffin, or at least a shroud. Whoever that man might have been, it hardly seems decent for his corpse to be carried in that way with no covering.

SOUND EFFECT: DOOR FLIES OPEN

247

MRS. BAXTER: (SCREAMS) There he is!

WATSON: Who, Mrs. Baxter?

MRS. BAXTER: That's Josef Meyer that they're carrying there. I just saw him from the front window.

HOLMES: I beg your pardon?

MRS. BAXTER: The man you've been looking for. I can see his face from here. It's him. He's dead, isn't he? I can tell.

HOLMES: Excuse me, madam.

MRS. BAXTER: What?

SOUND EFFECT: SCUFFLE.

MRS. BAXTER: Ouf! How dare you break into my house like this?

SOUND EFFECT: FOOTSTEPS GOING UP STAIRS. A DOOR OPENS AND CLOSES

MRS. BAXTER: I don't know who your friend is, but he's going to be arrested for trespassing, he is.

WATSON: My friend is Sherlock Holmes. You may have heard about him.

MRS. BAXTER: Oh. Then you are Doctor Watson, I take it? I've heard about you two. Read about you in the papers.

WATSON: I am, madam. Could you tell me something about the house opposite?

MRS. BAXTER: It's stood empty this past three months or more.

WATSON: And you have never heard any sounds come from there or seen lights?

MRS. BAXTER: I told you, it's empty.

248

HOLMES: I have it, Watson. It is all here in this newspaper. Apologies, Mrs. Baxter. You have done this nation a great service. Greater than you will ever be allowed to know. Accept the thanks of a grateful nation. Watson, let us meet Lestrade, inform him of what we have just learned, and make our way to Scotland Yard, where we can interview the constable who met the purported Josef Meyer last night.

WATSON: (CLOSE) "Purported"?

MUSIC: LINK

SCENE 3: SCOTLAND YARD

LESTRADE: I still find it incredible that the man who informed us of the lights and the argument taking place in an empty house should be found strangled inside that very house.

HOLMES: You are making one very elementary mistake, my dear Inspector.

LESTRADE: That being?

HOLMES: That the man who reported the incident to your constable is the same man whose body we discovered.

WATSON: Is it not possible that after he left the constable, he entered the house, where he was set upon and killed by those whom he had noticed earlier?

HOLMES: I doubt it very much. The house did, after all, appear to be empty and deserted when the good constable examined it. Ah, but speak of the Devil . . . .

LESTRADE: Constable Ruddock, this is Sherlock Holmes, who has been good enough to give us some small hints in the past regarding some of our more difficult cases, and his friend, Doctor Watson.

RUDDOCK: Pleased to meet you both, sirs.

HOLMES: You are the constable on duty who was addressed the other night by a Mr. Josef Meyer regarding a disturbance in an empty house on Lowman Road?

RUDDOCK: That is correct, sir.

HOLMES: And when you examined the house, was Mr. Meyer with you?

RUDDOCK: He was, sir.

HOLMES: And what did you see in the house?

RUDDOCK: Well, I couldn't see nothing, sir. All the doors and windows was locked, and when I looked through the windows, all I could see was black, sir. The house is a fair way off from the nearest streetlamp, and my lantern wasn't strong enough to see more than a yard or two inside the rooms.

HOLMES: So what did you say to Mr. Meyer when you had discovered this?

RUDDOCK: Well, sir, it's a funny thing, and somehow I forgot to put it in my report. When I had finished trying to look in through the back window, I turned 'round, and I was going to say to Meyer that he was imagining things. Well, blow my eyes, he'd scarpered. He wasn't there anymore.

LESTRADE: Blow your eyes indeed, Ruddock! Why did this not go in your report?

RUDDOCK: It sort of slipped my mind, sir.

LESTRADE: We will have words about this.

HOLMES: Later, Lestrade, later. Anyone can make a mistake. Now, Constable, can you describe this man to us?

RUDDOCK: Well, it was only by the light of the streetlamp, sir, and I didn't get that good a look at him, but he had fair hair, cut very short. A small man, much smaller than you or me, sir.

HOLMES: Moustache? Beard?

RUDDOCK: Clean-shaven except for a small moustache, sir. Fair, like his hair.

HOLMES: And how was he dressed?

RUDDOCK: Now that is something that did strike me, sir. Half-past-eleven at night, most folks in that area are in bed. It's not like it's the West End, where the toffs have parties and come home half-seas over at all hours. Begging your pardon, sir.

HOLMES: Granted.

RUDDOCK: Well, he wasn't drunk, I'd take my oath on that. But what struck me was the fact he was fully dressed – shoes, socks, collar and tie, and all. And yet he told me he'd been watching from his window in the house opposite and seen the lights and heard the noises from there. Would you expect someone to dress themselves up in that way if they were going out to look for help from the police on something like that, sir?

HOLMES: I agree, it seems unlikely. So he was wearing a collar and tie?

RUDDOCK: Yes, sir. I remember it most distinctly. That and the patent-leather boots. And the way he spoke – it wasn't quite right. Something queer about it. Sort of foreign.

LESTRADE: We want you to identify a body, Ruddock. Go to the mortuary in Holloway and ask to see the body of Josef Meyer.

RUDDOCK: He's dead, sir? The man I talked to the other night? I can't believe it.

HOLMES: Neither can we. Which is why we need your help in identifying him.

LESTRADE: And when you return, Ruddock, we will have words on this importance of making a complete report.

RUDDOCK: Sir.

SOUND EFFECT: DEPARTING FOOTSTEPS

HOLMES: Don't be too hard on him. Even without his identification of the corpse, we know that the body is not of the man who identified himself as Josef Meyer to your man. Slight build, heavy build; fair hair, dark hair; small moustache, full bushy beard; patent-leather shoes, hobnailed boots; slight accent, can hardly speak English.

WATSON: The two men seem to be exact opposites of each other.

HOLMES: No accident there, I am sure. These contradictions, seemingly pointing in opposite directions, may actually be a signpost pointing to a solution of this mystery.

LESTRADE: One of your theories, Mr. Holmes?

HOLMES: As yet, no definite theory, but a multitude of ideas. In the meantime . . . .

SOUND EFFECT: PAPER RUSTLES

LESTRADE: What is that?

HOLMES: A letter, in German. Tell me, does the name "Abigail" from Hamburg mean anything to you?

LESTRADE: I have never heard of her.

HOLMES: Now see here.

SOUND EFFECT: PAPER RUSTLES

HOLMES: This newspaper dated two days ago. Column four. The list of ships arriving at the East India Dock.

LESTRADE: *S.S. Abigail*, Hamburg. Arrived on Tuesday, and will sail this evening. Why is this important?

HOLMES: I strongly suspect that this ship is the bearer of the infernal machine or whatever means of destruction the dead man was meant to use in the assassination attempt on the Archduke. He would be unable to bring it in as a traveller, but as part of a ship's cargo, it

252

would be relatively easy for it to arrive in this country and be delivered – or, as I believe in this case, collected by the recipient.

WATSON: But how did you make the connection with the ship, Holmes?

HOLMES: Later. For now, let us make haste to the East India Docks. Lestrade, bring along several of your stoutest constables, and you may want to alert the River Police in case the *Abigail* tries to give us the slip.

MUSIC: LINK

SCENE 4: EAST INDIA DOCK

SOUND EFFECT: SOUNDS OF GULLS, WATER, MACHINERY, ETC.

HOLMES: There we are, the *Abigail*. She may not look like an impressive vessel, but I believe she carries the seeds of destruction. Consider the international situation should an attempt on the Archduke's life be made in this country, whether it is successful or otherwise.

WATSON: It would be war in Europe, for sure, and we here in Britain would not escape it.

HOLMES: Indeed so. Lestrade, I feel that I may have more success here than the uniformed police. Watson here is armed with his revolver, and I myself am carrying my loaded riding-crop, together with my swordstick. Should it become necessary, however, I will use my whistle to summon you and your men. (BEAT) And have no fear, Lestrade. When all this is over, should it come to the attention of the press, Inspector Lestrade will have all the credit, and Sherlock Holmes none.

LESTRADE: Most generous of you, Mr. Holmes. God speed. We are ready and waiting should you need us.

HOLMES: Come, Watson. Let us make our way to the *Abigail*.

WATSON: (LOW) Holmes, I do not have my revolver with me.

253

HOLMES: (LOW) I am aware of that. Nor is the stick I am holding my swordstick.

WATSON: (LOW) Then . . . ?

HOLMES: We proceed.

SOUND EFFECT: FOOTSTEPS

HOLMES: We are close enough.

WATSON: What are you doing, Holmes, holding up three fingers in that way?

HOLMES: I am waiting for the countersign of four fingers. Ah! You see it, Watson? On the poop. The master of the vessel, if I am not mistaken. I raise three fingers in reply and . . . .

SUSSBINDER: (OFF) Come aboard!

SOUND EFFECT: FOOTSTEPS UP GANGPLANK

HOLMES: *Guten Tag, Herr Kapitän.*

SUSSBINDER: Ah, you speak German, Inspector?

HOLMES: *Ein bißchen.* A little. However, I am not a policeman, let alone an inspector. My name is Sherlock Holmes, and this is my friend and colleague, Doctor Watson.

SUSSBINDER: *Zufrieden.* Otto Sussbinder at your service. Delighted to make the acquaintance of such a distinguished detective. And of you, Doctor. I have enjoyed your accounts of the cases which Mr. Holmes has undertaken in your company. Now, how may I assist you gentlemen?

HOLMES: I must ask you to return to Germany, carrying back to there the infernal machine which was to be collected by Tómaš Kiska.

SUSSBINDER: (LAUGHS) Mr. Holmes, there is no infernal machine. There never has been any infernal machine.

254

WATSON: But surely, Kiska was an anarchist?

SUSSBINDER: He was.

WATSON: And he was in contact with an anarchist group who would supply him with the means to destroy the Archduke on his visit here, to be delivered on this very ship?

SUSSBINDER: That is what he believed, yes.

HOLMES: (PAUSE) What rank do you hold in the police force of Hohe-Saxburg, Herr Sussbinder?

SUSSBINDER: Ah, you have guessed my little secret, Mr. Holmes. My congratulations. I am a captain in the police of the Archduchy of Hohe-Saxburg, with a special responsibility for thwarting the plans of anarchists.

HOLMES: And Kiska was in fact in contact with *you*, believing himself to be taking orders from a group of nihilists?

SUSSBINDER: Indeed so. You have it precisely. We had previously placed him in that room in Lowman Road opposite the empty house, to which we had keys – you do not need to know the details of how we obtained them, but I can let you know at some other time if you require the full story. One of our agents in this country used this empty house for meetings with Kiska at night.

HOLMES: A smaller man, fair haired, with a moustache, well-dressed?

SUSSBINDER: Indeed, that is a fair description of the man I will refer to as Gustav. Last night, he met Kiska to discuss the final details of how the supposed infernal machine was to be collected, and an argument ensued over money, as you might have expected. Kiska – you have seen the man's body, yes? – was a strong and powerful man, but Gustav, despite his size, is an extremely tenacious and skilful opponent, and was able to twist his riding-crop around Kiska's neck, and thereby kill him.

WATSON: The trachea was crushed. Death must have been swift.

SUSSBINDER: Having left the body where it fell, Gustave proceeded to take the sole candle which had illuminated the evening's proceedings, and decided upon a risky course – that of alerting the British authorities to the existence of Kiska. He therefore gave his name as the alias being used by Kiska, and told one of your English policemen that he had witnessed a suspicious happening in the empty house. As the policeman attempted to examine the interior of the house, Kiska escaped into the night.

HOLMES: And you intended us to discover that the man who had alerted the police was not who he said he was, and that we should discover the true identity of the dead man?

SUSSBINDER: Indeed so. There are those in your Government who are aware of the existence of Kiska, but were not aware of his presence in this country. I decided to make you a gift of him. We could, of course, easily have disposed of the body, and the man known as Josef Meyer would simply have disappeared.

HOLMES: And the whereabouts of the man you call Gustav?

SUSSBINDER: That, I am afraid, I will not tell you. He is, of course in strictly legal terms, a murderer, and has killed on English soil, but I ask you to ask yourselves, Mr. Holmes and Doctor Watson – are you really so anxious that he should face the gallows?

WATSON: For my part, I am ready to let him go free, given that he has likely saved Europe from war.

HOLMES: Good old Watson. The voice of England has spoken through you. We will make no further enquiries regarding Gustav.

WATSON: One question, Captain Sussbinder. When we entered the empty house, the floor, the table, everything was clean and swept. Why?

SUSSBINDER: Must you ask? We are Germans, and as you know, we Germans like everything to be just so. It was impossible for Gustav to be in a place as dirty as that house had become. (PAUSE) Now, if there is nothing further that you wish to know, I will bid you farewell. We sail on the tide.

HOLMES and WATSON: Farewell.

WATSON: How will you explain this to Lestrade?

HOLMES: Despite appearances, he is no fool. He will understand.

(FADE)

## SCENE 5: BAKER STREET

WATSON: Holmes, I can understand most of your reasoning, but how did you deduce that *Abigail* referred to a ship and not a person?

HOLMES: When I made my way into Mrs. Baxter's house, I was able to go straight to the room where Kiska had been lodging. Remember, we were told that the lights had been observed from his window, so it must have been one of the rooms at the front of the house on the first floor. One of them was locked, and Mrs. Baxter had told us that she had been into Kiska's room. That door was unlocked as I expected, and, by good chance, there was the newspaper, on the bed, open at the shipping page.

WATSON: Wonderful.

HOLMES: Elementary.

WATSON: And the deduction that his killer was no criminal, but an agent of the law?

HOLMES: Everything was too perfect. The man who talked to the constable, pretending to be Meyer, was the complete opposite of the Meyer lodging in Mrs. Baxter's house. The letter addressed to Kiska – had he been killed by one of his fellow anarchists, that letter would have been removed. The letter itself, though addressed to a Bohemian, presumably from a Bohemian group of nihilists, was written on German paper from a manufactory in Hohe-Saxburg. The very fact that the body, together with the incriminating weapon, and more importantly, the mark identifying its wearer as a member of a criminal society, was left for us to discover. The fact that there was no sign of forcible entry to the house. And, as you remarked, the cleanliness of the place. All this pointed to an operation conducted with Teutonic thoroughness. I therefore had no hesitation in

257

approaching the *Abigail*, though I confess to deceiving Lestrade to the extent of requesting constables for assistance.

WATSON: It could have turned out otherwise.

HOLMES: A possibility, true, but a remote one. And now, I must consider how to inform brother Mycroft of these happenings.

SOUND EFFECT: THE VIOLIN STARTS AGAIN, TUNELESS, BUT PLAYED WITH BRAVURA AND CONTINUES FOR A FEW SECONDS BEFORE IT STOPS.

HOLMES: (CLOSE) That is, of course, unless he already knows all about them.

SOUND EFFECT: THE VIOLIN STARTS AGAIN

# The Diogenes Club Poltergeist
# by Chris Chan

Readers who follow the exploits of Sherlock Holmes and myself will be familiar with the Diogenes Club, that remarkable gathering place for those antisocial men who wish to read quietly in a comfortable chair without having to deal with those most frustrating of creatures: Their fellow human beings. Holmes's brother Mycroft is a fixture of that peculiar assemblage of the resolutely unclubbable. Members of the Diogenes Club are strictly forbidden from speaking, and an atmosphere of absolute silence is rigidly imposed within its walls, except in the Stranger's Room. While the majority of men, including myself, might find the values of this club to be utterly alien to their own tastes, the world is composed of every conceivable sort of person, and the members of the Diogenes Club continue to bother no one and insist that no one bother them.

This rigidly enforced peace was shattered one overcast winter's day when Holmes received a telegram from Mycroft at breakfast. He read it, raised an eyebrow, and wordlessly handed it to me. It read:

*Sherlock –*

*Pay no attention to the letters from my fellow members of the Diogenes Club. Burn them unread.*

*– Mycroft*

"Why on earth would Mycroft want you to destroy letters from his fellows at the club?" I wondered. "And how could you possibly know that the letters *were* from members of the club without reading them first? Surely you don't know the names of every man who belongs to that bizarre organization?"

"As for your second question, the correspondence of men writing from the Diogenes Club is immediately distinguishable by the club's stationary, which is thicker than the standard envelopes and writing paper, and possesses a distinctive watermark. It's true that I only know a handful of the club's members' names, and at the moment I have no idea why Mycroft would be so anxious for me to avoid reading their correspondence. But if I may point out an important point, Watson, you are missing a much more important question."

"And that would be?"

"Why would members of the club be writing to me in the first place? One of Mycroft's fellows might conceivably choose to consult me about something, but more than one? Surely it is too much to believe that multiple members of that group would simultaneously feel compelled to write to me with different problems? Therefore, they must all be writing about the same issue. Now, there is no link between the club members other than the club itself. They come from all walks of life, and they mostly have no contact whatsoever outside the walls of the club. It follows, then, that there is some problem threatening the sanctity of the club. The members are not in the habit of consulting each other, so multiple members are sending letters of their own initiative, rather than one letter representing the entire group.

"We can further deduce that the problem is one that involves some crime or mysterious circumstance. If it were some simple matter, such as an overly talkative member, they could simply take the normal steps to remove the offender. But if there is a problem that would require my involvement, why would Mycroft request that I stay out of the matter? Normally, he would jump at the chance at letting me handle such a situation, because his deep-seated indolence would make him resent any call for him to investigate himself. I can only assume that Mycroft considers the problem at hand to be a situation that is unworthy of my modest powers, and that he feels so strongly about the matter that he decided to send me a telegram that would reach me before the morning post."

Holmes's theories were verified less than an hour later, when he received no fewer than nine envelopes which bore the watermark of the Diogenes Club stationery. After rifling through the sealed stack, he declared, "Clearly, Watson, the members of the club are under a great deal of distress."

I knew he was expecting me to respond with an incredulous. "How could you possibly know that, Holmes?" Perhaps it was a sudden impulse of recalcitrance, but I refused to provide him with the prompting question he obviously desired. After a few silent moments, Holmes looked up at me with an expression that was both slightly chiding and a gentle plea, and my resolve shattered. Reluctantly, I asked the question I had refrained from posing mere moments earlier.

"Quite simple, my dear fellow. Smell the sealed adhesive on these six envelopes."

I did so. "Brandy. Whisky. Whisky again. Beer. More whisky. Gin."

"Precisely. The men who composed these letters have been drinking profusely. But the members of the club never drink to excess – at least inside the walls of the building. Overconsumption of alcohol leads to loosened tongues, which leads to conversation, which is exactly what members come to the Diogenes Club to avoid. If six members required several strong drinks to write a letter to me, then something particularly upsetting happened there, something disturbing enough to make previously restrained men succumb to the comforts of the bottle. And I notice some important points on these two that do not smell of alcohol. The penmanship on both envelopes clearly shows the untidiness of a distraught mind. The stamps are askew. The ink has splattered a bit on both of these envelopes – clearly the pens were being held by people in a state of nervous agitation. Of course, the similar ink blots on the other six envelopes further prove that the men who wrote these letters drank to excess."

"Yes, but what is the cause of their distress?"

"That I cannot tell without opening the letters. And as curious as I am to figure out what is going on, my dear brother has specifically requested that I burn these envelopes unopened, and I would not dream of jeopardizing my relationship with my sibling over something so trifling as curiosity over the contents of some envelopes."

At that moment there was a knock at the door, and Mrs. Hudson entered with a telegram. Holmes tore it open, laughed, and tossed it to me.

*Sherlock –*

*On second thought, don't burn the letters. Bring them to me as soon as you get them.*

*– Mycroft*

"Mycroft certainly enjoys giving you orders," I mused.

"He has no doubt realized what can be deduced from this morning's correspondence, but for once Mycroft is a step behind me. He cannot determine who is behind whatever event is shaking up the Diogenes Club without seeing these envelopes, so I must bring them to him. It should only take Mycroft a few seconds to make the same deduction that I did about the identity of the party behind whatever is bothering the members of the club. Let us meet him in his rooms, Watson, and see what has caused this wave of unrest."

It was not until we were shaking hands with Mycroft in his sitting room that I realized that Sherlock Holmes had failed to explain exactly what in the unopened correspondence he had received was so revelatory.

261

I had no time to ask, however, since Mycroft took control of the conversation before I could speak.

"I heard from my sources that you led the police to make an arrest in the Gunton case," Mycroft told his brother.

"That's correct."

"Did you make the connection to the Barnett garroting from three years ago?"

"I wasn't aware of that case. Remember, I was pretending to be dead at that time. I was on the other end of the world and I was unable to follow the local crime news."

"Of course, of course. You need to have a word with your Scotland Yard friends. I suspect that Malvern may have been involved in both crimes. The signature is identical."

"I shall inform Lestrade to look into that immediately. But you didn't summon me here to talk about the Gunton case. What exactly is happening at the Diogenes Club, dear brother?"

Mycroft groaned and leaned back in his chair. "It's a terrible inconvenience. The calm and quiet of my sanctuary has been shattered. Many members of the club are convinced that there is a . . . a *poltergeist* disrupting the building."

"Excuse me?" Holmes responded as if he hadn't understood a word that Mycroft had said.

"A poltergeist, or some such rot. The outlandish belief that some malevolent supernatural being is haunting the Diogenes Club, wreaking havoc and upsetting the members."

"Surely a collection of grown men could not possibly give any credence to such a ridiculous supposition," I scoffed.

Mycroft frowned at me. "You forget, Doctor, that the membership of the Diogenes Club is not based upon being skeptical or level-headed. The sole criterions are to dislike unnecessary conversation and to be able to refrain from speaking. Many of the men who populate our membership may well be superstitious and possess a belief in 'ghoulies and ghosties and long-legged beasties and things that go bump in the night'. I wouldn't know. I've never shared two words with the vast majority of our membership, so I have no idea what sort of men they are. Frankly, until recently, I've never really cared about their personal thoughts or beliefs, and I hoped that they never extended any curiosity towards mine. Now, I am reluctantly forced to conclude that I am surrounded by hysterics."

Holmes pressed the tips of his fingers together and frowned. "Surely there must be some sort of reasons for this widespread delusion."

"Of course. It's nothing more than a series of practical jokes. Mean-spirited ones, but all easily explainable. Windowpanes, bottles, glasses, vases . . . anything that's fragile is shattering without apparent cause. The past week, members have been reading their newspapers, only have them catch fire while they were reading them. Members are being pelted with rotten food or splashed with icy cold water while they doze off in their chairs."

"There's absolutely nothing mysterious about that," Holmes scoffed. "The broken glass and china? A simple catapult would explain that. The newspapers? A magnifying glass focusing the rays of a light sources. The rotten food? All that would take is an arm with good aim, or perhaps the catapult again."

"What about the ice water?" I asked.

"Any mechanic or engineer could design a simple device shaped like a pistol that sprays a stream of water when you pull the trigger. Or possibly a smaller version of a syringe used to spray pesticide on plants."

"Of course, Sherlock. As expected, your train of thought is following mine precisely. Nothing that occurred cannot be explained by pranks known to any mischievous schoolboy. The mysterious disembodied voices that have been plaguing several members of the club at inopportune times – "

"Ventriloquism."

"Obviously. But a number of club members – and some members of the staff – insist that they've actually *seen* the poltergeist."

"Really? What does it look like?"

"Eyewitness descriptions vary, which is not surprising. They all agree that the supposed poltergeist can fly, and that an unearthly glow emanates from it. But after that point, the witnesses' testimony differs. Some people claim that it has a massive tail, others say three heads, others say enormous wings, or bright red eyes. No two descriptions match."

"How long has the poltergeist been active?"

"Just under a week. But the damage it has done to the club is incalculable."

I seized this opportunity to reenter the conversation. "You mean the physical harm caused by the destruction?"

"No, Watson! The noise! Due to all of the disruption, all of the chaos, the unthinkable has happened. Members of the club are actually . . . *talking to each other*. The Stranger's Room is filled to bursting with club members chatting, sharing their experiences about being pestered by the poltergeist, and their personal theories about its origins and what it's trying to accomplish with its hijinks. And the members of the club are carrying on their conversations elsewhere! They are interacting with each other socially, and even forming the beginnings of friendships!"

I attempted to keep my voice level. "And how does that pose a danger to the club?"

From the look on his face, Mycroft's evaluation of my mental powers had never been lower. "It means the end of all that we stand for! If a majority of the members of the club petition to amend the rules so that they can spend time together, they will destroy the spirit and purpose of the club. As we know it, the Diogenes Club will cease to exist! It will become a place of *socializing*, just like any other club in London!"

I realized that it would not be a wise decision to voice the thoughts that were currently running through my mind, and I worried that my facial expression would produce a similar effect to the one that I sought to avoid, so I rose with a quiet "excuse me" and crossed over to the window. Mycroft's well-known aversion towards moving longer distances than necessary played a pivotal role in his selection of the building across the street from his personal rooms as the site of the Diogenes Club. As I looked through the window and stared at the building across the street, I mentally noted how undistinctive it was. There was no sign identifying its purpose. Had I not known what was inside its walls, I would have walked past the building without a second thought, and had anybody asked me to take a guess as the structure's use, I would have been left at a complete loss.

Even as I watched, I was brought out of my meditations by the sound of shattering glass, followed by the sight of a man falling out of a top-story window of the Diogenes Club. As he fell, I saw a small object with an eerie green glow flying out the window, zigzagging through the air, and zooming away out of my line of sight.

Immediate action was clearly necessary. "Holmes! Mycroft!" I rapidly explained the situation as I bolted out of Mycroft's flat and sprinted down the stairs. Holmes was right behind me. Though I couldn't see him, I knew that if he did choose to follow us, Mycroft would be proceeding at a much slower pace.

I had neither enough time nor enough breath to tell Holmes what I had seen. Within moments, I was examining the man who had just defenestrated from the club. Fortunately, the building was not particularly tall, and the man had struck a fairly leafy tree on the way down, which had destroyed several branches, but had also slowed his rate of falling enough so as to substantially reduce the risk of fatal damage. After a basic check of his limbs, it was clear that both of his legs and his right arm were broken, though mercifully there did not seem to be any damage to his head.

The poor man was clearly suffering from shock. I gently leaned over him until I could make direct eye contact with him. "Sir, if you can hear me, you have sustained some serious injuries, but at the moment I do not believe that they will be life-threatening. Nor will they be permanently debilitating." The injured man didn't reply, but his eyes latched onto my gaze, so I concluded that he could hear me. "Can you tell me what happened to you? Why did you fall out the window? Did you jump, or were you pushed?" Those was probably more questions than I ought to have asked, but I was rather shaken from what I had just seen, and my bedside manner needed a little refinement.

The injured man blinked a few times and then sighed very softly. I crouched over him for a little over half-a-minute, until finally he spoke.

"*The . . . polt . . . er . . . geist . . . .*" After these two words, his voice trailed away and his eyes broke contact with mine.

"Will he be all right?" Holmes abruptly reminded me of his presence, causing me to start involuntarily.

"He's passed out, but he'll live and most likely recover, after a lengthy period of convalescence."

"I have summoned an ambulance, but it will be some time before it arrives. How are you feeling? Will you need a drop of brandy in order to recover yourself?"

My first instinct was to happily accept, but I immediately remembered that I still had a patient that needed my attention, and when the ambulance arrived I wanted to explain the injured man's condition without liquor on my breath. After I politely declined, Holmes took a moment to direct the gathering crowd to stand further back. Having finished, he leaned over to me and asked, "As you were running out of Mycroft's rooms, you mumbled something about a green glow. Would you mind explaining what you meant, please?"

I nodded and rapidly informed Holmes of the flying object with the unearthly aura that sailed out the window and into the street. "I've no idea what it was, Holmes. I'm quite certain that it wasn't really a poltergeist or any other paranormal creature, but for the life of me I couldn't possibly tell you what it really was."

I was grateful to observe that there was no incredulity or judgment in Holmes's face. He listened my eyewitness account, nodded, thanked me, and immediately left the scene, returning a little under five minutes later.

"Where did you go?" I asked.

"I summoned some much-needed assistance. Have you determined this injured man's identity?"

With a bit of self-reproach, I confessed that I hadn't checked his wallet or searched for any other form of identification.

"I can save you the trouble," Mycroft's voice boomed from behind me. "His name is Rufus Darbington, and he is one of the men who sent you a letter." Mycroft turned to Holmes. "Before this happened, you were about to show me the correspondence you received today. May I please see it now?"

Holmes swiftly withdrew the stack of envelopes from his pocket and passed it to his brother. Mycroft grunted something that I could only assume was an expression of thanks, and he rifled through the sealed correspondence, squinted at the writing on each one, and sniffed each envelope in turn.

"Darbington's is the one that smells of gin," Mycroft proclaimed. "He is very fond of some bizarre concoction known as a 'martini'. He has been drinking a great many of them the last few days."

"Now that you have had a few seconds to examine the evidence, no doubt you have arrived at the same deductions that I have," Holmes commented.

"Of course. I suspected him from the beginning, of course, but his letter confirms it."

I felt the need to re-insert myself into this conversation. "Excuse me, please, but what are you two talking about?"

"We will explain everything in a moment, Watson. The ambulance is arriving. As soon as this man is safely on the way to hospital, the three of us will – Mycroft, should we meet inside the Stranger's Room or your own flat?"

"My flat, I think. We can be assured again of utter privacy and of no ears to the keyholes there."

The moment the three of us were securely ensconced in Mycroft's comfortable chairs, Holmes began explaining everything to me.

"I realize that you didn't get a chance to examine the letters I received this morning, but I believe that I described them sufficiently enough for you to figure out *which* was the notable one, even if you couldn't possibly know *who* is the person who is currently our most prominent person of interest."

"And you haven't even opened the letters yet!"

"True, and it's certainly possible that there may be useful information inside of them. But use your powers of memory, Watson. Describe what you know of the letters."

I cast my mind back. "Nine letters. Six of them smell of various kinds of alcohol. I believe that at least one smelled of whisky – "

"For the moment, the types of alcohol consumed by those who licked the envelopes are irrelevant. What else?"

"Two more did not smell of alcohol, but the writing was sloppy and the stamps askew. The liquor-scented ones were messy as well."

"Precisely! Which leads to which important point?"

"Six plus two is eight. What of the ninth envelope?"

266

"Capital, dear fellow, capital! Of the nine envelopes sent to me today, only one was addressed in neat handwriting and did not smell of alcohol. I hasten to add that several of the envelopes that smelled of liquor also had messy handwriting on them. Clearly, the men who wrote the letters were distraught. It showed in their shaking hands in their excessive consumption of spirits. But only one man sent me a letter that did *not* betray any signs of distress. What does that mean to you?"

I took a breath and pondered my answer for a moment. "It means that the person who wrote the ninth letter was not upset like his colleagues were. It might be concluded that he is simply a preternaturally calm and unflappable person, or at least does a better job of disguising his distress from the world. But it might also imply a more sinister motive. This man may not be visibly nervous because he knows for a fact that he has nothing to be worried about, which would only be the case if . . . ." I realized that I was pausing for dramatic effect, and silently I chastised myself for doing so. "Maybe he knows the true facts behind the appearance of this supposed poltergeist. Perhaps he's the hoaxer who has been playing the unexpected pranks. I don't know for certain, but I perhaps the whole reason for writing a letter was to deflect suspicion. This was a miscalculation, because you and your brother were wary immediately."

Holmes laughed and his eyes twinkled with delight. "Don't forget to include yourself along with Mycroft and myself. It fooled none of us."

"I do have one more question."

"And that, no doubt, is 'Whose name is on the suspicious envelope?'" With a smile, Holmes once again removed the stack of correspondence from his pocket and handed me the top envelope.

Reading aloud, I declared, "'*Ian Dynell*'."

"What do you know of him, Mycroft? I realize that the nature of the Diogenes Club makes it unlikely that you would ever have a lengthy conversation – or even a short one – with him, but surely you would have done some research regarding his background before admitting him to membership?"

"I know precious little of Mr. Dynell, other than the fact that he is a solicitor's clerk, he's married with four energetic children, that his wife is very fond of talking, and they live with his wife's extremely opinionated mother."

"That explains why he might seek out the solace of the club."

"Indeed. I was surprised that he could afford the membership fees, as the well-worn state of his suit made it clear that he was a man of limited income."

"How long has he been a member?"

"A little under a month. Only a few weeks, in fact. He's the most recently inducted member."

I couldn't help myself from asking a question, even though I was certain that I already knew the answer. "Is there any sort of initiation ceremony for new members?"

Mycroft stared at me as if I'd asked him to knit a sweater for an elephant. "Of course not! In fact, one of the questions we ask prospective members is what they'd like us to serve at their welcoming banquet. If they fail to recoil in horror at the prospect of an evening of socializing, or if they don't ask if they can eat their banquet dinner alone or something like that, we know at once that they are not Diogenes Club material, and we deny their application for membership at once."

All I could manage was a very small nod.

"Perhaps we can speak to Mr. Dynell," Holmes said. "Do you know where he would be right now?"

"There's a chance that he's at the club. He's been in the habit of eating an early lunch most weekday afternoons and then returning at some point in the evening."

"Then may I suggest that we three cross the street to question him? Normally I wouldn't wish to disturb you, dear brother, but your presence will assure our entry."

As we entered the club, I noticed that there was no sign of the police, and mentioned the fact.

"There's no reason why they should be here," Mycroft replied. "None of the members want the authorities tramping about our sanctuary and asking impertinent questions. Besides, the members are well trained in scrupulously ignoring their fellows. I wouldn't be surprised if everybody simply failed to notice Darbington falling out the window. Now, remember the rules. No more talking from this point on, please. If you absolutely must communicate, use these pads of paper and pencils." Mycroft took those items from a pair of baskets on a nearby table and then handed them to us.

Holmes immediately began scribbling. *Shall we investigate the dining room?*

Mycroft didn't bother writing a reply. He simply nodded and gestured towards a pair of large oak doors. As we passed through, we saw a couple of elderly gentlemen sitting at a table and drinking. Both looked as if they had already imbibed well past the point of propriety, especially it being so early in the day. Mycroft wrinkled his nose, as if it was positively abhorrent to him to see two club members sitting in such close proximity to one another, even if they weren't speaking a single word.

268

Holmes's pencil flew across his pad of paper and showed it to us. *"These are Grove and Quarles, I presume?"*

Mycroft nodded.

*"How did you know their names?"* I wrote.

Holmes replied by scrawling, *"The men are clearly unnerved and using alcohol to steady their nerves. Clearly the type of men who would write to me to investigate a supposed poltergeist at their club. The ink stains on their right hands matching the ink on the letters further supports my conclusions. You will note that Grove is drinking brandy and Quarles is gulping down beer. I matched them to the names on the alcoholic odors on the envelopes. Simplicity itself."*

Mycroft pointed a large finger at a table in the corner. No one was seated by it, but there was a glass of water and a large bowl of some lumpy beef soup upon it on it. The bowl was only half full, and a great deal of the muddy-looking brown broth had spilled over all the floor-length white tablecloth. Holmes crossed over, examined the aforementioned items, as well as the saltcellar, the napkin, fork, and spoon, and frowned.

*"What's missing, Watson?"* he wrote.

*"The man eating this food?"* I scribbled back.

*"True, but what else?"*

After two more seconds, I had it. *"Where's the knife?"* I wrote.

Holmes nodded and looked thoughtfully at the table, and then lifted up the long white tablecloth that reached the floor. Underneath it was a very dead body with a table knife sticking in its throat. I took a moment to confirm that life was extinct, then stood to look at what Holmes was writing to Mycroft.

*"Dynell?"*

Mycroft nodded.

*"We shall have to summon the police now."* Holmes scribbled.

*"Nonsense. It's clear who did this. You just need to find the proof, and the police should be satisfied. They won't ask the club members any impertinent questions then."*

*"I just need to find the proof."*

*"Well you don't expect me to investigate, do you?"*

I joined the silent conversation, writing, *"How can you possibly know who did this?"*

*"Look at what's next to the body."*

As soon as I read Holmes's note, I noticed a large, bloodstained white napkin lying on the ground beside the corpse.

*"The sort of cloth worn by a waiter over his arm while serving. Dynell was stabbed by his own waiter while he ate, and the waiter used the cloth to protect himself from being spattered with blood."*

*"You can't be sure of that. There are a hundred – "*

Holmes didn't let me finish writing. *"A quick investigation will prove it."*

Grove and Quarles were still drinking silently. *"Shouldn't we question them? They could be witnesses?"*

Mycroft dismissed my idea. *"Useless. Diogenes Club members take no notice of each other, alive or dead. When Major Strausser had his fatal heart attack last fall in a library armchair, it was five days before the smell alerted his fellow clubmen to the fact."*

I was finding not being able to use my voice to be increasingly frustrating. *"Can I please start talking now? I'm running out of paper and the lead is wearing out on my pencil."*

*"Certainly not."* Mycroft wrote that two-word note with such authority that I didn't have it in me to question it.

Holmes crossed the room and opened a door, causing the sound of kitchen noises and the odors of cooking to fill the air. He motioned to the two of us and we followed him inside. A chef was calmly chopping vegetables.

Holmes scribbled another note and passed it to Mycroft, who nodded. Holmes then showed it to me, so I could see that it read, *"Where are the waiters?"* Holmes then showed the note to the chef.

The chef wiped his brow with the back of his hand and glared at Holmes. "Listen, gov. I know the rule about not talking in the club, but this is my kitchen and I set the rules. I can't write little notes when I'm filleting fish, can I? If you have a question for me, you can use your bloody voice."

"Very well," Holmes pocketed his notepad and pencil. "What is the name of your waiter, how long has he been working here, and where is he now?"

"His name's Canterville, he's been here for about a week because he's filling in for our regular waiter who's been ill, and he stepped out for a smoke."

"How long ago has it been since you've seen him?"

The chef's forehead creased. "Quite some time, come to think of it. At least ten minutes. Maybe fifteen."

"He won't be coming back." Holmes turned to Mycroft. "There's nothing for it now. I suggest that you bite the bullet and summon the police."

Mycroft made a sour face and took a spoonful of Lancashire hotpot from a casserole dish, presumably in order to comfort himself. "Very well. I shall not call for your friends Lestrade or Gregson, though. I happen to know an inspector whom I can trust to be completely discreet and keep inconvenient questions to a minimum."

"It doesn't matter to me whom you tell at Scotland Yard, Mycroft – only that you begin the search for this waiter. This supposed poltergeist is no simple prank. It is part of a far more dangerous and sinister plan."

I need not explain the events of the next hour. When the inspector Mycroft referred to earlier arrived, I was struck by the fact that I'd never before met an officer of the law so disinclined to assert his authority. The man was completely obsequious to Mycroft, and accepted his suggestions as to how to track the missing man down without question.

After the inspector left, the three of us settled in the Stranger's Room. I initiated the conversation by asking, "What do you intend to do to catch that waiter, Canterville?"

"We have already done everything that we ought to do, Watson. The official police are far more suited to a major manhunt than a private detective. They have the funds, the time, and the inclination to catch a killer who is almost certainly *not* named Canterville."

"What makes you so sure that it's an alias?" I asked.

"Perhaps you haven't read it, but there is a popular novella by Oscar Wilde titled *The Canterville Ghost*. I dare say that when our perpetrator applied for the job as a waiter, he consciously or unconsciously used a reference to a paranormal tale when planning a plot about a fake poltergeist."

"But what was the purpose of the whole charade? Simply to annoy the members of the Diogenes Club?"

"Oh, no. I'm convinced it was far more sinister than that. I must admit that I have only a fair guess at what the culprit's endgame was, though I can take some solace in the fact that brother Mycroft clearly has a better idea of the motive, judging from his posture."

Mycroft grunted in reply, then gave a tiny nod.

"Think less about the action – creating a fake poltergeist – and focus more on the *consequences* of the action, Watson."

"Many members of the club were scared."

"True, but that was not the main desired consequence. The ultimate goal was more than merely spooking the gullible. Consider what happened."

I pondered for a moment. "The Diogenes Club ceased to be a sanctuary for men seeking peace and quiet."

"Precisely dear fellow! Exactly!" Holmes beamed. "So what does that mean?"

"That members would be less likely to visit the club."

"Magnificent! And the desired result of that would be?"

271

I hesitated. "Fewer members would lead to reduced payment of dues. That would lead to financial problems for the club, which could conceivably lead to the eventual closure and the sale of the building. Could this whole charade have been driven by someone's desire to purchase the property?"

Holmes folded his fingers together. "An intriguing theory, Watson, but given the fact that the members pay annual dues, it would be months and months before the club would be short on funds."

"In any case," Mycroft added, "some of the club's members are sufficiently wealthy and dependent on the Diogenes Club as a refuge that they would gladly donate the necessary funds to keep it afloat in times of financial need."

At that moment, the dour concierge of the club entered the room, placed a salver with a pile of glowing matter and a note on the table next to Holmes, and shuffled away. I thought that he was far too dedicated to the club's theme of silence. It was only later that I learned that he was a lifelong mute.

"A-ha! My resourceful band of street urchins have managed to track down the object in question." Holmes held up the salver. "Behold the remains of the Diogenes Club poltergeist, Watson."

"What is that?"

"A form of rubber balloon, decorated with bits of glue and rubber to give it the appearance of a ghoul, and then painted with phosphorescent paint. The device was blown up, then released, causing it to fly around the room, making a shrieking noise as air escaped. A nervous person like Darbington could be startled by it to the point that he may have accidentally fallen from a window in a panicked desire to escape from it. Our culprit never expected that to happen. No, Darbington's injuries were not part of any plan. Neither was the balloon posing as a poltergeist planned to sail out of the broken window. Darbington's fall was a doubly tragic accident, because not only was the poor man injured, but Canterville, the mastermind of this plan, realized that his confederate Dynell was shaken up by the injury. I am quite sure that Canterville paid for Dynell's membership dues so that Dynell would serve as his assistant with the various pranks. Canterville himself took the role of a waiter so as to maintain an even lower profile. Perhaps his predecessor was paid off to feign sickness, perhaps he was mildly poisoned so as to give Canterville a chance to take over the job. Club members make a point of ignoring each other. They even more studiously ignore waiters. Dynell was guilt-striken over Darbington's injuries, doubtless wished to confess, and Canterville silenced him."

272

Holmes coughed, then continued. "You wondered, Watson, why I suspected a waiter. I was not inclined to write down my suspicions at that time, but I noticed numerous minute traces of phosphorescent paint on dozens of items in the dining room, such as eating utensils, saltcellars, candleholders, and napkin rings. I already suspected the use of a glowing device to simulate a poltergeist, and logically, a quantity of that paint would stick to the culprit's fingers. Who else would touch all of those items but a waiter? That is how I knew who was behind these disruptions."

Turning to his brother, Holmes asked, "So, Mycroft, why exactly was our man Canterville trying to empty out the club of its members? Surely he was up to some skullduggery where it would be in his interests to have as few potential witnesses as possible. And nothing of note ever happens within these walls. I remember a case where a man was drawn away from his place of business so a couple of scoundrels could dig in his basement to rob the bank next door. Could a similar principle be in play here? There is no bank next to the club. The only neighboring location of note is . . . your flat, dear brother."

"Precisely," Mycroft replied. "I'm in the middle of some tricky negotiations with a representative of a foreign government. In a few days, he is coming to my rooms for a secret meeting. I recently received some intelligence telling me that a trained assassin might be trying to strike my guest. I believe that Canterville is that assassin, and he planned to empty out the Diogenes Club so he could prepare for a strike. He wouldn't know the exact time of the meeting, but he could set up his rifle in the largely deserted building, and be prepared to take out the ambassador." Mycroft gave a little sniff that sounded suspiciously like a chuckle. "Little did he know that I have already taken precautions to protect my guest and myself. We had no intentions of making ourselves visible in the windows with the chance of being shot. This whole charade was laughably misguided from the beginning."

There is little more to tell. Darbington made a full recovery, aside from a slight limp in his left leg. Members of the club managed to take up a collection for Dynell's widow and children without saying a single word, and they easily raised enough to keep the Dynell family comfortable for several years. The man we knew as Canterville was captured and arrested the next morning, and Mycroft's meeting passed without incident.

Within a month, everything returned to normal at the Diogenes Club. Mycroft's fears that the members would begin forging amicable and talkative friendships proved unfounded. As the members who had been severely shaken by the antics of the "poltergeist" began to converse with each other, they overwhelmingly realized that they didn't really enjoy each other's company very much. The *status quo* of the Diogenes Club members ignoring each other was restored.

Holmes kept the "poltergeist" balloon, inflated it, and hung it in our rooms at Baker Street. "It is a reminder, Watson, that the unscrupulous can manipulate others with the possibility of the paranormal. We must remember not to dismiss the supernatural out of hand, but to thoroughly investigate such claims in order to determine if there is a more prosaic explanation."

# The Madness of
# Colonel Warburton
## by Bert Coules

*This drama was originally broadcast*
*on the BBC January 30th, 2002*

Following the BBC's ground-breaking audio production of the complete Canon, I was commissioned to write a series of follow-up adventures based on Doyle's intriguing throwaway references to other cases. "The Madness of Colonel Warburton" was the first of these.

I wanted to take Holmes and Watson into areas which their creator hadn't, and the world of spiritualism, the over-riding focus of the author's later years, was an enticing possibility. And there was a precedent: In *The Land of Mist*, he had been perfectly willing to let his maverick zoologist-explorer Professor Challenger not only research the subject, but also become convinced of its truthfulness. It's an intriguing novel, and for my money rather better than its popular reputation suggests.

A religious conversion seemed both inappropriate and unlikely for either Holmes or Watson, but perhaps there could be mileage in exploring the pair's attitudes to a movement which was drawing a lot of serious attention in late nineteenth-century England. Spiritualism, with its unique promise of hard physical proof to back up its claims, had a particular appeal for the scientific rationalist Victorian era: How would a scientific rationalist detective regard it? And how would his colleague, the romantic but ultimately feet-firmly-on-the-ground ex-army man, react to his friend's investigation?

A radio play-script isn't as easy to absorb as a story, but with luck the disjointed layout can disappear if the drama takes hold and you start to hear what you read. I hope that happens for you, and that you enjoy the experience.

Bert Coules<br>
July 2019

## THE CAST
*(in order of speaking)*

BESSMER: Smooth and sincere, but with a suggestion of the salesman or showman. Whatever his background, now occupying the lower fringes of gentility. Forties, fifties.

WARBURTON: Colonel James Warburton, hugely distinguished old soldier and man of integrity and honour. Sixties, seventies.

MRS. BESSMER: On the surface, a quiet, sympathetic, trust-inspiring woman, but with hidden depths and unsuspected talents. The same social background as her husband. Forties, fifties.

HOLMES: Sherlock Holmes, a detective.

WATSON: Dr. John H. Watson, a writer.

MICHAEL: Lieutenant Michael Warburton, the Colonel's only son and a rising star in his regiment. Early thirties.

SIR ROBERT: Upper-crust friend of Colonel Warburton. Sixties.

MAID: In the Bessmer household. Teens, early twenties.

MRS. FRYER: Grieving young mother. Educated, refined. Twenties.

MRS. COLE: From the respectable end of London society. Any age.

PC: Tired constable with a nagging wife, lumbago, and distressingly few opportunities to express himself. Any age.

WAITER: At a select London gentlemen's club. Any age.

SEXTON: Of a leafy suburban London church. Any age.

# The Madness of Colonel Warburton

*Of all the problems which have been submitted to my friend
Sherlock Holmes for solution, there were only two which I was the
means of introducing to his notice: That of Mr. Hatherley's thumb
and that of Colonel Warburton's madness . . . .*

– *Dr. John H. Watson,* "The Engineer's Thumb"

**TEASER. THE BESSMERS' PARLOUR. NIGHT.**

*A buzz of conversation and movement from half-a dozen people.*

BESSMER: Ladies and gentlemen.

*Silence falls. He has their attention.*

(*Backing off*) Fifty feet of rope. (*Vocal effort*)

*He pulls quite violently at the rope.*

Twenty feet of steel chain. (*Vocal effort*)

*The heavy chain clatters as he yanks on it.*

Sealed bandages over the eyes, ears, mouth, and other . . . natural
orifices. Would anyone care to examine the restraints?

THE SITTERS (*Variously*): No, by no means, of course not.

BESSMER: Colonel?

WARBURTON: Not necessary, thank you.

BESSMER: As you wish.

*He drops the chain.*

Are you quite comfortable, my dear?

MRS. BESSMER: Mm-mm.

BESSMER: Then I shall conceal you from view . . .

*He draws a heavy curtain across the alcove.*

. . . and we can begin. (*Suddenly low, solemn*) Friends – let us pray.

*Music: The opening theme.*
*Opening announcements.*
*The music fades into:*

## SCENE 1. THE SITTING ROOM AT 221b. DAY.

*Out of the music, close and disturbing:*

HOLMES: (*Tense breathing*)

*Glass chinks as a small bottle is replaced amongst others in a drawer.*
*The drawer is closed, and locked.*

(*The breathing turns into chuckling.*
*The chuckling grows into laughing.*
*The laughing develops an uneasy, uncontrolled edge.*)

*Suddenly, he breaks off – he can hear something. It's not audible to us.*

Ah! Unmistakeable. Right foot dragging. Must be tired. Top of the stairs. Pause. Rest. And on. On . . . On . . . And . . . *now.*

*The door opens revealing a tired Watson.*

Watson! Welcome home, welcome home, welcome home!

WATSON: It's good to be back.

*He closes the door.*

HOLMES: You had a bad journey. The train was late – no, you had trouble getting a cab.

WATSON: (*Approaching*) Not now, old man.

HOLMES: Yes, yes – trouble with the cab. Trouble with the cab. Trouble with the cab.

*Watson realises what's been going on.*

WATSON: Holmes . . . .

HOLMES: You had to wait in line behind two – no, three – other men, then had to lift your own suitcase on board. Three other men. Dreadful. (*He laughs*)

WATSON: Holmes, show me your arm.

HOLMES: Now don't lecture me, Doctor. I'm in too good a mood.

WATSON: Far too good. Come here.

*He grabs Holmes's wrist.*

HOLMES: (*Reacts*)

WATSON: Now . . . .

*He pushes back the sleeve.*
*Both men freeze. A long moment.*

HOLMES: I'm cutting down.

WATSON: Are you indeed.

HOLMES: Five percent solution. Better than seven, surely? I thought you'd be pleased.

*Cut to:*

## SCENE 2. THE BESSMERS' PARLOUR. NIGHT.

*Perhaps we're aware of a clock ticking.*
*An intimate conversation is taking place: Unhurried, untense, perfectly normal.*

279

WARBURTON: So, my dear. How is everything?

*He's talking to an elderly, refined woman.*
*This woman's voice appears courtesy of . . . .*

MRS. BESSMER: Now James, I've already told you. Stop fussing. It couldn't be nicer.

WARBURTON: There's plenty to occupy you, then.

MRS. BESSMER: Well I'm never bored, if that's what you mean. There are so many people to talk to. And there's always someone who needs my help.

WARBURTON: Now don't you go squandering your time on every lame dog, Elizabeth. I know what you're like.

MRS. BESSMER: Squandering my time? Don't be foolish, James.

WARBURTON: Oh, right. I suppose that's not really an issue.

MRS. BESSMER: No. Not really.

*Cut to:*

## SCENE 3. THE SITTING ROOM AT 221b. DAY.

*Continuing.*

WATSON: *Pleased*? Good God. (*Calmer*) No. No, what's the use? You've heard it all before.

HOLMES: That's true enough. Just as you've heard my reasons.

WATSON: Holmes, just because you don't have any work, you don't have to poison yourself with that filthy stuff.

HOLMES: Yes I do! My work is my oxygen. Take it away and I suffocate. I'm only alive when my brain has something to do.

WATSON: And you're seriously telling me that cocaine supplies that?

HOLMES: If only I could make you see. The clarity, the insight, the understanding. Without it . . . I can't live in your empty, everyday world, Doctor. It's like a prison.

*A moment.*

WATSON: Wasn't there *anything* while I was away?

HOLMES: Nothing of any interest. (*A moment*) I'm . . . sorry, Watson.

WATSON: Here.

*He holds out a bundle of letters.*

I brought up the post. There might be something.

HOLMES: Let's see.

*He takes the bundle and sorts rapidly through it, throwing the letters away.*

Nothing, nothing, nothing, social invitation, bill, nothing, nothing – ah . . . .

WATSON: What have you got?

*Holmes examines the envelope.*

HOLMES: Posted late last night in central London, but the writer lives out of town. A young man, well educated, with firm opinions. And the matter's important, but not urgent, because . . . ?

WATSON: . . . if it were, he would have sent a telegram.

HOLMES: Bravo, Watson. Bravo, bravo, bravo.

*A moment.*

WATSON: Well?

HOLMES: Well what?

WATSON: It's something important.

HOLMES: Oh yes.

WATSON: Then it could be a case.

HOLMES: It certainly could.

WATSON: Well then for the love of heaven open it!

HOLMES: I can't do that.

WATSON: Why not, for pity's sake?

HOLMES: Because it's addressed to you.

WATSON: (*An exasperated sigh*)

HOLMES: (*Chuckling*) Here.

WATSON: Thank you.

> *He takes the envelope, picks up a letter-opener and slits it open.*
> *He unfolds the letter and reads it, under:*

WATSON: It's from Michael Warburton.

HOLMES: A friend?

WATSON: Son of a friend. Well . . . .

HOLMES: An acquaintance.

WATSON: My old C.O. from the Berkshires – Colonel James Warburton.
Retired, now. This is about him.

HOLMES: Something's wrong?

> *Cut to:*

**SCENE 4. THE BESSMERS' PARLOUR. NIGHT.**

*Continuing.*

WARBURTON: So – everything's looking good, then.

MRS. BESSMER: "Good"? "Good" doesn't begin to describe it, my dear. It's simply . . . beautiful. Heaven is simply beautiful.

*Cut to:*

**SCENE 5. THE SITTING ROOM AT 221b. DAY.**

*Continuing.*
*Watson lowers the letter.*

WATSON: Yes. I think you could say that something's wrong.

*A violin passage takes us to:*

**SCENE 6. THE SITTING ROOM AT 221b. DAY.**

*Later.*

HOLMES: So, Mr. Warburton.

MICHAEL: Lieutenant Warburton, Mr. Holmes. I followed my father into the regiment.

HOLMES: Very good. Now, the facts, if you please.

MICHAEL: But surely you've seen my letter?

HOLMES: If you please.

MICHAEL: Very well. (*A breath*) My father is Colonel James Warburton. He's a soldier of great distinction, a man of intelligence and honour and the holder of the Victoria Cross. He is also absolutely convinced that his late wife – my mother – is communicating with him from beyond the grave.

HOLMES: A man's beliefs are his own affair, surely?

MICHAEL: Not if they affect the lives of other people, Mr. Holmes. On the advice of my dead mother . . . . (*He falters*)

WATSON: Go on, Lieutenant.

MICHAEL: On the advice of my dead mother, gentlemen, the old man's planning to give away everything he owns.

WATSON: To the regiment? To some charity?

MICHAEL: No, Doctor, not to a charity. He's giving the whole lot to the couple who bring him the messages from his wife.

*Cut to:*

## SCENE 7. THE BESSMERS' PARLOUR. NIGHT.

*After the séance: Drinks and chat.*

WARBURTON: Of course I'm sure it's her. I ought to know my own wife, man.

SIR ROBERT: Yes, of course.

WARBURTON: Besides, some of the things she says . . . No-one else could possibly know them. Everyone here says the same thing.

SIR ROBERT: Yes, I know. But even so. I mean, it goes against all reason.

MRS. BESSMER: (*Approaching*) You still have doubts, Sir Robert?

SIR ROBERT: Mrs. Bessmer.

BESSMER: (*Approaching*) You still have doubts, but you were open-minded enough to come.

SIR ROBERT: The Colonel here was very . . . persuasive.

BESSMER: We meet again on Saturday, Sir Robert. Come with an open mind and a clear heart and there could well be a message for you.

SIR ROBERT: For me?

MRS. BESSMER: We all have friends in the land of mist, Sir Robert. Companions, colleagues, loved ones. Will you come?

*A moment.*

SIR ROBERT: Yes. Yes, I will.

*Cut to:*

**SCENE 8. THE SITTING ROOM AT 221b. DAY.**

*Continuing.*

HOLMES: Does your mother actually appear at these séances?

MICHAEL: My mother is dead, sir.

HOLMES: Well then, does someone purporting to be your mother appear?

MICHAEL: No. As I understand it, there's just a voice in the darkness.

WATSON: Who is the medium?

MICHAEL: Her name is Mrs. Bessmer. It's her husband who runs things. That's all I know.

HOLMES: And you desire me to demonstrate to the Colonel that these Bessmers are frauds and the messages fake.

MICHAEL: Exactly so.

HOLMES: Hmm . . . Do you have any proof?

MICHAEL: Proof? I don't need proof. Good God, surely you're not suggesting that this business could be genuine?

HOLMES: I have no data. Until I do, I prefer to keep an open mind.

MICHAEL: An open mind?

HOLMES: The scientific approach. It's my way.

WATSON: For heaven's sake, Holmes.

MICHAEL: Well sir, it may be your way but it isn't mine. (*A moment*) Look . . . my father is . . . besotted with the Bessmers. He insists on singing their praises to anyone who will listen. His old friends, *my* friends . . . Dr. Watson, you understand what I'm saying.

WATSON: Yes, I'm afraid I do. The Colonel's making himself a laughing-stock.

MICHAEL: Exactly.

HOLMES: And you with him?

MICHAEL: I'll not deny it, but it's him I thinking of. His reputation, his good name . . . And beyond that, the honour of the regiment itself is at stake. I can't just stand by and let it happen.

HOLMES: I see.

MICHAEL: So if you can't help me, Mr. Holmes, I'll find someone else to snap him out of this insanity.

WATSON: Insanity? You think the Colonel's actually lost his mind?

MICHAEL: I wish I did think that.

HOLMES: What do you mean?

MICHAEL: If he were mad – certifiably mad – then he couldn't be held responsible for his actions.

HOLMES: And if there's no accountability, there's no shame? No disgrace?

WATSON: Exactly.

HOLMES: The military mind. Fascinating. (*Hearing something*) Ha!

WATSON: What's the matter?

HOLMES: I believe we're about to experience a visitation of our own.

*Suddenly, the door is thrown open.*
*A frozen moment.*

Won't you come in, Colonel? It's a little unfriendly to converse across the room – though I understand you're accustomed to somewhat greater distances.

*A moment. The Colonel says nothing.*

I am Sherlock Holmes. You might recall my associate, Dr. Watson.

WARBURTON: (*Approaching*) I know who you are. What has my son been telling you?

MICHAEL: Father . . . .

WARBURTON: Be silent, sir. You've no idea what you're dealing with. Mr. Holmes, has my son actually engaged you professionally?

HOLMES: He's enquired after my services. I've given him no answer, as yet.

WARBURTON: Excellent. Then we can consider the matter closed.

HOLMES: I think not.

WARBURTON: I beg your pardon?

HOLMES: Lieutenant, I'll give you my decision in the morning.

MICHAEL: Thank you, Mr. Holmes.

WARBURTON: I am not accustomed to being treated in this manner.

HOLMES: And now, good-day to you both. Watson.

WATSON: (*Crossing to the door*) This way please, gentlemen.

MICHAEL: (*Moving off*) Dr. Watson. Mr. Holmes. Father, are you coming?

*A tense moment.*

WATSON: Colonel?

WARBURTON: Very well.

*His footsteps move to the door.*
*He stops and turns.*

Mr. Holmes. This affair has implications beyond your understanding. I suggest that you keep your meddling nose out of matters which do not concern you. Good day.

*He goes. The door closes. A moment.*

HOLMES: Well, well, well.

WATSON: (*Approaching*) You were insufferably rude.

HOLMES: Yes, it's a useful technique sometimes. Well? What do you think?

WATSON: He's not mad. Just gullible.

HOLMES: Then you've made up your mind on the case.

WATSON: Holmes, the dead don't return in order to offer financial advice.

HOLMES: Perhaps not. We'll see.

*A violin passage takes us to:*

## SCENE 9. A STREET IN CENTRAL LONDON. DAY.

*Outside the Bessmer house.*
*Someone knocks at the door.*
*A maid opens it.*

MAID: Yes, sir?

BESSMER: (*Approaching from inside*) It's all right, Rose, I'll deal with this. Can I help you?

*The man on the step is a respectable, be-suited, quiet-spoken individual.*

HOLMES: Mr. . . . Bessmer, is it?

BESSMER: Maybe. Who wants to know?

HOLMES: Collins. Jonathan Collins. Perhaps I have the wrong house.

BESSMER: That depends, Mr. Collins.

HOLMES: I was told . . . (*Lower*) that you can . . . put me in touch with someone.

BESSMER: Who told you?

HOLMES: A client. Oh – I work at one of the City banks. Perhaps if I give you my card . . . .

*He fumbles for a card. He hands it over.*

BESSMER: Thank you.

HOLMES: A small establishment, but . . . select. Perhaps you've heard of us?

BESSMER: I have indeed. Please come inside.

*Cut to:*

## SCENE 10. A ROOM. DAY.

*Holmes and Bessmer approach.*

BESSMER: My wife is a wonderful woman, Mr. Collins. A wonderful woman who's been blessed with a wonderful gift.

HOLMES: Well, so I'm given to understand, yes.

BESSMER: Who is it you have in spirit?

HOLMES: I beg your pardon?

BESSMER: Who is it who's passed through the veil? Your own wife, perhaps? A parent?

HOLMES: Oh, I see. My sister, sir. Beatrice. Taken from me by illness.

BESSMER: It must have been a terrible blow.

HOLMES: Unendurable, Mr. Bessmer. I wasn't present at the . . . passing, you see. She called out for me, but I wasn't there.

BESSMER: Distressing.

HOLMES: She wanted to say something to me.

BESSMER: A message?

HOLMES: I can only suppose so. But . . . I wasn't there. It's eating me up, Mr. Bessmer! What was the message? What could it have been? I have to know! Can you help me? Tell me you can help me!

MRS. BESSMER: (*Appearing, slightly off*) We can help you.

HOLMES: (*In character, starts slightly*)

MRS. BESSMER: (*Approaching*) Have no more fear, Mr. Collins. You've come to the right place.

*Cut to:*

## SCENE 11. THE SITTING ROOM AT 221b. DAY.

*A moment.*

WATSON: Well? What happened then?

HOLMES: It was all disappointingly down to earth. They offered me tea and we sat and chatted.

290

WATSON: They were trying to put you off guard. So they could pick up useful information without your realising it, then . . . regurgitate it later, much to your astonishment.

HOLMES: I'd no idea you were such a fount of knowledge.

WATSON: You should try reading something other than the crime news for a change. The papers have been full of this damn business for ages. These people are everywhere. God alone knows where it all sprang from.

HOLMES: From two sisters in America back in forty-eight. Margaret and Katie Fox. A dead farmer spoke to them by rapping loudly on convenient surfaces.

*He demonstrates: Knock-knock. Knock-knock.*

WATSON: Good grief.

HOLMES: The entire movement sprang from there.

WATSON: I should have known you'd know all about it.

HOLMES: Not *all* about it. Not yet. But you're wrong about the questioning. Beyond Bessmer's first enquiry, there was none.

WATSON: Strange.

HOLMES: Not if they're genuine.

WATSON: For pity's sake.

HOLMES: Well, I shall find out tonight.

WATSON: Tonight?

HOLMES: For a trifling donation of forty guineas –

WATSON: (*Shocked*) How much?

HOLMES: – I'm invited to the next séance. Eight for eight-thirty.

*Cut to:*

## SCENE 12. THE BESSMERS' PARLOUR. NIGHT.

*The curtain is pulled closed.*

BESSMER: The medium is secured. We can begin. If you'll take your places.

*General movement, shuffling, sitting.*

HOLMES: (*Over*) There were six of us altogether, not including the Bessmers.

WATSON: (*Over*) Was the Colonel there?

HOLMES: (*Over*) Oh yes.

WATSON: (*Over*) Did he recognise you?

HOLMES: (*Over*) Please, Watson.

WATSON: (*Over*) Sorry.

BESSMER: Now, as you all know we have two new members of the circle with us tonight. Mr. Collins here has recently lost his sister to the spirit world –

THE SITTERS: (*Murmurs of condolence*)

HOLMES: Thank you, very kind.

BESSMER: – and Mrs. Fryer grieves for her daughter.

MRS. FRYER: Jane. Janey. (*She is close to tears*)

THE SITTERS: (*Murmurs of condolence*)

WARBURTON: You mustn't grieve, Margaret. She's not taken from you. She's just moved on, that's all. You'll see.

THE SITTERS: (*Agreement*)

MRS. FRYER: Thank you, Colonel. Thank you all.

BESSMER: They come, as you all have come, in search of The Great Truth.

THE SITTERS: (*A murmur of "Amens"*)

BESSMER: Mr. Collins, Mrs. Fryer, friends – if you'll put your hands flat on the table . . . .

MRS. FRYER: Like this?

BESSMER: That's the way. Now we all grasp the hands of the people next to us.

MRS. COLE: The circle of power.

HOLMES: Ah, yes, of course.

WATSON: (*Over*) Holmes this is the purest poppycock.

HOLMES: (*Over*) Is it?

WATSON: (*Over*) Well of course it is.

BESSMER: For the benefit of our new friends, I must explain that even though she's isolated behind the curtain, Mrs. Bessmer is under our supervision at all times. The least movement will be felt in the control ropes tied to her wrists. Colonel, you have yours?

WARBURTON: I have.

BESSMER: Mrs. Cole?

MRS. COLE: As safe as the Bank of England.

BESSMER: Very good. Now if we can all compose ourselves . . . (He takes a deep breath)

*The sitters settle into their places. Silence falls. A moment.*

HOLMES: (*Over*) We all sat there with our hands touching. Mrs. Bessmer was out of sight, tied up behind her curtain. Then Bessmer reached out behind him and turned out the lamp. It was pitch black.

*The atmosphere of the room for a long few moments.*

*Our senses are heightened in the darkness – we hear the clock ticking, the odd rustle of clothing, a throat being cleared.*
*Then, remarkably, these residual noises all cease and we are listening to a deep, pure, unsettling silence.*
*We listen. Nothing. Nothing. Nothing.*
*Then –*
*Crash!*
*Deafening in the silence, something falls to the floor just beyond the circle.*

THE SITTERS: (*Gasps*)

MRS. BESSMER: (*Starts to moan*)

HOLMES: (*In character*) Oh my dear Lord . . . .

BESSMER: It's all right, Mr. Collins. The power is upon her.

MRS. BESSMER: (*Louder moaning*)

MRS. FRYER: Mrs. Bessmer!

BESSMER: Don't be alarmed. This is perfectly natural.

MRS. BESSMER: (*A muffled cry. Then silence*)

*A long, tense moment.*
*Then, from the opposite side of the room to Mrs. Bessmer, unclear and unformed, the voice of a three-year old girl.*

Mummy?

MRS. FRYER: (*Gasps*)

MRS. BESSMER: (*Growing stronger and clearer*) Mummy? Mummy?

294

MRS. FRYER: Oh dear God.

MRS. BESSMER: Mummy?

MRS. FRYER: Jane? Janey darling – is it really you?

MRS. BESSMER: Course it's me, Mummy. Janey Janey Sugar Caney.

MRS. FRYER: (*Through tears*) I used to call her that! I used to . . . .

VARIOUS SITTERS: There. It's all right. You see? Didn't we say?

BESSMER: Talk to her, Mrs. Fryer.

MRS. FRYER: Yes . . . Yes. Er . . . Janey darling – are you . . . all right?

MRS. BESSMER: Course I am.

11. MRS. FRYER: Oh thank God. Thank God.

THE SITTERS: Amen. Praise the Lord.

*A moment.*

MRS. BESSMER: I have to go now, Mummy.

MRS. FRYER: No! No, you mustn't! Stay here with me!

MRS. BESSMER: I can't Mummy. They won't let me.

MRS. FRYER: What? Who won't let you? What do you mean?

MRS. BESSMER: I'll try to come again, Mummy. If they'll let me. Come every week. Come every week . . . .

MRS. FRYER: No! No . . . . (*She sobs*) Ah! Something touched me! Something touched my face!

THE SITTERS: (*Gasps*)

BESSMER: It was her spirit departing from the circle. You're very privileged to have felt it.

295

THE SITTERS: You're so lucky. You must have been very close. She sounded so lovely.

BESSMER: Let's compose ourselves, friends. I feel there's more to come.

*They settle again. Intense silence returns.*
*At last, from another part of the room:*

MRS. BESSMER: (*As Mrs. Warburton*) Good evening, James.

WARBURTON: My dear.

MRS. BESSMER: I have something for you.

WARBURTON: What do you mean, Elizabeth? Something for me?

MRS. BESSMER: There is too much doubt in the world, James. Too many people have closed their minds to the truth.

WARBURTON: People who should know better.

MRS. BESSMER: Yes. The power is strong tonight. Your belief makes it strong. Believe, James.

WARBURTON: I do believe.

MRS. BESSMER: I bring you something for those with no faith. I bring you proof.

*Then, from Mrs. Bessmer's original position:*

(*A muffled scream*)

WARBURTON: Elizabeth!

BESSMER: Don't break the circle! Stay where you are, all of you!

MRS. FRYER: Oh my God! Look!

THE SITTERS: (*Gasps*) Dear God. Heaven protect us. Oh my Lord . . . .

BESSMER: Keep calm. Keep perfectly calm.

*They try to keep calm.*
*An intense silence.*

HOLMES: (*Over*) There was something in the centre of the table. Something darker than the darkness. A shape.

WATSON: (*Over*) Holmes, what are you saying?

HOLMES: (*Over*) It moved. It was . . . growing. Stretching . . . .

WATSON: (*Over*) A trick.

HOLMES: (*Over*) It changed. It became . . . a form.

*Back in the scene:*

BESSMER: (*Hushed*) Nobody move. It won't harm us.

WARBURTON: (*Realising what it is*) No. No, she won't.

WATSON: (*Over*) Oh, now come on.

HOLMES: (*Over*) It was a figure. Kneeling in the centre of the table. There was something in its – in *her* hand. She laid it in front of the Colonel . . . And then – she was gone.

*A frozen moment. Then:*

THE SITTERS: (*React, relax*)

BESSMER: I'm going to put the light on.

*A match flares. A gas mantle pops.*

HOLMES: (*In character*) Mrs. Bessmer – is she all right?

*Bessmer opens the curtains.*

BESSMER: My dear?

MRS. BESSMER: Mm – mm – mmm . . . .

BESSMER: Wait.

*He loosens the sealed bandages.*

There.

MRS. BESSMER: (*Gasping for air*) What . . . ? What happened?

WARBURTON: This happened.

THE SITTERS: What? What is that? What did she give you?

WARBURTON: It's what she promised me. My proof. It's my wife's wedding ring. She was buried wearing it.

*A frozen moment. Then we . . . .*
*Cut to:*

## SCENE 13. THE SITTING ROOM AT 221b. NIGHT.

*We have caught up with the voice-overs.*

HOLMES: Well, Doctor?

WATSON: What kind of human being robs a grave for profit?

HOLMES: You're convinced it was some sort of trick, then.

WATSON: Of course it was a trick. You were in total darkness! They could have done more-or-less anything.

*He gets up and crosses to the sideboard.*

Were there any other . . . manifestations?

*He pours two drinks and returns, under:*

HOLMES: No, that was the grand finale.

WATSON: "Mr. Collins'" sister didn't show up then.

298

HOLMES: No.

WATSON: They hadn't had time to dig up enough details to make it convincing.

HOLMES: Yes, the same thought occurred to me.

WATSON: (*Returning*) Oh, so you're not completely on their side. Here.

*Holmes takes the drink.*

HOLMES: Thank you. I'm not on any side. Not yet.

WATSON: I'm pleased to hear it.

*A moment. They drink.*

So – what will you tell the Colonel's son? Will you accept the case?

HOLMES: Oh, didn't I mention that? I already have.

*He drains his drink.*

I'm going out. Don't wait up.

*Cut to:*

## SCENE 14. OUTSIDE THE BESSMER HOUSE. NIGHT.

*Very quiet and still.*
*An echoing hansom several streets away.*
*A distant barking dog.*
*Close, a burst of tapping.*
*It stops . . . And restarts.*
*Holmes is testing the window pane.*
*He tries a different spot. He stops.*

HOLMES: Hmm . . . .

*He tries to slide open the window.*

299

*(Grunts with the effort)*

*No joy. He gives up.*

Very well, then . . . .

*He unrolls a small burgling-kit.*
*Tools clink as he selects one.*

Now . . .

*He tries to force the window . . . .*

*(Effort)*

*. . . and finds it surprisingly resistant.*
*Nothing gives. Holmes desists.*

Well, well, well. Fascinating.

PC: (*Well off*) Oi! You!

HOLMES: (*Unfazed*) Ah.

*The PC – still off – blows his whistle.*

*Cut to:*

## SCENE 15. THE SITTING ROOM AT 221b. NIGHT.

WATSON: Wasn't that just a touch drastic? Burgling their house?

HOLMES: I didn't burgle it. I didn't get inside.

WATSON: Only because you were nearly caught by the police.

HOLMES: Give me some credit, Watson. I am more than a match for a
tired constable with a nagging wife and lumbago. Besides, he wasn't
the reason.

WATSON: Then what was?

HOLMES: The reinforced glass, the triple locks on the windows, and the case-hardened bolts on the back door. Our Mr. and Mrs. Bessmer value their security. What are they protecting, do you suppose? Their lives?

WATSON: Or their secrets. There's been a development.

HOLMES: Something happened while I was out?

WATSON: A message.

HOLMES: From our client?

WATSON: From his father.

HOLMES: O-ho. Another warning for me to back off?

WATSON: Actually, the message was for me.

HOLMES: Oh?

WATSON: The Colonel wants to see me. Tomorrow.

*Cut to:*

## SCENE 16. A GENTLEMAN'S CLUB. DAY.

*Two drinks are put down.*

WAITER: Gentlemen.

WATSON: Thank you. Your health, Colonel.

WARBURTON: Frankly, Doctor, I'm sick and tired of hearing about my health. The Berkshires.

WATSON: The Berkshires.

*They drink.*

WARBURTON: Now, Watson – I have a proposition for you.

*Cut to:*

## SCENE 17. THE SITTING ROOM AT 221b. DAY.

HOLMES: Splendid!

WATSON: You think so?

HOLMES: Don't you? It means I don't have to risk the disguise again. You'll be there as a legitimate invited guest. It couldn't be better. What's your objection?

WATSON: Suppose the Bessmers know who I am?

HOLMES: I'm sure they will. John H Watson, the famous crime-writer.

WATSON: And biographer of a certain celebrated detective. If I walk in to their house . . . .

HOLMES: Why should they make the connection? You said the Colonel hasn't told them I'm involved.

WATSON: No. But even so.

HOLMES: You'll simply be there as a friend of one of the regulars – and a possible convert . . .

WATSON: Huh.

HOLMES: . . . so why should they be suspicious?

WATSON: I still don't like it.

HOLMES: Alerting the Bessmers isn't what's worrying you, is it. What's really wrong?

*A moment.*

WATSON: You've already said it. The Colonel's invited me because he thinks I'll be convinced. He wants me to sing their praises in *The Strand Magazine*.

HOLMES: And you can't see that happening.

WATSON: Of course I can't. If I go, it'll be a betrayal of trust. I can't justify it.

*A moment.*

HOLMES: I've been making some enquiries of my own. A little discreet investigation into the other sitters.

WATSON: What were you looking for?

HOLMES: Discharged servants, garrulous neighbours, relatives given to gossip – any possible source for the Bessmers' private knowledge.

WATSON: And?

HOLMES: I found nothing. I need more inside information. Watson . . . .

*A solo violin, low and eerie. It runs under:*

## SCENE 18. THE BESSMERS' PARLOUR. NIGHT.

*The* séance *is getting under way.*
*The room is pitch dark and the mood is hushed.*

BESSMER: Open your hearts. Open your hearts and open your minds. And they will appear.

*The low, atmospheric music continues.*
*Through it, we become aware of the usual sounds: The clock, shuffling, a discreet cough, perhaps a dog or distant carriage from outside.*
*This all lasts until we can't stand it any longer. Then:*

MRS. BESSMER: (*A muffled cry*)

*The music cuts. Dead silence.*
*Then, from another part of the room:*

John? John? Can you . . . hear me?

303

*It's the voice of a gentle, cultured woman in her late twenties. It grows stronger, more definite.*

John?

WATSON: (*Sotto*) My God.

MRS. BESSMER: John? Aren't you there? Speak to me! Please!

*A tense moment.*

WATSON: Who is it?

MRS. BESSMER: Oh John. Have you forgotten me so soon? (*Close, intimate*) It's Mary. It's your wife.

*And in the darkness, the unmistakeable sound of a kiss.*

*Cut to:*

**SCENE 19. THE SITTING ROOM AT 221b. NIGHT.**

*Slam! A furious Watson shuts the door.*

WATSON: (*Approaching*) The Bessmers are crooks. I want them stopped.

HOLMES: You have proof?

*Watson is upset as well as angry.*

WATSON: In all the years we've worked together . . . . (*He can't go on.*)

HOLMES: Tell me what happened.

WATSON: They . . . (*He gets a grip.*) They presented me with Mary. They had the damnable gall to . . . conjure up my wife like some tenth-rate music-hall act.

HOLMES: You saw her?

WATSON: I saw nothing. I *heard* a lot of platitudes about love and faithfulness and heaven. And I felt . . . well, never mind what I felt.

304

And don't you dare ask me if it could have been real. I swear to you on everything I hold dear, my Mary was *not* in that room. You believe me?

*A moment.*

HOLMES: I believe you.

*A violin passage. It runs under:*
*A train rattles past, whistle blowing.*
*Train and music mix down to:*

## SCENE 20. A TRAIN. DAY.

*Clattering along.*

HOLMES: Beyond your first name and your wife's, were there any other private details?

WATSON: No, none.

HOLMES: Nothing they couldn't have discovered for themselves, then. Your names – even the fact that you had a wife, who died young – it's all a matter of public record.

WATSON: But what about the other sitters? "I heard things no-one else could possibly have known." They all said it. It's their main reason for believing. So the Bessmers must be getting private information from somewhere.

HOLMES: There is another possibility.

WATSON: There is?

HOLMES: Think about that atmosphere. The build-up, the expectation, the darkness, the tension. You must have felt it.

WATSON: Yes, I did.

HOLMES: And think about the others. The look in their eyes. The hunger. The need for reassurance.

WATSON: You're saying they're more than half-way convinced even before the séance starts.

HOLMES: And so they read more into the messages than is actually there. Exactly.

WATSON: Yes, that makes sense. It would help with the voices, too. They *want* them to be real.

HOLMES: And the result is instant faith.

WATSON: Instant riches too, at forty guineas a time. But I don't know . . . .

HOLMES: What's troubling you?

WATSON: The ring. What about the ring?

HOLMES: Ah yes. What about the ring.

*Cut to:*

## SCENE 21. A CHURCHYARD. DAY.

*The leafy outskirts of London.*

SEXTON: (*Approaching*) Here we are, gentlemen. The Warburton vault. It's been in the family for more than ten generations.

HOLMES: And the late Elizabeth Warburton is buried here?

SEXTON: And has been these thirteen years.

*Watson tries the locked iron gates.*

WATSON: How many people have a key to these gates?

SEXTON: Only the family.

HOLMES: So it wouldn't be possible to go inside the vault.

SEXTON: I'm afraid it's out of the question.

HOLMES: Ah.

SEXTON: I'm sorry your journey's been wasted.

HOLMES: My dear Sexton. It's been nothing of the sort.

*Cut to:*

## SCENE 22. AN OPEN CARRIAGE. DAY.

*Clopping along.*

HOLMES: Neither the ground nor the locks have been disturbed in a very long time. Capital.

WATSON: The ring was a fake, then. A duplicate.

HOLMES: Evidently.

WATSON: That must have involved a lot of work. Discovering the style, having it made, making sure it looked old and worn.

HOLMES: Our friends are thorough.

*The carriage starts to slow.*

Ah – I think we've arrived. Time for us to divide our forces.

*Cut to:*

## SCENE 23. A ROOM IN THE WARBURTON HOUSE. DAY.

*Bare and somewhat cavernous.*

WARBURTON: If you've come to see my son, Mr. Holmes, you should have sent word first. It would have saved you a journey.

HOLMES: The lieutenant is not here, Colonel?

WARBURTON: He's at a regimental dinner in London.

HOLMES: Well, perhaps you'd be interested to hear of my progress.

WARBURTON: I would not. What my son chooses to do is his affair. I'll have no part in it. Since I know that the Bessmers are genuine, why should I be interested in your futile attempts to prove otherwise?

HOLMES: Why indeed. Good day to you Colonel.

*He walks to the door. He opens it.*

WARBURTON: Mr. Holmes.

HOLMES: Colonel?

WARBURTON: Some truths are the better for not being dragged into the cold light of day. I ask you to remember that.

*A moment.*

HOLMES: Colonel.

*He goes, shutting the door.*
*Cut to:*

*A train whistles past.*
*Mix to:*

## SCENE 24. A TRAIN. DAY.

*Clattering along.*

HOLMES: What did you see on your walk around the gardens? Describe the house.

WATSON: Well, only the central part is occupied. The rest seemed to be empty. Wasn't in too good a state, actually.

HOLMES: Any signs of repair work?

WATSON: None at all, not recently. What about indoors?

HOLMES: The same. Fascinating, don't you think? The servants were interesting, too.

WATSON: You spoke to them?

HOLMES: I counted them. Tell Mrs. Hudson you'll be dining alone tonight. I have work to do.

*The train for A moment.*
*Then Cut to:*

## SCENE 25. THE SITTING ROOM AT 221b. NIGHT.

*Watson is relaxing in his fireside chair.*
*He lights a cigar and draws on it.*
*He exhales unhurriedly.*
*The door opens. It's Holmes.*

HOLMES: Ah, Watson.

WATSON: You missed an excellent dinner.

*Holmes closes the door.*

HOLMES: (*Approaching*) Look at this.

*He brandishes a document.*

WATSON: What is it?

HOLMES: A copy of the Colonel's will. His *first* will, before the recent changes in favour of the Bessmers.

*Watson takes the will.*

WATSON: How did you get hold of this?

HOLMES: It was simple enough to find out the name of the Colonel's solicitor. I went round to his office . . . .

WATSON: At this time of night? (*Accusing*) Holmes . . . .

HOLMES: . . . where I discovered him working late. He was delighted to see me, happy to reminisce about the time I saved one of his clients from the gallows – and only too pleased to do me a small favour in return.

WATSON: Ah. Sorry.

HOLMES: You know, you can be far too suspicious sometimes. (*Deadpan*) I didn't need these at all.

*He tosses down his rolled-up burglary toolkit. It clanks.*

(*Chuckles*)

WATSON: (*Chuckles*)

HOLMES: Now – read . . . there.

*He indicates.*

WATSON: Let me see . . . (*He reads. A moment*) Well, it's unusual, but is it significant?

HOLMES: I think it's extremely significant.

WATSON: You do? Why?

HOLMES: Get your hat. I'll explain on the way.

*Cut to:*

## SCENE 26. AN ANTE-ROOM, THE CAFE ROYAL. NIGHT.

*From within an adjoining room, a gathering of boisterous young officers.*

OFFICERS: (*A buzz of drunken chat and laughter*)

*A door closes and the sounds are cut off. Michael Warburton has emerged.*

HOLMES: Good evening, Lieutenant Warburton. My apologies for interrupting your dinner.

MICHAEL: Good Lord, man, never mind that. What have you found out?

HOLMES: I believe I can prove to the Colonel that he's being deceived.

MICHAEL: You believe? Is your proof good enough to convince him or not?

WATSON: That's hard to say. His conviction is very deep-seated. It's based on something far stronger than simply the facts.

HOLMES: But then, that's exactly what you're counting on, isn't it.

MICHAEL: What?

HOLMES: You don't want me to disabuse your father. You've never wanted it. That's not why you engaged me.

MICHAEL: What are you talking about?

HOLMES: You had to be seen to be taking action.

WATSON: How would it have looked to the regiment if you'd just stood by and let your father give away his entire estate?

MICHAEL: Are you making some sort of accusation?

HOLMES: It would have looked suspicious in the extreme. And so you came to me – and engaged me to uncover the very fraud that you yourself were perpetrating.

MICHAEL: This is outrageous.

HOLMES: The Colonel's house was the vital clue.

MICHAEL: The house? What about the house?

WATSON: Your father's will – his old will – was quite specific. You were – (*to inherit . . . .*)

311

MICHAEL: How the devil do you know what was in my father's will?

HOLMES: Knowing things is my business. You were to inherit the house and the land on condition that you never sell them.

MICHAEL: Of course I wouldn't sell them. That house has been in our family for generations.

HOLMES: And now it's all but derelict. It would take a fortune to restore it – leaving you with nothing. You could say goodbye to your high life.

MICHAEL: You're saying I cooked up this whole business just to get rid of the house?

WATSON: You fed private information to the Bessmers. You supplied the duplicate wedding ring. You did everything in your power to make the séances convincing.

MICHAEL: I've never set eyes on the Bessmers.

HOLMES: What was your arrangement with them? What was your cut going to be when they sold the estate? What price did you put on betraying your father?

MICHAEL: By God, sir! (*He controls himself with an effort*) All right, that's enough. I've listened to you, now you can listen to me. There's not one single shred of truth in anything you've said. The thought that I would do that to my father . . . I have more cause to be grateful to my father than you can ever know. If you don't believe me then let's go now, right now, to these Bessmers and see if they recognise me. And while we're there I'll beat the truth out of them. I should have done that from the start. Well? Are we going?

*A long moment.*

HOLMES: No. It isn't necessary. Lieutenant, you have my profound apologies.

*Cut to:*

## SCENE 27. A SIDE STREET. NIGHT.

*Not busy.*

HOLMES: (*Breathes deeply*)

WATSON: What the devil was that all about?

HOLMES: I was wrong.

WATSON: Well, I realised that much. But what's changed your mind?

HOLMES: Weren't you listening to him?

WATSON: Of course I was. But you must have heard more than I did. What was it?

HOLMES: It's not important. The question now is what do we do next?

WATSON: Do we have to start all over again?

HOLMES: Of course not. I've solved the case.

WATSON: You have?

HOLMES: Well, to be strictly accurate, Lieutenant Warburton solved it for me. But what now . . . ? (*A moment*) Watson . . . .

WATSON: I know that tone. You need my help but you're not sure if I'll go along with it.

HOLMES: Am I really that transparent?

WATSON: Only to me. What is it? Another burglary?

HOLMES: I'm afraid it's something rather more . . . upsetting.

WATSON: You want me to go to another one of those damned séances.

HOLMES: That's . . . part of it.

WATSON: Part of it . . . Are you sure this time?

HOLMES: Quite sure.

WATSON: You can definitely put a stop to the Bessmers?

HOLMES: Yes, I can.

*A moment.*

WATSON: Right. What do you need me to do?

*A violin passage takes us to:*

## SCENE 28. THE BESSMERS' PARLOUR. NIGHT.

*A private gathering: only Watson, the Colonel, Bessmer, and Mrs. Bessmer, already trussed up in her alcove.*

BESSMER: Are you comfortable, my dear?

MRS. BESSMER: (*Slightly off*) Mm-mm.

BESSMER: Excellent.

*He draws the heavy curtain shut.*

Now if we could take our seats . . . .

*As they do so:*

WATSON: This is very good of you, Mr. Bessmer.

BESSMER: The Colonel is one of our greatest champions. And any friend of his . . . .

WATSON: The other night. When Mary came through . . . It was just . . . overwhelming.

WARBURTON: Same for me, first time.

WATSON: But with all those others there . . . Strangers. I mean, I just couldn't . . . You understand.

MR. BESSMER: There's no need to explain, Doctor. It's an intensely personal experience. We understand completely.

WATSON: It's really very good of you.

WARBURTON: You quite sure you want me here, Watson? I'd be perfectly happy to go. Wait outside or whatever.

WATSON: No, Colonel. You're used to all this, I'm not. I'd be grateful if you'd stay.

BESSMER: Now, gentlemen – you have the ropes securely?

WARBURTON: Perfectly.

BESSMER: Doctor?

WATSON: Yes.

BESSMER: And you're quite satisfied with the restraints?

WATSON: I'd have been perfectly content to forego all this, Mr. Bessmer.

BESSMER: (*Sitting*) Oh no, that would never do. You must be sure that whatever happens, my wife is not directly responsible. Now if you're both ready?

WARBURTON: Ready.

WATSON: Ready.

BESSMER: Excellent. Then I'll turn out the lamp.

*He does so.*

And if we link our free hands . . .

*Movement as they do so.*

. . . then the circle is complete. Free your minds. Open your hearts. And the spirits will come. They will come.

*A long moment. The clock ticks. Eventually:*

MRS. BESSMER: (*Moans. Then sudden silence.*)

*A moment. Then, from another direction:*

John?

WATSON: (*Gasps*)

MRS. BESSMER: John? Are you there?

*Silence.*

BESSMER: Answer her, Doctor.

WARBURTON: Call her to you.

MRS. BESSMER: John?

WATSON: Mary?

MRS. BESSMER: Oh John, it's so good to talk to you. I've missed you so much.

WATSON: Mary, is it really you?

MRS. BESSMER: Oh, it is, it is. Oh my dearest love.

WATSON: It seems so . . . fantastic.

MRS. BESSMER: Always believe, John. It's your belief that makes it possible. You do believe?

WATSON: I want to. I want to so much.

MRS. BESSMER: I can help you believe.

WATSON: How?

MRS. BESSMER: The power is strong tonight. Your faith can make it stronger.

316

WATSON: What's going to happen?

WARBURTON: Don't question it, Watson. Just do as she asks.

WATSON: All right. I shall.

BESSMER: Compose your mind. Empty your heart of all doubt and pain. Call to her.

WATSON: Mary. Mary. (*He gasps*)

WARBURTON: What happened?

WATSON: Someone touched my shoulder. I felt it.

BESSMER: Don't break the circle. Can you still feel our hands?

WATSON: Yes. (*Gasps*) My God. It happened again.

BESSMER: She's trying to materialise. Are you still holding the ropes?

WATSON: Yes.

WARBURTON: Yes.

WATSON: And again!

MRS. BESSMER: (*Closer*) John. Stay calm. Believe. Believe.

WATSON: I . . . believe.

MRS. BESSMER: Release your hands, my love. Come to me.

WATSON: Where?

MRS. BESSMER: Beside you. Here. Can you feel my touch?

WATSON: Yes. Yes!

MRS. BESSMER: Then hold me. Hold me as you used to.

317

WATSON: Yes . . . .

*His chair scrapes as he stands.*
*Ethereal clothes rustle as he takes her into his arms.*

MRS. BESSMER: Now kiss me, John. Kiss me, my love.

*And Watson's whole manner changes:*

WATSON: I don't think so, thank you.

*Click-click! A pair of handcuffs is slammed shut.*

MRS. BESSMER: What the – ?

BESSMER: What's going on?

WARBURTON: Watson?

WATSON: Everyone stay calm.

MRS. BESSMER: (*Struggling*) Let me free!

WATSON: (*Struggling*) Including you, please, madam. (*A vocal effort*)

MRS. BESSMER: You're breaking my arm!

WATSON: No I'm not, but you'll break it yourself if you don't stop struggling. Well?

MRS. BESSMER: All right. All right! (*She slumps with a sigh*)

WATSON: That's better. (*He gets his breath. Then he calls*) I've got her, Holmes.

HOLMES: (*Slightly off*) You underestimate yourself, Doctor.

*Suddenly deafening, a fiery flare hisses and burns.*

ALL: (*React in shock*)

HOLMES: What you've got is all three of them.

318

*A violin flourish takes us to:*

## SCENE 29. THE BESSMERS' PARLOUR. NIGHT.

*Slightly later.*
*A gas mantle pops and burns.*

HOLMES: That's better. Magnesium flares have their uses but they're hard on the eyes.

BESSMER: You're trespassing. You broke in like a common thief.

HOLMES: I'll be sure to mention it to the police when they arrive. Well, well. Quite a haul. Two confidence tricksters – and their accomplice.

WARBURTON: If this is your idea of a joke, sir . . . .

HOLMES: There's no point in pretending, Colonel. I know too much.

WARBURTON: So this whole evening was just a charade.

WATSON: Colonel, I'm sorry. It was the only way.

MRS. BESSMER: You've made a big mistake, the pair of you. You're finished, Warburton. Now it'll all come out, your sordid little secret.

BESSMER: We'll ruin you and your worthless son.

WARBURTON: I don't think so.

*A sudden flurry of movement as he produces a small pistol.*

WATSON: No!

*BANG!*

MRS. BESSMER: (*Cries out*)

*BANG!*

BESSMER: (*Cries out*)

319

*And two bodies hit the floor.*
*A frozen moment. Then:*

HOLMES: Give me the gun, Colonel.

WARBURTON: Keep your distance, Holmes.

WATSON: Colonel . . . .

WARBURTON: You too, Doctor. And you can spare me the pitying look. They were vermin. If you know everything, you know that.

HOLMES: I never said I knew everything.

WARBURTON: Then be good enough to tell me exactly what you *do* know.

HOLMES: I know that the Bessmers were no more in touch with the next world than I am. And I know how they made your messages and your ring so impressively accurate. Their knowledge came from an impeccable source. *You.*

WARBURTON: Go on.

WATSON: We also suspect that you've been feeding the Bessmers information on your various friends before you persuaded them to come to the séances.

HOLMES: And that you gave a helping hand in the dark by releasing your control on the medium. Are we right?

WARBURTON: Quite right. And do you know why?

HOLMES: Because the Bessmers were blackmailing you.

*And at last it's out in the open.*

WARBURTON: (*A sigh. A long moment. Then:*) I never realised what a relief it would be to have it known. I almost feel I should thank you.

HOLMES: Somehow they discovered the secret you've worked for so long to keep hidden. The secret you've spent a fortune to conceal.

WARBURTON: You really do know everything, then.

WATSON: No. We know that this secret concerns your son. Beyond that, we know nothing.

WARBURTON: My son . . . It was a foolish . . . indiscretion, many years ago. He's repented it ever since.

HOLMES: And you've successfully kept it from the eyes and ears of the world.

WARBURTON: Not just the world. Mr. Holmes – the regiment. Michael has a glorious career in front of him. If the news had become known, he would have been finished. And the regiment itself – it would have been . . . tainted.

WATSON: And the Bessmers threatened you with exactly that.

WARBURTON: In return for their silence, I had to go along with their preposterous lies. I had to convince friends – valued friends – of the wonder of it all. And to my lasting shame, I had to profane the memory of my wife for the sake of their . . . play-acting.

HOLMES: Eventually, you ran out of friends to introduce. The Bessmers saw your usefulness coming to an end . . . .

WARBURTON: And they demanded my very home. A final payment.

HOLMES: And you gave it. At the cost of your own reputation.

WARBURTON: What was that to me? Do you have a son, Mr. Holmes?

HOLMES: No.

WARBURTON: Well perhaps if you had, you would understand. (*A moment*) Look at this scene. Not exactly the glory of the battlefield, eh Doctor?

WATSON: No, Colonel.

321

WARBURTON: No. Damaging to the regiment.

WATSON: I'm afraid so.

WARBURTON: Unless of course it was the work of a lunatic.

WATSON: Colonel?

WARBURTON: Someone not responsible for his actions. Then the only blame would be on him. Don't you agree?

HOLMES: (*Gently*) Colonel, we know perfectly well that you're in your right mind.

WARBURTON: I take the liberty of disagreeing with you, sir – and I venture that this will prove me correct. For the Berkshires. And for my son.

*Bang! Splatter!*
*And the Colonel falls dead.*
*A long moment.*

*Then a slow violin solo takes us to:*

## SCENE 30. THE SITTING ROOM AT 221b. EVENING.

*An evocative hansom clops by outside.*
*Holmes and Watson relax by the fire, pipes alight.*

WATSON: Was it difficult?

HOLMES: What?

WATSON: Convincing the police that the Colonel was insane.

HOLMES: The Scotland Yard brain runs on predictable tracks. No gentleman in his right mind would kill twice and then put a pistol to his own head in front of witnesses – therefore he was not in his right mind. Exactly as your Colonel intended.

WATSON: Do you suppose he planned to shoot them anyway? Even if we hadn't exposed the whole thing?

HOLMES: Why else would he have taken the gun? They'd driven him to his limit.

WATSON: Will it have to come out? The blackmail, the family secret?

HOLMES: I don't see why it should.

WATSON: Thank you.

HOLMES: "Some truths are the better for not being dragged into the cold light of day."

WATSON: Who said that?

HOLMES: A good man of my acquaintance.

*A moment.*

WATSON: Will you tell me something?

HOLMES: What?

WATSON: Well, two things actually. How did she get out of those ropes and chains?

HOLMES: It's a question of accumulated slack.

WATSON: Accumulated slack.

HOLMES: The longer the rope, the easier to slip it off. Chain's the same. Actually, the hardest thing is stopping it falling off before you're ready.

WATSON: You almost sound as though you're speaking from experience.

HOLMES: (*A chuckle*) What's the second thing?

WATSON: What was it Michael Warburton said that put you onto the solution?

HOLMES: Oh, that. "I have more cause to be grateful to my father than you can ever know."

WATSON: And that gave you the whole story?

HOLMES: Let's say it put all the other pieces into place. I'd considered that the Colonel might have been co-operating with the Bessmers, but I dismissed it. Why should he? It never occurred to me that he might have been protecting his son.

WATSON: Until that moment.

HOLMES: Exactly.

WATSON: Then it's a good thing that you did provoke him. I doubt he'd have said it otherwise.

HOLMES: True enough.

*A companionable pipe-puffing moment.*

HOLMES: Will you tell *me* something?

WATSON: Of course, if I can.

HOLMES: Do *you* understand?

WATSON: I'm sorry?

HOLMES: "Perhaps if you had a son, you would understand." Do you?

WATSON: Don't you?

*A long moment.*

HOLMES: Not yet.

*He rises and crosses to his desk.*
*He unlocks the drawer.*
*The bottles clink as he removes one.*

Good night, Watson.

*And Watson makes no comment.*

WATSON: Good night.

*Music: Closing Theme.*
*Closing announcements.*
*The music ends.*

*The End*

# The Return of the Noble Bachelor

## by Jane Rubino

"But as the Duke's second son, should he not have been 'Lord *Robert* St. Simon?'"

Sherlock Holmes had listened with a smile as I read the letter aloud. "I am flattered by the interest that our American cousins have taken in my career," he said, when I had finished. "But as they have forsworn rank for the more pragmatic aristocracy of wealth, we must not be surprised when they are occasionally puzzled by our canons of style and address. And, as I recall Watson, it was not just in your account that he was identified as 'Lord St. Simon'. The society papers did the same."

"Perhaps I should have made some mention of the elder brother's death?"

Holmes shrugged his shoulders. "It had no bearing on our case. Your narrative was none the worse for leaving it out, and our client was certainly none the better for being the heir."

Ten years have passed since Lord St. Simon's short-lived union with Miss Hatty Doran, and yet, a decade has not lessened the interest among our American cousins, for the lady in the case was a California heiress. One may recall that not an hour after the two were pronounced man and wife, the bride vanished, and the groom retained Holmes to find out what had become of her. Happily, the lady's whereabouts were quickly discovered. Sadly for Lord St. Simon, she was discovered in the company of a prior husband, who had been presumed dead. For a season or two, the deposed groom's disappointment was the subject of gossip and mirth among fashionable London, until a fresh set of scandals eclipsed the St. Simon affair.

To his credit, our client did not allow his injured pride to overwhelm his sense of what was right, and he renounced all claim to a considerable dowry. The enormity of this sacrifice cannot be underestimated. Holmes was entirely correct when he observed that the death of the Duke's eldest son had not improved our former client's situation in life. The Duke's passion for horses and cards (and more unsavory indulgences, it was said), had threatened to leave his successor encumbered with debt that might only be satisfied by breaking the entail to an estate that had been preserved for many generations.

Until his premature death, that successor had been our client's elder brother, David Arthur Cecil DeVere St. Simon. A stroke of good luck had given the young man expectations beyond those which were at the mercy of his imprudent father, for a bachelor uncle had bequeathed to him a modest estate at Birchmoor and twenty-thousand pounds. Young Lord St. Simon had the good sense – or foresight, perhaps – to wait only upon his majority to draw up a will, assigning the real property to Lord Robert, and any residue of the fortune, in equal shares, to Lord Eustace and Lady Clara St. Simon.

As fate would have it, young Lord St. Simon died not two years later, and Robert St. Simon became heir to whatever might survive his father's extravagant vices. Even as he prepared to marry Miss Doran, his father was holding off creditors through the sale of some valuable portraits and several items of Qianlong porcelain that had been wedding presents from his wife's family.

As Holmes had observed, my account of the St. Simon marriage was none the worse for omitting these irrelevant details. I raise them here because, as chance would have it, not a week after I received the letter regarding our former client, Holmes was to receive a letter from the gentleman himself.

"'*My dear Mr. Sherlock Holmes,*'" read my friend. "'*I find myself once again in need of your judgment and discretion in a sensitive matter that was brought to my notice only last night. If it is convenient, I will call upon you this morning at ten o'clock.*' I hope," Holmes remarked, as he tossed the black-bordered sheet to me, "that your American correspondents have kept up with recent events."

The recent event to which Holmes alluded was the death of our client's father only the month before. Lord St. Simon was now his Grace, the Duke of Balmoral.

The gentleman arrived promptly at ten o'clock. A decade had made few, though perceptible, alterations in his appearance. Sorrow and disappointment (for there had been one or two unsuccessful petitions after Miss Doran) had etched a few lines into the pale face, and the hair, formerly grizzled at the temples, was now completely gray. A gold-rimmed *pince nez* had replaced the eye-glasses, and the silver-knobbed walking stick seemed as much necessity as affectation. His manner had altered as well. Though forthright as before, he seemed less aloof.

Holmes rose. "Your Grace," he greeted. "Please accept my condolences on the death of your father."

"Yes, yes, thank you," he said, and glanced around the room. "Very little has changed. I am glad to see that. I will sit, I think." And then, laying his black-bordered topper and stick on a side table, he lowered himself into the basket chair. "I trusted you once, Mr. Holmes, and you did not fail – though I would have preferred a different result."

Holmes took a chair opposite the Duke. "You may trust me now."

The gentleman removed his *pince nez*, scrutinized the lenses, wiped them with a black silk handkerchief, and put it back upon his nose. At last, he said in a low voice, "I don't suppose, Mr. Holmes, that you believe in ghosts?"

"No."

"Nor do I."

"That's settled, then."

"It would be, were the verdict confined to this room. But when a gentleman's – that is – " He paused. "It is my mother. She declares that she has seen my father's ghost – three times, in fact. Twice last week and again yesterday."

"But, as there are no ghosts, she must be mistaken."

"She *must* be, and yet she insists that she is not, and will not be contradicted."

"And what is it you wish me to do?"

"I would wish, Mr. Holmes, that you might offer some theory that would explain why delusions should suddenly overtake most rational creature who ever lived. But my wishes must yield to those of my mother. It was she who insisted that I retain you."

"To do what, precisely?"

"To locate this ghost, intercept him, and discover what it is he wants of her."

Holmes settled back in his chair and pressed his fingertips together. "Where does your mother claim to have seen this apparition?"

"Walking in the street."

"Always in the street?"

"Yes."

"Pray, what were the circumstances?"

"For the past three months, Mother has been living in town – "

"Forgive me, your Grace. You father died last month, at your family estate. Your mother was not present?"

"No." The gentleman hesitated, and then said, "The late Duke's proclivities – as I am sure you have heard – were often indulged at the expense of domestic harmony. There was no formal separation, but for several years, my parents frequently lived apart, Father at Walsingham, and Mother at our residence in town, until our family was compelled to sell it. Since then, Mother has been welcomed into the home of an old family friend, Lady Alicia Whittington, who resides in Devonshire Place."

"Lady Alicia Whittington," Holmes repeated. "I seem to recall the name from the reports of your wedding to Miss Doran."

"Yes, Mr. Holmes. That – event – was a very small affair, and only two guests were not family: Lord Backwater, who was a friend from my university days, and Lady Alicia, whom I've known since childhood."

"Pray, continue."

"It seems that last week – Wednesday, to be precise – Lady Alicia, in the company of her attendant, Miss MacKinnon, and Mother were returning to Devonshire Place by way of Weymouth Street. Their carriage had just passed Portland Place when Mother happened to glance out of her window and spied a gentleman across the street, walking slowly in the direction opposite their own. She states that he was tall and pale, dressed in a black overcoat and black Homburg, and though she got no more than a glimpse of him, she said that his bearing, his gait, his features – which she saw only in profile – were identical to my father's. On the following day, they again found themselves traveling along Weymouth Street – "

"At the same hour?"

"Yes. The coachman had been instructed to stop at the corner of Harley Street so that Miss MacKinnon might enquire at a chemist's about some preparations recommended by Alicia's doctor. Mother and Lady Alicia remained in the carriage, and as Miss MacKinnon approached the shop, that same tall, black-garbed gentleman held the door for her, and then proceeded on foot – "

"Walking in the same direction as the previous day?"

"Yes. Mother got no more than a glimpse of him before he raised his umbrella, yet she insists that it was my father."

"Did you speak with Miss MacKinnon? What does she say of the encounter?"

"She said that there was a great deal of foot traffic, and that she recalls a gentleman holding the door for her, but she scarcely noticed him and would not recognize him again."

"Had she known your father?"

"No."

"And the third incident?"

"Yesterday. They were once again returning to Lady Alicia's residence when some congestion in the vicinity of Portland Place brought the coach to a halt. Mother was seated backward, and happened to glance out just as the same gentleman, this time walking in their direction, passed not three feet from the carriage window. Mother said that his hat brim was pulled low over his forehead, and his complexion was ghastly white, but that she did see his face clearly."

"Did he see her?"

329

"No. She said that he seemed like a man in a daze, not mindful of his surroundings at all."

"And what did she do?"

"She alighted and called out to him – called him by his Christian name. Loudly enough, it seems, to be heard over the commotion of the street. It is – " He gave a discreet little cough. " – quite out of character for my mother to make such a public display."

"And did he respond?"

"Mother said that upon hearing his name, he turned around and glanced at her in a puzzled fashion, and then a look of horror passed over his features and he darted past her and through a swarm of pedestrians – "

"One moment, your Grace – he did not run *away* from her, but toward her and then beyond – moving in the same direction as he had been walking on the two prior occasions?"

"Yes, so she said."

"And her companions – did they see this apparition?"

"No. Miss MacKinnon thought that Mother had left the coach because she had wearied of sitting idle, and wanted a breath of air. When Mother cried out, Miss MacKinnon and the coachman both got down and found her pointing into the crowd and uttering my father's name. Together they were able to urge her into the coach, and, as the congestion had begun to ease, they made their way back to Devonshire Place. Miss MacKinnon tended to her charge and then went down to Mother, who declared that she had seen the ghost of my father, not only that afternoon, but twice before. Miss MacKinnon was sufficiently alarmed to send off a wire, urging me to come to London at once. I arrived last evening and spoke to the coachman and Miss MacKinnon, but neither could account for my mother's extraordinary behavior. I then spoke to Mother, who related the three incidents as I have described them to you. I thought, perhaps, that a night's rest would moderate her account, but we spoke again this morning, and her story does not change."

"Forgive me, your Grace," I said, "but the reports of the late Duke's passing stated that he had been in sound health for a man of his years, and that his death came as quite a shock to those who attended him."

"Yes. His doctors had diagnosed a mild case of bronchitis, and so he would not have any of us sent for. And yet, only five days after the first symptoms had appeared, he was gone."

"When a person has not been present at the death-bed of a loved one, such confusion – the belief that one has seen the deceased – is not uncommon."

"My mother is the very soul of rationality, and she is no stranger to grief. Indeed, if she were disposed to see the ghost of a loved one who died

330

. . . ." The gentleman looked down at the gloved hands clasped upon his knee.

"She would have seen that of your late brother," Holmes concluded.

"Yes. David was Mother's favorite, and of the two deaths, I daresay his was the greater blow. He died while traveling abroad, and I have heard it said that when a loved one is lost in war, or abroad, or at sea, the survivors often will imagine that they have seen him afterward. For many weeks after we received word of David's death, Mother confined herself to her chamber, weeping over his photographs and insisting that not an item of his clothing was to be discarded. And yet, she never claimed to have seen his ghost."

Holmes was silent for some minutes, and then said, "You say that you spoke to your mother, and to the coachman and the maid. Did you not speak to Lady Alicia?"

"No, Mr. Holmes. In fact, I have neither seen nor spoken to Alicia for many years. Miss MacKinnon is not her maid, you see, but a private nurse who has attended Alicia for the past five or six years at least, ever since a nervous complaint – one that had been discernable even at the time of my wedding – left her an invalid."

"Yet she is able to drive out at least three times in the last week."

"Well, yes, and I thought it odd but, from something Mother said, I gather that Alicia's physician encourages her to take the fresh air whenever she feels strong enough and the weather is fine. Otherwise, Alicia confines herself to her rooms and, as a rule, sees no one but Doctor Trevelyan and her nurse."

"Doctor Percy Trevelyan?" I asked.

"Yes."

Holmes betrayed nothing of his surprise upon hearing the name of a former client. "She makes an exception to this rule for her Grace," he said.

"Well, yes, but Mother is more than a guest. She frequently takes on some of Miss MacKinnon's duties, and I daresay no nurse could be more skilled, nor more devoted. Mother loves Alicia like a daughter. Indeed, there had been a time when . . . ."

"When they anticipated a closer relationship?"

The Duke (for so I must begin to call him) nodded. "At the time of his passing, David and Alicia were engaged to be married."

"And she is 'Lady Alicia Whittington' still."

"Yes, Mr. Holmes, she never married," the client said, with a sigh. "Thirty years have gone by, and she is Lady Alicia Whittington, still."

"Your elder brother must have been a remarkable young man to inspire such an attachment," I said.

"Indeed, he was, Doctor. I could not have wished for a more splendid, clever, affectionate brother or friend. He was two years my senior, as were Lord Alfred and Lady Alicia Whittington – they were twins. The Whittington estate bordered ours, and from the time we were children, until David and Alfred went off to university, you would be hard-pressed to find a merrier, livelier, and, on occasion, more – " he paused. "Well, we were no strangers to mischief. It seemed the most natural thing in the world that David and Alicia should become attached to one another, and a month or two after he and Alfred entered their last year at university, David proposed, and Alicia accepted him, and they were to marry the following June."

"Your brother have scarcely been of age at the time," said Holmes.

"Yes, he was just twenty-one."

"That is rather young for marriage."

"Well, yes, and I believe that Mother had some misgivings on that score, but my father had long pressed for the match, and, I suspect, for the same reason that Lady Whittington argued for delay. She was fond of David, but his prospects were not – not what they ought to have been – and Alicia's fortune was quite large."

"And the lady's father?"

"The Earl had been an invalid for some years and in fact, died two months after the engagement, and Lady Whittington then entreated the couple to delay the wedding and so it was put off until autumn. And then . . . ." He fell silent and his gaze drifted toward the fire. "Poor Alicia! To lose everyone who is dear to you in a few short years – father, fiancé, mother. And her brother, in a manner of speaking, for after David's death, Alfred left the family estate in the hands of the stewards, and has wandered the Continent like a vagabond ever since, returning to England only once, for Lady Whittington's funeral."

"When did that occur?" asked Holmes.

"Five years after the Earl's death. I cannot express, Mr. Holmes, what it is to scarcely recognize one who had been nearly as close as a brother. That bold, fine-looking, high-spirited, companion of my youth was gone entirely and he was – well, you might say he was a ghost of what he had been. Guilt will do that, I suppose."

"Guilt?"

"Alfred blamed himself for David's death."

"Indeed!"

"Yes. From the first, those two were the firmest of friends and the fiercest of rivals, one always trying to best the other. David was gifted, mind you, but Alfred was brilliant, fearless, determined to be first in everything. I recall the time that David laid down a challenge, a race to climb a great oak that sat on the boundary between the Whittington estate and ours. David sprang up, but Alfred was ahead of him in an instant, while Alicia and I stood on firm ground and begged them to descend. David lost his grip and the fall left him with a gash on his forehead and a few broken bones, and Alfred and Alicia took turns at his bedside, she to read from his favorite novels, and Alfred to coach David in his studies so that he would not fall behind." He paused for several minutes, his expression melancholy. "I ramble," he said at last. "These sad details, this old history, can have no bearing upon the matter at hand."

"Details are rarely of no consequence, your Grace," said Holmes. "And there is little of the present that does not retain some mark of the past. You must leave me to determine which details are relevant and which are immaterial. You said that Lord Alfred Whittington felt responsible for your brother's death?"

The Duke nodded. "I have called him brilliant, but 'driven' might be a better term, and I believe that the strain of his studies had begun to work on him even before the Earl's – well, I haven't been entirely frank, Mr. Holmes. But, of course, it was only a rumor, and rumors – "

"Often have some basis in truth."

"It was rumored that the Earl's death was not a natural one."

Holmes leaned forward in his chair. "Foul play?"

"No. A suicide, so it was whispered 'round. It is not what you may suspect," he hastened to add. "There was no dishonor, nor debt, but only Alfred knew the real motive – the Earl left him a letter to be read after his death, and it was said to be a confession – an admission that he'd taken his own life. It seemed that the sum total of all – the letter, the strain of study, a succession that came with responsibilities that he was not prepared – indeed, was disinclined, I think, to assume – drove Alfred toward physical and mental collapse. By the time of his graduation, he was in such a precarious state that his doctors insisted that only a long holiday and complete change scene could prevent an irreversible breakdown. And so, the wedding was postponed once more, and Alfred, David, and a party of friends set off on a long tour of the Mediterranean.

"They had been gone for a few months when their travels took them to Greece, where Alfred decided – quite against the advice of his friends and the local guides – to explore a set of caverns along the coast. David would not let him go alone, and so, careless of the time, the two of them made their way from one cave to the next, and did not allow for the incoming tide. David was drowned and Alfred barely escaped with his life. It was not until a month later that David – his remains – were recovered. And – " He paused for some time and then said, in a low voice. "The sea had not been kind."

For a long time, Holmes pondered the gentleman's statement in silence, and then said, "And since your brother's death, Lord Alfred and Lady Alicia have seen each other only that one time, at their mother's funeral?"

"Well, no, there was one other occasion. Some months after Lady Whittington's passing, Alfred wrote to Alicia and asked if they might pass a month together at Baden. Alicia departed in good spirits, determined to assure Alfred that she did not blame him for the tragedy and hopeful that she might bring him home with her. But she returned alone and miserable. She would say nothing of Alfred, nothing of their reunion, and began to withdraw from society and her former pursuits, choosing to live as a recluse long before her health compelled her to do so. My parents – from different motives, to be sure – advanced the notion – but it . . . was not to be . . . ."

"The notion that you and Lady Alicia might marry."

"Well, yes. And I did, in fact, make her an offer of marriage, which she refused. I confess, I was somewhat surprised. I had always been quite fond of Alicia, and I know that she liked me, and cared for no one else, but for some, as I well know, no man on earth can take the place of the first and only love."

"Did Lady Alicia attend your father's funeral?"

"No. I understand from Mother that the state of her health has put travel quite out of the question. There was no one but Mother, my younger brother and sister, and myself."

"What was your mother's conduct at Walsingham, prior to the funeral and afterward?"

"She was quite resigned, quite calm, and took on all of the arrangements herself, but within a week of the funeral, she returned to town."

"And you have remained at Walsingham?"

"Yes. There are a great many matters of business that the Duke – that had been left unattended, and of course, there is my own estate at Birchmoor, which I cannot neglect."

"And you have no theory at all that might explain the appearance of this ghost?"

"I have given you the material facts, Mr. Holmes. I am at a loss to explain how they conjure up spirits."

Holmes rose and paced the room for some minutes, his expression grave. "I will have to speak to her Grace, of course, but I would like to turn over the matter in my brain for an hour or two first. Please advise her that we will call at three o'clock."

"At three. Very well. I must prepare you," said the Duke, as he took up his hat and stick, "that my mother is a formidable woman."

With that final remark, he offered his hand to us both and departed.

"Well, well," said Holmes as he threw himself back into his chair. "What do you say, Watson? Is human nature not a strange mixture? This pretty puzzle brings out a sympathetic element of the gentleman's character that we did not see before."

"We did not know the details of his family's sad history."

"What do you say of the mother's conduct?"

"It is bizarre, certainly."

"And yet, her son declares that she is the soul of rationality."

"That rationality may be compromised by the anxiety and exhaustion of caring for her invalid friend," I said. "If Lady Alicia is Trevelyan's patient, she must be seriously ill."

"He has come up in the world, I hear, since he was a client."

"Indeed, he has. A few years ago, he and an American colleague gave a joint presentation on an obscure neurological condition that took a prize, and advanced the careers of both. In England, he is now regarded as one of the top men in his field."

"So your theory is that the Duchess suffers from delusions brought on by exhaustion?"

"It's certainly possible. How do you view the problem?"

"Oh – the problem is solved."

"Solved! Then what is the answer?"

"Oh, I do not have the answer, merely the solution. I have, in fact, four possible solutions, but I must first assemble and sort through the facts before I can come up with the answer."

"You don't agree with my theory, then?"

Holmes sat back in his chair and pressed his fingertips together. "If we grant that the demands of Lady Alicia's affliction have put a strain upon the Duchess, that may explain *why* she claims to have seen a ghost – it does not necessarily determine what she *did* see. A figment of imagination? Quite possibly. But now, let us, for the sake of argument, take the position that it is not, and that she did, indeed, see something walking along Weymouth Street. Then there are only four possible explanations. The first is that, by coincidence, her Grace spied a gentleman who bore a strong resemblance to her husband."

"The second?"

"That much the same occurred, but by design."

"Design?"

"On each occasion, Lady Alicia's carriage was proceeding along the same route, at the same time of day. If it is known that the Duchess

335

accompanies her friend, someone may have assumed the appearance of her late husband and placed himself where he will be seen."

"For what purpose?"

"I have not enough data for that."

"What else?"

"It may have *been* her late husband."

"My dear Holmes!"

"You recall Jonas Oldacre? He did not feign his own death solely to avenge himself on an old lover, but also to elude creditors, and begin life anew under another identity."

"But, surely, the Duke could not deceive the widow and children who made arrangements for his funeral! And, even if he *did* manage such a charade, a man who hopes to elude his creditors would not go walking around London in the middle of the afternoon."

"Yes, well, there is the fourth possibility," said Holmes as he reached for his clay pipe. "It may, indeed, have been a ghost."

For the next two hours, Holmes smoked and ruminated, and at last, laying aside his pipe, he sprang from his chair and rummaged around his desk for his big map of London and spread it out upon the carpet. "Come, look here, Watson," he said, when I had knelt beside, him. "Here we have Devonshire Place, which becomes Upper Wimpole Street, and moving eastward, Harley Street and then Portland Place. All of them intersected by Weymouth Street. Now it is not only in this vicinity that the Duchess saw her ghost, but on all three occasions, her carriage was moving in the same westward direction."

"Returning to Lady Alicia's residence on Devonshire Place."

"And on all three occasions, the ghost walked eastward, on a course that was the reverse of the Duchess's. Even yesterday, though he *had* been walking in her direction, when confronted, he chooses not to run *away* from her, but past her, in the same direction he had taken twice before."

"I confess, Holmes, that save for the fact that one of them is a ghost, I see nothing suggestive or strange in the fact that two parties should cross paths upon an active street at the busiest time of day."

"But," replied Holmes as he rose and tossed the map onto his desk, "do you not find it strange that Lady Alicia, who is too frail to receive her oldest friend from childhood, goes rattling across London at least three times in a week? If she is only taking the air, why not a quiet morning turn around the park, instead of along active streets at the busiest time of day? And, if she goes out only when the weather is fine, why, when they stopped at the chemist's, does this ghost open an umbrella after he held the door for the nurse?"

336

"You are right! Last Thursday was dirty and wet!"

"It is nearly three," said Holmes, with a glance at his watch. "I am in danger of possessing too many facts – let us hope that her Grace may help us to eliminate those that are immaterial."

Devonshire Place was on the border of medical London, with a few consulting rooms set among several handsome two-storied private residences. As we approached Lady Alicia's address, Holmes pointed toward the drawn shades at the upper windows.

There was no bell, and the door was opened upon our first knock by a stone-faced maid, who took our coats and deposited us to a spacious, elegantly furnished sitting room, but one which showed very few signs of use. "Her Grace will be down directly," she said, and withdrew, closing the door, soundlessly.

"Do you hear it, Watson?" Holmes asked in a low voice.

"I hear nothing."

"That's it – it is utterly still. No bell at the door, not a footfall, nor the rattle of a tea cart. Silent as a tomb."

Our conversation was interrupted by the entrance of a lady who could only have been the Duchess. She must have been seventy-one or -two, yet she had the upright carriage and brisk step of a much younger woman, and the blue eyes that appraised us from behind the silver-rimmed spectacles were forthright and clear. The eyes were red-rimmed, however, bearing the unmistakable traces of tears and exhaustion, and her complexion was unnaturally pale.

Still, the voice was firm when she addressed Holmes with, "My son told you what I saw?"

"A ghost."

"My husband's ghost."

"And you are certain of that, your Grace?"

"Do you mean to ask whether I am mad? I assure you, sir, if I were inclined toward madness, the trials of my marriage would have driven me to the state long ago."

"I do not think you are mad, ma'am."

"Then perhaps you think me senile."

"No, ma'am, I only ask whether you are certain that what you saw was a ghost and not a man who bore some resemblance to your husband?"

"When you were married to a man for more than fifty years, you do not mistake him for a stranger. If I did not see my husband, I saw his ghost or his twin, and he had no twin. He had no male relations at all."

"Now, you saw this ghost on three occasions and on each occasion, you had been driving out with Lady Alicia."

"Yes."

337

"Did you go out today?"

"No."

"And yet, it is excellent weather for a drive."

"Lady Alicia is not well enough today."

"If I may ask – what is the nature of Lady Alicia's malady?"

"Your friend will agree," she gave a nod in my direction, "that if a patient desires privacy, those close to her – particularly those who have been the object of vulgar curiosity in the past – know the importance of respecting it."

"Quite so. Now, the purpose of these drives is solely Lady Alicia's health, is that correct? There is no particular destination."

"What do these questions have to do with my husband's ghost?"

"I merely observe that both your route, and your ghost's, seem to follow a rather fixed course. Each time you spotted him, he was walking along Weymouth Street. Your ghost is a rather parochial creature, wouldn't you agree, to keep to such a narrow district."

"Surely, Mr. Holmes, if my husband's ghost confines himself to a fixed location, it should not be difficult for you to intercept him. You did, after all, produce a dead husband once before."

"To your family's disadvantage, I am afraid," said Holmes, gravely. "Now on the second occasion, your carriage had stopped at the corner of Harley Street so that Miss MacKinnon might make a purchase at a chemist's. There, you saw your husband hold the door for her – forgive me, but I seem to forget the name of the chemist."

"Luddington and Son. My husband was walking out of the shop as she entered and he held the door for her."

"Very civil of him," Holmes murmured, and then after a brief pause, he said, "On the first two occasions, you saw this ghost only at a distance, but yesterday you were near enough to see his features clearly."

"As near as I stand to you."

"Your son said that his hat was set low upon his forehead."

"It was not a mask. It did not cover his face."

"And when you called out to him by name, he turned and appeared to recognize you."

"Yes."

"Quite so. Now, if I understand my commission, ma'am, I am to apprehend this being and discover why he appears to you."

"Yes. And," she added, her features softening, "to tell him that if it is forgiveness he seeks, I forgive him."

"You believe that he seeks your forgiveness?"

"Why else would he come so near, and yet not have the courage to approach? What have I left to give him that he did not wring from me in life?"

"And how shall I identify him, ma'am?"

The lady went to a small writing desk in the corner and removed a cabinet size photograph from a drawer and handed it to Holmes.

The subject was a gentleman looked squarely into the camera. He was dressed in a dark greatcoat, and held a hat in one hand and a walking stick in the other. In the stooped shoulders and trace of petulance about the mouth, I saw some resemblance to our client, but the white hair had not thinned with age, and the countenance bore few traces of a lifetime's worth of dissolute habits. "This cannot be recent. The Duke appears to be in his early sixties or so."

"This was taken three years ago when he was seventy-one. My husband was one of those fortunate creatures who wore his years and his excesses quite lightly. Not unlike Mr. Wilde's Dorian Gray. Indeed, I would not be surprised if a fiendish portrait of my husband should turn up in one of Walsingham's attics." She paused and for a moment, her lips trembled. "Find him, Mr. Holmes. Find him and tell him that I forgive him and wish that death may bring him more peace than he left to those who survive him."

"Give me your opinion, Watson," said Holmes as we departed. "Did you find the Duchess to be unusually close-mouthed on the subject of her friend's affliction?"

"Her husband's sordid history and her son's unfortunate wedding have made her very sensitive to what she called 'vulgar curiosity'."

"Perhaps. Did anything else about the lady's narrative strike you?"

"No – her account was in keeping with that of her son."

"Nothing at all?"

"Well, she gave the name of the chemist. Luddington and Son."

"She gave something more. According to the Duchess, this apparition did not merely stop to open a door for the nurse – he did so as he emerged from the shop. Now, what business has a ghost in a chemist's shop? It is one thing to go wandering around our fair metropolis, but what need has he for potions and pills? Perhaps Luddington and Son can put some flesh and bone upon our ghost."

Luddington and Son was a compounding chemist and dispensary on the corner of Harley and Weymouth Streets. The window displayed a variety of the latest patent medicines, and within, it was all glass shelves and polished linoleum floors that smelt of camphor and lemon oil. We made our way along a narrow aisle to the counter at the back of the shop, and a tap at the bell brought a pale, black-haired fellow bustling from the dispensary.

"Good afternoon," Holmes greeted him. "My name is Sherlock Holmes – "

"The detective! And then you must be Doctor Watson!" The fellow reached across the counter to shake my hand. "Why I have read all of your tales! What wonderful adventures they are!"

"Perhaps," said Holmes, with a wry smile, "you may play a role in one of them." He drew the cabinet from his breast pocket and handed it to the fellow. "I am retained by a client to locate this gentleman, and I have learned that last week, he was seen leaving this shop."

The fellow took the spectacles that were perched upon his brow and settled them before his eyes. "Oh, yes! I remember him well! He came last week to enquire about two compounds, one for a tonic and another for a lineament."

"His name?"

"Oh – I cannot recall – something quite common – I am certain that I wrote it down in the register." He removed a large flat ledger from a shelf and laid it on the counter. "It is not his name that I remember, it was the odd coincidence. No sooner did he walk out of the shop than a lady entered and asked after much the same items. I told her what I had told the gentleman – that I could certainly make up the orders, but it might take several days to obtain the tincture of lobelia. Of course, I was bound to tell them both that I could not vouch for the efficacy of either the tonic or the cream, but I suppose when a loved one is suffering, some will try anything."

"These compounds were not for the two customers, then?"

"Oh, I think not – both seemed in good health, though the gentleman must have been sixty or thereabout, and white as milk."

"And what ailments are these remedies used for?"

"The lineament is said to ease contracture of the muscles, and the tonic is sometimes a last measure for severe asthma or congestion of the lungs. I have heard that veterinarians will use it for lock-jaw, though I do not believe that was the gentleman's trade."

"How do you know that?"

"I deduce it!" declared the fellow. "He was to come for the items yesterday, but he did not. Instead, he sent around a note this morning, directing me to deliver them to the Fitzroy Sanatorium."

"An asylum?" said Holmes.

"Not for the mad, no. It is a sort of retreat for incurables."

"On Portland Place, if I recall."

"No, sir, just beyond, on Charlotte Street."

340

"An old, rambling structure."

"Oh, no, sir, quite new, and very well appointed, but small, no more than a home hospital. I don't believe there are more than a dozen patients. Well-off ones, too, for it is five guineas a week, and that is for nursing and board only."

"Are there no doctors on staff?" I asked.

"No, the patients or their families must employ their own, or have the administrator, who is a specialist, agree take on the case."

"One of the patients is an acquaintance of mine, I believe," said Holmes. "Lady Alicia Whittington."

"That I cannot tell you, sir, for their relations and the staff are very careful about keeping the names of the patients from the public. The newspapers, you know. I am sorry if your acquaintance is a patient, for those who are admitted are very near the end."

"And the administrator who is a specialist – would that be Doctor Percy Trevelyan?"

"No, Doctor Agar. Doctor Moore Agar," replied fellow, turning the pages of a register as he spoke. "I know Doctor Trevelyan, and would not be surprised if one or two of his graver cases were to be sent there. Ah, here it is!" he cried, pointing to an entry in the register. "The gentleman who gave the order – the gentleman in your photograph – was named Mr. Harmon."

"And you're certain that Mr. Harmon was this man?" Holmes held up the photograph once more.

The man glanced at the image and nodded. "The hat and stick were not the same, but yes, it is the same fellow. Mr. John Harmon."

Holmes thanked the gentleman and pocketed the photograph.

"The Fitzroy Sanatorium sounds like institutions that have begun to appear on the Continent," I said, as we left the shop. "There are one or two in Lyons, managed by nursing sisters – they call it a *hospice*. Her Grace was wrong, then, when she said that she would not mistake a stranger for her husband. Evidently, this John Harmon is no more than the unhappy relation of an invalid patient. What the Germans call a *doppelganger,* perhaps – " I stopped abruptly, for my friend had suddenly turned on his heel and dashed back to the shop.

After several minutes, he returned, his expression more grave than I have ever seen it. He said not a word all the way back to Baker Street, and when he had thrown off his coat, he went to the desk, scribbled a couple wires, dispatched them with page, and then sank into his chair and stared into the fire.

Then, abruptly, after a half-hour's silence, he said, "I hope you didn't want your tea, Watson, and I cannot even promise your dinner. We shall

341

be going out again very shortly, and I daresay we may be gone for some time."

Holmes had scarcely uttered this remark when sharp peel of the bell drew him to the window. "I must trouble you to take up your coat again, Watson. We mustn't keep the Duchess and her son waiting."

We threw on our coats and hats, and descended to find mother and son sitting side-by-side in Lady Alicia's carriage. Holmes handed up a note to the coachman and then climbed in beside me.

"Your wire was quite urgent, Mr. Holmes," said the Duke.

"I thought it best to bring the matter to a close as quickly as possible."

"To a close?"

"Yes. I was engaged to locate the ghost. I have done so. I was further engaged to convey your forgiveness, ma'am, I think it would be better if I took you to him and let you offer that yourself."

The lady's expression could not be seen through her veil, but her son stared at Holmes as though he were mad.

"I have given the address to the coachman. I believe you know the place, ma'am. The Fitzroy Sanatorium."

The lady started, her gloved hands clutched at the folds of her mantle.

"A sanatorium?" said the gentleman.

"A small, private hospital for the gravely ill, those who can no longer be adequately cared for at home. When you spied the ghost, your Grace, you were not on some leisurely outing, but visiting this asylum on the advice of Doctor Trevelyan, and in the company of Miss MacKinnon, to begin arrangements for Lady Alicia's admission as a patient."

The gentleman turned to his mother. "You said that Alicia was too weak to receive visitors, but – gravely ill! I had no idea! How could you have kept this from me!"

"It was Alicia's wish. When it was made clear to her, the course that this illness would take, she gave instructions to her attorneys and Doctor Trevelyan and to me. She wanted no one to know."

"Am I 'no one'? I am her oldest friend in all the world! It is unforgivable – "

"Robert," said his mother, tersely. "There is no better authority than I upon the subject of how long and how often we are expected to forgive."

"I think," said Holmes, gravely, as the carriage drew up to the sanatorium. "that you may soon find occasion to put that principle to the test, your Grace."

The sanatorium was a newly built structure, well set back from the bustle and flow of traffic. It had been laid out as a peaceful little villa with a small garden in front, surrounded on all sides by a wrought-iron fence. A broad portico overhung an entrance which was so well recessed that, not until our party stepped up to the door, we were able to make out the modest brass plaque which read: *Fitzroy Sanatorium.*

Our knock was answered promptly by a page, who admitted us to a spacious entry hall with a lift at one end and a stairway at the other. "Mr. Sherlock Holmes to see Doctor Agar," said my friend, as he placed his card upon the salver.

The page nodded ushered our party through a side door and deposited us in small room that appeared to serve both as a consulting room and office, furnished with the traditional oak and leather, but brightened somewhat with fresh flowers and a half-dozen restful landscape paintings on the walls.

After a moment, the door swung open and one of the most imposing men I have ever seen entered the room. He was taller than Holmes, and far broader, with a mane of white hair brushing the collar of his rather disheveled attire, a deeply lined face, square and formidable jaw, and beneath a thicket of graying brows, black eyes that smoldered with the grim resignation of one who is too well acquainted with suffering.

The dark gaze surveyed our party. "Your Grace," he said, with a stiff bow to the lady. "We have no appointment. Which of you is Mr. Sherlock Holmes."

"I am," said my friend. "Have I the honor of addressing Doctor Moore Agar?"

"I am Doctor Agar. You may wish to reserve judgment, Mr. Holmes, before you pronounce it to be an honor."

"I have been engaged by her Grace to find the ghost of her late husband," said Holmes. "I have reason to believe he is here."

"Mr. Sherlock Holmes, the nature of my work leaves me with little tolerance for levity."

"Oh, it is no jest," said Holmes. "This is the gentleman's photograph."

He held it up, and the doctor studied it, his unruly brows knitted in concentration. "I do not believe in spirit photographs," said he, "nor in spirits walking about. But there is a gentleman here who resembles this subject. He appealed to me not long ago on behalf of a cousin who had been cared for at an establishment in Lyons. He transported the patient here little more than a fortnight ago, and at great toil and expense, for the patient has got to the stage where he is incapable of voluntary movement. He is no ghost, ma'am, nor is he your husband. He calls himself John Harmon, though I suspect that is an alias."

"John Harmon?" echoed the bewildered lady.

"Is he here now?" asked Holmes.

"Yes. Mr. Harmon leaves his cousin's side only to take a few hours rest, or to hunt up some useless palliative."

"Would you have any objection to introducing her Grace to this gentleman?"

"I *will* meet him," said the lady. "Whether you object or not."

I daresay if any of us had said it, we would have been met with a stern refusal and shown the door. But, as her son had told us, the Duchess was a formidable woman.

"Very well. But I caution you, he is having a bad time of it, and will not withstand browbeating or temper."

With that, Doctor Agar threw open the door and ushered us toward the lift, which the lady regarded dubiously and then declared that she was well able to manage a flight of stairs. The doctor then offered her his arm, and we followed the pair up the stairs and along a broad, carpeted corridor flanked by a half-dozen closed doors. As we passed down this hallway, we caught the sound of a sob or a groan, but from the last, which was our destination, there was only silence.

"Your Grace," said Holmes to the lady as we stood at the door, "I ask you to remember what you said about the extent to which we are called upon to forgive."

She gave him a sharp glance and then, stepping past us, she turned the knob and entered the room.

The chamber was more a suite than a room, with a comfortable sitting area, bright curtains, and a few upholstered chairs. Yet the pall of despair could not be done away with, for on the iron-framed bed lay a pale, emaciated figure whose slight movements of the jaw and the closed eyelids were all that hinted of life. The flesh of his face was taut and muscles of the arms that lay above the coverlet were emaciated and pale. At the far side of the bed, a gray-haired man knelt, his head upon the patient's breast, clutching one of the patient's skeletal hands in his own.

"Mr. Harmon," said the doctor, gently, and the man raised his head, a lock of hair falling over his brow. He looked upon us and then his gaze fixed on the Duchess and he stumbled to his feet and staggered back. Though there was no more than the light from one of the lamps to illuminate the chamber, we could see that the person who faced us was the man in the photograph.

For a moment, the silence was broken only by a slight sound from the patient, as soft as a child's whimper. The Duke gasped and dropped into a chair beside the door, but the lady advanced to confront the apparition. With one gloved finger, she reached up, lifted the lock of hair from the gentleman's forehead, and traced the remnant of a scar just below his hairline. She then snatched off one glove, drew back her arm and struck a resounding blow across the man's face.

"How could you!" she cried. "David! How could you!"

The Duchess dashed her fists against his shirt front, and then clung to him and began to sob, uncontrollably. "My son! My son!"

"I beg you – " the man's voice was hoarse and exhausted. "I beg you, Mother. Noise distresses him so!"

The Duke pushed himself to his feet and stared at the stranger. "What – who is this imposter, Mr. Holmes?"

Holmes addressed the man. "You are David Arthur Cecil DeVere St. Simon?"

The man gave out something between a sigh and a groan. "I am."

"And this," Holmes added, with a nod toward the figure upon the bed, "is Lord Alfred Whittington."

"Yes."

"Alfred!" The Duchess approached the figure, and then leaned over him and took his drawn face in her hands. "Can it be . . . ?"

"What is the meaning of this?" demanded the Duke. "If you are David – for God's sake! What have you done to Mother – to our family? To Alicia? Thirty years!"

"I know what I have done and that no explanation I give will excuse it. You have every right to hate me."

"Doctor," said Holmes, "if you would summon a nurse to sit with the patient, we might do better to work out this matter in the privacy of your consulting room."

Agar stepped out to fetch a nurse, and the fellow who had called himself John Harmon leaned over the bed and pressed his lips to the patient's forehead and whispered, "I shall not be gone long, Alfred."

"Perhaps," said Holmes, when we were all settled in Agar's office, "it would be the easiest course if I were to relate the history of the events which bring us to this point, and if there are facts which I overlook, you, your Grace, and you, sir – " he said, addressing St. Simon (for so I will call him for the sake of simplicity if not accuracy,) "may interject where I go wrong."

"First, I must know – " the Duchess addressed Doctor Agar, who stood leaning against the door. "The affliction that Alfred suffers – it is the same as Lady Alicia's?"

The doctor nodded. "And, from what little I know of the history, that of their father, who was an invalid from early middle age. The malady is a hereditary one and it goes by more than one name. Some call it fatal familial choreiform disease, and others know it as Huntington's Chorea, after the American doctor who wrote a very thorough description of the

345

condition. The nervous system breaks down and all that it controls –
movement, breathing, digestion, intellect – breaks down with it. The
chance of a sufferer passing it to the offspring is said to be fifty-percent.
There is no cure."

"This malady, which kept the Earl confined to his bed," said Holmes,
"and the predilections of the late Duke, as well as the difficulties these
circumstances imposed upon their wives, did not make for very congenial
households. The two eldest St. Simons and the two Whittingtons found
relief from the unhappiness at home in the companionship of one another.
As the children advanced toward adulthood, the Duke – from selfish
motives, I am sorry to say – pressed and goaded his eldest son toward a
marriage with Lady Alicia, whose fortune was well into six figures. At
last, you, sir, relented, and made the lady an offer of marriage which she,
having a very genuine affection for her childhood companion, accepted.
But there was one complication. You were not in love with the lady. You
were in love with her brother."

"Mr. Holmes!" cried our client.

"It is why you, your Grace, had reservations about the marriage."

"I think you must concede, Mr. Holmes, that the observations of a
mother, when it comes to her children, may be as keen as those of a
detective."

"It's true," declared St. Simon, almost defiantly. "Alfred and I were
in love. And what was to be done about it? How were we to live among
those who would have thought of our love as shameful – even criminal. At
university, you cannot imagine how many hours were spent dreaming up
plans for escape, where we might go, and what we would do, and how we
might get free of that other cloud which hung over both of us, that day
when a father's passing would thrust upon us obligations that neither had
ever wished for. Even before the Earl's death, we spoke of taking a sort of
grand tour after our graduation, running off to Italy – anywhere – never to
return. Youthful fancies."

"At some point," said Holmes, "they became more than fancies,"

St. Simon nodded. "He was ambitious in everything – studies, sport,
mischief. Alfred did nothing by half measures. Study alone might have
brought him down. But then the Earl died."

"He left a letter, describing this terrible affliction and, I believe, his
decision to end his own life," said Holmes. "And, perhaps, a sobering
caution that Lord Alfred must be the one to disclose this secret to his sister,
and to warn her that neither of them must ever risk having children of their
own."

"Yes, Mr. Holmes. The odds were too great that it might be passed
down. With the contents of that letter, and his studies and his new role as

heir, Alfred was left in such a bad way that his physicians said that it would be months in hospital or months on holiday, he must choose. Everyone urged the latter, and so we set off. And then, some months later, you received word of my death. As with many lies, there was some truth to it. Alfred did go off to the caves, not to explore, but to do as his father had done, to bring an end to matters. He left a note for me, very much like the one his father had left for him. '*It will appear to be an accident,*' he wrote. '*I haven't the stomach to wait and see how the coin falls.*' I found the note well before I was meant to – thank God! – and went after him and told him that where he went, I would follow. He laid out everything about this wretched affliction, and it did not sway me. Alfred said that it would get very bad, there would be no escaping from it, and made me swear that when it came to that point, I must leave him, and I swore to it. No man ever told a greater lie."

We were all silent for several minutes, and then Holmes said, gently, "There was the other lie, of course. That you had died that day in the caves."

"Yes. The escape we had dreamed of, and coming at such a time! One would die, and the other would be too devastated by guilt to ever return to face his survivors."

"And you were chosen as the casualty," said Holmes, "because your mother had – despite his shortcomings – a husband, and three other children, while Lady Whittington would be losing her only son. And, also, because your death would benefit your brothers and sister. They would inherit the money and property that you had left to them in your will."

"Money and property that my father could not squander," St. Simon added. "It lessened my feelings of guilt, somewhat, to think that I had done something material to offset the effects of my father's extravagance. Alfred sent directions to his stewards regarding the estate, and drew from the income when we needed money, but we rarely did. There are all sorts of things a fellow can do in this world if he has the will, and I daresay we tried them all. And so a year passed, and then two, and then five, and we told one another that if half of the offspring succumbed to this terrible affliction, half escaped it, and that Alfred would be among that lucky half. And then the first symptoms appeared."

"Near the time of Lady Whittington's death," said Holmes.

St. Simon nodded.

"Alfred had never been able to bring himself to show their father's letter to Alicia, but some months after Lady Whittington's funeral, he summoned Alicia to the Continent and disclosed all."

"And Lady Alicia returned from this visit morose and changed and withdrawing from society altogether. And," Holmes added, directing his

347

remark at the Duke, "declining a proposal of marriage that, had circumstances been different, she would have been happy to accept. But she would not inflict the torment of her decline upon you, nor the anxiety of wondering whether this infirmity would pass to your children."

The Duke dropped his face into his hands and let out a groan.

"And now, we come to the present," said Holmes. "On the Continent and in London, the condition of brother and sister have deteriorated to the point where they can no longer be cared for at home, and separately, they turn to Doctor Agar's establishment. And one day, your Grace, you catch a glimpse of a tall, pale figure who strongly resembles your late husband. You see him again the next day and again a week later, when you confront him on the street. You produce a photograph of your late husband, taken when he was seventy-one. I estimated his age to be sixty or thereabouts, but that was because the Duke had the dubious good fortune to look much younger than his years. Now, when the chemist is shown that same photograph, he pronounces it to be the image of his customer, John Harmon. You sir," he said with a nod toward St. Simon. "can only be fifty-two or -three, but I suspect the burden of caring for your gravely ill companion has left its mark, which is why the chemist took you for the man in the photograph."

"You are wrong, Mr. Holmes," said St. Simon, quietly. "Caring for Alfred was never a burden. When you love someone, it never is."

"At any rate, as we were leaving the chemist's, I was struck by the significance of what he had said. John Harmon. You recall that I returned to the shop, Watson."

"Yes."

"Now your son had told me, your Grace, that when you confronted this apparition, you called out to him by his Christian name, whereupon he turned, and appeared to recognize you and then fled. Why would a fellow named 'John Harmon' react so when you called out your husband's Christian name? Because eldest sons are often named for the father. And so I returned to ask the chemist if his patron happened to remove his hat, which, in fact, he did, and the chemist recalled seeing what appeared to be the remnant of a scar just at the hairline. It happened when you took a fall. You were laid up for weeks, and Lord Alfred would keep you current with your studies, and Lady Alicia would sit at your bedside and read Dickens because it was your favorite."

"Yes, Mr. Holmes," St. Simon nodded.

"*Our Mutual Friend*, if I remember aright," said Holmes. "John Harmon's body '*had been discovered floating in the Thames in an advanced state of decay and much injured.*' Of course, Harmon isn't dead – he assumes an incognito and carries on."

348

"Victims of drowning were not uncommon in that region. It did not tax our resources too severely to have one of them passed off as young Lord St. Simon. We carried on as well, traveling as relatives, as partners in business, as employer and clerk, and finally as patient and nurse. When Alfred was no longer able to write, I wrote his letters for him, directions to the stewards, his correspondence with Alicia, and read him her letters which, for the past few years, Mother, were in your own dear hand."

He took his mother's hand and kissed it. "I can't think of anything more to be said. I cannot even say that if I had it to do over again, I would do things much differently. I can only hope that a day may come, when you, Mother, and you, Robert, can forgive me."

There was a brief pause, and then the Duchess said, "I see nothing wrong with this day. It's as good a day as any."

"If there's nothing more, you must excuse me. I must get back to Alfred. I don't like – " his voice choked and he turned away for a moment. "I don't like to be apart from him for long."

"One moment!"

The Duke had listened to this recital, sitting stiffly in his chair, his hands clasped upon the knob of his cane. Now he rose and looked at his brother. "There is one thing more."

He approached St. Simon and laid his hands upon his brother's shoulders. "I wish with all my heart that the circumstances were not so grave – that you and Alfred had been more certain of our love for you, and allowed us to do for you both – but he will want for nothing now." He removed his *pince nez* and wiped them with his handkerchief. "I am very glad to see you again, David."

The Duchess rose, and I saw some of her brisk resolution return. "Doctor Agar, Alfred's suite is quite large, and I think room may be made for Alicia."

"It is not done, ma'am. We have separate wings for male and female patients."

"I daresay you did not rise in your profession by doing things as they have always been done. They came into this world together, and it is only right that they should be together now. I will go up with you, David, and see how it can be managed. Robert, will you come?"

"Yes, in a moment."

The Duchess took her eldest son's arm and walked for the door, stopping only to look up at Holmes. "Thank you, sir."

"Indeed, ma'am, I am afraid I have failed you. I did not produce a husband this time."

"No, sir. You did much better."

349

"I will excuse myself as well," said Agar. "I have patients who cannot be neglected. It has been an honor to meet you, Mr. Holmes."

"You may wish to reserve judgement until we are better acquainted," replied Holmes with a smile.

We were left alone with our client. "When we first met, Mr. Holmes, your researches cost me a wife, and now they cost me a Dukedom."

"I cannot provide you with a wife, your Grace, and I cannot answer for your status. That may be up to a gentleman named Harmon, who, I suspect, might prefer to have matters remain as they are."

"And if he does not," said the Duke, philosophically, "I am no worse than I have been in the past."

As fate would have it, our noble client's situation did change, and in a rather surprising fashion. Lord Alfred and Lady Alicia Whittington died within a day of one another, not long after these dramatic events, and when Lady Alicia's will was read, it was discovered that she had left her entire fortune to "the dear friend of my childhood, Robert Walsingham DeVere St. Simon."

"I believe," Holmes said, some weeks after the conclusion of the case, "that should you ever give an account of this tale, you may have to alter so many of the names, and withhold so many of the facts, that it will never satisfy the public. You would do better, I think, to convert the whole matter into a ghost story. If nothing else, it should divert your American readers who, I understand, are rather fond of such tales."

# The Reappearance of
# Mr. James Phillimore
### by David Marcum

The north wind was in our faces as we trudged homeward along Baker Street. It pushed dead leaves that danced with whispering rustles around our feet, along the pavement, and against the buildings. An October cold snap had descended on London several days before, along with brilliant blue autumn skies. We had enjoyed a refreshing change from the rains that had assailed us just days earlier, but now the clouds were building once again, and very shortly we would be inundated.

We had just reached the coffee house at the corner of Portland Mansions when we encountered a woman headed south. She had been walking with steady purpose, scanning passers-by with a peculiar intensity. When she spotted my friend Sherlock Holmes, she pulled up with recognition.

"Mr. Holmes!" she cried, causing several people nearby to look up and our way from their own inner distractions. "Your landlady said that you were out. It *is* you, isn't it?"

Holmes frowned – a not-uncommon reaction when called out by strangers in public. While it could not be denied that my literary endeavours of the late 1880's and early 1890's had substantially increased his fame, making him much more recognizable and enabling him to increase his caseload substantially, he still felt that my efforts had deprived him of a certain amount of necessary anonymity. And I had to agree – although it must be noted that any anonymity that he desired was also often undone by his own insistence upon wearing his Inverness and fore-and-aft cap in both the city and the country, all the year round. However he had justifiable reasons for this, rightly believing that he could not be kow-towing to fashion if the needs of a case suddenly called him into action. "This coat and hat enable me to instantly begin an investigation – to be dressed to follow someone, travel to high or low places, and stay out for days if necessary. Imagine, Watson, if I were sankoing down the street attired in a topper and tails when I suddenly caught sight of a wanted man. Could I drop everything and pursue him in those clothes? What if the merry chase led me to Limehouse, or Dartmoor – and I still in my formal-wear? Nonsense!"

He was right, of course, and this had been proven dozens upon dozens of times. It didn't hurt that Holmes cared nothing for fashion's – or society's – dictates. His was a Bohemian soul, and he wore what he wanted without regard to others' opinions. On this day, it was a fortunate thing, as he was both identified by a new client, and he was also properly dressed – better than I was – for the rains that were arriving, with the first drops hitting around us even as we paused to talk to the strange woman.

Seeing that we were at the door of the coffee shop, I suggested that we quickly adjourn inside. It was warm and welcoming as always, with the old wooden floorboards creaking as we passed across them. Behind the counter, Mrs. Brett, the owner, smiled our way. About our age, Holmes and I had both known her since she opened the shop nearly two decades earlier, around the time that Holmes was able to explain a small mystery that had vexed her. Now a settled and middle-aged wife and mother of three, she had built up the business with a skill to be admired. While Holmes led the woman to a quiet table, I said hello to our long-time friend and ordered three of her moderate blends – aware that some of the darker roasts might keep me awake for days.

Soon, with three hot mugs in hand, I joined the others and was able to see the woman from the street in better circumstances. She was around sixty years old, and rather matronly in a plain but pleasant way. She was moderately dressed, without any bright colors or noticeable jewelry. She carried a sensible bag, and her expression denoted intelligence. I was glad to see it, for her initial approach on the street had suggested that she was impulsive and overwrought. Clearly something was worrying her to have caused such a forward introduction.

I could hear the intensity of the rain increase outside, and I knew that we were in for it over the next few days. When this storm blew away, the last remaining bits of summer would have truly departed.

"While you were serving us," Holmes told me, "Mrs. Harlow introduced herself." I glanced at her ring finger, which was bare. A widow, perhaps?

"She hasn't related any other facts, however." He turned back to the woman. "How can we help you?"

Mrs. Harlow took a sip of the coffee and held the hot mug cupped in her hands for a moment, clearly enjoying the heat in her fingers. Then, realizing that the silence was becoming awkward, she squeezed her eyes shut, took a deep breath, set down the mug, and began.

"I live at Number 12, The Arbour, in Highgate," she said. At that, Holmes seemed to show a spark more interest, but perhaps only someone who knew him as well as I would have noticed.

"I bought my house there two years ago," continued Mrs. Harlow, "when my husband passed away. He was a supervisory clerk at a bank in the City, and he wisely maintained an insurance policy that paid quite handsomely when he died. Sadly, we were never blessed with children, and after he was gone, I began to feel the need for a change. A house agent who had been a friend of my husband's arranged for the sale of our old house and the purchase of the new one. I had considered traveling, but I realized that I'd like nothing better than to settle into my new home. And now . . . ." She closed her eyes again, and a tear suddenly ran down one cheek.

"There, there," I said, laying my hand on hers. "Whatever it is, I'm sure that we can help. What caused you to seek us out today?"

She dabbed at her eyes with a small handkerchief, produced from her bag. "After living so peacefully in my new home, I'm suddenly terrified of it. After . . . after last night, I didn't know what to do. I recalled you, Mr. Holmes, from when you once helped a friend of mine, Mrs. Horace Mortimer, and so I hurried around, without even making an appointment. When your landlady said that you weren't there, I turned away in despair. I . . . I believe that she called to me that you would be back soon and that I could wait, but I was so despondent that I simply needed to walk. Then I saw you both coming my way, and it seemed to be a miracle."

I could tell that Holmes was becoming impatient, but he'd learned over the years that often a story has to be told in its own way. I patted Mrs. Harlow's hand one more time and then withdrew my own. She was ready to continue.

"My little house is one of a row, not more than twenty years old. It consists of just two stories – a sitting room and parlor and kitchen on the ground floor, without a cellar, and a couple of bedrooms upstairs. It's cozy and comfortable, and I've filled it with objects that please me. Books, and interesting little curios that I obtain – selectively, I assure you – during explorations to various parts of London. I live a very quiet and satisfying life, with only my cat to keep me company.

She gave a small sob, and then continued. "It has been thus for many months, until . . . until five days ago, at which time I began to have . . . *visitations.*"

Holmes shifted in his seat and leaned forward, his hands resting on the table, fingers intertwined, coffee ignored. "What sort of visitations?" he asked. "Surely you don't mean to imply something along the lines of a spirit or ghost?"

She rocked a bit and chewed her lip before saying with a low cry, "Mr. Holmes, I simply do not know! I would have never thought that I could be afraid of such a thing, and yet – I have seen things that I cannot explain!"

Seeing that we were listening intently, she continued. "It began innocently enough, last Monday night – although at the time it was rather upsetting, as I didn't realize how much worse things could become. I was awakened by a noise in the night, in the hallway outside my bedroom. I sleep with the door closed, and my cat, Molly, was with me. I'm normally a light sleeper, and it was no wonder that such a sound would disturb me. It was a distinct thump, as if someone were walking in the darkness had inadvertently knocked against the small table standing outside my bedroom door.

"I gave an inadvertent cry, certain that a robber had entered the house. I was quite fearful and uncertain as to what I should do. But then, instead of hearing footsteps making a quick escape, I heard a moan, a terrible sound that started low, almost like the wind, but then grew in volume and intensity until it was nearly a scream. I didn't imagine it – it was no dream. Molly heard it as well, and instantly the hair on her back stood out while she cringed against me and hissed at the terrible sound. And then – it stopped abruptly, as if whomever – or whatever – had created it met with some great violence. Then, with another a painful groan, it vanished entirely.

"My heart was pounding, and I cowered in bed for the longest time. Molly seemed to calm herself after a while, but I never truly did. Morning light was beginning to peep through the windows before I managed to make myself arise. Only then did I remember that my door, while closed, had not been locked – for who locks themselves in their bedroom at night when living alone? Or perhaps that is a perfectly sound reason to do so, but it hadn't ever occurred to me before, and while the door had a lock, I'd never had a key for it, from the day that I moved there.

"I examined the hallway and saw no signs of an intruder. The small table was as I'd left it. I crept around the house for an hour or so, looking for evidence of a break-in, or half-expecting someone – or some*thing* – to jump out at me from every door or recess that I passed. It was a terrible feeling – this home that I'd loved from the beginning, and which was to me the coziest of havens – now suddenly an unfamiliar and dangerous threat.

"I was too ashamed to call the police, for even I could see that no one had broken in, and there was no sign of damage or proof that anyone had been there. Possibly you, Mr. Holmes, could have read much that was invisible to me, but I simply never thought of you. Instead, I relayed a message to the locksmith – I am on the telephone – and requested that he provide me with a key to my bedroom that very day. He seemed curious, and came around within the hour, but I provided no answers to his unvoiced questions.

"That day was so long, and it was dark as well – not quite raining, but with fitful and unceasing winds rattling around. I would look out the windows at the low clouds scudding by, my unease growing. I've never gotten to know any of my neighbors, and I've lost track of the few friends that I had when my husband was alive. I realized just how alone I was. I couldn't even go next door and ask if they had heard anything in the night – I had never met them, and they would think that I was touched in the head. Well, I suppose that I could have asked them, but it simply seemed impossible.

"And so Tuesday night came, and I followed my usual routine, cooking a small supper and carrying out the usual household chores. I tried to read, but every knock and thump from the rising wind outside distracted me. Finally, when I could avoid it no longer, I went up to bed.

"Somehow I fell asleep, comforted perhaps by my now-locked door. And yet, it was almost as if I'd known that the previous night was only the beginning. Around four in the morning, without any warning or preparation, my door was suddenly subjected to three very loud knocks – pounding, really, as if by a giant fist. And then, there was a low laugh – sinister, and slightly wheezy. It seemed to resolve itself into a repetition of sibilant whispers. Gradually they became loud enough for me to recognize their pattern: '*Get out!*' they hissed. '*Get out!*' Eventually they peaked in intensity before fading away.

"Once again, Molly beside me had been as frightened as I was. And yet, this time instead of cringing, she stood and walked down the bed, as if willing to fight. However, I was not so brave, making no effort to do anything but hide beneath my covers, weeping and wishing for morning.

"Wednesday was much the same, as has been each day since then. The daylight hours pass with a sense of dread and impending disaster, while the nights have been one terrifying incident after another. That night, nothing happened for so long that I began to believe it had ended – and yet, a sudden scream an hour or so before dawn woke me from a troubled slumber. After several moments nothing else happened, and I foresaw another wakeful wait for morning. Then I heard a terrible dragging noise on the door. It was over in seconds, and only when I exited hours later did I see that the woodwork had been damaged from the top to the middle, as if it had been raked by claws.

"Thursday night, I was awakened again by loud pounding on the door, followed by maniacal laughter. It was almost a comfort that nothing further occurred. And yet, when I went out in the morning, I found that a series of naked footprints, one after another, had been *burned into the floor*, leading from the top of the stairs to my doorway. I touched them and they were cool, but the floor where they lay was most definitely burned, and there was ash on my fingers. Likewise, at eye level on the wall across from my bedroom door was the word *Leave*, burned along the wallpaper.

"I know what you're thinking, gentlemen: Why in God's name was I putting up with this for so long? But I truly had nowhere else to go, and up until then I had feared approaching the police, as I had no real evidence – even the scratches on my door could have been made by me. My former sister-in-law had a mental affliction in which she made greater and greater efforts to inflict self-harm, pretending that she was being victimized by others, if she felt that she wasn't getting enough attention, and I saw over the years how she was treated and not believed. Even the footprints could have been something that I constructed in a warped effort to bring myself to someone's awareness. I only wish that I had gone yesterday morning, before this . . . this malevolent phantom escalated the affair to a new level!

"Last night, as I again prepared myself for another long night of waiting to see how I would be disturbed, I realized that I hadn't seen Molly for an hour or so. I went to the rear of the ground floor, into the kitchen, and saw that her food hadn't been eaten. I was more puzzled than I can say, and I searched high and low, calling her name. I knew that she couldn't have slipped out, because I hadn't opened the door in days – in fact, since the visit of the locksmith. Her absence made me more and more concerned, and angry as well, as if my willingness to fight back against this . . . this *thing* was finally awakening. Instead of going to bed last night, I lit all the lamps, found the largest knife that I owned and, carrying it into the sitting room, I placed myself in a chair, ready to confront whatever it was that was terrorizing me.

"Periodically through the night, I would pass through the house, terrified with every step and expecting to encounter the intruder, calling for Molly, and looking for anything unusual. But I never saw a sign of her, or my intruder. Eventually this morning came, and I was relieved – I seemed to have broken the cycle. And yet, it was a very hollow victory, for my only companion had vanished.

"As today wore on, I puttered about. I usually have very few chores, and so eventually I found myself back in the sitting room, reading a book, and becoming more and more sleepy. In mid-afternoon, I awoke with a start, with the vague sense that I'd heard a noise, like the sound of a door shutting in another part of the house. Rousing myself, for I'd slept deeply and I still felt as if I were halfway between wakefulness and drowsing, I picked up the knife and went to examine the house.

"I'd only reached the front hall, however, when I saw her – Molly – before me, on the floor near the front door. I dropped to my knees, the knife clattering to the woodwork beside me. She was dead – stiffened, and with a look of rage on her face, as if she'd fought whatever it was that killed her. The fur was bunched at her throat, and her head was . . . it was at an odd angle, as if her neck had been twisted and broken!"

356

At this point, Mrs. Harlow broke down, sobbing silently into her handkerchief. I glanced at Holmes. His gaze was intent, and there was an angry flame burning in his eyes that revealed his outrage at the circumstances faced by this poor woman.

"It was then that I knew I couldn't stay," said Mrs. Harlow. "I had remained for so long, but then I stood and fled, somehow remembering to grab my coat, hat, and bag. Thankfully I locked the house behind me, but I could have just as easily forgotten. I walked for quite a bit, only stopping to have a cup of tea and a bite to eat when I felt myself becoming weak. I was considering finally approaching the police when I thought of you, Mr. Holmes. I made my way to Baker Street, and then fortunately I saw you both on the street." Her voice faded away, as if every bit of her energy had been used up remembering the terrors of the last few days, and now she was trustingly placing the matter in Holmes's hands.

He thought for a moment, and then said, "I know that it will be difficult, and frightening, but can you return there, and wait for Dr. Watson and me to prepare ourselves?"

A look of terror filled her eyes. "I cannot! I can't be alone there. Can't you return with me?"

Holmes smiled and reached to pat her hand. "You won't be alone. Dr. Watson and I have something to do first, but in the meantime, we'll send you with a lad that I know, by the name of Philip Barsby."

Young Philip was one of Holmes's Irregulars, that group of lads – and occasionally lasses – who often served as his eyes and ears. I recalled passing Philip earlier as we had walked toward home. "His appearance," Holmes continued, "may not provide the greatest confidence, but there is no one more true and sure. But you must remember," he said, his tone changing, "that neither of you should speak to each other. Don't say a word. Whatever is in the house must believe that you have returned there alone. Do you understand?"

She nodded, uncertain, but willing to take the lifeline thrown to her.

"I don't believe that you will be in any immediate danger, but it's essential that the house be reoccupied as soon as possible. I assure you that we will settle this in a very short amount of time."

She nodded, and then her eyes widened momentarily. Tears formed, and I have no doubt that she was again seeing her poor cat lying dead in the hall where she had left it. So vivid had been her description that I could envision it there as well, and I felt her pain at being asked to go back. Holmes was not indifferent.

"I wouldn't ask you to return if there was any other way," he said. "But you may have left the place untenanted for too long already, and

357

whomever wants you to leave must believe that you're still defenseless, and without aid, if he is to reveal himself."

"So," she asked, eyes wide, "you don't believe this to be some kind of monster?"

Holmes frowned. "Of course not. But if we have any hopes of putting a stop to this, we must hurry. You will return to Highgate with our young friend, as soon as I round him up, while Dr. Watson and I will repair to Baker Street and carry out our plans from there. Within the hour, the doctor will present himself at your home in the guise of a gas inspector."

With that, I raised an eyebrow, but Holmes continued without pause. "You will enter, Watson, making a great show of explaining that you are checking for leaks. Putter about, make some noise, and then return to the front door, where you will noisily say goodbye. But you will *not* leave. Rather, you will also remain in the house, quietly, and no further conversation will pass between any of you, whatsoever. That is most important. Mrs. Harlow, is there somewhere that the doctor and our young friend Philip can wait unobserved until tonight?"

She nodded. "The parlour, by the front door, is rarely used, and there is are comfortable chairs for reading."

"No reading, Watson. I'm afraid that you must both wait in darkness. And no smoking either, old fellow."

"I understand." And I did. It was rather like that terrible night in '83 when Holmes and I had hidden in a bed chamber where violent death had occurred before, knowing that the killer was waiting patiently in the adjacent room. There had been a ventilator constructed high in the wall where death would slip through, and any indication that we had replaced the room's regular occupant, as revealed by smoke from our pipes or cigarettes, would have ruined Holmes's scheme. The villain had never realized that we were there, and his murderous plot recoiled on him in a most fitting and satisfactory way – but not before Holmes and I had a few terrifying moments where our own deaths were entirely possible.

Holmes stepped outside to locate Philip Barsby, and I continued to speak softly to Mrs. Harlow, assuring her that my friend would soon find a solution. I didn't mention that he had seemed to recognize the address, and I looked forward to learning from him its significance.

In a moment, Holmes returned and waved toward us from the door. I nodded to Mrs. Brett behind the counter and then gave Mrs. Harlow my arm. Outside, Holmes introduced Mrs. Harlow to Philip, a bright boy of perhaps ten. He carefully instructed that Mrs. Harlow should arrive at the front of her house alone, and then let Philip in discretely through the back door. He made it quite clear that there should absolutely be no conversation between them to indicate that Philip was inside the house. I

358

felt that the boy was trustworthy in this matter, but I wondered if Mrs. Harlow could remain silent. I assured her that I would soon join them, and that Holmes had a good idea of what to do. Then we put them in a cab and sent them away. Then, with the cold rain in our faces, we dashed for our rooms up the street.

I knew that Holmes already had some sense of what had occurred, but I didn't know yet how he came to any conclusion. I could only grasp with certainty that when Mrs. Harlow had stated her address, he seemed to show some additional interest, as if he'd recognized it. When we had entered the front hallway of our lodgings, and were shaking out our wet coats at the bottom of the stairs, I asked him to elaborate.

"Very good, Watson," he said as we started upstairs. "You see that this narrative, consisting of a series of events that are all self-contained within that small household, and with a very limited cast of characters, could have occurred anywhere. The only facts that might have a wider significance are the profession of the late husband or that specific address. How did you decide to ask about one over the other?"

"I hadn't given any thought to her late husband's job at the bank," I confessed, entering the sitting room and turning to face him. "Instead, I saw your interest when she mentioned her address."

"Ha!" he barked. "I must learn to guard against your growing observational skills," he said, "lest I become careless and give away other secrets before they can be dramatically revealed." He dashed into his room, only to immediately return carrying a shabby overcoat and a leather folder of the type used by workmen recording observations. "This shall be your disguise," he said. "Nothing too elaborate." I took the items from Holmes, who then said, "Make sure that you bring your service revolver."

I patted my coat. "As you know, I learned years ago never to step out without it."

"Good man. Be on your way soon. Don't look for me, but I will be nearby." And he walked toward the door, stopping to pick up his loaded riding crop from the nearby stand.

"But Holmes," I asked, "*why* were you interested in the address?"

"You'll find it in my commonplace books," he replied. "But don't dawdle – that poor woman is counting on you to join her soon. It's the Phillimore matter. You'll find it filed under '*F*'."

"Phillimore starts with a '*P*'," I called, but he was already gone.

His filing system was always more curious than could be comprehended by lesser mortals, but I suspected that he had listed it under '*F*' because he considered it to be a *Failure*. However, cases that he often judged to have unsatisfactory endings usually seemed, to me at least, to be astounding successes. Still, he would see something in those affairs that

359

irritated him – a deduction made later than he would have liked, or his initial pursuit seemingly wasted time while he followed a false trail before comprehending the truth – and so forever after it would be labeled in his mind as a defeat. The Phillimore case of two years before had certainly been perceived that way by the public. When the man disappeared, Holmes had been consulted, and at the end he admitted that he had no solution. Afterwards, he'd accepted the good-natured chiding of the police, without revealing that he had in fact truly arrived at a solution, and rather easily at that. Yet he chose to hide it, rather than expose a man's carefully constructed secret.

I found the book for the letter '*F*' and carried it to the dining table. I knew that every minute was important, and that Mrs. Harlow and Philip Barsby might, even at that moment, be entering her Highgate home. But I wanted to understand what Holmes had remembered, and he apparently felt that it was safe for her to return there, at least initially, if she could muster the courage.

Holmes's scrapbooks are not books at all, but rather a loose collection of documents somewhat enclosed in front-and-back covers. There are attached pages, but more are loose than not, and tucked between every leaf are other scraps of paper – photographs, receipts, handwritten notes, and brochures – along with other odd and unexplained items like feathers, or strips of papyrus with curious hieroglyphics upon them, or swatches of cloth. Each has a story, and relays some fact to Holmes that is often meaningless to others. In flipping through the sheets, I found his notes related to Phillimore, immediately after a small booklet describing the history of an ancient London church.

I scanned Holmes's neat handwriting and saw immediately why he had been alerted by Mrs. Harlow's story – the address that she gave us was the very same where James Phillimore had disappeared just over two years earlier, probably within a month or so before she purchased it.

The case was quite the nine-days wonder at the time, and it wasn't long until Holmes was consulted by our old friend, Inspector Lestrade. Phillimore, a bachelor who worked for a nearby wine merchant, had stepped outside one spring morning and called to a passing constable. He hurriedly made some explanation about a mysterious package that he'd received, and asked the constable to whom he should report it. Then, as a shower was about to begin, and before the constable could answer, Phillimore excused himself for a moment, indicating that he was going to step back inside for an umbrella. He turned and passed in, partially pushing the door to but not entirely closing it – and vanished.

After a few moments, the constable, Wilkins, became impatient, but rather than simply walking on, he knocked and called several times before entering the house. Inside, he found that James Phillimore had seemingly disappeared without a trace. Wilkins pushed the door shut, locking it and taking the key that was still in the lock with him while he searched the house, moving methodically from room to room. Wilkins was known to Holmes and me as being one of the more responsible of the bunch, and it was proven this his examination of the house was quite effective while he listened carefully to make certain that no one was moving around in places where he was not then occupying. The house was a small one, and I didn't take long to ascertain that it was mysteriously empty.

The windows were all locked, and there was a bar on the inside of the back door that absolutely could not have been replaced if Phillimore had exited by that route. Realizing that something was happening beyond his experience, Wilkins unlocked and re-opened the front door to blow his whistle. Within a few moments, several other officers had joined him, and before long Lestrade was there as well. A plethora of constables then swarmed through the place, and no sign of Phillimore was found.

Routine investigation revealed a number of documents left on Phillimore's desk, including a number of threatening letters that had been mailed to him at that address from central London over the preceding week, all written by a mysterious man named "Willoughby". Each was vague, promising that he would die for what he had done – without providing any details as to what exactly that might have been. Of this Willoughby there was no trace.

Phillimore, a quiet and anonymous man of around forty years, had led a routine life, moving from work to home and back again. He was engaged to be married to a middle-aged spinster named Sylvia Amherst, but the relationship had been long-standing, and there was no apparent urgency toward formalizing the arrangement. With no apparent clues, the public became fascinated with the story, especially as it somehow found its way into the newspapers, despite the efforts of the police to keep it quiet. Several anonymous letters to the editor were published, all calling for Holmes's intervention. With no other direction to turn, Lestrade summoned Holmes and me, and was immediately chided by my friend for waiting so long. He wasted no time in examining the entire house, which had remained locked and guarded since Phillimore's disappearance, while the inspector and I waited patiently in the sitting room off the front hall. We could hear Holmes exploring the building, upstairs and down, and then back again. Eventually he joined us, agreeing with Lestrade that Phillimore hadn't exited by the windows or the back door. With that, he indicated that he would continue his investigation, and we departed, leaving Lestrade markedly unsatisfied.

Over the next couple of days, Holmes built up a greater picture of Phillimore – a bland fellow, living life with a sameness that never varied from day to day and year to year. We met with Miss Amherst, and found her to be a singularly unpleasant person who gave us to understand that if we found her errant fiancé, she would quickly place him under a much firmer thumb than how he'd previously found himself. She let it slip through implication that it had only been through the threat of a breach of promise suit that they'd remained engaged as long as they had.

When we were back outside, both rather shaken at being in the presence of such a harridan, Holmes announced that it was time to settle this. He then hailed a cab and directed us to the Charing Cross Hotel.

In the lobby, a boy of ten or so approached us. It was young Abel Foster, one of Holmes's irregulars who often drew this sort of assignment, as he was from a middle-class home, and thus had both better manners and shoes. He informed us that Mr. Willoughby was still in his room, and how to find it. I started to ask how Willoughby had been located, but Holmes was already headed upstairs.

We knocked on the door of Number 412, which opened to reveal a rather plain middle-aged man with his brown hair combed low on his forehead. He peered at us curiously, but stepped back with a start when Holmes greeted him as Mr. Phillimore and asked if we could step inside.

Phillimore seemed to be trapped between amazement and nervous laughter when he realized that he'd been discovered, and that his use of the name "Willoughby" had been revealed. As expected, he wanted to know how he'd been found. Holmes explained that during his searches of the house, he'd found various footprints throughout belonging to Phillimore, as identified when matched with shoes belonging to the missing man, along with a number of constable's prints, along with the inspector's, the left of which had a marked inward twist. Oddly, some of those belonging to Phillimore had been mixed in with those of the constables in the ground floor entry hall. In fact, in a few cases these had lay *on top of* the constable's prints. Following some of Phillimore's tracks back from the front door, Holmes discovered that they had come from the closet underneath the stairs.

While Lestrade and I had waited in the sitting room, he had given the closet a more intense examination, aware that Phillimore couldn't have simply hidden there while Wilkins searched the house, as he would have been quickly discovered. Further examination of the space had led Holmes to discover that it had a false back, with room enough behind it for a man to hide, although just barely. This was confirmed by seeing that Phillimore's footprints were also there in the scattered dust.

362

Holmes had then realized what must have happened: Phillimore, planning to vanish, had waited until he saw a constable passing by. He called to him to obtain his attention, and then, with the excuse of retrieving an umbrella, he went back in the house, leaving the door open. He hurried to the closet, stepped inside and, closing the door behind him, he moved further back into the secret chamber. There, he had a constable's jacket and helmet hidden, and he put them on and waited.

Holmes revealed then that he'd consulted with the various constables who had been at the scene that morning and verified that no one had been allowed in or out of the house but the police. Lestrade confirmed that the house had been locked up tight since. With this in mind, Holmes was certain that the evidence of the footprints was unaltered.

With the testimony of the constables also confirming that no one else had been in the house that morning, Holmes knew that Phillimore had waited until the house was full of policemen searching for him. Then, disguised as one of them, he simply kept his head down and walked purposely out to the street, where he strolled away and vanished.

"Amongst the papers in your desk was a recent receipt for a theatrical costumer, located near your place of employment. The clerk there verified that they had rented a constable's coat and helmet to a man named Willoughby, and that they were returned later the same morning that you disappeared. Very conscientious, Mr. Phillimore, since you could have simply dropped them in any convenient alley. Perhaps more responsible of you was when you provided a required address – which turned out to be this hotel. You could have lied, but you had to tell them something, and this was what suggested itself to you. And then there's the use of the name Willoughby – not very imaginative, I'm afraid – using it to rent the costume, as well as your room here at the hotel, and also on the threatening letters that you forged to yourself. Though disguised, the handwriting is unmistakable as your own. What significance does the name Willoughby hold for you? I was able to ascertain that as well. As James Phillimore, you've slowly but surely been emptying your bank accounts, making regular payments – never large enough to attract attention – to the accounts of someone named Willoughby."

"That was my great-uncle's name – Thomas Willoughby," Phillimore replied with a rueful smile. "When I concocted this plan, it seemed fitting somehow to use that name, both on the letters, and as my new identity. Several months ago, you see, I received a rather substantial and unexpected inheritance from him. Realizing the freedom from responsibility that the funds now provided, I found that I had the itch to break out of my routine and see the world."

"But why this complex subterfuge?" I asked. "If you could now afford it, you could have simply quit the shop, sold the house, and bought a ticket."

Phillimore shrugged. "What can I say? I wanted to set forth as a different person – to be reinvented as an entirely different man. And Sylvia – that is, Miss Amherst . . . ." He drifted off.

"Yes," Holmes nodded. "She is rather unpleasant."

Phillimore stared for a moment, as if feeling that he should defend her, before nodding. "She has always threatened to bring action against me if we should part. She is quite a . . . vengeful person. She would never have rested. Rather than that hanging over me, wherever I went, I decided that it was simply another reason to vanish entirely. Besides, I can assure you that she would much rather go forward as a jilted and broken-hearted fiancée – chewing on the grievance will sustain her for years!"

He smiled as he said it, but then a silence descended upon us, and his face settled into that bland forgettableness that was certainly its normal state. After a few minutes, Holmes glanced at me with an interrogative expression. "Well, Watson? No crime has been committed here. Do you think my little reputation can stand a bit of tarnish if we let this one remain unsolved, allowing Mr. Phillimore – that is, Mr. *Willoughby* – to follow his own path from here on out?"

"I think so," I agreed, "if you do."

And so, with Phillimore – as I continued to think of him – showing quite a bit of relief, we took our leave, and the matter played out for several more weeks in the press before fading and joining those other cases that are seemingly solution-less, but in actuality do have an explanation, if only one knows where to look and whom to ask.

Holmes's short written *précis* of the affair didn't deviate from my recollection. Yet, as I was about to close the scrapbook, I noticed a second sheet tucked behind the first, headed *Phillimore – Continued.* On this was only one cryptic sentence, written in Holmes's distinctive hand: *House at Number 12, The Arbour, Highgate Sold 17 October, 1895.*

That corresponded to the approximate date that Mrs. Harlow had purchased the house, not long after Phillimore vanished. No surprise there – and yet, why did Holmes feel the need to document it?

Realizing that precious time was slipping away, I pulled on the shabby overcoat and, tapping my pocket where my service revolver rested, I walked down and out to the street, where one of the cabbies that we knew, Bert Deacon, was passing. He waved and seemed oblivious to the driving rain. Giving him Mrs. Harlow's address, I settled back for the journey up to Highgate.

364

Deacon dropped me at the end of the block. The rain had diminished a bit, but the wind was rising. I walked slowly toward the remembered house, admitting to myself that I'd only given the neighborhood cursory attention when visiting there with Holmes two years earlier. Now, with the cold rain falling steadily and in the dim evening light, I was even less inclined to spend any time looking at it with any great intensity from the outside. I stopped in front of Number 12, put my foot on the single front step, and rang the bell.

Almost before I could withdraw my hand, Mrs. Harlow answered, her eyes wide with fear. "Good evening, ma'am," I croaked in my best Cockney accent – not entirely a terrible effort, but not worth trying to recreate here within this printed record. "We're checking the gas connections in the neighborhood – "

"Yes, yes," she interrupted, a bit shrill, and pulling me forward. "Come right in."

Knowing that Holmes had put me in disguise for a reason, I'm sure that he thought that the house was being watched. Mrs. Harlow's nearly panicked welcome of me was far too sudden – she might alert someone that my visit was more planned than the business-like and unexpected intrusion that it was supposed to portray. I needed to calm her down.

Inside, she quickly shut the door. The entry hall, much as I remembered it from two years earlier, was lit by a small gaslight. As my eyes adjusted, I saw young Philip standing in the shadows to the left, in the door of the small parlour. I nodded to him, and Mrs. Harlow began to whisper, hissing, "When I returned, just a few minutes ago – "

I held up my hand abruptly, and she stopped speaking. Then, holding a finger to my lips, I finished my prepared speech, in case someone was already in the house, listening. After all, we knew that there was a secret space behind the walls of the under-stairs closet, and it hadn't yet been searched. "Good evening, ma'am," I growled. "Sorry to bother you so late in the evening, but we've a report of a gas leak in the neighborhood. Have you noticed anything unusual? Have you smelled any gas?"

She shook her head, and I said, to remind her to speak, "What's that, ma'am? I'm a bit hard of hearing."

"No," she said, her voice almost a croak. Her hand was still on my arm, and I realized that she was trembling. "Not a thing."

"Where are the pipes? I asked. "In the cellar?"

"No," she said, calming a bit. "There is no cellar. They are out back, in an area near the small garden."

"Ah, then," I replied, making a few heavy footsteps across the hall. "Let me just see if I smell anything." I took a quick and noisy turn toward the back of the house, and then returned to where Mrs. Harlow was watching. "Nothing inside then. I'll just give it a check outside and then speak to your neighbors. Sorry to intrude." And I opened the door before immediately slamming it shut – while I remained inside.

Then I put my finger to my lips once again and nodded toward the parlour, on our left. As she led me in, Philip stepped aside and I removed the heavy coat that had served to minimally disguise me. She took it from me and then stepped close, indicating that she wanted to speak. Leaning toward her, she breathed with a quiver in her faint whisper, "When I returned home, only a few minutes ago, Molly was gone!"

I immediately remembered that, when she had fled the house earlier, the body of her cat had been left behind on the hall floor. I wanted to ask further questions, and to return to the hall and examine the scene to see if I could observe any signs of how it had been removed, but I realized that I needed to follow Holmes's instructions. Therefore, I simply nodded, I hope reassuringly, and indicated that I would now be taking a seat in the darkened room, as planned.

She pursed her lips a bit, as if she'd expected me to rush to examine the scene, or to somehow notify Holmes of this development, or to at least ask questions in my own strained whisper. However, when it was apparent that I was going to stay in the parlour with Philip, she mouthed the word, "Tea?" and I shook my head. She then set my coat on a small divan near the front window and walked out – quite stiff as she passed from the room, as if expecting a blow to fall at any second from a figure lurking just outside, or fearing that someone would jump from the dim surroundings with a heart-stopping scream –or perhaps she was just irritated with me as well.

And so began one of those long nights of waiting for something to happen. I only spoke to Mrs. Harlow one other time that evening, whispering so softly that I barely formed words, telling her that she should repeat her typical nightly routine, going to bed and locking the door behind her. Holmes hadn't specifically mentioned this, but it seemed to make the most sense. And as for Holmes himself? I had no idea where he was or what he was doing, but I assumed, having known him for so long, that he would reveal himself when the time was best.

We heard as she made her dinner, and I regretted not eating something earlier, when I'd had the chance.

Around ten o'clock, Mrs. Harlow walked to the front door, ostensibly to check the lock, but actually to peer into the dark parlour and raise a hand, as if saying farewell to each of us. I acknowledged with my own wave in return, and then I heard her go up the stairs, her pace slow and her feet dragging, as if she were climbing a gallows. Philip and I sat in darkness. In a moment, from deeper in the house, came the muffled sound of her bedroom door closing and the lock turning. Seconds later, I heard the sound of a sob, as if she had finally given way to the terrible grief that had gripped her throughout the day.

But it occurred to me then that, while I was correct to hide as soon as I'd pretended to leave, as per Holmes's instructions, I hadn't been able to search the house, and that she might very well be in danger. Whatever had been terrorizing her had been content so far to do so at night when she was safely in her room, while it had the full run of the rest of the house. But she had been away today for an hour or so, and during that time, her bedroom was undoubtedly accessible. What if she was being attacked right now? The intruder, having hidden itself in her bedroom, could wait until she locked the door, believing herself to be safe, and then she would turn around, only to discover . . . .

Just the thought of it made me stand before I realized it. Philip glanced at me in surprise, but good lad that he was, he didn't make a sound. I was nearly on my way to pound up the steps, calling Mrs. Harlow's name and telling her to open the door, when I stopped myself. Creeping to the hall door, I held my breath, trying to calm my heart and ignore the blood rushing in my ears, hoping not to hear any indications that some type of violence was occurring just a few feet above me.

But the house was silent, without even the typical creaks and settlings that one so often ignores, but nevertheless occur steadily. Even the lady's sob had only occurred once. Finally believing that she was in truth safe behind her locked door directly above us, I crept back to my chair, nodding reassurance to Philip.

There was no thought that I would sleep, but I did wish again that I'd thought to provide myself with something to eat. I was aware that food was certain to be found at the rear of the house, just a short excursion along the hall to the kitchen. But of course there was really no question but that I would remain where I was. I had been hungry before, and I knew that I'd survive it, as would my young companion.

I had just checked my watch to see that it was a little after one o'clock when I heard it – a sound barely noticeable above the steady fall of the rain outside. At first I wasn't sure that I'd heard anything at all. Perhaps there had been a noise out in the street. But I became convinced that it was real, and that it had been inside the house – a low thump, such as what a door makes when it's closed.

I arose slowly, cursing as my knees cracked. However, I was certain that my aging joints couldn't have been heard even five feet away. I glanced at Philip, and he nodded – he'd heard the noise from the other part of the house too. Walking forward with careful steps, and grateful that the house seemed solid and that creaking boards wouldn't betray my movement, I paused at the hall door, the boy waiting behind me, looking warily around the door-frame at the stairs.

I nearly fell back, with the primitive part of my brain reacting in terror at the sudden and unexpected hellish vision before me. It was tall, well over six feet, but it would have been even taller if it had possessed a head. Arms dangled at the sides, flopping forward and backward as it came to the base of the steps from somewhere in the back of the house. Then it turned and started up, rising from one step to the next, making no effort to grab the bannister for support. The shoulders were very broad, and only served to emphasize the absent head. But the twisted and mutilated aspect of the figure was only the merest part of its horror. For as it climbed, a hideous moan was building from within it, a low tone to a shriek. Even as I watched, it progressed into a terrifying ululation that pierced my ears. And throughout, perhaps the most terrifying of all, it appeared to glow with an inner fire that rippled and shimmered across its surface with every movement.

And yet, this light didn't appear to illuminate the stairs around it. It was self-contained, as if the figure burned with its own inner radiance, seemingly pulling an unholy fire from some other dimension that only barely pierced our own. Altogether, it was a hideous sight, and I wondered what Mrs. Harlow would have thought if she'd actually encountered it, rather than simply hearing its scream and movement from the other side of a locked door.

And yet, this phantom climbed the stairs, an action wherein its physical being interacted with solid materials – Verily, it *had* to touch each physical step to propel itself upward. There was nothing supernatural about that. It didn't float above the floor, or choose to suddenly glide, or apparate from one place to another, appearing instantaneously outside the poor woman's door. It pushed itself, one step at a time, up from the ground floor, and as I watched it do so, I recalled a similarly glowing figure from nearly a decade before that had to run across the fog-shrouded wastes of Dartmoor in order to pull down its terrified prey, rather than simply materializing from the ether, as one would expect a vengeful spirit to do. That had been a real beast that could be killed – and this was certainly the same.

Yet, even as I felt for my gun, I saw another movement in the hallway beyond the stairs. The headless monster had just reached the top and had turned out of sight when a second figure appeared, also moving to the foot of the steps at a near run. While not nearly as frightening as what had just preceded it, the other was no less disturbing. It was a normal man, or at it was least shaped like one. But while the first had glowed with an unholy fire that seemed to undulate with every movement, the second was a black void, a darker darkness against the lesser of the unlit hallway. It mounted the steps lightly and ascended two at a time. Believing that I dimly understood, I followed, motioning Philip to stay back until the danger had passed.

What I saw as I reached the top of the steps and turned to face down the hallway filled me with dread. The tall headless figure, still producing the nerve-tearing shrieks, had somehow managed to wedge its hands into the doorframe itself, and was lunging back and forth to the sound of cracking wood. Meanwhile, I was shocked to see that there appeared to be a second set of arms hanging from the creature's shoulders, swaying each time it tugged at the door. An entry was quickly being forced, and inside I could hear the terrified moans of Mrs. Harlow.

Then the door broke free and flew back into the room on its hinges. The figure made no move to enter, but rather stood there, swaying and moaning, it's horrible cries gradually coalescing into understandable words: *"Get out! Get out!"*

I raised my revolver, intending to shoot it down, intent on stopping that hellish shrieking and hoping that my bullets could destroy it, even as we had once fired on and killed the deadly Baskerville hound. Only then, just before I pulled the trigger, did I notice the black figure standing between me and the monster. It had planted its feet and, shoulders thrown back, and it yelled in a well-recognized voice, "Enough!"

As if a door had been slammed on a terrible storm, the sudden silence was shocking. The tall monster froze, both sets of arms dangling down from its great shoulders, while beyond in the bedroom we could hear the quiet weeping of our client.

"Watson," said Holmes, revealed now to be the figure in black. "Come forward. But keep your distance from this villain. He is a cornered rat, and might very well try anything." As I moved nearer, Holmes shifted slightly to the left, and I saw that he held his riding crop. Reaching forward, he prodded the broad shoulders of the creature, only dimly outlined by the light coming from the street window past him at the end of the landing.

"Mrs. Harlow," called Holmes. "We are here, and we have a gun trained on your persecutor. He is nothing other than a very evil man. Please light your lamp." The creature shifted then, as if planting its feet to either dash past us desperately, or even to throw itself through the window behind it and out to the street.

"Halt!" cried Holmes. "Watson, if he moves again, shoot him in the leg."

The figure settled back then – a collapse of apparent defeat, and with a very definite movement, but an action with a better intention than escape,

369

and therefore I didn't shoot him. Without being told, the intruder dropped a metal pry bar at his feet. Light appeared from the bedroom as the lamp was lit, better illuminating the tall shape, and suddenly negating the unearthly glow that had been spread across its clothing, revealing instead a series of dull whitish stripes – some sort of luminescent chemical smeared onto the cloth.

Holmes took a cautious step closer and, making a more forceful jab this time with his riding crop, he pushed again at the figure's shoulders. With the sound of rubbing cloth, the whole structure started to slide, falling to the floor and revealing a rather harmless looking plain man, half-turned in our direction, and blinking rather stupidly in the dim light.

"Phillimore!" I said, nearly lowering my revolver, before Holmes snapped in response.

"Not James Phillimore. Rather, his cousin, Edward Harding."

Moving closer, I could see that, in spite of whatever name that he was called, this was the man whom we had located two years before, in a room at the Charing Cross Hotel.

Beside me, Holmes was dressed entirely in black, and I could see that he had darkened his face as well, so that he would be nigh invisible in the darkness. He reached into his coat and pulled out a police whistle. After several long bursts, I heard a curious thump, and within moments we were joined by Inspector Lestrade and a brace of constables as they scrambled up the stairs.

"Is she all right?" was the inspector's first question.

Holmes nodded, wiping the lamp-black from his face with a handkerchief. "I don't think that he intended her any permanent harm – at least not yet. Convincing her to abandon the property was his goal. Isn't that right, Harding?"

"I have nothing to say," said the man whom I had believed to be James Phillimore, quite a bit more surly and harsh than his previously portrayed personality would have suggested.

"No matter," said Holmes. "I know most of the story, and we'll soon have the rest of it out of you. Constables – please remove him to the sitting room downstairs. We'll join you shortly."

The officers moved past us and took Harding into custody. Kicking the construct that had fallen from his shoulders out of the way, they quick-marched him in front of us and down the stairs. I moved past Holmes and Lestrade to the bedroom, where I found Mrs. Harlow nearly in hysterics. However, she soon understood that she had simply been harassed, although to a remarkably terrible degree, by a man and not a monster, and she rallied most satisfactorily.

She asserted that she was feeling strong enough to join us in a moment and hear the explanation from the man being held downstairs, and we left the room to wait for her while she dressed. As her door closed, Holmes lit one of the lamps standing on a side table and then leaned down to pick up the item knocked from Harding's shoulders. In the light it was obvious that it consisted of a headless construct simulating broad shoulders, attached to a set of straps that had held it onto Harding's frame, fitting over his own head and giving him the illusion of great height. It was draped in an oversized shirt and dark coat, and the arms hanging from the sides were tied off at the wrists and filled with what turned out to be sandbags, causing them to dangle and swing in the odd way I'd observed when he'd climbed the stairs.

"Devious," muttered Holmes, tossing it aside once more.

"Mr. Holmes," said Lestrade, "Who is that man?"

"All will be revealed," replied my friend vaguely. Before he could be asked to elaborate, the bedroom door opened, and Mrs. Harlow joined us. I looked to see that Philip was standing at the top of the stairs. I hoped that he had stayed away when there was a chance of gunfire, but I doubted it.

Downstairs in the sitting room, we found the constables standing on either side of the man identified as Edward Harding. Two more had joined them, and another was standing by the front door. The prisoner was in a straight-backed chair, and I was glad to see that his hands were now manacled.

"There's really no need for you to explain much of anything, Mr. Harding," said Holmes. "I've waited quite a while to make your acquaintance once again, but I didn't expect that it would be in this fashion, or so fittingly at this location." He turned to me. "Would you care to enlighten the Inspector, Watson, as to our first encounter with the gentleman two years ago?"

I then related how, at the time of the mysterious disappearance, Holmes had tracked the man that we believed to be Phillimore from his hiding place behind the closet to the Charing Cross Hotel . . . and let him go. Lestrade exhibited a variety of emotions as the story was revealed, from surprise and wonder to frank irritation when learning that Holmes had discovered the solution but hadn't bothered to share it with him. While agreeing that no crime had been committed, he was properly resentful that the case had been allowed to remain open on Scotland Yard's books for so long, being logged as something of an embarrassment to them.

"And to you too, Mr. Holmes," he added, although like me, he certainly realized even as he said it that such a consideration would be of no consequence whatsoever to the consulting detective.

371

"I didn't see the harm in it then," replied Holmes with a frown. "Men disappear all the time, and there is no law against it. I'll grant that this method seemed eccentric, and overly complicated, but people's motivations are often that way. But it was only later that I realized that I'd been duped."

"How so?" I asked.

"It was when I recalled that the man we believed to be Phillimore was still legally the owner of this house. Did he simply choose to walk away from his investment here, or did he somehow have a plan to sell it? Out of curiosity, I checked the records and saw that it had sold quite soon after his supposed disappearance. But if he had truly disappeared, how could any legal affairs such as sale of the property be carried out? There was no body to prove that he had died, so in the eyes of the law he *wasn't* dead. There were no apparent heirs to have him declared deceased in order to take possession of the house. And yet . . . the house *had* sold.

"I did a bit more research, learning that the woman who bought the house – *you*, Mrs. Harlow – had no connections to Phillimore, so it wasn't a legally contrived transfer. I also found that, in fact, ownership of the property had been transferred to one Edward Harding – this man – some three weeks *before* Phillimore's disappearance, and it was he who sold you the house. The arrangement was accomplished through an attorney in Southwark named Shaplow. I arranged an appointment with him, only to discover that he was quite infirm, although stubbornly refusing to give up his practice – the perfect man for such a scheme.

"I managed to convince him to reveal to me that he'd never actually met James Phillimore – the man had never visited his office – or witnessed any signatures, but instead he'd simply filed, for a substantial fee, a set of signed property transfer papers that were presented to him by his client, one Edward Harding. These being legal documents, they had to be recorded under the true names. Therefore, Harding was the owner of Phillimore's house at the time of the man's disappearance, and it seemed quite probable that Phillimore had no knowledge that his house had just been stolen out from under him before he vanished.

"Old Shaplow could only provide the vaguest description of Harding, and it was of no practical help whatsoever. When I subsequently searched for more about the elusive Mr. Harding, it was as if he no longer existed – as if he had disappeared too. I could prove through various records that he'd been born, and I discovered that he was Phillimore's cousin, the son of the missing man's late aunt. He had no other living relatives besides Phillimore. Harding himself had seemingly vanished two years before Phillimore's disappearance, following his near-arrest in connection with an extensive embezzlement scheme, but there were no indications as to his current whereabouts.

"It was then that I suddenly looked at Phillimore's disappearance from a slightly different perspective, and realized that there was no proof, other than the acknowledgement that Watson and I received at the Charing Cross Hotel, that the man we had confronted there *actually was James Phillimore*. There were no photographs in Phillimore's house to show his appearance – if there had been, Harding had removed them so that there could be no positive identification – and if any images of Phillimore had existed in Miss Amherst's possession, no one had thought to retrieve them from her. To be certain, I did revisit her soon afterwards, and she confirmed that she had no photographs of her missing fiancé. I made certain during that visit to obtain her description of him, but it was singularly vague and unhelpful – it could have been the man that we met at the hotel, and it could have been the attorney's client, Harding. What I learned from Phillimore's former co-workers was just as useless. They could have been describing any medium-sized man with brown hair and plain features. Harding looks very much like their representation of Phillimore – hardly a surprise, considering their family connection.

"I felt then that I could piece together the situation quite well by that point. Phillimore had come into an unexpected inheritance from his great-uncle Willoughby – a man who was also *Harding's* great-uncle. Harding, who had already fled from his previous identity to avoid prosecution several years earlier, was apparently disqualified from receiving a share since he'd vanished, and couldn't legally claim it without reappearing. He conceived of the idea of taking what his cousin had inherited by arranging things so that Phillimore would seem to have vanished.

"After he cleverly arranged the disappearance to seem as mysterious as possible, he would leave a trail for me to follow, especially prepared with the types of clues that I'm known to observe – the footprints in the dust, for instance, and the costume shop receipt for the constable uniform, which laid a clear trail to Willoughby at the Charing Cross Hotel. Harding additionally made sure that I was involved by repeatedly writing anonymous letters to the editors of various newspapers regarding the disappearance, in spite of the police efforts to keep the affair quiet, and then he further specifically demanded that I be involved. There was really no way that I wouldn't examine the house and see what I was supposed to see. I would find him, blindly following the trail that he had constructed, and then he would hope to convince me with his seemingly harmless story that he – as Phillimore – just wanted to start anew, and that he should be allowed to stay hidden with the assets that he'd already transferred to different accounts under the name 'Willoughby' – again without his naïve cousin's knowledge through the use of forged documents.

"There was always a chance, of course, that I'd simply wash my hands of the matter and notify the police that Phillimore had been found, in which case he could still hope to flee. No doubt a plan was already in place for that eventuality as well. If nothing else, he'd simply return to whatever identity it was that he'd held since vanishing as Edward Harding – which is likely what he's done over the last two years, sinking back into that life when 'James Phillimore' was found at the Charing Cross Hotel, and I trustingly fell for his scheme like a fool, giving my blessing that his version of Phillimore should be able to go away and start over fresh, leading a brand new life. I allowed him to slip away, with the stolen inheritance and other resources that he'd siphoned away from his ignorant and trusting cousin." He turned to the prisoner. "When I realized that I'd been fooled, Mr. Harding, I set out to find you, but you had truly vanished. You had gone down a hole and pulled it in behind you. Yet, I've never stopped looking. Imagine my surprise when you reappeared here, at the house where it all began!"

"But Mr. Holmes," said Lestrade, puzzled. "If what you say is true, then we still don't know where the *real* James Phillimore is located."

"Ah, but I fancy that we will shortly." He turned to Harding, who had listened the entire time with his lips so tight that they appeared to have vanished. "Would you care to share the rest of your cleverness, or shall I?"

The man seemed determined to stand mute, and so Holmes continued. "It really is a unique tale, and I'd think that you'd be quite proud of the discovery. I only became peripherally aware when I was looking at the records of the sale of the house. I saw that it was built in the mid-1870's, upon the ruins of a much older church that had stood here in Highgate since the middle ages. I – "

"The brochure!" I interrupted. "In your scrapbook, next to your notes on the Phillimore investigation!"

"Exactly!" cried Holmes. "You didn't think to read the brochure when you refreshed your memory, thinking it was simply adjacent to my notes, but it was actually a part of the case. When looking into the records of the previous ownership transactions, I saw that this property, and the other houses around it, were built on what had originally been a church, and I was curious enough to obtain further information. As I assembled various facts, I learned that the crypts of the church still exist, underneath this row of houses. In fact, they can still be entered from a locked gate at the north end of the block. You stated, Mrs. Harlow," he said, turning toward our client, "that the house has no cellar."

She cleared her throat. "That's true."

"Not exactly," Holmes countered. "It wasn't constructed to have a cellar as such, but the crypt is located directly beneath us. In fact, I've only discovered tonight that the hidden chamber behind the closet wall itself opens yet again to a further narrow stairway, obviously constructed around the time that the house was built, leading down into the spaces below. When someone was able to get in and out despite the locked doors, I theorized another entrance, and thought that the hidden chamber behind the closet might have an additional opening – something that I should have seen two years ago." He turned to Harding. "How long have you known of the crypt?"

Still the man refused to answer, but his expression had become more calculating and watchful, as if he was concerned as to which direction Holmes's explanation was taking.

"You've certainly been using it to get in and out of the house this past week. I wonder if your cousin knew as well, or if it's something you figured out later. Apparently," Holmes continued, "you remained in contact with the real James Phillimore, even after disappearing as Harding and taking on a new identity. How did you explain to him why you had disappeared – or was he even aware of it? Your crime wasn't widely reported at the time. Did you remain in touch with him after you fled as Harding, or did you only re-establish relations later, after he received the inheritance from your mutual grand-uncle, when you decided to take it away from him? No matter. You were clearly the man whose footprints were in the closet, and who wore the rented constable uniform, and who left a trail for me to find from this house to your room at the Charing Cross Hotel. That will be enough to hang you."

Lestrade cleared his throat. "Yes, Inspector," Holmes continued. "I will explain. When I heard Mrs. Harlow's story this afternoon, giving this address, and specifically how someone was gaining access to it, in spite of locked doors, I immediately recalled what I had incidentally learned about the crypts while trying to track down the truth behind Phillimore's disappearance of the last couple of years. It reminded me that one might be able to get into the houses by way of that route. This evening, after Watson and young Philip returned here to keep guard, I found the builder who first constructed these houses twenty years ago. He confirmed that such an entry was possible, if someone had discovered the existence of the crypts and had made alterations in one of the houses to access them.

"The builder and I entered the crypt, exploring under this row of houses until we found the crude wooden steps that had been built to lead up to the foundations of this very address. That was when I summoned you and your men, Lestrade. After that, Watson, we placed the crypt entrance under observation. As expected, a man surreptitiously made his way in a little after midnight. We followed and watched as he, ignorant of our attention, climbed the steep steps up and into the bottom of this house. He was carrying something – which turned out to be that contraption that he'd strapped on to look like a giant headless monster. He ascended the crude steps into the space built into the back of the hidden closet. We immediately followed, and I pursued him the rest of the way up the stairs while Lestrade and his men came through and then waited downstairs in the hall. I was in time to see Harding carrying out his most bold and threatening move yet, attempting to force his way into Mrs. Harlow's presence to terrify her into abandoning the house – at least long enough for him to carry out an adequate search."

"But for what?" asked the lady herself, now quite recovered, and clearly very angry at the prisoner seated before her. "What is it that he seeks? And why now, after I've lived here for two years?

"That specific answer still eludes me," replied Holmes, "although it may have something to do with the man who first owned this house from the time that it was built in the 1870's. You'll have heard of him, Lestrade. Elias Bates."

I saw a light of recognition pass across the inspector's face. Sensing my confusion, he answered, "Bates was a most notorious fence, Doctor – made all the worse by the fact that he simply couldn't be caught. We knew what he was up to, but his methods always proved too much for us. Do you mean to say, Mr. Holmes, that this was *Bates'* house? And that he was the one who first built the secret closet, and the passage behind it, in order access the crypt, and then use it for his own illegal purposes?"

"Undoubtedly."

Lestrade nodded and sat back, as if all now made sense.

"When age overtook Bates," continued Holmes, "he simply closed up his operation, retired, and moved away. As you know, he died in Surrey several years ago, having never once been jailed. Years later, long after Bates had left London, the house was purchased innocently enough by James Phillimore, and it seems that he somehow discovered both the closet and then the access behind it to the crypt below while in the process of making himself at home. He foolishly shared that knowledge with his cousin Harding, who then made use of it over the course of the past week to enter the house while attempting to intimidate Mrs. Harlow into leaving." He glanced at Harding. "Now, having circled back to the lady's question, would you care to explain why you would do such a contemptible thing?"

Harding licked his lips, darting his eyes from Holmes to Mrs. Harlow and back, before speaking for the first time. "It started out innocently enough. I had some of James's papers, after he . . . disappeared, but I had

376

never took the time to look through them. When I finally did, I saw something – a diary from this Elias Bates fellow. James must have found it in the house, likely left behind, and tucked it away. It was quite old, and reading between the lines, so to speak, it seemed to reference a cache of jewels that Bates had hidden here – or so it seemed to me. James had never mentioned this diary to me while he was – before he disappeared. After reading it, I decided that he must have been trying to find the jewels himself. They may not even be here – Bates may have taken them with him when he moved away – but there was always a chance that they could still be hidden somewhere about, if only someone took the time to seek them. I decided to see if I could find them. But the diary was vague, and I had no idea just where to look. And this woman here – she never seemed to leave or go anywhere so that I could get in and search the house! Or if she did go out, it was at random times, so that I could never count on getting in and being allowed any peace.

"I didn't want to hurt her, but I was getting frantic. I have . . . I have some debts that are due. The other night, I decided to sneak in after she'd gone to bed, and look all night if necessary. I came in through the crypt, just the way that James had discovered when he'd moved here, and I set about exploring, looking for some clue. But I accidentally bumped the table outside of her bedroom, and when I heard that she'd awakened, I froze. Then, not knowing if I could get back downstairs and out through the passage before she came out of the bedroom, I made as if I were some sort of ghost. Hoping that she was too scared to investigate, I then escaped down and out through the passage.

"After I'd had a chance to think about it, I realized that I might be able to scare her away for a much longer period of time, and I began to try more and more elaborate attempts each night. And yet, she refused to budge, no matter what I tried. Claws on the door. Flammable chemicals painted in the shape of footprints, and written as a warning. Nothing worked – she never went anywhere!"

"So," said Holmes coldly, "you escalated the stakes and killed her cat."

"I did. I left the closet slightly open during the day, and lured the cat in with some food. Then I caught it and killed it. I would have brought it back out that night, but she never went upstairs. So I waited and waited until I heard her sleeping the next day and then crept out, leaving it where she'd find it in the hall." He licked his lips in a curiously reptilian fashion. "It worked," he said, showing no apparent remorse. "She left."

Without a word, Mrs. Harlow rose and stepped forward. Then she slapped him, the force of it creating a loud *Crack!* and turning his head violently. Before he could react, both constables pushed down forcefully on his shoulders, apparently preventing him from rising if Mrs. Harlow wished to give him another. Instead, however, she sobbed and stepped back, turning away from him.

"I wonder if your cousin knew what he was letting himself in for when he shared the secret of the crypt with you," said Holmes. "He probably did it innocently enough – I've found no evidence that the real James Phillimore was as reprehensible as you are, Harding. The poor man never knew that sharing that curious knowledge would eventually lead to his death."

"Now hold on," said Harding, holding a hand to his face, still red from the vicious slap. "James planned his disappearance on his own. After he received the inheritance, he felt trapped – just as I told you when I pretended to be him in the hotel room. He knew that I had changed my name and taken a different identity, and he decided that he wanted to do the same thing. He asked my advice, and he arranged everything – including the payments to Willoughby."

"Then why were *you* the man who carried it out?"

"He . . . he was afraid. That he couldn't bring it off. He was never bold like me. He asked me to take his place in the house and pretend to be a constable."

"Then why the rest of it?" I asked. "Why leave clues leading to the hotel, and arrange that Holmes be involved at all. Why not simply vanish through the secret stairs and into the crypt?"

"We . . . wanted a witness, someone eminently trustworthy, and sympathetic, in case something ever came up, legally, to verify that someone had seen James *after* he disappeared – that he was still alive, but without giving away the secret. To testify if needed that he hadn't truly vanished."

Holmes nodded. "Strangely, that part makes sense. I learned that there were some irregularities with your great-uncle's estate, wherein the sales of various additional properties had to be arranged after the initial inheritance. In case Phillimore's legal participation was required, you could discretely contact the attorney handling the estate, show up to sign whatever was necessary, a summon me there to verify that *you* were actually James Phillimore, and that I was still keeping your secret and that all was above-board – even if you were choosing to live in anonymity.

Harding nodded. But then Holmes asked, "Where, then, *is* the true James Phillimore? After you staged the disappearance, your part was finished, and he was free to assume his new life. But how could he do that, as *you* had arranged for control of the accounts where his inheritance had been placed, and *you* were now the owner of this house?"

Harding was startled. "Oh, yes," Holmes continued. "You took over ownership of this house. Where does that fit in your explanation of selflessly helping your cousin?"

Harding again licked his lips, glancing from one to the other of us in rapid succession. He seemed to be coming apart before our very eyes. He began to speak, talking faster and faster, as if drowning us in words would make his story more believable. "He fell soon after we made our plans. He hit his head. And I realized that the inheritance, and everything else that he had, would be lost. I couldn't reveal myself as his cousin to make a claim on his estate as his only living relative – not without resuming my identity as Harding. And even if I did, the family relationship didn't seem strong enough to establish me as his heir. His plan for a new identity was already in place, and I simply took advantage of it."

Holmes shook his head with a smile. "You should have simply stood mute, Mr. Harding. Now you've opened the door. No, no, it really won't do. Certainly your cousin died, and I expect when we examine the body – and we will – we'll see that he did die from a blow to the head, but I seriously doubt that he fell. You forget, I had already long ago worked out your plan to take everything he had, and that you had done so several weeks *before* his disappearance. You had already taken ownership of this house, through the forged papers at the attorney's office. Your cousin James was still among the living then – he was still going to work every day, and he was still affianced, however unhappily, with Miss Amherst. He had in fact spent the entire day prior to his disappearance at work, and showed no signs of agitation. He was clearly a man who didn't realize that he'd been fleeced of everything that he owned, and that he was living on borrowed time.

"He may have come up with the original idea to disappear, as you say, but once you realized that what he intended, you saw a way to make it work to your advantage. You killed him and took his place."

Harding made a growling noise in his throat and tried to lurch to his feet before being slammed back once again by the massive hand of one of the constables. Holmes ignored him, turning instead to Lestrade. "Inspector, you're as aware as I am of just how difficult it is to dispose of a human corpse. I would advise that a thorough search be made of the crypt below. That seems to be the most likely place. I suspect that you'll find Mr. Phillimore buried somewhere, either in a shallow grave, or tucked in with one of the other permanent residents. Perhaps he'll be hidden behind or underneath some rocks. But be careful – it's possible he's been covered in quick-lime, and I'd hate for any of your men to accidentally plunge their hands into it, or stir it up and breathe the dust."

Lestrade waited until morning before sending a team into the crypt, armed with digging tools and powerful torches. They entered through the gate at the end of the street, as directed by the builder who had assisted Holmes the previous evening. He led them down into the dank passages. Holmes and I, on the other hand, walked along the street to Mrs. Harlow's house, where she let us in and joined us at the closet door beneath the steps. We left her there, standing in the hall, while we passed through and down the rude stairs into the chamber below. Holmes pointed out some aspects of their reinforced construction, obviously added at some point after the house was initially built. Then we stood there, watching the police lanterns moving this way and that through the forgotten crypt, but ever closer, in the distant darkness, waiting for word about the discovery of James Phillimore's body. It wasn't long in coming. Within a quarter-hour, the poor man had been found, buried under a loose cairn of stones seemingly borrowed from other graves, his head crushed by a far heavier blow than could have never come from a simple fall. The autopsy would reveal a twisted and broken neck as well. As expected, the corpse was covered underneath the rocks in quick-lime, in the mistaken belief that it would hasten decomposition – although it did do a great deal to prevent any signs of decay that might reveal the body's location.

Harding's arrest and reappearance under his own name set off something of a frenzy, as one past crime seemed to lead to another, like peeling the layers of an onion. The capital crime, however, superseded the lesser, and he met his fate on a cold morning a few months later at Newgate Prison, after his pathetic attempts to claim insanity were quickly disproven.

If Elias Bates hid a cache of jewels in either the house or the crypt, it was never found, although I understand that intruders are regularly caught trying to conduct illegal treasure hunts underneath the row of houses where the ancient church once stood.

Mrs. Harlow, despite the week of terror that she'd been forced to endure, recovered quickly, along with the realization that she needed to find friends and interests away from her home. She began to interact with her neighbors, and from there her influence began to spread, eventually leading her to establish the highly respected mission in the East End for which she has since become well-known. More importantly, she took an interest in young Philip Barsby, orphaned at a young age, and eventually adopted him.

I ran into her a month or so later, not having seen her since the events of that terrible October night. She informed me that her cat was doing well, as if I would know of what she spoke. Seeing my ignorance, she laughed and said that she wasn't surprised. She'd had a feeling, when Holmes had brought her a kitten just days after Harding's arrest, that he wouldn't be advertising the fact.

As she walked away, I considered how I would address this act of kindness when I saw Holmes that evening. But then I reconsidered. Obviously he hadn't wanted it to be known, and I found that just the knowledge of his gesture was satisfying enough, without making him aware that I knew. Sometimes friendship is allowing someone else to keep his secrets.

# The Miracle Worker
## by Geri Schear

*January 24<sup>th</sup> 1898*

I<sub></sub>t is always a delight to hear from Bea, and all the more so when she has a puzzle to share. Over breakfast I read her note, which arrived hand-delivered this morning:

> *A peculiar situation had come to my attention. Possibly a case. Will call upon you at 11 a.m. B.*

"Lady Beatrice never fails to brighten the day," Watson said. "Do you wish me to be present?"

"Most certainly. A peculiar situation, she says. Bea has a better understanding of what constitutes a case than most Scotland Yard detectives. A keener wit, too."

"Her insights are certainly unique," the doctor agreed. "I cannot say I always agree with them, or her methods, but we, and this nation, would have suffered a grave loss without her assistance last spring. Well, well, this promises to brighten a dull Monday morning."

Bea arrived on the first chime of the hour and sat with us in our sitting room by the fire. However, before she could relate the particulars of the case, we must first endure Mrs. Hudson's hovering, and the pouring of the coffee, and ensuring that Lady Beatrice was quite warm enough, was she quite sure, etc., etc.? Finally, my patience expired and I dismissed the old woman with a succinct, "That will *do*, Mrs. Hudson." This earned me some tutting from Watson and an amused raised eyebrow from Bea, though I believe I had been the very epitome of patience. Still, for several minutes after our landlady's departure, Beatrice continued to sit in silence, her coffee untouched.

"Bea – " I urged, at last.

"Forgive me," she said, roused from her reverie. "I have an odd tale to tell you, and I'm trying to determine how best to relate the details so you will not think me a fool."

"I assure you, anyone who knows you could never make that error," I replied.

"You have not yet heard my story," she replied. "Well, I shall simply tell you, and let you decide for yourself.

"I have had a friend since childhood by the name of Caroline Becket. She comes from an ancient Catholic family, of which she is the last survivor. We were much thrown together as children because our fathers shared an interest in medieval history. My late father, an intellectual of great renown, was often consulted by various academics. Gilbert Becket, Caroline's father, was one of these. His area of interest was St Thomas à Becket. He was trying to prove that his family was related to the saint. During those afternoons, while the men conducted their research, Caroline and I became close. She is very bright and curious. We have remained friends, although our interests led us into very different directions. As you know, I am scientifically curious, and I have devoted my life to acquiring knowledge and exploring the world."

"I take it your friend Caroline is less adventurous?" Watson asked.

"Considerably so. She was always devout. She spent much of her youth visiting the poor and performing works of charity. I confess, I found the intensity of her beliefs rather tedious at times, but despite that, we remained good friends.

"When she was eighteen, her father died, and Carrie prepared to join a religious order. However, she was found to have contracted consumption and, as a consequence, the sisters refused to accept her. She instead retreated to seclusion to her estate in Greenwich, where she lives a life of prayer and contemplation. She has a few devoted servants, a confessor who visits her weekly, and she permits me to visit her on rare occasions."

"Depression and withdrawal from society are not unusual in that condition," Watson said. "I suppose she is fortunate to have the comfort of her religion."

I snorted. "Some comfort if it deprives her of all human society. Even a misanthrope such as I must seek the stimulation of other minds from time to time. Forgive me, Bea. We interrupted your story."

She finished her coffee and set down her cup. "It's perfectly all right. I agree with you. I cannot see anything comforting in the life my old friend is living, but I suppose it is not for me to say. Caroline's condition has deteriorated considerably and I do not think she has very much time left to suffer.

"Last week, I received an unusually exuberant letter from her. She had been 'uplifted in spirit' – her words – by a visit from her confessor, Father Devlin. He is an elderly priest who has been attending her for many years. He is as blameless a creature as any man I know."

"That's hardly a ringing endorsement," I said.

"True," she replied, with a dry laugh. "However, I have never had cause to mistrust him. In her letter, Caroline said he told her of the return to England of a missionary whose work she has supported for many years.

383

Tom Beckett has spent the last fifteen years in the South Pacific, and his work among the Polynesians is renowned. It is claimed he has healed some of those unfortunate enough to have fallen victim to leprosy. Caroline has corresponded with him for several years, and has supported his ministry with what must be, I'm sure, generous donations."

"I have read about him," Watson said. "There was an article in *The Times* a few months ago. I am no Roman, but I confess I am awed by all I have heard. Leprosy is a vile disease. I encountered it during my military service."

For a moment, I thought he would say more, but he did not. From his expression, I believe that his memories were particularly unpleasant. Not surprising. My own encounters with the disease, though few, are also disagreeable.

"And now this remarkable man has returned to England?" I said. "Why so, if he is doing such splendid work, and where he is needed?"

"One of many questions I have been asking myself," Lady Beatrice replied. "Another is why a man who has been corresponding for many years with his benefactress should fail to notify her of his return. But let me continue to relate the events as they unfolded.

"Knowing my friend's tendency towards melancholy, and her interest in Beckett's ministry, Father Devlin thought it would lift her spirits to know that the man was in London, not five miles from her home, and that he would soon be preaching in his very church.

"Caroline was, of course, in raptures. She is too humble to be bothered by Beckett's failure to notify her of his return. She wished only to meet him. Father Devlin said it would take some time to arrange – the man is much in demand – but he would do his best. In the meantime, Caroline begged me to go and hear him speak and report back to her. I confess, I was reluctant to waste an evening on such an errand, but she is a very good friend, and she has never asked me for any favour. Besides, I was curious, and so I went."

"You went alone?" Watson asked.

"Certainly."

"I would have been delighted to escort you," the doctor said. "I would have liked to have heard about the man's experiences with lepers."

"You would have been disappointed," Bea replied. "Mr. Beckett – he is a lay preacher, not a priest – spoke little about the South Pacific or his experiences there. His focus was on faith and sacrifice.

"It was a normal Mass at first, very well attended, full of dock workers and their families."

"I thought Lady Caroline lives in Greenwich?" I asked.

"So she does, but her confessor, Father Devlin's parish is St. Mary's in the docklands."

"I see. Pardon my interruption. Pray continue."

"When it was time for the sermon, Beckett was introduced. He is about forty years of age, not quite six feet tall, with fair hair, a deeply tanned complexion, and has a musical speaking voice.

"As I said, he spoke about sacrifice and service. His words worked the crowd up into quite a religious frenzy. Three people came forward and declared their back pain was completely healed. Two others vowed their blurred vision had cleared."

"Hysteria," Watson commented. "I have seen it before. You can convince a man of anything if you rouse his passions sufficiently. Such 'cures' seldom last."

"So I thought, too. I did not see anyone grow an amputated leg, or a blind man regain his sight. Father Devlin was troubled, but had no explanation for it. He is a simple man, however, and is not a sceptic like myself. However, that was not what caused my consternation. About halfway through the sermon, Beckett stopped suddenly as if he were in a fit or a trance and said, 'Precious Lady, daughter of Gilbert . . . I am sent you by God. I am Thomas, your blessed . . . Doubt me not . . . .' I wrote it down exactly as he spoke the words."

Lady Beatrice handed her notebook to me. The phrases were clearly written in her elegant handwriting.

"I asked to speak with Beckett after the meeting," she continued, "but was told he was fatigued and needed to rest. Instead, I went to Caroline to report on my evening. I found her and her staff in a state of agitation. There was so much confusion with everyone talking at once, it was difficult to understand what had alarmed them. At length, I learned that earlier that evening, at what seemed to me the very moment when the missionary was in an apparent trance miles away, an apparition had appeared to Caroline and her maid, Mary. He was described to me as looking exactly like Dr. Tom Beckett, whom I had seen at that very moment. Caroline described him – a man she had never seen with her own eyes – in minute detail, and he spoke the exact same words that I had heard. Holmes, I questioned my friend and her maid very closely. I have known Caroline most of my life, as I said. Her integrity is beyond reproach. Mary has served her for almost twenty years. She is as reliable as any maid I've ever known. I have no doubt they believe utterly what they reported to me. I am at a loss to explain it."

"So a man appears in front of hundreds of people, and is simultaneously witnessed at the exact same moment five miles away before two women of unimpeachable character," Watson said.

I chuckled with delight. "Quite the merry puzzle," I said.

"She is my friend, Holmes," Beatrice said with some asperity. "You must excuse me if I do not see it as merely a merry puzzle."

"My apologies, Bea," I replied. "I do forget myself at times."

She sighed. "No, the fault is mine. It is a puzzle, and of course you are intrigued by it. I am, too, at least to a degree, but I cannot help feeling uneasy for my friend."

"You believe there is some skulduggery afoot?" Watson asked. "Forgive me, but I have to play devil's advocate – were there ever a less appropriate time to use that phrase? – but is it possible she really did have some sort of divine experience?"

"Watson!" I cried with a laugh. "You must be in jest. You do not believe in miracles, surely?"

"I have seen things I cannot explain. It is hubris to assume that mankind has all the answers."

"Well, Caroline would certainly agree with you," Bea said, "but I share Holmes's cynicism. This Tom Beckett seems far too good to be true to me."

"Perhaps," Watson said, "But I cannot see any rational explanation for the mystery."

"There is a dearth of facts," Lady Beatrice said, speaking my own thoughts, "and one cannot draw conclusions without them."

From her bag she produced a cheap pamphlet. This she handed to me, and said, "These were circulating around the church. You may make of it what you will. I have also asked Father Devlin to call upon you this afternoon. You may count upon his discretion."

I glanced at the pamphlet and handed it to Watson.

"Ah yes, I've seen this sort of thing many times in the course of my work, Holmes," the doctor said. "Many of my patients, failed by medicine, turn to the many proffered 'cures' and religious 'healers' who abound. This one seems no different."

"*Christ's ministry made manifest in London*" proclaimed the banner. "*The spirit of Thomas à Becket returned in Tom Beckett, preacher and healer. Many have been cured, more have been saved. Come to hear him speak at St. Mary's Church . . . .*"

"Perhaps this Tom Beckett means to follow the path of the ancient pilgrims," Watson added. At my blank expression, he added. "As in *The Canterbury Tales*."

"Chaucer, Holmes," Beatrice added.

"I am not familiar. This is literature?"

"And history. You are familiar with Thomas à Becket?"

386

"I have heard the name," I replied. "I cannot say it means much to me. Is it relevant?"

"Good heavens," Watson exclaimed. Briefly, he explained how the twelfth-century Archbishop of Canterbury had been murdered in the cathedral by henchmen who believed they had been sent to do the will of Henry II. Becket refused to defend himself, and died on the steps of the altar. He was subsequently canonised. He was associated with miracles and it became the custom for pilgrims to visit the cathedral. Chaucer immortalised the pilgrimage with his *Canterbury Tales*.

"The custom continues to this day," Watson concluded, "though I suppose it is less common."

"I don't see how any of this is relevant to the case," I said, dismissing history to the cobwebs.

"Only insofar as Caroline shares her family's interest in the saint. It's why she first became so interested in Tom Beckett."

"Humph. You said your friend corresponded with him – "

"She received her last letter from him two months ago, on November 20th. I borrowed it for you to study."

I clapped my hands together in delight. "Splendid! Splendid!" I cried. "I wonder you even need my help. You are more than capable of investigating this case on your own."

"You are too kind," she replied, "but I am too close to the situation. Besides, I must be realistic. There are places you can go that I cannot. You will help me, won't you, Holmes?"

"You may count on me, of course," I replied. I am unsure why Watson smiled so broadly. Some foolish romantic notion, no doubt.

The letter was written in a strong hand with black ink on cheap bamboo paper. Between the expected encouragement to "*wait on the Lord*" and "*have faith*", I found a dry wit, and a gift for describing the life of the Islanders in a respectful, compassionate tone. I could see why Lady Caroline was impressed with this man, and why she felt compelled to support him.

"If you don't need the letter, I should like to return it before Carrie realises it's missing," Bea said. "I, ah, did not tell her that I was borrowing it."

"I understand," I replied, as I placed it in her hand. "Is it possible for me to examine the room where this remarkable encounter occurred?"

"Not overtly. Nor, I'm afraid, can I arrange for you to speak with Caroline – at least, not as Sherlock Holmes. However, she offers meals to anyone who stops by the kitchen and claims to be hungry . . . You could, perhaps, find a way to explore the house then."

After Beatrice left, I sat by the fire in silent reverie. Watson didn't disturb me for some time. It is one of his more admirable qualities, his gift for silence. At last he coughed and, when he had my attention, he said, "What is it that troubles you, Holmes?"

"Any number of things, my dear Watson. The very best we can hope for is that Tom Beckett is indeed a man blessed by God and can perform miracles."

"And the worst?"

"That he is a dangerous predator. That Lady Caroline will die disappointed. And that I have set you and Bea in his path."

This afternoon, the good priest arrived promptly at two o'clock, and greeted us with a gentle smile that even I could not fail to return. He is a tiny man, scarcely five feet in height, with white hair that is wild and spirited. His face is red from long days spent out of doors. Apart from hours spent on his bicycle visiting his parishioners, he also spends as much time as he can in his garden. His wrist and boots made this plain, though his astonishment when I pointed it out was most gratifying.

"Lady Beatrice told me you were a wonder, Mr. Holmes," he cried, "and so you are! A rare wonder!"

He greeted us with a discreet crossing of his hand and the words, "A blessing on this house," which made me feel oddly humble. There was a simplicity to the man's faith that I could not deny. I am no great champion of orthodox religion, no matter its orientation, and adhere to my own private beliefs, but I respect true devotion when I see it. I believe I saw it in Father Devlin.

"Lady Beatrice asked me to call upon you gentlemen," said the priest, "With regards to Tom Beckett. I will gladly answer any questions you have, but I will speak no slander. You must expect nothing of me but simple truth."

"Would all visitors to these rooms could make the same claim," I said, smiling. "Please make yourself comfortable, Father. May we offer you a beverage of some sort?"

"I wouldn't refuse a cup of tea," he replied. "The day has a chill, and I've been out in it for many a long hour."

The tea was brought and we sat together. I began by asking how Father Devlin first encountered Tom Beckett.

"He called upon me last Wednesday evening and said he had but stepped off a ship. I must say I was astonished to see him."

"Why so?"

"Well, like most people, even those not of the Faith, I was very familiar with his name. His work in the Pacific is renowned. He has been doing noble, even heroic, things there. I thought he would be there until the end of his days. I said as much to him, but he said that God had, to his sorrow, called him home."

"How extraordinary," Watson said. "For what purpose?"

"He said he did not know. The Almighty spoke to him in a vision and commanded him to come home. He was not given a reason."

"Did he not ask for one?" I said.

Father Devlin chuckled. "I have never had a vision of the sort Beckett described, but I understand one does not argue with God."

"Pah!" I snorted. "What sort of divinity discourages intellectual discourse?"

"I'm inclined to agree," Watson said, to my surprise. "Is there not a verse – '*Come, let us reason together, saith the Lord*'?"

Father Devlin chuckled. "Isaiah 1:18. Please, gentlemen, I am only a messenger, and a poor one at that. I confess, I would have debated the matter with the Heavenly Father myself, had I been chosen. But perhaps that is why I was not."

"What can you tell me about Beckett?" I asked. "I understand he is not a priest?"

"No, he is a layman. I know nothing of his background. All I can say is he speaks a simple language, but is extremely charismatic." He frowned. "I'm not sure I'm being helpful."

"You're doing very well," Dr. Watson said. "Did you speak to him about Lady Caroline?"

"Yes, I knew she was a frequent correspondent of his, and a generous supporter of his ministry. She has, from time to time, read to me excerpts of his letters. I assumed that he would want to visit her at once. Frankly, I was surprised that he didn't go to see her before he came to me, but he said he felt God wanted him to wait."

"Indeed?"

"I invited him to stay with me, but he said he felt he must stay among the common men that he had met on board ship, and minister to them. I could hardly argue the point."

For all his words, I read the disquiet in the gentle man's eyes. I said, "He delivered the Sunday sermon – was that his idea or yours?"

He hesitated. "Do you know, I'm not sure."

"I see . . . Did he speak at every service?"

"No, just the late evening one. He said he was unused to speaking so much, and would prefer to deliver his address only once. I thought he might be a little nervous. After all, there's a difference in speaking before a church of London parishioners and an assembly of South Pacific islanders in the open air. I was inclined to be flexible."

389

"And you weren't suspicious?"

He hesitated. "No, but I became . . . unsettled when, in the middle of his address, people began to moan and several began to cry out that they were healed. I understand that such things sometimes happen in Evangelical churches, but we are not accustomed to them in the middle of a Catholic Mass."

"How did Beckett react?" Watson asked.

"He hardly seemed aware. Indeed, I might say the man was in another state of awareness altogether."

"Do you mean a trance?" Watson asked.

"So it seemed to me, Doctor, though I have never seen such a thing before. I confess, my initial reaction was annoyance, may God forgive me. Am I too suspicious, too lacking in faith?"

"Some questions are beyond even Sherlock Holmes," I replied, "but I am intrigued by your doubt. I think you have an instinct for . . . well, I am loathe to use the word, but let us say, *sin.*"

"I have encountered it in my sixty years on this earth," the priest replied. "Rather more than I would care to own. Yes, I know sin."

"Do you sense it in Mr. Beckett?"

He hesitated. "I will only say that there was sin in the church last night." Setting down his teacup, he joined his hands, as if in prayer, and said, "My primary concern is for Lady Caroline. She is a good and kind woman. She is so eager to finally meet a man whose correspondence has meant much to her. Lady Beatrice urges caution, and I understand why. But what if she's wrong? Beckett claims God has sent him on a mission. Who am I to say otherwise?"

"Do you believe Beckett is a holy man?" Watson asked.

The priest struggled and at last said, "I do not know. Forgive me, gentlemen. I know your intentions are honourable, but I must trust to God."

"Even if God has sent us to tell you this is foolishness?" Holmes said.

"If that is the case, the Lord will make it clear to me. I am a humble man and I need a little more than a dream or an intuition. I trust that you will help Lady Caroline to the best of your considerable ability, Mr. Holmes. I will help you as much as I can, but understand, I serve a higher master."

"Do you have any suggestions for us?" Watson asked.

"Just one. Lady Caroline's condition has deteriorated considerably over the past few months. Indeed, I believe she has little time left. Her physician, Dr. Martin, is a fine man, but he is kept very busy looking after the people of the dockside. I think I could persuade Lady Caroline to engage a personal physician, one dedicated to her care, if you might be available, Dr. Watson? I had been considering such a thing in any case. It would enable you to spend time in her home, to keep an eye on things."

"You would be at risk of the contagion, would you not, Watson?" I asked. "I would not subject you to harm."

"I have faced such risks in my daily practice over the years, Holmes. I will take all necessary precautions, I assure you. If I can lend comfort to the poor woman, I would be happy to do so. I'm not busy at present. Would my being there assist you, do you think?"

"I think your presence would be invaluable," I replied. "You would have the run of the house, and could ensure Bea's safety, should it prove necessary."

*January 25<sup>th</sup>, 1898*

This morning, Watson and I called upon Bea and apprised her of our plan.

"I think that is a splendid idea," she said. "I am very glad to know you will be there to look after Caroline, Doctor. Mary tells me a nurse was hired some weeks ago, but I haven't met her."

"Do you know anything about her?"

"The butler, Burleigh, tells me she is trained in the Nightingale method, and was hired from a reputable agency. I haven't confirmed that information for myself. When do you go to meet Caroline, Doctor?"

"Father Devlin thought you and he might perform the introductions. He hoped your joint recommendation might sway her to accept my services."

"Caroline is very humble. She will feel she does not deserve care unavailable to the poor." She sighed. "Well, we can but try."

A busy afternoon, but ultimately fruitless. Lestrade less helpful than usual, if that is possible. Have put the Irregulars to work. And so to bed.

*January 26<sup>th</sup>, 1898*

My morning began as yesterday evening ended. At least Watson fared better.

Apparently it took less than fifteen minutes to convince Lady Caroline that the Good Doctor was essential to her well-being. Although my friend downplayed his role in the proceedings, Bea was effusive in his praise, not sparing the poor fellow's blushes.

"He was so gentle and kind," she said, "that Caroline could hardly refuse his aid. I have no doubt that Dr. Martin is a decent-enough fellow, but he cannot have Watson's delicacy. In any case, it was only moments before she relented and said if it meant so much to me then of course she would consent." She bit her lip, a rare sign of emotion, and said, "I made her cry, Holmes."

"It was for the noblest of reasons, my dear Beatrice," I said. "I am sure Watson would agree."

"I do, most heartily," Watson said. "The poor woman obviously needs care. She is dying, but she need not be as uncomfortable as she has been. Your intervention was well meant, and can only serve her well. I fear she doesn't have very long. You should not distress yourself."

"You have met the staff?" I asked Watson.

"Yes. There are few indeed for a house of that size. None made much impression, save the latter, and she in a most negative manner. She may claim to have been trained as a Nightingale, but I have grave doubts that that is the case."

"Why so?"

"She is slovenly, and she drinks – both of which are utterly against Miss Nightingale's code of conduct. She was most displeased to see me, I should add, and protested that she could care for her Ladyship's needs perfectly well on her own. However, the other staff were very happy to have a physician present, and relieved to see their mistress receive proper care. Nurse Roberts is not popular among them. I would have dismissed her, but Beatrice suggested I discuss it with you first."

"Yes, I think we should keep her *in situ* for the moment. Who knows what we may learn from her?"

"I should add there are other staff who tend the grounds, or who work on an as-needed basis," Bea said. "They do not live in. Caroline is anxious that no one else contract her illness. Even with visitors, such as Father Devlin and myself, she takes great care."

"That is to be commended. I hope you will both exercise all caution."

"You may be sure of it," Watson said.

"When does your residency begin?"

"This evening. Tom Beckett is to call upon Lady Caroline tomorrow afternoon."

"Is he, indeed? Bea, can you arrange to be present?"

"Yes, I move in this afternoon. I told Caroline I want to be near her in her last days. She knows she doesn't have much longer."

"Excellent."

"We have our assigned tasks, then, Holmes," Bea said. "May I inquire what you will be doing while the doctor and I are in Becket House?"

"Working the docks," I replied.

I have, in my time, essayed a number of different professions. I have been a cabby, a blacksmith, a bookseller, and, memorably, a mortician, but few professions eat at the bones like the dockworker. Aside from the sheer intensity of the labour, there is the bitter cold, the danger, and the relentless demands of the tasks to contend with. All day and a good part of the night, I laboured alongside dozens of other poor souls. At last, with the moon high in the sky, I and several of my comrades took refuge in The Pelican for a pint and a plate of sausage and mash. Both tasted sweet after twelve hours of filthy, back-breaking labour. Still, my efforts were rewarded for the information I gleaned.

While it was yet dark, I made my way to Becket House. The Norman façade glowered over me as I crept up the icy driveway. My caution seemed unnecessary, however. I encountered no one. Once I reached the main door, I made a complete circuit of the building, heading in a counter-clockwise direction. Beatrice had told me there were five entrances, but I found a sixth, a once-sealed postern gate, almost invisible, concealed in the shadow of the east tower. It had, but late, been hidden behind a wall of ivy. No wonder Beatrice had missed it. In recent weeks, someone had hacked the ivy away, exposing it to anyone with keen eyes.

The gate swung open easily. I cautiously made my way inside and found myself in a narrow hallway that lead to a winding stone staircase.

With my weapon in my hand, and wishing I had the ever-faithful Watson at my side, I made my way up the stairs until I found myself on the topmost floor of the home in a small chamber. I emerged behind the chimney. The panel that concealed the compartment where I stood from the room beyond had been recently oiled. It would slide back silently – no doubt a remnant from the turbulent times of the Civil War when it was used to hide priests from the Roundheads. I was about to remove the panel and enter the small chamber beyond when I beheld soft footsteps and then the glow of a lamp. A moment later a familiar voice said, in amused tones, "Holmes?"

"Beatrice?"

I stepped out into the room, a little annoyed at being so easily discovered.

"How did you know I was there?" I asked.

"I could smell your pipe tobacco," she replied.

"Tsk, I should be more cautious."

"How did you get into the house?"

I explained my means of entrance and she listened solemnly. I then asked her to explain her own behaviour.

"I told you the Beckets were staunch Catholics of old. When Carrie told me she had seen a vision in this room, I surmised it might contain a priests' hole. I came looking for it. It seems we came to the same conclusion from a different angle."

"I said you could solve this little mystery without me," I said, chuckling.

"Finding an explanation is one thing. Convincing Caroline is another matter entirely. She will not be persuaded by logic and cold, hard facts. We need to unmask this charlatan . . . ."

She broke off and seemed distressed.

"What is it?"

"It's just . . . her faith has been the one constant in her life. Are we wrong to take that from her? Now, especially, when she is so close to the end?"

"We are not taking anything from her, my dear Bea. We are protecting her from a fraudster."

"No. No, you are right, of course. How do you suggest we proceed?"

"We let him put his plan into motion and then unmask him."

*January 27ᵗʰ, 1898*

This morning, I made my way to the kitchen and begged a breakfast in return for some work. Both were immediately offered. The food was excellent and plentiful. The work was easy enough: Manual labour, chopping wood, and so forth. I played the part of a genial fellow, eager to please, and willing to work. In return, both the cook and the butler were happy to keep me occupied for the day and see that I had my meals.

After the staff sat for lunch, the house sank into a siesta. With only one woman to look after, and she an invalid, there was little enough to do. The nurse, a slovenly, tipsy woman, with a face like lard and an expression like sour milk, stomped away to tend her unfortunate patient. Watson and Beatrice were in the dining room, finishing their meal. I waited until they left and made their way upstairs, and then I rendezvoused with them in the small room with the priests' hole, as we had arranged.

"Well, Holmes," Watson said in a low voice. "You and Beatrice have been having adventures without me?"

"Do not feel too left out, Watson," I replied. "Of all of us, I suspect you are the only one who had a decent night's sleep."

"Well, I suppose that's something," he said.

"How fares your patient?"

"She lingers," he replied. "That's the best that can be said for her condition. She isn't in great distress, but neither is she restful."

"What do you make of that nurse?"

394

"If she's a Nightingale, I'm a Labrador retriever," he scoffed. "She hasn't the slightest idea about caring for a patient, nor even the most rudimentary tenets of hygiene."

"So it was she who found the entrance to the room for whomever impersonated Beckett, do you think?" Beatrice asked.

"I doubt she has the wit. I suspect she has been following someone else's directions," I said.

"Beckett should be here in about half-an-hour. Doctor, you and I should go and get Caroline. Holmes, we'll see you in the sitting room. I've told Burleigh who you are. He will find a reason to justify your presence."

With his hand on the doorknob, Watson hesitated and said, "I want it on the record that you're both going to look very foolish if this man turns out to be a genuine miracle worker."

"Bea and I shall share the lightning bolt, shall we not?" I said.

The lady smiled enigmatically. "You know my regard for you, my dear Holmes," she said, "but in this instance, I shall repent, stand with Watson, and you may face perdition alone."

"The curse of the true independent mind," I said, sighing heavily.

"The truly independent mind admits all possibilities," Watson retorted. "Even miracles."

Despite the gravity of her condition, Lady Caroline refused to meet her illustrious guest in her bedchamber, and elected to come down to the sitting room. I put the wood that I had spent the morning chopping to good use in building a merry fire. The room was soon cheerful and warm.

Watson, I was surprised to see, carried her in his arms. She wore a scarf wrapped around her nose and mouth to prevent her contagion from spreading, but despite her pallor and frailty, her eyes glowed.

The Good Doctor placed her gently on the chaise-longue, and covered her with a warm rug. Beatrice smiled her thanks to him, and sat at her friend's side, holding her hand.

"You are all so kind to me," Lady Caroline said. "How blessed I am to be surrounded by such kind and caring friends."

There was an ethereal quality to her. Some small, disloyal part of me, in defiance of logic, whispered that she was already seeing angels. I silenced such nonsense with a reminder that this is what going without sleep will do to a man.

She and Bea sat together, the one so pale, fragile, and ghostly, the other vibrant, robust, and keenly aware of the world and her place in it. Bea's eyes met mine and I read her anger towards the man who would shatter the peace of her dying friend.

Moments later, the butler announced the priest and Tom Beckett. They joined us and nodded their greetings. I stayed in the background tending the fire and remaining as inconspicuous as possible. The priest made a cross on the dying woman's forehead with oil and murmured prayers in Latin. The tanned, fair-haired fellow bowed low and then knelt at her feet.

"We meet at last, my dear lady," he said. "God sent me to you."

"I stayed awake all night in prayer," Lady Caroline said. "My dear friends are so worried for me. Beatrice is afraid I will be made a fool of and will sign over my fortune to you."

"She does not understand true faith," he replied in a soft voice. "I forgive her."

"She understands the mind," the sick woman said, "and the heart, and human frailty. My dear Bea would not see me come to harm, nor those I care for either." She broke off and coughed long and hard. Watson held a handkerchief to her mouth, and I saw it stained with blood. The "nurse" cowered against the wall, and Beckett turned his head away.

Bea took a washcloth and bathed her friend's face. Lady Caroline smiled at her, and at Watson, and then she said, "I have not much time."

She turned to Beckett and reached out her hand to him. "You brought papers for me to sign?" she asked.

He drew them from his jacket. "But we should pray first," he said.

"I have prayed," she replied, taking them. Then, turning her head and looking directly at me, she said, "You may need these, Mr. Holmes." She placed the papers directly into my hand.

"Lady Caroline . . . ." Beckett began.

"God warned me not to trust you. You would have me sign away this house and my entire fortune. But what, then, would become of dear Mary, and Mr. Burleigh, and all my dear companions who have looked after me these many years? No, I do not think my true friend, Tom Beckett, would ask such a thing of me. Mr. Holmes . . . ."

"Yes, Lady Caroline?"

"Remove this man from my sight, if you will."

Through the window I saw that the police stood ready, awaiting my signal.

"Stupid woman," Beckett cried, suddenly revealing his true nature. Then something happened for which I have no explanation. Three black birds appeared. Crows, I thought them, but Watson has since told me they were Cornish choughs. I can only imagine someone left a window or door open, though why anyone should do so on a bitter January afternoon, I cannot imagine. It seemed as if they appeared from nowhere. They descended upon the villain's head. They pecked at him as he screamed.

396

Blood streamed from his face and neck. Even as I dragged him from the building, the birds did not relent. Together with the policemen we got him into the van, and the birds vanished as mysteriously as they had appeared.

"A late Christmas gift for you, Lestrade," I said. "Have you detained his brother?"

"An hour ago, Mr. Holmes. Nasty pair of villains. Been looking for them for a long time."

"You should take this woman, too, Inspector," Watson said, as he handed the Roberts woman into Lestrade's custody. "She's just as involved as your other prisoners."

"She is, indeed," I agreed. "I shall make my farewells to Lady Caroline and follow you to the Yard shortly, if you do not object, Lestrade."

"No need to hurry, Mr. Holmes. None of these birds are going anywhere." The inspector chuckled at his jest.

By the time the doctor and I returned indoors, Lady Caroline was breathing her last, a beatific smile on her lips. I have witnessed many deaths in my lifetime, but none so . . . joyous.

Beatrice closed her friend's eyes, and stood. "There now, my duty is ended. She is at peace."

"Amen," the priest said.

Outside, snow began to fall, yet I vow I could smell roses.

"Beatrice?" I said. "Are you wearing perfume?"

"Not I, nor any woman present. It aggravated Carrie's cough."

"There cannot be roses blooming in January," Watson said.

"Surely she is with the saints," the priest said, blessing himself.

Bea wiped her eyes. She looked utterly spent. "Thank you for all your help, my dear Holmes," she said. "Dr. Watson. I suppose you need to go to Scotland Yard?"

"Yes, but there is no need for haste. If you have need of us . . . ?"

"No, you are most kind. Perhaps we can meet at Baker Street next week, after the funeral?"

*February 8ᵗʰ, 1898*

Beatrice joined us for coffee late this morning. It is a filthy day, and her boots were caked with the worst of London's mud. Still, she seemed in good spirits and has recovered her usual vivacity.

"How went the funeral?" Watson asked.

"So well attended that mourners spilled into the churchyard, and down the street. Crowds came from all over Greenwich, as well as the docks, both men and women. She was so well loved. You would hardly

397

imagine it, a woman who never left her home, and yet her good works secured her reputation."

"I hardly knew her," Watson said, "but she greatly impressed me with her kindness and her gentle manner. Certainly her staff were devoted to her."

"I wish I could be more like her," Bea said. "I fear I am far too much the cynic."

"For my part, Bea," I replied, "I would not have you any other way. Your keen wit and extraordinary intellect are what make you so remarkable. Were she here, I am sure your friend would agree."

"Hear, hear," Watson replied.

Bea flushed slightly and said, "What happened at Scotland Yard? What did you learn about those ruffians?"

I sipped my coffee and leaned back in my chair. "Oh, I knew about them long before I faced them in Scotland Yard. It may surprise you learn, my dear Beatrice, that as soon as you told me about a man seeming to appear in two places at the same time, with unimpeachable witnesses in both places, I immediately surmised twins were one of the most likely hypothetical solutions. The Sullivans have been swindling people all over England and, indeed, Scotland, for several years, using their extraordinary physical similarity to deceive the innocent. Often, they included John's wife, Myrtle – the woman you knew as Nurse Roberts – to aid them.

"Thanks to the efforts of the Irregulars, and my time working on the docks, I was able to identify the culprits. My only question was how James Sullivan managed to get into Lady Caroline's chamber.

"So unsettled were the men by the curious attack upon John by the birds that they readily confessed. Myrtle had been persuaded, much against her will, to play the part of the nurse. To her fell the task of finding the priests' hole."

"I'm surprised she had the wit to discover it," Watson replied.

"She didn't," Bea said. "Mary told her about it one evening, just in idle conversation. I asked her at the funeral, and she admitted as much."

"Ah," I said. "That explains it. Well, once they had a means of access, it was an easy matter for one brother to deliver the sermon while his twin 'appeared' before Lady Caroline, speaking identical words, which were designed to excite her interest."

"How could they know I would be present at the service?" Bea asked.

"They did not. That was a happy coincidence. But they knew someone would be sure to report back to her, probably the priest. The rest, they thought, would be easy."

"How did they come up with this scheme?" Bea asked.

"John, the one who had the unfortunate encounter with the birds, was the brains of the operation. He read the article about Tom Beckett in *The Times*, and concocted the plan. He rues it now. The birds have scarred him for life. He will never again be mistaken for his twin. In any event, all three admitted their wrong-doing. Myrtle first, and then the brothers. They'll be sent down for a considerable time, if I have anything to do with it."

"Excellent."

"The one who delivered the sermon at the Mass took a big risk," Watson said. "How could he be sure that anyone would react so powerfully to his words, and claim to be cured?"

"For the simple reason that they were paid to do so," I said with a chuckle. "When I worked the docks, I met several men who told me about the shillings they had been paid for their acting. 'Money for old rope,' one of them put it. I can't say I disagree, certainly compared with a shift on the docks."

"It was a very strange case," Watson said. "I still don't understand how Lady Caroline suddenly changed her mind about Beckett like that."

"She said she received insight during prayer," Bea said. "It must have been profound – not only that she knew the erstwhile Beckett was a fraudster, but that she recognised you, Holmes."

"That's true," Watson said.

"She has left Becket House to the Dockland workers, for Father Devlin to administer. Her fortune has gone to her staff and the real Tom Beckett. She left me her father's library, and her home in France. We spent many happy summers there. And she left gifts for both of you." She handed us both a neatly-wrapped package, one addressed to Dr. John Watson, and the other to Mr. Sherlock Holmes.

"Good heavens," Watson said.

Watson opened his gift first and stared in astonishment at the contents. He said nothing, but waited for me to open mine. My gift was identical, a set of cufflinks depicting a coat of arms, bearing three red-beaked crows.

"Cornish choughs, Holmes!" Watson said. "Those are the very birds that attacked Sullivan."

"They are indeed, Doctor," Bea said.

"And the coat of arms?" I asked, though I suspected I already knew the answer.

Bea said, "It is that of Thomas à Becket."

# The Hand of Mesmer
## by Dick Gillman

### Chapter I – A Chance Meeting

It was one afternoon in August 1898 that Holmes had asked a favour of me, as he was engaged on a case that required his complete and full attention. I had been charged to deliver, by hand, some legal papers to the chambers of a solicitor in Lincoln's Inn. So pleasant was the day that I determined, after depositing the papers, to stroll some little distance east before hailing a cab to return to Baker Street.

It was as I was passing Barts that I heard my name called out in the street. I looked around to see a fellow on the opposite kerb, waving his cane and rather energetically shouting, "Watson! Watson! It is you!"

It took me a moment to place him but then realised that it was a fellow from the hospital that I had met around the time when I first made the acquaintance of Holmes. Crossing the street, he held out his hand in greeting. "Doctor Watson! It has been some years but I am pleased to see you." Smiling, he asked, "Are you still sharing rooms with Holmes in Baker Street?"

I shook his hand and remembered that the person before me was Charles Beech, a colleague of Stamford's. "Yes, we have managed to share amicably, for the most part, without coming to blows. Are you still at Barts?"

Beech nodded. "Yes . . . and once more making your acquaintance is the best thing that has happened to me for some considerable time. I wonder if I might call upon you and Holmes, say, tomorrow evening? Perhaps at seven o'clock? I am in grave need of some sound advice."

The man before me now looked both eager and troubled in equal measure. Seeing his demeanour, I readily agreed. "Why of course, Beech. I am sure Holmes would be amenable."

On hearing this, Beech brightened and hurried on, calling out, "Tomorrow at seven. Thank you, Watson!"

I didn't know what to make of this encounter. Here was a man that I had barely known and hadn't seen for years, who was clearly in need of Holmes's counsel. Indeed, so much so, that he'd almost invited himself to our rooms! It troubled me and, on hailing a cab, I sat, unsettled, for the whole of the journey back to Baker Street.

On my return, I found Holmes slouched in his chair, drawing contentedly upon his favourite briar. Hardly had I sat down when he enquired, "What has stirred you so, Watson? It can hardly be the errand that I required you to undertake. Your face and respiration tell all – you are clearly ill at ease." I sat with a slight frown upon my face as he continued, "The way that you are holding your leg tells me that, despite the warm weather and the respite that it brings, you are in some pain, as you have walked from the cab at a pace that declares your urgency to return."

Of course, my friend was quite correct, for I was still unsettled and had hurried from the cab in my eagerness to tell Holmes of my meeting with Beech.

Easing myself back into my armchair, I smiled. "A visitor is to call tomorrow evening at seven o'clock. He is a gentleman named Beech who wishes to consult you on a matter which, by his manner, seems to be of some importance to him."

Holmes frowned. "Beech . . . a common enough name, but as your return route here may well have passed close to Barts, the only Beech that I know and with whom you and I share some commonality is that friend of Stamford's. I take it that it is he?"

I reached for my pipe and began to fill it, nodding as I did so. "Yes. He gave me not an inkling as to the nature of his business, but he was, indeed, most eager to call."

Holmes sat back and smiled. "Then we must wait and see what intrigue the fellow presents us with."

The following day, Holmes moped about our rooms, flicking through various newspapers before tossing them to one side in disgust. Having completed all aspects of his previous case, his mind craved stimulation, and I was indeed grateful when, after dinner, seven o'clock came and the bell in the hallway below announced the arrival of our visitor.

Holmes's mood had brightened and he sat, eagerly waiting for Mrs. Hudson's knock on our sitting room door. On hearing it, Holmes leapt from his chair and stood, at the ready, to welcome our guest. Mrs. Hudson nodded towards me and then announced, "A Mr. Charles Beech to see you, Mr. Holmes."

He strode forward, muttering a brief "Thank you" before holding out his hand to Beech, directing him to sit before us.

As I'd noticed the day before, the man had changed little from the fellow I'd first met at Barts. He was slim and tall, with a thin face and dark hair, slightly slicked back, and with evidence of the odd grey hair now appearing at his temples. He sat and seemed a little nervous in the presence

401

of my friend. Sensing this, Holmes began, "Watson tells me that you wish to consult me on some matter, Mr. Beech. How can I be of service?"

Beech sat and tapped the fingers of each hand against each other in a delicate, clapping motion. "I am unsure as to where to begin. I am now a registrar at Barts and work under the direction of Sir Lionel Wood. I've been happy in my position until, perhaps, four months ago."

Holmes sat forward a little. "Is this the same Sir Lionel that is a figure of some importance in the field of mental illness?" asked Holmes.

Beech nodded. "Indeed so, Mr. Holmes. He has written several articles on the subject which have appeared in both *The British Medical Journal* and *The Lancet*."

I nodded as I recalled that I had, indeed, read some of these with great interest.

Beech continued. "It is his reputation and import that makes this particularly difficult for me. I fear that he has been deceived by a visiting doctor from the Imperial Novorossiya University in Odessa, a Doctor Mikhail Shukhov. He claims to be a master of Mesmerism, and I fear that it is Sir Lionel who has fallen under his spell."

At this I sat up, asking, "Do you not believe in Mesmerism, Beech?"

Beech turned towards me, his face most serious. "I do, Watson. I believe that the mind may be influenced by external stimulation and encouraged to heal itself through relaxation, but this dogma of 'invisible fluids' within the body that can be directed by using Mesmer's techniques? I am unconvinced – so much so that I want to cry out 'Fraud!' – but I dare not."

Holmes looked most serious. "Yes, it does put you in something of an impossible position, Beech. I would welcome the opportunity to observe this Shukhov fellow."

At this, Beech brightened. "Ah, I had hoped that might be the case." He then delved into his jacket pocket and held out to Holmes two coloured pieces of card. "Shukhov is to give a demonstration of Mesmerism tomorrow evening at seven o'clock at Barts. Would that be convenient for you and Watson?"

Holmes looked across to me and raised a questioning eyebrow. I nodded in return. "Yes, we will be there. I look forward to it!"

Rising from his armchair, Holmes extended his hand, saying, "Good evening, Beech. You must excuse Watson and me, for we have much to consider." With that, he guided a somewhat bemused Beech to our sitting room door.

With the door now closed and hearing Beech's footfall on the stairs, Holmes returned to his armchair, rubbing his hands with glee. "This is most interesting, Watson. Tell me what you know of Mesmerism."

I sat back and began to fill my pipe. "Well, my knowledge on the subject is far from perfect, but, as I recall, Franz Mesmer was a German doctor who developed a theory which he called 'animal magnetism'." I lit my pipe before adding. "To some, his theories were plausible, whilst to others, he was seen as a complete fraud and, I believe, he died, in some obscurity, earlier this century. His theory has also became known as 'Hypnosis' – not a term that he used, preferring 'Mesmerism'."

Holmes nodded, asking, "And what are your views on this 'Mesmerism'?"

Drawing on my pipe, I considered Holmes's question. "I believe that the mind can be placed in a trance-like state and become suggestible. Often, sensations of pain can be suppressed, and I have myself witnessed Indian religious men having large needles passed through their flesh whilst in a trance, seemingly without pain." Holmes again nodded and waited for me to continue. "Indeed, there are, I believe, ancient texts from different civilizations – the Greeks, Chinese, and even the Egyptians – that refer to individuals entering trance like states brought on by various rituals."

Holmes frowned, asking, "How are such trances brought about?"

I pursed my lips before answering, "In some cultures it can be drug-induced, but Mesmer used his own presence and body to induce the trance, staring intensely at the subject whilst either holding their hands or by making flowing movements with his own hands around their body."

I paused and I could see that Holmes was seeking more. "Mesmer explained the 'science' of his discoveries using the notion of a mysterious, invisible fluid that coursed around the body. Any blockage of the flow caused physical symptoms and, by entering a trance, the blockage was removed and the flow was once more restored."

Holmes gave me a sceptical glance, enquiring, "Do you adhere to this theory?"

I shook my head. "No, but a lot remains unexplained. Mesmerism, as a tool, requires further study and, perhaps, we might be further enlightened by this fellow, Shukhov."

## Chapter II – An Evening at Barts

Little happened the following day, but I was intrigued to see that Holmes had decided to research further into Mesmerism, as a small pile of reference books were untidily stacked beside his armchair. I took the opportunity to tease him, asking, "Are you now convinced of the efficacy of this treatment?"

Holmes lowered the tome that he was reading and could clearly see the mischief in my expression as I awaited his reply. "I believe that there

403

is merit in some elements of this 'treatment', but the explanation of the mechanism of its function borders on the fantastic. But let us not disappoint the good doctor!"

With that, Holmes rose from his chair, grasping his overcoat as he rushed towards the stairs. I blinked and then made haste to follow my friend towards our rendezvous with Doctor Shukhov.

After a brief cab ride, we arrived outside Barts and, on tossing the cabby a shilling, we hurried inside. As we made our way deeper into the building, Holmes pointed towards a poster which gave details of the demonstration by Shukhov and designated its venue as being a small lecture theatre attached to the Department of Neurology. On seeing this, Holmes made a sharp turn and then hurried onwards along a glazed corridor.

Arriving before a partly open pair of stout doors, he handed our previously obtained tickets to a young fellow who directed us to two seats some small distance from the central stage of the lecture theatre. Looking about me, I saw that the area was laid out in tiers of seats arranged around an oval stage or demonstration area. This arrangement was reminiscent of the many times that I had sat and observed either dissections or operations during my training at University.

Within minutes, the doors closed and a respectful moment of quiet fell as a tall, slim fellow with iron grey hair appeared from an entrance to the side of the stage. He was, I would say, some fifty years old, well presented, and in evening dress. However, it wasn't his appearance that claimed my attention, for I was surprised to see that he was leading a young lady, dressed in a white robe, by the hand.

He paused and then took her to a single chair that had been placed centre stage. Releasing his grip, he then addressed the room. "Good evening, gentlemen and esteemed colleagues. My purpose tonight is to demonstrate the power of Mesmerism. In order to do this, I have brought with me a young subject whom I have found to be extremely susceptible to my Mesmeric rays."

On hearing this, I looked blankly towards Holmes, as this was the first mention of such an effect. He raised an eyebrow slightly and then returned his gaze towards Shukhov. For the next ten minutes, Shukhov expounded upon Mesmeric "$N$" rays and how they could not only affect human patients, but might also be absorbed by inanimate objects.

I heard Holmes repress a snort of derision but continued to listen to the doctor's lecture. It was when Shukhov sought to involve his "patient", the young lady in the white robe, that Holmes sat a little further forward in his seat.

404

Shukhov now gestured to an assistant off-stage who then appeared carrying a small side table, upon which stood a tumbler and a carafe of water. This was placed beside Shukhov, who then poured a glass of water and held it before him, saying, "I hope you will accept that this is simply a glass of tap water. It has not been adulterated with any narcotic. Indeed, I will prove it."

Putting the glass to his lips, Shukhov took a long draw of water from it before replacing it on the side table. "Now, I will infuse it with "$N$" rays and you will see the startling effect upon my young patient. She came to me suffering from a stutter and a mild form of mental seizure which, after my treatment, has now disappeared."

Shukhov took a pace back and stared fixedly at the glass of water. His expression took on a most intense glare and he moved his trembling hands around the glass, as if something was, indeed, leaving his body and being transferred. After perhaps a minute of this, he took the glass and gave it to the girl who, in turn, drained half of it.

Within moments, her whole demeanour seemed to change and she sat rigid, gripping the arms of the chair with white knuckles. Shukhov looked around the lecture theatre at the amazed faces. "Gentlemen, you will see that the patient is now in a trance. She has drunk the water that was infused with energy, the animal magnetism of Mesmer, and is aware of my voice, but little else."

Shukhov waited a few moments for the gathered audience to marvel at his demonstration before he reached behind the lapel of jacket and held up something that I thought might only be visible to those in the front row of the theatre. "Here, gentlemen, is a needle. It is my intention to pass it through the flesh of my patient's neck and she will feel no pain."

On hearing this, there was a hushed gasp from the assembled audience. Shukhov went towards the young girl and led her, like some performing creature at a circus, to the edge of the first row of seats and proceeded to pinch the flesh of her neck, and pass the needle through it. Leaving the needle in place, he proceeded to process around the theatre so all might see.

I must say that I was repulsed by this obvious showmanship. I leant towards my friend, whispering, "This is monstrous, Holmes! I am appalled!"

He nodded. "Indeed, Watson, and it may not be as it appears. I hope to speak to this fellow before we leave." I looked towards Holmes and his face was, indeed, grim.

Shukhov continued his demonstration, where he sought to infuse various objects with "animal magnetism". He wakened his patient and then returned her to a trance state whenever she touched one of the "charged"

405

objects. Finally, the demonstration was at an end, and Shukhov bowed to a good deal of applause before leaving the stage.

As we left the lecture theatre, Holmes caught my sleeve as he observed Beech standing some feet away. Moving towards him, he called out, "Beech! Might I ask a small favour of you?"

Beech turned and smiled, saying, "Of course, if I am able."

Holmes had something of a wolfish grin about him as he replied, "I would very much like to meet this fellow Shukhov. Immediately, if at all possible."

Beech pursed his lips. "I believe he has been invited to take a glass in the refectory. This way."

Holmes and I followed him and we were soon enjoying canapes and a glass of claret whilst rubbing shoulders with many senior figures of the hospital. Beech manoeuvred his way through the assembled dignitaries until we were standing not a yard from Shukhov. He appeared to be expounding on some point to a bearded figure who was nodding enthusiastically. Holmes, I noticed, had moved even nearer and I stared as he appeared to stumble into Shukhov, causing him to almost spill a full glass of claret.

Holmes looked aghast as he turned to face the man. "Apologies, Dr. Shukhov. My balance is not all that it might be, but I was so enthralled by your demonstration that I was eager to pass on my congratulations."

Shukhov looked shocked for a moment but then beamed at the compliment. "Ah, no harm done. But I do not think that we have been introduced?"

Holmes reached out his hand towards Shukhov, saying, "My name is Sherlock Holmes, and this is my friend, Doctor John Watson. I was indeed impressed by your demonstration this evening, particularly so when you were able to infuse the glass of water with 'animal magnetism'. Tell me, does this work at a distance?"

Shukhov again beamed. "Why yes. We have even been able to reflect the rays using a mirror!"

Holmes stood back, amazed. "I am in awe, Doctor Shukhov! An acquaintance of mine, Doctor Beech, tells me you are from the University in Odessa. Did your experiments begin there?"

Shukhov nodded. "Yes, I began to develop my theories there before bringing them first to Paris, and then to London."

Holmes smiled. "Odessa is a wonderful place. I had reason to visit there some months ago and, as it happens, I had the pleasure of meeting Professor Dmitri Mendeleev. His work in the field of biology never fails to astound me – and of course, I visited the new theatre of opera and ballet.

It was such a great pity when it was damaged by fire so soon after it was completed."

I looked towards Shukhov who now appeared to be a little uncomfortable. "Quite so, Mr. Holmes, a great shame. Well, I must . . . ."

Shukhov was unable to finish his sentence as Holmes grasped his forearm, saying, "I wonder if I could invite you to a small *soiree* that I am holding in my rooms at 221b Baker Street, tomorrow evening? The reason being that I have invited a doctor friend who has premises in Harley Street and his clientele, it seems, suffer greatly from the conditions which your treatment seeks to alleviate."

At the mention of Harley Street, Shukhov's manner seemed to change markedly. No longer did he wish to leave Holmes's company, instead replying, "Well, Mr. Holmes, that is a most generous offer. What time would be convenient for me to attend?"

Holmes smiled. "Would eight o'clock be suitable? I think we all will be assembled by then."

Shukhov nodded, saying, "Excellent. I look forward to it."

Nodding, Holmes turned and strode from the room with me, feeling a little nonplussed, behind him. As he strode down the corridor I tugged at his sleeve, asking, "What in heaven is going on, Holmes? I thought you were intent on exposing this fellow."

Holmes continued to walk on but replied, "It is just a question of rope, Watson. I am giving this fellow just a little more before the noose tightens."

Chapter III – A *Soiree* of Revelation!

During our cab ride, Holmes would say no more, despite my questioning looks. I had to wait until we were once more ensconced in Baker Street before he would enlighten me further. Sitting in his armchair, his pipe now fully alight, he began thus. "This Shukhov is a fraud, Watson. He has blinded those around him with pseudo-science and by deception."

I frowned. "He is a showman and some of his claims seem to be somewhat fantastic, but you witnessed that dreadful display of his power for yourself!"

"Power?" cried Holmes. "You have seen what he wanted you to see – but I saw more!" Holmes's eyes burned as he continued, "What you did not observe was the small puncture mark to the side of where the needle had been inserted. Shukhov was clever in trying to mask it with his thumb as he paraded the girl for all to see."

I frowned again, unsure of the implications of this. "Was the mark of some relevance, Holmes?" At once, I regretted asking the question, as he

407

reached for the bell rope and pulled strongly upon it, crying, "Well, let us see!"

Within moments, Mrs. Hudson appeared and Holmes addressed her. "Mrs. Hudson, I have often seen you leave Baker Street wearing a variety of fine bonnets. Might I trouble you for the loan of a large hat pin – the larger the better?"

Mrs. Hudson gave Holmes a querying look. "Well . . . yes, of course, Mr. Holmes."

Holmes smiled and we waited patiently whilst she disappeared downstairs and then returned with a truly fearsome example, some four inches in length. "Thank you, Mrs. Hudson. I will take great care of it and return it to you in the morning."

Turning his back on us both, he disappeared into his bedroom. Mrs. Hudson returned below stairs and I waited patiently. After two or three minutes, Holmes returned, brandishing the hatpin in a most cavalier fashion. "You will recall, Watson, that Shukhov was able to pass his needle through the flesh of the girl's neck, somewhat in this fashion."

I stood agog as he took the hatpin and placed it against the web of flesh between his thumb and forefinger. "Holmes! Are you mad?" I cried, expecting him to grimace and cry out as he pierced the flesh – but he appeared to not have even noticed the pain!

Observing my distress, Holmes now withdrew the hat pin and then took up the whisky decanter, splashing a little onto his handkerchief before wiping away the blood that oozed from the wound. "So, Watson. Did I disappear into my bedroom to infuse myself with 'animal magnetism'? I think not, but I did avail myself of a little cocaine, injected close to the point where I was to insert the hatpin."

I stumbled into my chair, eyes wide as I muttered, "A local anaesthetic! The girl. The mark on her neck. Shukhov had . . . ."

Holmes nodded. "Yes, he had injected the site on her neck before entering the stage. I took the opportunity to grasp the item I perceived to be in Shukhov's jacket pocket as I engineered to stumble into him. His pocket contained a syringe case, much like my own."

I blinked, saying, "Then it is all a pretence, and the girl must be part of it!"

Holmes returned to his chair and took up his pipe. "Quite so. The man is indeed a fraud, and I believe that we must expose him, publicly." Taking a long draw on his pipe, Holmes continued, "He is no man of science. What do you know of Dmitri Mendeleev, Watson?"

I did not even have to think for a single moment as I replied, "He is the 'father' of the Periodic Table, a chemist . . . But you said his work was in the field of *biology*!"

Holmes had a grim look on his face as he nodded. "Yes. It was not through politeness that he agreed with me. It was through ignorance, and the new theatre of opera and ballet in Odessa remains intact!" Holmes contemptuously blew out a cloud of smoke before continuing, "I believe *this* man has taken on the persona of Doctor Shukhov, choosing to have hailed from a university far from London – hence his *bona fide* would be unlikely to be checked. However, it is a task that I will endeavour to accomplish in the morning."

With that, Holmes drew up his legs and sat motionless, lost to the world.

True to his word, Holmes sat at the breakfast table and dashed off not one, but four telegrams that he placed upon his battlefield of breakfast dishes before ringing for Mrs. Hudson. I took it that one of the telegrams was to the University in Odessa, but I was curious as to whom the three others were addressed.

"Are you seeking yet further verification of Shukhov?" I asked, not wanting to peer too closely to read what he had written.

Holmes smiled, thinly. "No, Watson. I needed to have a plausible person to act as an incumbent of Harley Street. Does anyone spring to mind?"

"Mycroft!" I shouted gleefully, feeling sure that he would indeed enjoy being part of this deception to bring a villain to justice. "What of the two others, Holmes?"

"I wanted to invite Beech, but also I wanted to let Lestrade have sight of this fellow – not to arrest him, but to be made aware of his practices." answered Holmes.

I frowned, asking, "Is that not something of a gamble? Lestrade isn't a man who is comfortable in the same circles as Beech, and certainly not those of Mycroft."

At this, Holmes laughed heartily and then patted me on the shoulder, saying, "Indeed not, but never fear. I have asked him to say nothing and to pretend to be a friend of yours." I frowned and then chuckled at the very thought of it.

The day seemed to pass quite quickly and Holmes busied himself with the details of the evening's *soiree*. He had refilled the decanters and made sure that the dining table was clear of the usual clutter of chemical apparatus that seemed to perpetually reside upon it.

I was intrigued when he disappeared mid-afternoon, re-appearing with four, small, brown-paper wrapped parcels. The first two of these he unwrapped and revealed a small bell-jar, some six inches in height and, perhaps, some four inches in diameter. Next to this he placed a flat,

409

circular, wooden base with a central dowel spindle, topped by a sharp pivot. It was upon this that he carefully placed a large compass needle. Once it had settled, he placed the bell jar over it, thus ensuring that its direction would not be affected by any draughts or air currents within the room.

I was indeed curious as I watched him assemble this, asking, "What is the relevance of the compass? We know that Baker Street runs north to south."

Holmes smiled, "It is part of an illusion that I wish to create this evening, Watson. You will see soon enough!"

The contents of the other two packages remained hidden and Holmes disappeared into his room with them, taking the compass with him.

It was little before five o'clock that Mrs. Hudson knocked gently upon our door and then entered, holding a telegram in her grasp. Holmes was still in his bedroom, so I relieved her of it. Calling out to Holmes, I advised him of its arrival. He didn't emerge, simply replying, "Be a good fellow, Watson, and read it to me."

I tore open the envelope and the content was, indeed, enlightening. "It is from the University of Odessa, Holmes. Doctor Shukhov sends his regards, saying, *"I am grateful for your concern, Holmes. Examine the left hand of your imposter. I lost half of my smallest finger in childhood. Shukhov."*

On hearing this, Holmes's bedroom door opened and he emerged with a grim smile of satisfaction upon his face. "It is as I thought, although we shall play his game to the end."

We ate an early dinner almost in silence, enjoying roast gammon with a savoury white sauce, boiled potatoes, and carrots. This was followed by an excellent seasonal fruit tart served with Devon Cream. After retiring to dress for our guests, we arranged the room so that there was sufficient space for Shukhov to stand while giving access to the dining table. Sitting upon it, centre stage, if you will, was the compass encased in its bell jar. What purpose that was to serve had not, as yet, been revealed to me.

At a few minutes before eight o'clock, the distinctive tread of Mycroft Holmes was heard upon the stairs, the ringing of our bell having been deemed as unnecessary. On arrival in our rooms, Holmes took Mycroft to one side for a brief moment to appraise him of what was to happen during the evening. I noticed Mycroft nodding his approval and, indeed, patting his brother on the forearm, an almost unique gesture of fraternal affection.

Following on from this, in swift succession, the rest of our guests arrived. Shukhov, I saw, was most pleased to be placed centre stage.

Holmes now rose. "Good evening, gentlemen. It is my pleasure to introduce to you Doctor Shukhov, our eminent guest from the Ukraine who will, I hope, demonstrate his skills in Mesmerism. Unbeknownst to him, I would like to volunteer myself as his subject. I think my friend from Harley Street, Mr. Mycroft Hudson, will find this most illuminating."

I had placed myself next to Lestrade who, on hearing this, looked puzzled and was about to interrupt when I placed a restraining hand on his forearm and gently shook my head. Lestrade frowned, but thankfully held his tongue.

Shukhov rose and, after a brief introduction of himself and Mesmerism in the broadest of terms, then turned his attention to Holmes. "You will understand, Mr. Holmes, that not everyone is susceptible to Mesmerism, so please bear with me if I am not fully successful."

Holmes nodded and smiled, adding, "I am confident in your abilities, Doctor Shukhov, after witnessing your previous demonstration. I was intrigued when you suggested that 'animal magnetism' may possess some of the properties of traditional magnetism. With that in mind, I have set up on our dining table a compass beneath a bell jar to see if we might observe this phenomenon."

I watched Shukhov closely and saw a slight expression of unease pass across his face. "Perhaps so, but as I say, Mr. Holmes, it depends on the susceptibility of the subject. Let us begin."

Shukhov drew his chair up to that of Holmes so that their knees now touched. He then stared intensely at Holmes and, whilst doing so, he passed his hands around Holmes's head, shoulders, and torso. As I watched, it seemed like a transformation had occurred. Holmes's whole expression changed and his vision became glazed and his body slumped.

I looked again at Shukhov, whose countenance seemed to hold some degree of wonder also. Standing, he led Holmes to the dining table and the chair before it. Seating Holmes, he then placed his leaden hands either side of the bell jar. "Now Mr. Holmes, I want you to extend your animal magnetism towards the compass. Press forward with your mind."

Holmes's body stiffened. As one, we all looked towards the bell jar. Nothing appeared to happen but then, slowly, the compass needle began to turn. At this, the whole room gasped. The needle stayed deflected until Shukhov whispered, "And now relax and return the force to your body."

At this, Holmes's body began to droop and, once more, our attention was rivetted on the bell jar and the compass needle within it. I was amazed to see that as Holmes relaxed, so the compass needle returned to its original position.

Shukhov mopped his brow and returned Holmes to his seat. Placing both his hands on Holmes shoulders, Shukhov now encouraged gently him to awaken.

411

Within seconds, Holmes appeared as normal and seemed unaware of what had occurred. Looking at our shocked faces, he enquired, "Pray tell me, was the demonstration a success? I confess that I feel invigorated by it. I think this calls for a little brandy!"

Holmes's offer was readily accepted by all, and for several minutes we stood, talking amongst ourselves regarding what we had just witnessed. Holmes now called Mycroft to him, saying, "Dr. Hudson, do you consider that your patients might benefit from the relaxation brought about by Mesmerism?"

Mycroft nodded. "I have many who suffer from depressive illness and the like that would gladly pay twenty guineas for such a treatment."

I was not surprised to see Shukhov almost lick his lips at the prospect. "I'm grateful for your confidence, Doctor Hudson. I am at your service."

Mycroft nodded, adding, "I would like to invite two or three of my patients to one of your demonstrations, Shukhov, so that they might witness, first hand, your skill. Perhaps Mr. Holmes would be amenable to be involved, as he seems to be particularly susceptible to your Mesmerism?"

Both Shukhov and Mycroft now turned towards Holmes with an enquiring look. Holmes appeared to consider the proposal for a moment before nodding in agreement. Shukhov seemed particularly pleased, saying, "I am due to give a second demonstration at St. Bartholomew's in two days' time. Would that be too soon, Mr. Holmes?"

Holmes shook his head. "No, that is quite convenient, I shall be pleased to assist."

With a round of goodbyes, the evening finished successfully. Poor Lestrade was indeed perplexed, but as our guests left. I noticed that Mycroft had summoned a cab and was now inviting Lestrade to join him. As a result, I was confident that Mycroft would explain all.

## Chapter IV – A Friend of Little Alfie's

It was as we sat and smoked to release the tension of the evening with Shukhov that I found that I couldn't contain myself any longer. "Tell me, Holmes, truly, that you too haven't fallen under the spell of that charlatan!"

He almost exploded with laughter as he explained, "Great heavens, no, Watson, although I am encouraged that my performance was so convincing!"

Whilst greatly relieved, I was still eager to know how what we had seen had been achieved. "How was it done? How were you able to control the deflection of the compass with your mind?"

412

Holmes smiled once more and then rose from his chair, disappearing into his bedroom. Within a minute he had returned and in his grasp was a maze of wires. "It is all the fault of the Danes, Watson, that I had to wear this contraption. But that is too strong. Rather, blame one Dane in particular, a certain Hans Christian Oersted."

I had to consider this statement for perhaps five seconds before I realised how the deception had been achieved. "Electromagnetism! But how did you manage to control it, for your hands had been placed on the table, beside the bell jar?"

Holmes smiled. "I had anticipated that Shukhov would place my hands near the compass. With that in mind, it was necessary to devise another method of completing the circuit." Holmes drew on his pipe, continuing, "I had wound a large coil of copper wire that was connected to a dry battery and had placed it beneath my clothing. Placing a small switch within my shoe, I merely pressed down upon it to energise the coil. As I stiffened my body, at Shukhov's command, I allowed current to flow."

Whilst I was pleased with what had been achieved both by Holmes and by Mycroft, my thoughts now turned to how Shukhov might be exposed as a fraud. "I was greatly amused when Mycroft was revealed as Doctor Hudson, but what have you in mind for the second demonstration with Shukhov?"

Holmes again smiled before tilting back his head and slowly blowing out a thin stream of blue smoke towards our now almond-coloured ceiling. "I am, as yet, unsure, but it will be necessary to also reveal the complicit role played by the young girl in the deception."

Having said this, my friend closed his eyes and retreated into that inner sanctum where he would consider a myriad of possibilities.

In the day prior to the second demonstration by Shukhov, Holmes did little in the way of preparation. However, after a brief visit to Carlin's, the tobacconists, I returned to find him deep in conversation with Little Alfie, the smallest and youngest member of the gang of street urchins that were sometimes Holmes's eyes and ears. Upon hearing my return, voices were lowered and I was just in time to see Holmes pass Alfie a florin. With a joyful "Watcha, Doctor Watson!" Little Alfie hopped down from our sofa and scampered his way back down the stairs to Baker Street.

I looked toward my friend, but he was now hidden from view behind his copy of *The Times*. It was evident to me that he did not wish to be disturbed.

I slept fitfully that night and, in the morning, I could barely manage to consume my usual full English breakfast. Holmes, however, was patently content with his cup of coffee and seemed eager to pile homemade strawberry preserves onto his thickly buttered toast.

Between mouthfuls, he asked, "Did you know, Watson, that the term 'Hypnosis' was coined in the eighteenth century by the Englishman, James Brand, with its origins from the Greek god Hypnos, the god of sleep?"

I looked at my friend and answered, rather testily, "Well, I believe that he must be taking a holiday somewhere quite remote, for he was not present in my bed chamber last night!"

Holmes laughed but, after regarding my fragile demeanour, took pity on me and did not bother me further. By mid-morning, I had revived sufficiently to take a cup of Darjeeling and to engage my friend in conversation.

"You know," I said, "there is some serious science hidden beneath this miasma of Mesmerism. Indeed, this Hypnosis has been used on both animals and humans to the extent that limbs have been removed with no other form of anaesthesia. It is, indeed, an area not to be scoffed at as quackery."

Holmes turned to me and nodded in agreement. "Indeed so, but it is charlatans like Shukhov that bring it into disrepute." Holmes drew on his pipe and then asked of me, "What do you imagine Shukhov's response will be to my apparent ability to deflect the compass needle, Watson?"

I sat and thought for a moment. "Well, given his ego and desire for the limelight, I would imagine that he would not want to be outshone. Consequently, he will want to be able to show that he too can cause the effect."

Holmes nodded in reply. "Yes, you mirror my thoughts exactly. But how will he attempt to achieve it?"

I pursed my lips. "Perhaps . . . perhaps a permanent magnet sewn into the sleeve of his jacket?" I suggested.

Holmes seemed to consider this for a moment. "A possibility, but I think that would be too crude. Image the consternation if he were to suddenly find a fork or a spoon attaching itself to his jacket sleeve! We shall have to bide our time to see how ingenious the doctor has been."

It was a little after six o'clock when a knock at our sitting room door, followed by a scuffle, announced Mrs. Hudson with Young Alfie firmly in her grasp. "I'm sorry, Mr. Holmes, but I found this young ruffian sneaking up the stairs."

Little Alfie was wriggling in her grasp, shouting, "I weren't sneakin'! Mr. 'Olmes ses I were to come at six!"

Holmes approached, saying, "It's quite alright, Mrs. Hudson. I was expecting Alfie. Do you have it?"

414

Mrs. Hudson released her grip on Alfie, who now produced a small cardboard box, tied with string and punctured along both long sides, as if done with a pencil. "'Ere you are, Mr. 'Olmes, just what you ses."

Holmes took the box and then delved into his trouser pocket to produce a silver sixpence, which he flicked with his thumb towards Alfie. Reaching out a grubby hand, the little lad grabbed it in mid-air and then scuttled off down the stairs.

I admit that my curiosity was piqued, but I had no opportunity to enquire further as Holmes hurried to his room and swiftly closed the door.

By half-past-six, we were both dressed for the evening and standing in Baker Street, waving to attract an approaching cab. Once installed, I noticed that Holmes had a small parcel in his lap and appeared to be eager to sit away from me in the cab. This I thought to be most unusual behaviour. Indeed, as we entered Barts, he kept his cane partly raised, as if maintain a barrier between him and any passing person or obstacle. Once at the entrance to the lecture theatre, he disappeared to prepare whilst I met Beech at the door, and we entered together.

Beech had reserved two seats for us adjacent to the stage, which was arranged as before, except for a large table and three chairs which had been placed centrally. As I watched, an assistant came from the wings and placed the bell jar and compass upon the table. I now understood, or so I thought, the reason why Holmes wanted to avoid any contact as he carried this fragile item.

At precisely seven o'clock, the lecture theatre doors closed and Shukhov made his grand entrance to suppressed applause. Behind him came his two acolytes, the young girl in her white robe and, beside her, Holmes in full evening dress.

Shukhov began thus. "Good evening, gentlemen. This is the second of my demonstrations of the power of Mesmerism. I have with me this evening not one, but two subjects whom I have discovered to be most susceptible to Mesmerism."

At this he turned and led forward the young girl. Asking her to sit, he then faced her, with knees touching, just as he had done with Holmes. As we watched, Shukhov made flowing gestures with his hands and, as he did so, the girl's expression changed to one that was completely blank. Her eyes stayed sightless and her body slightly slumped.

Turning to the audience, Shukhov announced, "You will observe that this subject is almost lifeless and in a complete trance-like state. She can only follow my commands. I will now pass this needle . . . ."

Shukhov was not to finish the sentence as Holmes now approached and stood by the girl's side, saying to the audience, "Gentlemen, you have seen how Doctor Shukhov has induced a trance and has complete control of his patient."

Reaching up to her face, Holmes gently held her lower jaw and opened her mouth. Shukhov could only stare as Holmes now reached into his jacket pocket whilst saying, "She is completely docile and unaware, even when I place this live mouse in her mouth."

Holmes now held the small, squirming form by its tail and moved it towards the girl's face. A blood curdling scream came from the girl as she fled towards the exit and into the waiting arms of a burly constable. Holmes calmly replaced the mouse in his jacket pocket and turned to Shukhov, exclaiming, "You, sir, are a fraud. You lie, cheat, and hide behind ethereal Science to line your own pocket! You are even low enough to harm the girl, your 'patient', to enhance your reputation and further your own greed."

I thought Shukhov might truly explode. His face was puce as he stood and visibly shook. "How dare you say such things that are plainly untrue! I am a respected academic from the University of Odessa and . . . ."

Again, his sentence went unfinished. "No sir, you are not!" Holmes reached into his inside jacket pocket and produced the telegram he had received from the university. "This is a telegram I received from the *real* Doctor Shukhov at The University of Odessa, saying. '*Examine the left hand of your imposter. I lost half of my smallest finger in childhood. Shukhov.*' Show me your hand, sir!"

Immediately, almost instinctively, Shukhov placed his left hand behind his back, shouting, "No, Holmes! I am Shukhov, and I have the power of animal magnetism! I can prove it!"

Holmes stood back and looked Shukhov in the eye. "If you truly have this power, you will walk free and I will publicly apologise."

I gasped that Holmes should take such a risk. Shukhov now addressed the audience, who sat in stunned horror. "Gentlemen, both my identity and my honour have been impugned. I will now prove to you that what I say is true."

Shukhov now approached the bell jar and once more stared at it fixedly, his hands outstretched, quivering. We crowded around to look. To my dismay, as he slowly moved his hands around the glass jar, the compass needle slowly followed.

Shukhov turned in triumph towards Holmes, and, in a raised voice, he mocked him. "I know what you are thinking, Holmes. You believe I have a magnet sewn into my clothes, but we shall see!" With that, Shukhov threw off his jacket, unbuttoned and tossed aside his waistcoat and then slowly, dramatically, rolled up his shirt sleeves. There was nothing present but flesh.

416

Slowly, he turned and, with his arms now bared, he once again fixed the bell jar with an almost fanatical stare. With hands quivering, he began to move them slowly around the jar. Again, the compass followed his movements.

I fell back in my seat in horror and disbelief, crying, "No . . . it cannot be!"

Shukhov turned and sneered at Holmes. "Well, Mr. Holmes?"

Holmes looked like a broken man and Shukhov gloated. "Is there anything further before your public apology, Holmes?"

Holmes shook his head, saying, "It appears that I was wrong, Shukhov, but I would like to see you repeat the experiment . . . with only your left hand."

It was now the turn of Shukov to stumble. "That is not necessary, I have shown you that I am able to control the compass with only my mind."

Holmes was now his old self and I realised that he had once again demonstrated his acting skills. His voice was strong as he questioned, "Simply with your mind, Shukhov? Then there should be no difference which hand you use to guide the flow of *magnetism!*"

Shukhov's face had now turned ashen. I thought for a moment that he might comply with Holmes's request but, suddenly, he sprinted from the stage and, most unfortunately for him, into the waiting arms of a second constable.

Holmes now turned and faced the patently confused audience. "Gentlemen, I am afraid the demonstration is at an end. The mysteries of Science continue and, in Mesmerism, there is much to learn. The human psyche is loathe to give up its secrets easily, and we must beware of blind alleys and false prophets. I bid you a good evening." With that, Holmes left the stage.

Leaving the lecture theatre, I watched as the audience, to a man, looked bemused and uncertain as to what had occurred. As I waited for Holmes, I was joined by Mycroft, who was elated, whilst Beech was still clearly mystified. I was, indeed, curious, but I could extract nothing from Mycroft except a simple "Masterful," which was praise indeed towards his brother.

Holmes finally appeared and, on delving into his jacket pocket and passing a small, white mouse to Beech for safekeeping, Holmes led Mycroft and me out of Barts.

Once more back in Baker Street, Holmes opened a box of Havanas whilst Mycroft and I settled back with glasses of Holmes's own barrel, a single malt whisky. Perhaps now we could reflect on what had transpired in the last hour.

417

I frowned, asking, "What was the significance of Shukhov's left hand, apart from the fact that he possessed a complete little finger?"

Holmes drew on his cigar and then waved it in my direction. "You may recall our discussion on hidden magnets?" I nodded and waited for him to continue. "I was of the opinion that the only way that the compass could be moved was by a magnetic field or, less likely, simply a piece of iron – for a compass needle is, in itself, a magnet."

Taking another draw on his cigar, he took from his waistcoat pocket a small snuff box and offered it to me. I thought this most unusual and held up my hand to decline. Holmes smiled, saying, "It is not snuff, Watson."

Frowning, I took it from him and was immediately surprised by its weight. Opening it, I found that its content was indeed not snuff but a supremely fine, grey dust. "What is this?"

Holmes chided me. "Come, Watson. What natural force has been uppermost in our minds today?"

"Iron!" I cried, my outburst being sufficient to disturb a small amount of the powder onto Mrs. Hudson's rug. Still frowning, I asked, "But what was its purpose?"

Holmes's lips were thin as he explained. "Whilst I was unobserved, I sprinkled a small amount onto the table before the demonstration had begun. You, perhaps, may not have noticed that Shukhov's appearance had changed slightly since he was our guest here in Baker Street."

I thought back but couldn't bring to mind any difference between the man we had seen this evening and his appearance during our previous encounter. Observing my blank expression, Holmes continued, "This evening, he was wearing a large gold ring on his right hand, set with an equally large, dark stone. I observed, as he rested his hand on the table, that the stone now had a dusting of iron powder upon it."

"Lodestone!" I said. "The dark stone was Lodestone, the magnetic mineral used for navigation by the Vikings as a compass."

Holmes nodded. "Exactly. Shukhov could influence the compass with the hand wearing the ring – his right, but not with his left!" I sat back, elated, but was now curious as to what might be the fate of Shukhov and his young "patient".

On asking Mycroft, he replied, "As Shukhov is not one of Her Majesty's subjects, and has sought to criminally deceive us, he will, undoubtedly, be deported forthwith." Mycroft paused before continuing. "As to the girl, it could be argued that she had been coerced, threatened, or any other sinister reason for her participation. I very much doubt whether a criminal case will be brought against her, for it would, no doubt, expose senior members of the medical profession to ridicule."

418

I nodded and we sat together to finish our cigars, in relative silence, before finally bidding Mycroft farewell. Once he had departed, Holmes and I sat quietly, each, I believe, reflecting on the day's events.

After some little time, Holmes turned to me, saying, "The human mind is a complexity that is capable of great insight and creativity, Watson, but also of great wickedness. We understand so little about it, and yet, we are now fast approaching the twentieth century." Holmes paused and gazed into the far distance, whilst saying, "In respect to the human mind, I find myself drawn to an observation by Friedrich Nietzsche, '*There are no facts, only interpretations.*'"

With that, Holmes drew up his knees to his chest, withdrew from the world, and would say no more.

# About the Contributors

The following contributors appear in this volume:*
**The MX Book of New Sherlock Holmes Stories**
**Part XVII – Whatever Remains . . .**
**Must Be the Truth (1891-1898)**

**Kareem Abdul-Jabbar** is a huge Holmesian, the National Basketball Association's all-time leading scorer, a Basketball Hall of Fame inductee, and a *New York Times* bestselling author. In 2016, he received the Presidential Medal of Freedom, the USA's highest civilian honor, from former President Barack Obama. Currently he is chairman of the Skyhook Foundation, which "gives kids a shot that can't be blocked", a columnist for *The Guardian* newspaper, and a cultural critic for *The Hollywood Reporter.* He has written a number of books, and is a two-time NAACP aware-winning writer and producer. With Anna Waterhouse, he is the author of *Mycroft Holmes* (2015), *Mycroft and Sherlock* (2018), and *Mycroft and Sherlock: The Empty Birdcage* (2019).

**Hugh Ashton** was born in the U.K., and moved to Japan in 1988, where he remained until 2016, living with his wife Yoshiko in the historic city of Kamakura, a little to the south of Yokohama. He and Yoshiko have now moved to Lichfield, a small cathedral city in the Midlands of the U.K., the birthplace of Samuel Johnson, and one-time home of Erasmus Darwin. In the past, he has worked in the technology and financial services industries, which have provided him with material for some of his books set in the 21st century. He currently works as a writer: Novelist, freelance editor, and copywriter, (his work for large Japanese corporations has appeared in international business journals), and journalist, as well as producing industry reports on various aspects of the financial services industry. Recently, however, his lifelong interest in Sherlock Holmes has developed into an acclaimed series of adventures featuring the world's most famous detective, written in the style of the originals, and published by Inknbeans Press. In addition to these, he has also published historical and alternate historical novels, short stories, and thrillers. Together with artist Andy Boerger, he has produced the *Sherlock Ferret* series of stories for children, featuring the world's cutest detective.

**Brian Belanger** is a publisher and editor, but is best known for his freelance illustration and cover design work. His distinctive style can be seen on several MX Publishing covers, including *Silent Meridian* by Elizabeth Crowen, *Sherlock Holmes and the Menacing Melbournian* by Allan Mitchell, *Sherlock Holmes and A Quantity of Debt* by David Marcum, *Welcome to Undershaw* by Luke Benjamen Kuhns, and many more. Brian is the co-founder of Belanger Books LLC, where he illustrates the popular *MacDougall Twins with Sherlock Holmes* young reader series (#1 bestsellers on Amazon.com UK). A prolific creator, he also designs t-shirts, mugs, stickers, and other merchandise on his personal art site: *www.redbubble.com/people/zhahadun.*

**Sir Arthur Conan Doyle** (1859-1930) *Holmes Chronicler Emeritus.* If not for him, this anthology would not exist. Author, physician, patriot, sportsman, spiritualist, husband and father, and advocate for the oppressed. He is remembered and honored for the purposes of this collection by being the man who introduced Sherlock Holmes to the world. Through fifty-six Holmes short stories, four novels, and additional Apocryphal entries, Doyle

423

revolutionized mystery stories and also greatly influenced and improved police forensic methods and techniques for the betterment of all. *Steel True Blade Straight.*

**Chris Chan** is a writer, educator, and historian. He works as a researcher and "International Goodwill Ambassador" for Agatha Christie Ltd. His true crime articles, reviews, and short fiction have appeared (or will soon appear) in *The Strand, The Wisconsin Magazine of History, Mystery Weekly, Gilbert!, Nerd HQ*, Akashic Books' *Mondays are Murder* web series, *The Baker Street Journal*, and *Sherlock Holmes Mystery Magazine.*

**Bert Coules** BSI wandered through a succession of jobs from fringe opera company manager to BBC radio drama producer-director before becoming a full-time writer at the beginning of 1989. Bert works in a wide range of genres, including science fiction, horror, comedy, romance and action-adventure but he is especially associated with crime and detective stories: he was the head writer on the BBC's unique project to dramatise the entire Sherlock Holmes canon, and went on to script four further series of original Holmes and Watson mysteries. As well as radio, he also writes for TV and the stage.

**Anna Elliott** is an author of historical fiction and fantasy. Her first series, the *Twilight of Avalon* trilogy, is a retelling of the Trystan & Isolde legend. She wrote her second series, *The Pride & Prejudice Chronicles*, chiefly to satisfy her own curiosity about what might have happened to Elizabeth Bennet, Mr. Darcy, and all the other wonderful cast of characters after the official end of Jane Austen's classic work. She enjoys stories about strong women and loves exploring the multitude of ways women can find their unique strengths. She was delighted to lend a hand with the Sherlock & Lucy series, and this story, firstly because she loves Sherlock Holmes as much as her father does, and second because it almost never happens that someone with a dilemma shouts, "Quick, we need an author of historical fiction!" Anna lives in Pennsylvania with her husband and their four children. Learn more about the Sherlock and Lucy series at *www.sherlockandlucy.com*

**Steve Emecz**'s main field is technology, in which he has been working for more than twenty years. Following multiple senior roles at Xerox, where he grew their European eCommerce from $6m to $200m. Steve worked for eCommerce provider Venda, mobile commerce platform Powa, collectAI in Hamburg (Artificial Intelligence) and is now back in London with CloudTrade. Steve is a regular trade show speaker on the subject of eCommerce, and his tech career has taken him to more than fifty countries – so he's no stranger to planes and airports. He wrote two mystery novels (one a bestseller) in the 1990's, and a screenplay in 2001. Shortly after, he set up MX Publishing, specialising in NLP books. In 2008, MX published its first Sherlock Holmes book (Alistair Duncan's wonderful *Eliminate the Impossible*), and MX has gone on to become the largest specialist Holmes publisher in the world. MX is a social enterprise and supports two main causes. The first is Happy Life Children's Home, a baby rescue project in Nairobi, Kenya, where he and his wife, Sharon, spend every Christmas at the rescue centre in Kasarani. In 2014, they wrote a short book about the project, *The Happy Life Story*, with a second edition in 2017. The second is the Stepping Stones School, of which Steve is a patron. Stepping Stones is located at Undershaw, Sir Arthur Conan Doyle's former home.

**Mark A. Gagen** BSI is co-founder of Wessex Press, sponsor of the popular *From Gillette to Brett* conferences, and publisher of *The Sherlock Holmes Reference Library* and many other fine Sherlockian titles. A life-long Holmes enthusiast, he is a member of *The Baker Street Irregulars* and *The Illustrious Clients of Indianapolis*. A graphic artist by profession, his work is often seen on the covers of *The Baker Street Journal* and various BSI books.

**Paul D. Gilbert** was born in 1954 and has lived in and around London all of his life. He has been married to Jackie for thirty-nine years, and she is a Holmes expert who keeps him on the straight and narrow! He has two sons, one of whom now lives in Spain. His interests include literature, ancient history, all religions, most sports, and movies. He is currently employed full-time as a funeral director. His books so far include *The Lost Files of Sherlock Holmes* (2007), *The Chronicles of Sherlock Holmes* (2008), *Sherlock Holmes and the Giant Rat of Sumatra* (2010), *The Annals of Sherlock Holmes* (2012), *Sherlock Holmes and the Unholy Trinity* (2015), *Sherlock Holmes: The Four Handed Game* (2017), and *The Illumination of Sherlock Holmes*, to be published 2019.

**John Atkinson Grimshaw** (1836-1893) was born in Leeds, England. His amazing paintings, usually featuring twilight or night scenes illuminated by gas-lamps or moonlight, are easily recognizable, and are often used on the covers of books about The Great Detective to set the mood, as shadowy figures move in the distance through misty mysterious settings and over rain-slicked streets.

**Dick Gillman** is an English writer and acrylic artist living in Brittany, France with his wife Alex, Truffle, their Black Labrador, and Jean-Claude, their Breton cat. During his retirement from teaching, he has written over twenty Sherlock Holmes short stories which are published as both e-books and paperbacks. His contribution to the superb MX Sherlock Holmes collection, published in October 2015, was entitled "The Man on Westminster Bridge" and had the privilege of being chosen as the anchor story in *The MX Book of New Sherlock Holmes Stories – Part II (1890-1895)*.

**Arthur Hall**, who also has stories in Parts XVI and XVIII, was born in Aston, Birmingham, UK, in 1944. His interest in writing began during his schooldays and served as a growing ambition to become an author. Years later, his first novel *Sole Contact* was an espionage story about an ultra-secret government department known as "Sector Three" and has been followed, to date, by four sequels. The sixth in the series, *The Suicide Chase*, is currently in the course of preparation. Other works include five "rediscovered" cases from the files of Sherlock Holmes, two collections of bizarre short stories, and two novels about an adventurer called "Bernard Kramer", as well as several contributions to the ongoing anthology, *The MX Book of New Sherlock Holmes Stories*. His only ambition, apart from being published more widely, is to attend the premier of a film based on one of his novels, ideally at The Odeon, Leicester Square. He lives in the West Midlands, United Kingdom, where he often walks other people's dogs as he attempts to formulate new plots. His work can be seen at *arthurhallsbooksite.blogspot.com*, and the author can be contacted at *arthurhall7777@aol.co.uk*

**Stephen Herczeg** is an IT Geek, writer, actor, and film-maker based in Canberra Australia. He has been writing for over twenty years and has completed a couple of dodgy novels, sixteen feature length screenplays, and numerous short stories and scripts. Stephen was very successful in 2017's International Horror Hotel screenplay competition, with his scripts *TITAN* winning the Sci-Fi category and *Dark are the Woods* placing second in the horror category. His work has featured in *Sproutlings – A Compendium of Little Fictions* from Hunter Anthologies, the *Hells Bells* Christmas horror anthology published by the Australasian Horror Writers Association, and the *Below the Stairs*, *Trickster's Treats*, *Shades of Santa*, *Behind the Mask*, and *Beyond the Infinite* anthologies from OzHorror.Con, *The Body Horror Book*, *Anemone Enemy*, and *Petrified Punks* from

Oscillate Wildly Press, and *Sherlock Holmes In the Realms of H.G. Wells* and *Sherlock Holmes: Adventures Beyond the Canon* from Belanger Books.

**Christopher James** who also has a poem in Part XVIII, was born in 1975 in Paisley, Scotland. Educated at Newcastle and UEA, he was a winner of the UK's National Poetry Competition in 2008. He has written two full length Sherlock Holmes novels, *The Adventure of the Ruby Elephant* and *The Jeweller of Florence*, both published by MX, and is working on a third.

**Steven Philip Jones** has written over sixty graphic novels and comic books including the horror series *Lovecraftian, Curious Cases of Sherlock Holmes*, the original series *Nightlinger, Street Heroes 2005*, adaptations of *Dracula*, several H. P. Lovecraft stories, and the 1985 film *Re-animator*. Steven is also the author of several novels and nonfiction books including *The Clive Cussler Adventures: A Critical Review, Comics Writing: Communicating With Comic Book , King of Harlem, Bushwackers, The House With the Witch's Hat, Talisman: The Knightmare Knife*, and *Henrietta Hex: Shadows From the Past*. Steven's other writing credits include a number of scripts for radio dramas that have been broadcast internationally. A graduate of the University of Iowa, Steven has a Bachelor of Arts in Journalism and Religion, and was accepted into Iowa's Writer's Workshop - M.F.A. program.

**Roger Johnson** BSI, ASH is a retired librarian, now working as a volunteer assistant at the Essex Police Museum. In his spare time, he is commissioning editor of *The Sherlock Holmes Journal*, an occasional lecturer, and a frequent contributor to The Writings About the Writings. His sole work of Holmesian pastiche was published in 1997 in Mike Ashley's anthology *The Mammoth Book of New Sherlock Holmes Adventures*, and he has the greatest respect for the many authors who have contributed new tales to the present mighty trilogy. Like his wife, Jean Upton, he is a member of both *The Baker Street Irregulars* and *The Adventuresses of Sherlock Holmes*.

**Michael Mallory** is the Derringer-winning author of the "Amelia Watson" (The Second Mrs. Watson) series and "Dave Beauchamp" mystery series, and more than one-hundred-twenty-five short stories. An entertainment journalist by day, he has written eight nonfiction books on pop culture and more than six-hundred newspaper and magazine articles. Based in Los Angeles, Mike is also an occasional actor on television.

**David Marcum**, who also has stories in Parts XVI and XVIII, plays *The Game* with deadly seriousness. He first discovered Sherlock Holmes in 1975 at the age of ten, and since that time, he has collected, read, and chronologicized literally thousands of traditional Holmes pastiches in the form of novels, short stories, radio and television episodes, movies and scripts, comics, fan-fiction, and unpublished manuscripts. He is the author of over fifty Sherlockian pastiches, some published in anthologies and others collected in his own books, *The Papers of Sherlock Holmes, Sherlock Holmes and A Quantity of Debt*, and *Sherlock Holmes – Tangled Skeins*. He has edited nearly fifty books, including several dozen traditional Sherlockian anthologies, including the ongoing series *The MX Book of New Sherlock Holmes Stories*, which he created in 2015. This collection is now up to 18 volumes, with several more in preparation. He was responsible for bringing back August Derleth's Solar Pons for a new generation, first with his collection of authorized Pons stories, *The Papers of Solar Pons*, and then by editing the reissued authorized versions of the original Pons books. He is now doing the same for the adventures of Dr. Thorndyke. He has contributed numerous essays to various publications, and is a member of a number of Sherlockian groups and Scions. He is a licensed Civil Engineer, living in Tennessee with his wife and son. His irregular Sherlockian blog, *A Seventeen Step Program*, addresses various topics related to his favorite book friends (as his son used to call them when he was small), and can be found at *http://17stepprogram.blogspot.com/* Since the age of nineteen, he has worn a deerstalker as his regular-and-only hat from autumn to spring, and often summer as well. In 2013, he and his deerstalker were finally able make his first trip-of-a-lifetime Holmes Pilgrimage to England, with return Pilgrimages in 2015 and 2016, where you may have spotted him. If you ever run into him and his deerstalker out and about, feel free to say hello!

**Will Murray** is the author of over seventy novels, including forty *Destroyer* novels and seven posthumous *Doc Savage* collaborations with Lester Dent, under the name Kenneth Robeson, for Bantam Books in the 1990's. Since 2011, he has written fourteen additional Doc Savage adventures for Altus Press, two of which co-starred The Shadow, as well as a solo Pat Savage novel. His 2015 Tarzan novel, *Return to Pal-Ul-Don*, was followed by *King Kong vs. Tarzan* in 2016. Murray has written short stories featuring such classic characters as Batman, Superman, Wonder Woman, Spider-Man, Ant-Man, the Hulk, Honey West, the Spider, the Avenger, the Green Hornet, the Phantom, and Cthulhu. A previous Murray Sherlock Holmes story appeared in Moonstone's *Sherlock Holmes: The Crossovers Casebook*, and another is forthcoming in *Sherlock Holmes and Doctor Was Not*, involving H. P. Lovecraft's Dr. Herbert West. Additionally, a number of his Sherlock Holmes stories have appeared in various volumes of *The MX Book of New Sherlock Holmes Stories*.

**Sidney Paget** (1860-1908), a few of whose illustrations are used within this anthology, was born in London, and like his two older brothers, became a famed illustrator and painter. He completed over three-hundred-and-fifty drawings for the Sherlock Holmes stories that were first published in *The Strand* magazine, defining Holmes's image forever after in the public mind.

**Tracy J. Revels**, who also has stories in Parts XVI and XVIII, has been a Sherlockian from the age of eleven. She is a professor of history at Wofford College in Spartanburg, South Carolina. She is a member of *The Survivors of the Gloria Scott* and *The Studious Scarlets Society*, and is a past recipient of the Beacon Society Award. Almost every semester, she teaches a class that covers The Canon, either to college students or to senior citizens. She is also the author of three supernatural Sherlockian pastiches with MX (*Shadowfall*, *Shadowblood*, and *Shadowwraith*), and a regular contributor to her scion's newsletter. She also has some notoriety as an author of very silly skits: For proof, see "The Adventure of the Adversarial Adventuress" and "Occupy Baker Street" on YouTube. When not studying Sherlock, she can be found researching the history of her native state, and has written books on Florida in the Civil War and on the development of Florida's tourism industry.

**Roger Riccard** of Los Angeles, California, U.S.A., is a descendant of the Roses of Kilravock in Highland Scotland. He is the author of two previous Sherlock Holmes novels, *The Case of the Poisoned Lily* and *The Case of the Twain Papers*, a series of short stories in two volumes, *Sherlock Holmes: Adventures for the Twelve Days of Christmas* and *Further Adventures for the Twelve Days of Christmas*, and the new series *A Sherlock Holmes Alphabet of Cases,* all of which are published by Baker Street Studios. He has another novel and a non-fiction Holmes reference work in various stages of completion. He became a Sherlock Holmes enthusiast as a teenager (many, many years ago), and, like all fans of The Great Detective, yearned for more stories after reading The Canon over and over. It was the Granada Television performances of Jeremy Brett and Edward Hardwicke, and the encouragement of his wife, Rosilyn, that at last inspired him to write his own Holmes adventures, using the Granada actor portrayals as his guide. He has been called "The best pastiche writer since Val Andrews" by the *Sherlockian E-Times.*

**Jane Rubino** is the author of A Jersey Shore mystery series, featuring a Jane Austen-loving amateur sleuth and a Sherlock Holmes-quoting detective; *Knight Errant, Lady Vernon and Her Daughter*, (a novel-length adaptation of Jane Austen's novella *Lady Susan*, co-authored with her daughter Caitlen Rubino-Bradway, *What Would Austen Do?*, also co-authored with her daughter, a short story in the anthology *Jane Austen Made Me Do It, The Rucastles' Pawn, The Copper Beeches from Violet Turner's POV*, and, of course, there's the Sherlockian novel in the drawer – who doesn't have one? Jane lives on a barrier island at the New Jersey shore.

**Geri Schear** is a novelist and short story writer. Her work has been published in literary journals in the U.S. and Ireland. Her first novel, *A Biased Judgement: The Diaries of Sherlock Holmes 1897* was released to critical acclaim in 2014. The sequel, *Sherlock Holmes and the Other Woman* was published in 2015, and *Return to Reichenbach* in 2016. She lives in Kells, Ireland.

**S. Subramanian** is a retired professor of Economics from Chennai, India. Apart from a small book titled *Economic Offences: A Compendium of Crimes in Prose and Verse* (Oxford University Press Delhi, 2012), his Holmes pastiches are the only serious things he has written. His other work runs largely to whimsical stuff on fuzzy logic and social measurement, on which he writes with much precision and little understanding, being an economist. He is otherwise mainly harmless, as his wife and daughter might concede with a little persuasion.

**Charles Veley** has loved Sherlock Holmes since boyhood. As a father, he read the entire Canon to his then-ten-year-old daughter at evening story time. Now, this very same daughter, grown up to become acclaimed historical novelist Anna Elliott, has worked with him to develop new adventures in the *Sherlock Holmes and Lucy James Mystery Series.* Charles is also a fan of Gilbert and Sullivan, and wrote *The Pirates of Finance*, a new musical in the G&S tradition that won an award at the New York Musical Theatre Festival in 2013. Other than the Sherlock and Lucy series, all of the books on his Amazon Author Page were written when he was a full-time author during the late Seventies and early Eighties. He currently works for United Technologies Corporation, where his main focus is on creating sustainability and value for the company's large real estate development projects. Learn more about the Sherlock and Lucy series at *www.sherlockandlucy.com*

428

## The MX Book of New Sherlock Holmes Stories
## Whatever Remains . . .
## Must Be the Truth
## Part XVI – (1881-1890)
*and*
## Part XVIII – (1899-1925)

**Josh Anderson** is twenty-four and lives in Wales, UK. He enjoys running, tennis, video games, and reading, and is currently training to be an English teacher. His favourite Sherlock Holmes author is James Lovegrove. This is his first story.

**Derrick Belanger** is an educator and also the author of the #1 bestselling book in its category, *Sherlock Holmes: The Adventure of the Peculiar Provenance*, which was in the top 200 bestselling books on Amazon. He also is the author of *The MacDougall Twins with Sherlock Holmes* books, and he edited the Sir Arthur Conan Doyle horror anthology *A Study in Terror: Sir Arthur Conan Doyle's Revolutionary Stories of Fear and the Supernatural*. Mr. Belanger co-owns the publishing company Belanger Books, which released the Sherlock Holmes anthologies *Beyond Watson*, *Holmes Away From Home: Adventures from the Great Hiatus* Volumes 1 and 2, *Sherlock Holmes: Before Baker Street*, and *Sherlock Holmes: Adventures in the Realms of H.G. Wells* Volumes I and 2. Derrick resides in Colorado and continues compiling unpublished works by Dr. John H. Watson.

**S.F. Bennett** has, at various times, been an actor, a lecturer, a journalist, a historian, an author and a potter. Whilst some of those things still apply, she has always been an avid collector, concentrating mainly on ephemera and other related items concerning Sherlock Holmes and British science-fiction of the 1970's. To date, she has written articles on aspects of The Canon for *The Baker Street Journal*, *The Sherlock Holmes Journal*, and *The Torr*, the journal of *The Sherlock Holmes Society of the West Country*. When not collecting, she can be found writing science-fiction and mystery stories, and has contributed to several anthologies of new Sherlock Holmes pastiches. Her first novel was *The Secret Diary of Mycroft Holmes: The Thoughts and Reminiscences of Sherlock Holmes's Elder Brother, 1880-1888* (2017). She is also the author of *A Study In Postcards: Sherlock Holmes in the Golden Age of the Picture Postcard* (*Sherlock Holmes Society of London*, 2019).

**Bob Bishop** is the author of over twenty stage plays, musicals, and pantomimes, several written in collaboration with Norfolk composer, Bob McNeil Watson. Many of these theatrical works were first performed by the fringe theatre company of which he was principal director, The Fossick Valley Fumblers, at the Edinburgh Festival Fringe between 1982 and 2000. Amongst these works were four Sherlock Holmes plays, inspired by the playwright's lifelong affection for the works of Sir Arthur Conan Doyle. Bob's other works include the comic novel, *A Tickle Amongst the Cornstalks*, an anthology of short stories, *Shadows on the Blind*, and a number of Sherlock Holmes pastiche novellas. He currently lives with his wife and three poodles in North Norfolk.

**Andrew Bryant** was born in Bridgend, Wales, and now lives in Burlington, Ontario, Canada. His previous publications include *Prism International*, *Existere*, *On Spec*, *The Dalhousie Review*, and second place in the 2015 *Toronto Star* short story contest. His first Holmes story, "The Shackled Man", was published in *The MX Book of New Sherlock*

*Holmes Stories – Part XIII.* The story in this collection, "The Blue Lady of Dunraven", is situated at Dunraven Castle, a few miles from where he was born, and he remembers walking the house and grounds as a child. Tragically, the Castle was demolished in 1963, robbing the nation of a fascinating and mysterious historic landmark. Hopefully, The Blue Lady wanders the ruins still.

**Thomas A. Burns, Jr.** is the author of the *Natalie McMasters Mysteries*. He was born and grew up in New Jersey, attended Xavier High School in Manhattan, earned B.S degrees in Zoology and Microbiology at Michigan State University, and a M.S. in Microbiology at North Carolina State University. He currently resides in Wendell, North Carolina. As a kid, Tom started reading mysteries with The Hardy Boys, Ken Holt and Rick Brant, and graduated to the classic stories by authors such as A. Conan Doyle, Dorothy Sayers, John Dickson Carr, Erle Stanley Gardner, and Rex Stout, to name a few. Tom has written fiction as a hobby all of his life, starting with The Man from U.N.C.L.E. stories in marble-backed copybooks in grade school. He built a career as technical, science, and medical writer and editor for nearly thirty years in industry and government. Now that he's truly on his own as a novelist, he's excited to publish his own mystery series, as well as to contribute stories about his second-most-favorite detective, Sherlock Holmes, to *The MX anthology of New Sherlock Holmes Stories.*

**Nick Cardillo** has loved Sherlock Holmes ever since he was first introduced to the detective in *The Great Illustrated Classics* edition of *The Adventures of Sherlock Holmes* at the age of six. His devotion to the Baker Street detective duo has only increased over the years, and Nick is thrilled to be taking these proper steps into the Sherlock Holmes Community. His first published story, "The Adventure of the Traveling Corpse", appeared in *The MX Book of New Sherlock Holmes Stories – Part VI: 2017 Annual*, and his "The Haunting of Hamilton Gardens" was published in *PART VIII – Eliminate the Impossible: 1892-1905.* A devout fan of The Golden Age of Detective Fiction, Hammer Horror, and *Doctor Who*, Nick co-writes the Sherlockian blog, *Back on Baker Street*, which analyses over seventy years of Sherlock Holmes film and culture. He is a student at Susquehanna University.

**Harry DeMaio** is a *nom de plume* of Harry B. DeMaio, successful author of several books on Information Security and Business Networks, as well as the ten-volume *Casebooks of Octavius Bear – Alternative Universe Mysteries for Adult Animal Lovers.* Octavius Bear is loosely based on Sherlock Holmes and Nero Wolfe in a world in which *homo sapiens* died out long ago in a global disaster, but most animals have advanced to a twenty-first century anthropomorphic state. "It's Time" is Harry's first offering treating Holmes and Watson in their original human condition. A retired business executive, consultant, information security specialist, former pilot, and graduate school adjunct professor, he whiles away his time traveling and writing preposterous articles and stories. He has appeared on many radio and TV shows and is an accomplished, frequent public speaker. Former New York City natives, he and his extremely patient and helpful wife, Virginia, and their Bichon Frisé, Woof, live in Cincinnati (and several other parallel universes.) They have two sons living in Scottsdale, Arizona and Cortlandt Manor, New York, both of whom are quite successful and quite normal – thus putting the lie to the theory that insanity is hereditary.

**Matthew J. Elliott** is the author of *Big Trouble in Mother Russia* (2016), the official sequel to the cult movie *Big Trouble in Little China, Lost in Time and Space: An Unofficial Guide to the Uncharted Journeys of Doctor Who* (2014), *Sherlock Holmes on the Air* (2012), *Sherlock Holmes in Pursuit* (2013), *The Immortals: An Unauthorized Guide* *to* Sherlock *and* Elementary (2013), and *The Throne Eternal* (2014). His articles, fiction, and reviews have appeared in the magazines *Scarlet Street, Total DVD, SHERLOCK,* and *Sherlock Holmes Mystery Magazine,* and the collections *The Game's Afoot, Curious Incidents 2, Gaslight Grimoire, The Mammoth Book of Best British Crime 8,* and *The MX Book of New Sherlock Holmes Stories – Part III: 1896-1929.* He has scripted over 260 radio plays, including episodes of *Doctor Who, The Further Adventures of Sherlock Holmes, The Twilight Zone, The New Adventures of Mickey Spillane's Mike Hammer, Fangoria's Dreadtime Stories,* and award-winning adaptations of *The Hound of the Baskervilles* and *The War of the Worlds.* He is the only radio dramatist to adapt all sixty original stories from The Canon for the series *The Classic Adventures of Sherlock Holmes.* Matthew is a writer and performer on *RiffTrax.com,* the online comedy experience from the creators of cult sci-fi TV series *Mystery Science Theater 3000* (*MST3K* to the initiated). He's also written a few comic books.

**David Friend** lives in Wales, Great Britain, where he divides his time between watching old detective films and thinking about old detective films. Now thirty, he's been scribbling out stories for twenty years and hopes, some day, to write something half-decent. Most of what he pens is set in an old-timey world of non-stop adventure with debonair sleuths, kick-ass damsels, criminal masterminds, and narrow escapes, and he wishes he could live there.

**Tim Gambrell** lives in Exeter, Devon, with his wife, two young sons, two cats, and seven chickens. He contributed "The Yellow Star of Cairo" to *Part XIII* of *The MX Book of New Sherlock Holmes Stories,* and has a story in the forthcoming collection *The Early Adventures of Sherlock Holmes* from Belanger Books. Outside of The World of Holmes, Tim has written extensively for Doctor Who spin-off ranges. He has recently had two linked novels published by Candy Jar Books: *Lethbridge-Stewart: The Laughing Gnome – Lucy Wilson & The Bledoe Cadets,* and *The Lucy Wilson Mysteries: The Brigadier and The Bledoe Cadets* (both Summer 2019). He also has a novella, *The Way of The Bry'hunee,* for the Erimem range from Thebes Publishing, which is due out in late 2019. Tim's short fiction includes stories *in Lethbridge-Stewart: The HAVOC Files* 3 (Candy Jar, 2017), *Bernice Summerfield: True Stories* (Big Finish, 2017), and *Relics . . . An Anthology* (Red Ted Books, 2018). Further short fiction will feature in the forthcoming collections *Lethbridge-Stewart: The HAVOC Files – The Laughing Gnome,* and *Lethbridge-Stewart: The HAVOC Files – Loose Ends* (both due later in 2019).

**Jayantika Ganguly** BSI is the General Secretary and Editor of the *Sherlock Holmes Society of India,* a member of the *Sherlock Holmes Society of London,* and the *Czech Sherlock Holmes Society.* She is the author of *The Holmes Sutra* (MX 2014). She is a corporate lawyer working with one of the Big Six law firms.

**Arthur Hall** also has stories in the companion volumes, Parts XVI and XVIII.

**Paul Hiscock** is an author of crime, fantasy, and science fiction tales. His short stories have appeared in several anthologies and include a seventeenth century whodunnit, a science fiction western, and a steampunk Sherlock Holmes story. Paul lives with his family in Kent, England, and spends his days chasing a toddler with more energy than the Duracell Bunny. He mainly does his writing in coffee shops with members of the local NaNoWriMo group, or in the middle of the night when his family has gone to sleep. Consequently, his stories tend to be fuelled by large amounts of black coffee. You can find out more about his writing at *www.detectivesanddragons.uk.*

431

**Christopher James** also has a poem in the companion volume, Part XVII.

In the year 1998, **Craig Janacek** took his degree of Doctor of Medicine at Vanderbilt University, and proceeded to Stanford to go through the training prescribed for pediatricians in practice. Having completed his studies there, he was duly attached to the University of California, San Francisco as Associate Professor. The author of over seventy medical monographs upon a variety of obscure lesions, his travel-worn and battered tin dispatch-box is crammed with papers, nearly all of which are records of his fictional works. To date, these have been published solely in electronic format, including two non-Holmes novels (*The Oxford Deception* and *The Anger of Achilles Peterson*), the trio of holiday adventures collected as *The Midwinter Mysteries of Sherlock Holmes*, the Holmes story collections *The First of Criminals*, *The Assassination of Sherlock Holmes*, *The Treasury of Sherlock Holmes*, *The Schoolroom of Sorrow*, *An East Wind*, and the Watsonian novels *The Isle of Devils* and *The Gate of Gold*. Craig Janacek is a *nom de plume*.

**Kelvin I. Jones**, who has stories in Parts XVI and XVIII, is the author of six books about Sherlock Holmes and the definitive biography of Conan Doyle as a spiritualist, *Conan Doyle and The Spirits*. A member of *The Sherlock Holmes Society of London*, he has published numerous short occult and ghost stories in British anthologies over the last thirty years. His work has appeared on BBC Radio, and in 1984 he won the Mason Hall Literary Award for his poem cycle about the survivors of Hiroshima and Nagasaki, recently reprinted as "Omega". (Oakmagic Publications) A one-time teacher of creative writing at the University of East Anglia, he is also the author of four crime novels featuring his ex-Met sleuth John Bottrell, who first appeared in *Stone Dead*. He has over fifty titles on Kindle, and is also the author of several novellas and short story collections featuring a Norwich-based detective, DCI Ketch, an intrepid sleuth who investigates East Anglian murder cases. He also published a series of short stories about an Edwardian psychic detective, Dr. John Carter (*Carter's Occult Casebook*). Ramsey Campbell, the British horror writer, and Francis King, the renowned novelist, have both compared his supernatural stories to those of M. R. James. He has also published children's fiction, namely *Odin's Eye*, and, in collaboration with his wife Debbie, *The Dark Entry*. Since 1995, he has been the proprietor of Oakmagic Publications, publishers of British folklore and of his fiction titles. He lives in Norfolk.
(See *www.oakmagicpublications.co.uk*)

**David Marcum** also has stories in the companion volumes, Parts XVI and XVIII.

**Mark Mower** is a member of the *Crime Writers' Association, The Sherlock Holmes Society of London* and *The Solar Pons Society of London*. He writes true crime stories and fictional mysteries. His volumes of Holmes pastiches include *A Farewell to Baker Street, Sherlock Holmes: The Baker Street Case-Files*, and *Sherlock Holmes: The Baker Street Legacy* (all with MX Publishing) and, to date, he has contributed many stories to the ongoing series *The MX Book of New Sherlock Holmes Stories*. He has also had stories in two anthologies by Belanger Books: *Holmes Away From Home: Adventures from the Great Hiatus – Volume II – 1893-1894* (2016) and *Sherlock Holmes: Before Baker Street* (2017). More are bound to follow. Mark's non-fiction works include *Bloody British History: Norwich* (The History Press, 2014), *Suffolk Murders* (The History Press, 2011) and *Zeppelin Over Suffolk* (Pen & Sword Books, 2008).

**Josh Pachter** (1951-   ) is a writer, editor, and translator. His short fiction has appeared in *Ellery Queen Mystery Magazine*, *Alfred Hitchcock Mystery Magazine*, and many other periodicals, anthologies, and year's-best collections. *The Tree of Life* (Wildside Press, 2015) collected all ten of his Mahboob Chaudri stories. He edited *The Man Who Read Mysteries: The Short Fiction of William Brittain* (Crippen & Landru, 2018) and *The Misadventures of Nero Wolfe* (Mysterious Press, 2020), and co-edited *The Misadventures of Ellery Queen* (Wildside, 2018) and *Amsterdam Noir* (Akashic, 2019). His translations of stories by Dutch and Belgian authors appear regularly in *Ellery Queen Mystery Magazine's* "Passport to Crime" Department. In his day job, he teaches interpersonal communication and film history at Northern Virginia Community College's Loudoun Campus.

**Tracy J. Revels** also has stories in the companion volumes, Parts XVI and XVIII.

**Brenda Seabrooke**'s stories have been published in sixteen reviews, journals, and anthologies. She has received grants from the National Endowment for the Arts and Emerson College's Robbie Macauley Award. She is the author of twenty-three books for young readers including *Scones and Bones on Baker Street: Sherlock's (maybe!) Dog and the Dirt Dilemma*, and *The Rascal in the Castle: Sherlock's (possible!) Dog and the Queen's Revenge.* Brenda states: "It was fun to write from Dr. Watson's point of view and not have to worry about fleas, smelly pits, ralphing, or scratching at inopportune times."

**Roger Silverwood** was educated in Gloucestershire before National Service. He later worked in the toy trade and as a copywriter in an advertising agency. Roger went into business with his wife as an antiques dealer before retiring in 1997, and he now leads a fairly happy existence with his wife Mary in the town of Bromersley in South Yorkshire. The Yorkshire author excels in writing crime books and is known for his sensational series featuring the fictional Detective Michael Angel.

**Shane Simmons** is the author of the occult detective novels *Necropolis* and *Epitaph*, and the crime collection *Raw and Other Stories*. An award-winning screenwriter and graphic novelist, his work has appeared in international film festivals, museums, and lectures about design and structure. He was born in Lachine, a suburb of Montreal best known for being massacred in 1689 and having a joke name. Visit Shane's homepage at *eyestrainproductions.com* for more.

**Mark Sohn** was born in Brighton, England in 1967. After a hectic life and many dubious and varied careers, he settled down in Sussex with his wife, Angie. His first novel, *Sherlock Holmes and the Whitechapel Murders* was published in 2017. His second, *The Absentee Detective* is out now. Both are available from Amazon.com.
*https://sherlockholmesof221b.blogspot.co.uk/*
*https://volcanocat.blogspot.co.uk/*

**Robert V. Stapleton** was born and brought up in Leeds, Yorkshire, England, and studied at Durham University. After working in various parts of the country as an Anglican parish priest, he is now retired and lives with his wife in North Yorkshire. As a member of his local writing group, he now has time to develop his other life as a writer of adventure stories. He has recently had a number of short stories published, and he is hoping to have a couple of completed novels published at some time in the future.

**Kevin P. Thornton** has experienced a Taliban rocket attack in Kabul and a terrorist bombing in Johannesburg. He lives in Fort McMurray, Alberta, the town that burnt down in 2016. He has been shortlisted for the *Crime Writers of Canada* Unhanged writing award six times. He's never won. He was also a finalist for best short story in 2014 – the year Margaret Atwood entered. We're not saying he has luck issues, but don't bet on his stock tips. Born in Kenya, Kevin was a child in New Zealand, a student and soldier in Africa, a military contractor in Afghanistan, a forklift driver in Ontario, and an oilfield worker in North Western Canada. He writes poems that start out just fine, but turn ruder and cruder over time. From limerick to doggerel, they earn less than bugger-all, even though they all manage to rhyme. He also likes writing about Sherlock Holmes and dislikes writing about himself in the third person.

**Gareth Tilley** is a writer whose works include several scripts for Imagination Theatre's *The Further Adventures of Sherlock Holmes.* One of these was included in *Imagination Theatre's Sherlock Holmes*, where the contributor royalties benefit the Stepping Stones School at Undershaw, one of Sir Arthur Conan Doyle's former homes.

**Thomas A. (Tom) Turley** has been "hooked on Holmes" since finishing *The Hound of the Baskervilles* at about the age of twelve. However, his interest in Sherlockian pastiches didn't take off until he wrote one. *Sherlock Holmes and the Adventure of the Tainted Canister* (2014) is available as an e-book and an audiobook from MX Publishing. It will also soon appear in *The Art of Sherlock Holmes – USA Edition 1*. In 2017, two of Tom's stories, "A Scandal in Serbia" and "A Ghost from Christmas Past" were published in Parts VI and VII of this anthology. "Ghost" was also included in *The Art of Sherlock Holmes – West Palm Beach Edition*. Meanwhile, Tom is finishing a collection of historical pastiches entitled *Sherlock Holmes and the Crowned Heads of Europe*. The first story, "Sherlock Holmes and the Case of the Dying Emperor" (2018) is available from MX Publishing as a separate e-book. Set in the brief reign of Emperor Frederick III (1888), it inaugurates Sherlock Holmes's espionage campaign against the German Empire, which ended only in August 1914 with "His Last Bow". When completed, *Sherlock Holmes and the Crowned Heads of Europe* will also include "A Scandal in Serbia" and two additional historical tales. Although he has a Ph.D. in British history, Tom spent most of his professional career as an archivist with the State of Alabama. He and his wife Paula (an aspiring science fiction novelist) live in Montgomery, Alabama. Interested readers may contact Tom through MX Publishing or his Goodreads author's page.

**I.A. Watson** is a novelist and jobbing writer from Yorkshire who cut his teeth on writing Sherlock Holmes stories and has even won an award for one. His works include *Holmes and Houdini*, *Labours of Hercules*, *St. George and the Dragon* Volumes 1 and 2, and *Women of Myth*, and the non-fiction essay book *Where Stories Dwell*. He pens short detective stories as a means of avoiding writing things that pay better. A full list of his sixty-plus published works appears at:
*http://www.chillwater.org.uk/writing/iawatsonhome.htm*

**Matthew White** is an up-and-coming author from Richmond, Virginia in the USA. He has been a passionate devotee of Sherlock Holmes since childhood. He can be reached at *matthewwhite.writer@gmail.com.*

**The MX Book of New Sherlock Holmes Stories**
*Edited by David Marcum*
(MX Publishing, 2015-   )

"This is the finest volume of Sherlockian fiction I have ever read, and I have read, literally, thousands." – Philip K. Jones

"Beyond Impressive . . . This is a splendid venture for a great cause!
– Roger Johnson, Editor, *The Sherlock Holmes Journal,*
The Sherlock Holmes Society of London

*Part I: 1881-1889*
*Part II: 1890-1895*
*Part III: 1896-1929*
*Part IV: 2016 Annual*
*Part V: Christmas Adventures*
*Part VI: 2017 Annual*
*Part VII: Eliminate the Impossible (1880-1891)*
*Part VIII – Eliminate the Impossible (1892-1905)*
*Part IX – 2018 Annual (1879-1895)*
*Part X – 2018 Annual (1896-1916)*
*Part XI – Some Untold Cases (1880-1891)*
*Part XII – Some Untold Cases (1894-1902)*
*Part XIII – 2019 Annual (1881-1890)*
*Part XIV – 2019 Annual (1891-1897)*
*Part XV – 2019 Annual (1898-1917)*
*Part XVI – Whatever Remains . . . Must be the Truth (1881-1890)*
*Part XVII – Whatever Remains . . . Must be the Truth (1891-1898)*
*Part XVIII – Whatever Remains . . . Must be the Truth (1898-1925)*

**In Preparation**
*Part XIX – 2020 Annual*

*. . . and more to come!*

# The MX Book of New Sherlock Holmes Stories
## *Edited by David Marcum*
(MX Publishing, 2015-   )

*Publishers Weekly* says:

Part VI: *The traditional pastiche is alive and well . . . .*

Part VII: *Sherlockians eager for faithful-to-the-canon plots and characters will be delighted.*

Part VIII: *The imagination of the contributors in coming up with variations on the volume's theme is matched by their ingenious resolutions.*

Part IX: *The 18 stories . . . will satisfy fans of Conan Doyle's originals. Sherlockians will rejoice that more volumes are on the way.*

Part X: *. . . new Sherlock Holmes adventures of consistently high quality.*

Part XI: *. . . an essential volume for Sherlock Holmes fans.*

Part XII: *. . . continues to amaze with the number of high-quality pastiches . . .*

Part XIII: *. . . Amazingly, Marcum has found 22 superb pastiches . . . This is more catnip for fans of stories faithful to Conan Doyle's original*

Part XIV: *. . . this standout anthology of 21 short stories written in the spirit of Conan Doyle's originals.*

Part XV: *Stories pitting Sherlock Holmes against seemingly supernatural phenomena highlight Marcum's 15th anthology of superior short pastiches.*

# The MX Book of New Sherlock Holmes Stories
## *Edited by David Marcum*
(MX Publishing, 2015-  )

## MX Publishing

**MX Publishing** is the world's largest specialist Sherlock Holmes publisher, with several hundred titles and over a hundred authors creating the latest in Sherlock Holmes fiction and non-fiction.

*www.mxpublishing.com*